THE GILDED TORCH

BOOKS BY IOLA FULLER

LOON FEATHER

THE SHINING TRAIL

THE GILDED TORCH

IOLA FULLER

THE

GILDED

TORCH

G. P. PUTNAM'S SONS
NEW YORK

©1957 by Iola Fuller McCoy

Published on the same day in the Dominion of Canada by Thomas Allen, Ltd., Toronto.

Library of Congress Catalog
Card Number: 57-6731

Second Impression

MANUFACTURED IN THE UNITED STATES OF AMERICA

For Ray and Paul
and
In Memoriam
Mary W. Hyslip

PART I

PART I

1

IT wanted three quarters before eight on every one of the carefully regulated gold, silver, and bronze doré clocks of Versailles. The sun had just banished the soft haze of an early May morning, to blaze against serried glass panes until the broad white palace seemed aglow with fairy lights. The dazzling façade could easily be that of an imaginary palace of crystal, magically built to astound the eye by vastness and to charm it by delicacy of detail. Though still unfinished in this year of 1678, it was assured, arrogant, a perfect assertion of monarchy and of the two passions of the fourteenth Louis—magnificence and order. Already it was a royal dwelling unrivaled outside the Orient, comparable to nothing in the western world since the fall of the Caesars.

At this very moment, as if the lacelike wrought-iron gates of the Place d'Armes had some magnetic power, hundreds of Frenchmen and foreigners in carriages, sedan-chairs, on horseback or on foot, were being drawn toward them along three converging avenues. The travelers, gazing toward the gates in hope or dread, were struck anew every morning by the magnificence of the vista, even more by its rigid symmetry. The three arched windows of the king's bedroom, the actual as well as the symbolic center, were flanked by two vast identical wings, whose balanced harmony of columns, railings, and lesser courts was suitably framed by immense formal gardens, where amid the flashing of cascades and fountains stood so many classical statues that seemingly all the ancient deities of forest and river had met here to do honor to the greatest of modern kings.

On the crowded Cours-la-Reine, the highway from Paris, bewigged heads were being thrust out of gilded carriages to watch a solitary horseman riding against the crowd. He circled them all, reckless and unseeing, until half a league away, he met another horseman in a small open space.

"*Mordieux,* Victor, you are all right?" He rode close enough to embrace the other with a brief laying of the arm over the shoulder. Being Normans they were less demonstrative than other Frenchmen.

"*Oui*. Why not?" Catching a glance at the mended tear in his sleeve, he added, "Oh, I got a scratch."

The first nodded, wheeled his horse, and fell in slightly behind, keeping that position as they rode toward Versailles, a sample of elite horsemanship. The identical fine gray horses marked them as members of the King's "gray musketeers," or rather as former members, for their brilliant matching uniforms set them farther up the scale. Their sky-blue coats, brocaded in gold and silver, with red and gold cuffs; their hair held back in military fashion by knots of black ribbon; their wide-brimmed beavers surmounted by curling white plumes; their gold-embroidered and fringed baldrics supporting swords ornamented at the *garde* by a cluster of red and gold ribbons—and above all, a special gallant bearing—identified them as picked men, officers in the King's crack household troops: the famous Blue Guard.

Both guardsmen were tall for Frenchmen, with the fair hair and skin of their native Normandy, like the men who had followed William the Conqueror to the field of Hastings. Their hats shaded faces not only alike in being very young and both wise and ingenuous but in features; for Victor and Marc, the younger sons of the Marquis de Lorennes, were identical twins.

"I knew something was wrong," said Marc. "So I came to find you. What happened?"

Victor glanced at him. *Parbleu!* Why did that woman pick such a way to make him pay a card debt, demanding secrecy even from his brother?

"It was nothing." He waved a yellow leather glove. "Some fools attacked me. Only two of them. So I defended myself," he added gaily. "You know the rule."

Marc nodded. It had been taught them by a famous teacher: attack an enemy alone, defend yourself against two, do not yield to three, but flee without shame before four. "Where did this happen?"

"Leaving—a courtyard where I had an errand," Victor evaded. "Before I could mount, two men pushed me as if by mistake, and then came at me with drawn swords. We did a little hacking and slashing, and I got this scratch. Then I caught the sword of one of them, a masked fellow in violet, and sent it flying over the hedge. I took him by the belt and sent him flying over after it. The other melted away into the darkness. My sword had blood on it, so I must have touched him."

"*Vrai dieu!* You sound like Monsieur d'Artagnan himself," said Marc solemnly.

Victor laughed, but thought, *Touché.* It was a good augur on this particular day to dispose of those rascals in the style of the redoubtable D'Artagnan, their father's friend and their earliest instructor in fencing. He had been determined that if the twins ever died in duels it would be by no common sword; so on their fifth birthday he had placed little foils in their hands. From then on he had flavored his strict teaching with stories of the duels he reckoned in hundreds, for no one had worn out more swords than he in the service of France. His finest one, presented to him by Louis XIII, now hung at Victor's side, his choicest possession, the keenest of Toledo blades, the engraved hilt set with an emerald in a circle of pearls. Before going into his last battle, D'Artagnan had called the two of them to fence before him. He had grunted and scolded, but they knew he was quite content with them. He had awarded the sword to Victor as the more aggressive, though both were flawless in technique.

"Did you recognize them?" asked Marc.

"Who? Oh. No, it was too dark."

"*Eh bien,* enemies will crop up easily along your path now. At least twenty lieutenants your senior aspire to captaincy of the Guards. Yet suddenly, the post is yours."

"Nonsense! Two guardsmen wouldn't set on me at once," said Victor. "But it's over now." He stroked his sleeve. "Damned shame to get a hole in good cloth. I'll have Monsieur Tourneau put in a new sleeve. He's cursed slow in getting my captain's scarf embroidered." He was scowling, but his eyes glowed.

Marc smiled. This uniform, the most dashing next to the King's, was a constant delight to Victor, an arbiter of fashion in their circle. And the distinctive scarf of an intimate member of the King's household would give it the final touch of perfection.

"And by the way," Victor added, "Monsieur Villette asked when you were coming in to finish your 'experiment.' It's spread all over the back room, and crowding his apothecary supplies. I told him you'd clear it out this afternoon. Don't forget, you go back on duty tomorrow."

"As usual," said Marc dryly, "you are neatly arranging all my time that the King doesn't use." Victor opened his mouth in surprise, but Marc hastened on, "Did you see Father in Paris?"

"No. I rode around to his usual lodgings, but the porter said he had already started for Versailles in another nobleman's carriage. His own was dirty and the horses tired from those three days of abominable roads from Rouen."

Marc glanced around. "Then he might be in almost any of these carriages. He knows everyone."

"The stupid porter didn't notice the armorial bearings or the livery. I've been keeping an eye out for him, but I may have missed him inside the city. Let's push on a little faster."

It was an ideal morning. An early light rain had laid the dust, but had not turned the earth to mud. As they passed each coach, the two young men turned to look at the occupants, touching their plumed hats. "We look like mounted police officers in search of a nun escaped from a convent," laughed Victor.

"A nun going toward Versailles? *C'est impossible!* Women go the other way—from the palace to a convent, when the King tires of them."

But Victor was serious again. "Father wrote us he would come in time to see us before we go on duty."

"Before *you* do, Monsieur le Capitaine. I have one day yet that is mine."

"How long will you bask in being a hero of the siege of Ghent?"

". . . which terminated gloriously for French arms," recited Marc sonorously, and then grinned. "I'd have cut a poor figure in His Majesty's Guards, with a lame foot."

"That lame foot has been healed for some time," retorted Victor. "Your reluctance to come back—" he hesitated —"it's not because I will be your commanding officer?"

Marc laughed. "Like every lieutenant since men fought with rocks and clubs, I'll feel that my commanding officer does not appreciate me. *Mais non,* it is not that."

"You wanted more time to mess around with those flasks and—what do you call them? Retorts?" accused Victor. "A smelly mess. Of course, when you start making gold from lead, don't forget to share it. My purse could stand fattening."

"There's more to alchemy than that." Marc realized as he spoke that his interest in alchemy, like other studies he had taken up, had at least two facets. He enjoyed pursuing a subject to its known limits, as he had once studied fortification. But just as urgent was the need to do something of his own. All their lives Victor had made the decisions, little or big, and he had followed along with only occasional discontent. Of late, though, he had felt so restless that even his current enthusiasm did not fill the need. Of course, Victor might marry soon. I can make plans of my own then, he thought. And yet I don't really want anything to change. And I'm uneasy about Victor's trip to Paris. He never kept anything from me before.

Victor was still mumbling about alchemy. "You started loafing around that shop because Monsieur Villette was an old servant of Father's, and now your money is all going up in smoke instead of into diversions proper to your rank."

Marc took the criticism without rancor, knowing that whenever one of them criticized the other, it was done from a desire that the other appear perfect to all the world.

"*I* can find enough to do without turning alchemist," Victor ended with a grunt.

"*Mais oui.* A man like Monsieur le Capitaine has so many responsibilities," teased Marc. "He has to lord it through the Bois in the blue and gold of His Majesty's Guards. He has his gallantries, his ballets with Monsieur Lulli, his theatricals. Now that you're Monsieur le Capitaine, if you compose a miserable couplet to a jig tune, they'll call you a great poet."

Victor smiled. He didn't mind being teased. Until autumn at least, God willing, he was to be temporary Captain of the Guards, while M. le Duc de Luxembourg was away with the army. He would have a taste of the dish every guardsman aspired to from the time he was first accorded his musketeer's tunic. He didn't feel conceited, merely lucky. He knew how often Louis XIV awarded an accolade to one in pleasure over some trivial service, while many another could devote a lifetime and receive nothing. This particular honor came from an incident at the siege of Ghent. Under the eyes of the King himself, the courage of the household troops had brought another victory against the Dutch. Marc had been wounded and Victor had got a bullet through his hat. After the battle, when the enemy, by permission, had sent out servants to gather up the dead, Victor had caught, lurking near the King's quarters, a man dressed as a valet, who had confessed to being a Dutch officer and a spy. The King had rewarded Victor's alertness by this captaincy on the spot.

"I think," said Marc, "His Majesty is giving you a glimpse of the heights you may aspire to if you always serve him as well. The Captain of the Guards often receives the governorship of a fortress."

Victor nodded. *"Eh bien,* what else is there but to serve the King well, and hope for appropriate rewards? Would it have suited you better if we had stayed with the Jesuits and learned to be priests?"

Marc shook his head, his white plume swaying in emphasis. "No. Not that. My hand fits a sword better than a cross. But this court life! It doesn't satisfy one—it only keeps one from being satisfied with anything else."

"But what would you have?"

"I haven't decided. But I'm tired of doing always the same thing, on duty and off. Every occupation, every pleasure is regulated. Isn't there more to life than marching fifth instead of ninth in a procession, or sitting down when someone else must stand up?"

"Oh, you're in one of your moods," said Victor.

"No. I mean it. Maybe alchemy has given me a new light on things."

Victor asked scornfully, "What kind of light, *nom de dieu?*"

"I don't understand it myself. But I admire the alchemists, patiently working through so many ages, in spite of ridicule and persecution— and not just to change base metals into gold. They have a vision of man wielding power we haven't even glimpsed yet."

Victor rolled his eyes heavenward. *"Mon dieu,* what a speech!"

Marc continued his own train of thought. "I wish I knew more than what I have read by myself. If only one of our army years might have been spent instead at the Sorbonne!"

"Not for me," said Victor, yawning. "I would die of ennui trying to win laurels on Parnassus. I am as suited to the court as a fish to the Seine. I like my daily contacts with the great nobles of France, and with men of genius like Racine, Corneille, Lulli."

"I wonder what they might write if they could be freed from eternally portraying the royal perfections?"

"What better subject is there?"

"I say we're missing something by being caught up in this kind of life."

"You'll miss more if you don't stop such talk. You'll find yourself out of favor."

"Oh, I can depend on the influence of my prominent brother." Marc saluted mockingly and spurred his horse to avoid the halfhearted kick Victor aimed at his leg.

The end of the cortège of carriages ranged the length of the great iron grille enclosing the courtyard. Some were discharging their passengers; others, of a rank to have the "honors of the Louvre," which

14

gave them the entree to Versailles's Place d'Armes as well, were awaiting their turn at the wrought-iron gates. Not finding their father, the guardsmen rode inside. The vast court was, as usual, filled with animation. On the ground huge blocks of granite and slabs of marble were being hewn into shape by marble cutters from the Pyrenees, Italy, or Greece. Gendarmes, guards, light-horsemen, musketeers, and mounted grenadiers were lining up for parade. Teams of fine horses swung carriages around to unload rainbow-hued courtiers, like bright flowers from elaborate baskets.

A black horse wheeled out of the courtyard melee and pranced toward Victor and Marc. Its rider leaped down and came toward them in the musketeers' blue short coat with its silver cross on the breastplate. Dreux's swagger, even more than his swarthiness, revealed his Gascon origin. He jerked a quick salute, but added familiarly, *"Pardieu!* Where have you been?" Without pausing for an answer he added, "This is your first morning as captain. Everyone's talking about it."

"What are they saying?" Victor interrupted.

"You can guess. Most are surprised that you have been raised over them. Me, I'm glad for you. I'd give a lot just to be in the Guards."

"We wish you could," said Marc. "Isn't there any way?"

Dreux grinned. "You know better. I have three years as a cavalry officer, but not one year of nobility, much less two hundred. Not to mention having no money, and being a Huguenot."

"Well, cast off your heresy and enter the true church," said Victor lightly. "And get some money from the conversion fund. Some people are converted three or four times, under different names."

"You sound as if it's as easy as changing your shirt," commented Marc.

"Well, anyway," said Dreux, "You're not the ones to convert me. You merely neglect your prayers in Latin while I neglect mine in French." He glanced around at the swarms of servants. "Where's your man?"

"Old Jacques doesn't know we are out," said Marc.

"I'll take care of your horses, then. I'm free until nine o'clock."

As they dismounted and handed him the reins, he added, "Can you come to my rooms tonight after you're off duty? I've got a new recipe." A gourmet, Dreux collected new dishes and concoctions.

"Not tonight," said Victor. "Father is on his way here, and will want us with him after the King releases me by going to bed."

15

Dreux nodded. "Later on, then."

While Dreux led the three horses away, the two boys hurried with the tide toward the Cour des Princes at the left of the Cour Royale, reserved for the royal family. Victor was straightening his coat as, rounding the end of L'Aile du Midi, the wing that housed the Orleans family, he collided with a small black-caped figure crouched under a window.

"A thousand pardons!" He set the little fellow on his feet, startled when he recognized the impish face of the club-footed Duc du Maine, eldest son of Louis XIV and Madame de Montespan. "A million pardons, Your Highness."

"Granted."

"What are you doing out here alone, sir?"

From the folds of his cape, the little Duc produced a bunch of fire-crackers. "I'm going to set these off under Monsieur's window."

They grinned. It was always fun to stir up the excitable, foppish younger brother of the King. "Well, go ahead. We won't tell." They bowed and drew away.

"He'll see me. I can't get away very fast."

They exchanged glances and turned back, unable to resist a good prank. "You touch them off," said Victor, "and we'll pick you up and run."

"*A la bonne heure!*" Dangling from a chain on one arm the lad had a small metal box with a live coal, which he touched to the string of firecrackers. As they caught and sputtered, he tossed them upon the window ledge. Victor caught him up and ran, Marc making way for them through the crowd pouring into the various entrances. Around the first corner, they waited. After a few seconds, when nothing had happened, Victor peered back around the corner, the little Duc close at his side. At that instant the firecrackers popped, singly at first, and then with a resounding fusillade. The window flew open, and a petulant, half-feminine voice shrieked, "What devil did that? Oh, phew—" His Royal Highness, Duc d'Orleans, was choking in the smoke. "My nerves! My skin—I'll get wrinkles!"

The Duc du Maine fell heavily against Victor, pushing him beyond the corner, in full view from the window.

"Who's there?" screamed Monsieur, and then realizing that people were staring at him with his head in a nightcap, he slammed down the window, cutting off his own petulant voice like a snuffed-out candle flame.

16

"Sorry I lost my balance," said the Duc. "And thank you very much. That will be enough to spoil Uncle Philip's day."

"Where is your tutor?" asked Victor severely.

"The Abbé isn't up yet. I'm going to Madame Scarron's—I mean Madame de Maintenon's room as soon as she is awake." His ugly face glowed with the adoration the illegitimate princes and princesses had for their governess. It was said that their father, the King, was beginning—somewhat differently—to share their regard. "You won't tell on me?"

Victor and Marc bowed together. "On the honor of a guardsman." Victor added, "And you won't tell on us?"

The Duc made them a bow that would have become an accomplished courtier twice his age. "On my honor as a prince."

2

AS they entered the vestibule where the broad Marble, or Queen's, Staircase rose to branch into two flights at a fountain-decked landing, Marc hesitated. "I think I'll go see M. Lulli." He glanced toward the wing where the less exalted personages lived. "Good luck to you, Captain!" He bent in a deep, sweeping salute, his hat plume almost brushing the marble floor.

"Merci bien." Victor returned the salute, and then, his mind leaping eagerly forward to this day's duties, he joined the crowd moving toward the marble stairs.

It was just about eight o'clock and the broad flight of marble steps, no more polished and no more hard than the courtiers who trod upon them, were beginning to echo from the high red heels of noblemen freshly shaven and bewigged for the ceremony of the Sun King's rising. As in the sky, the colors changed slowly, for it was early enough that the courtiers could pause in little clusters to whisper the latest news and scandal of the court, passed on either by word of mouth or the new issue of the *Mercure Galant,* which a few were carrying under their arms. Inside the *Mercure* a few had folded the *Gazette de Hollande,* in which one could find many things that could not be printed in France. They offered each other rare tidbits of scandal as importunately as they themselves were being offered the wares of booksellers, drapers, perfumers and clockmakers, who kept shop on the staircase landings, for the King's house was as open as a mill.

Victor hurried upward toward the King's bedroom, his right hand moving gracefully to the plumes of his beaver as he saluted those whose rank demanded it, or returned the salutes of lesser men. A few sleepy-eyed courtiers called warm congratulations, but more than a few gazed after him, missing the quick jest, the tongue that usually flicked rapier-like among them and was as much respected as his sword.

Actually, this morning Victor was more than usually subdued. A small flat package in his gold-braided pocket reminded him of the dreaded errand he must do before going to his post, even though he could hardly spare the time.

Near the fountain on the landing, he felt a tug at his sleeve, and turning, saw the graceful, delicate old patrician, M. le Duc de la Rochefoucauld, in the blue and gold *justau'corps à brevet* of a king's favorite.

"I just want to congratulate you, *mon fils,*" said the melancholy Duc. *"Eh bien,* I want to make sure, too, that I stand in the good graces of the new captain."

"Sir, one who is known throughout the court as simply 'the King's friend' will never need my good graces."

Polite laughter came from a group of nobles leaning against the marble balustrade, and one of them, the short, fat Duc de Sully, asked, "How did it happen? Who is your patron? Scarron's widow?"

"No patron—except Lady Luck."

"And good enough," giggled Sully. "How does Marc feel about it?"

Victor said lightly, "Marc has always said I would go farther in the world than he. I was born fifteen minutes ahead of him, and he has always ascribed it to superior enterprise on my part."

"You've gone far enough already," yawned a courtier in green velvet, wiping sleep from dissipated eyes. "To receive an honor others have considered themselves lucky to obtain when they have grown old in harness. And you're how old? Eighteen?"

"But it's only until Monsieur de Luxembourg can leave the army——"

The courtier waved a languid hand. "Yet if De Luxembourg should fall——"

Victor looked up quickly, for the tone had given the word both shades of meaning: fall in battle, or fall from favor. But he decided

18

to take it as a joke. "Even then, I have no hopes. A heavier purse would outweigh me."

"Don't mind us, *mon fils,*" said La Rochefoucauld. "Old people are fond of giving good advice, to console themselves for being no longer able to give bad examples. But we mustn't detain you. Come, I'll walk up with you. Not too fast—remember my gout."

Victor tried to restrain his impatience, as they slowly mounted. Both sides of the staircase bubbled and seethed with gossip:

". . . The *Mercure* says that Madame de Montespan is giving a lottery tonight, at the *appartements.* The King pays for it, of course. She wants to let it be known that they are 'friends' again."

". . . A thousand double pistoles that the other one will win him in the end."

"Taken. That pious old woman is nothing but the governess of his bastards—pardon, I mean the 'legitimated princes.'" The bitter tone resulted from Louis's insult to all nobility: his decree raising Montespan's brood to princes of the blood royal, ranking them above even the most ancient peerage.

"She merely started as a governess. She's Madame Scarron no longer, but a marquise now—Madame de Maintenon, with a rich estate. Her reward—for entertaining the King in her apartment every afternoon—while he *talks* to her."

Cynical laughter broke out.

"What twaddle!" said La Rochefoucauld. "You and Marc come to my rooms this evening. We'll have some good talk, instead of this." He waved a contemptuous hand over the staircase.

"I'm sorry we can't, sir," said Victor, not very sincerely. The Duc's rooms were usually full of bores and idlers. "His Majesty is having *appartements.*"

"*Ciel!* I had forgotten. I'll have to attend, too. And I'm so tired of gambling—a polite way of picking pockets."

"And mine have been picked clean," admitted Victor. "By the way, Father will be here sometime this morning."

"Splendid! But *pardieu,* what rashness to stay away so long! He should present himself before His Majesty at least once a year."

"He doesn't like to come to Paris since my mother died."

"Yes, yes." The Duc took out his snuffbox and put it back unused. "Those were my happiest days, when you lived near me in the Rue du Seine, and your mother had one of the most brilliant salons in Paris. *Tout le même,* your father shouldn't seclude himself on his estate. The

19

King ought long ago to have awarded him the Order of the Holy Ghost—his services entitle him to it, but if he won't appear at court—!" The Duc lifted his narrow shoulders. "Is there something special now that motivates this visit? Your marriage perhaps to Madame's new maid of honor?"

Victor smiled. "Not much escapes you, sir!"

"Only a blind man could have failed to see your amorous glances. Her birth is nothing, of course, but her money—ah, that will help to regild your escutcheon. Who is she, exactly?"

"Her father is a rich magistrate of Rouen. He bought her a place at court."

"It's a sad thing that the ancient nobility has to marry rich wives to survive." The Duc sighed.

Victor glanced up the stairs desperately.

At this moment, something clattered on the marble above them, and Victor expertly caught a gold-headed cane that came sliding past his boots. "The Prince de Conti falling over his stick again."

"Go along." The Duc gave him an affectionate push. "He'll want to congratulate you. I'll watch for your father."

Louis-Armand de Bourbon, Prince de Conti, helped by a half-dozen hands, was already back on his feet. Graciously accepting his stick, he returned Victor's salute. "Thank you, Monsieur le Capitaine." He stressed the title lightly. *"Bonne chance,* Victor. Glad you have the post. You won't give the rest of us a chilly eye. I like a decent modesty."

"Your Highness, my modesty would be like that of a short man stooping to go under a doorway."

"Ce sacré Victor!" The Prince's smile made his amiable face a strange partner of his ugly body. He appreciated the sally, for he was so short that Victor, on the step below, still topped him. Victor waited for a nod of dismissal. Time was passing and he still had to get rid of that accursed package. He swayed as if to move along with the crowd, but the Prince stopped him. "Oh, I'm so deucedly absent-minded," he said, as if it were something to be proud of. "Monsieur le Capitaine, may I present my friend, Monsieur le Sieur de la Salle?"

Victor turned in surprise. In all the confusion on the staircase, he had not noticed that De Conti was accompanied by a stranger in scarlet and gold, who now bowed gracefully. "May I have the honor of adding my felicitations to those of His Highness?" The cultivated Norman voice had none of the courtier's fawning.

20

Victor, returning the salute with a polite murmur, was about to try to escape when he noticed the stranger's hands, nearly hidden beneath the masses of lace, but unexpectedly brown and muscular. His glance traveled upward to the strikingly handsome face of a man in his early thirties. Framed by black hair worn without a wig, and set off by intelligent black eyes, it had so much character that beside him the courtiers' features looked corroded. It was hard to place one so obviously at home out of doors as in a drawing room. Upon his scarlet coat he wore no gems, and his waistcoat was innocent of ribbons, but he had an air of reserved self-confidence that had nothing to do with rank. He was not a bourgeois, for his hat bore a plume. Since the Prince had called him Sieur, he must belong to the lowest, the untitled, nobility. Clearly he was a gentleman, and an unusual one.

De Conti fumbled in his waistcoat pocket, brought out an enameled box, tapped it, and took a pinch of scented snuff between his fingers. "Monsieur de la Salle comes from your own city of Rouen, Victor. The name La Salle comes from one of the family estates." The Prince brushed snuff from his malines lace ruffles. "The family name is Cavalier." The Prince sneezed gently. "He is serving France well as an explorer in the New World."

La Salle's bow conveyed the right balance between polite deprecation and gracious acceptance of the judgment of so noted a speaker. "Your Highness is most kind."

"Everyone needs a friend at court. I'm glad to be yours."

So this La Salle was one of those explorer fellows. Victor felt vaguely disappointed. What attraction could such a life have for a gentleman? At least he had found a friend of impressive rank. But if he had come to ask for something, an even better sponsor might be some lower-placed man more popular with the King. The house of Condés and Contis was enormously influential, both through birth and through the distinction of having made France a first-rate military power. But the King did not like these princes. They were too wealthy, too talented. Yet His Majesty might be agreeable to De Conti just now, for he wanted to marry him to his illegitimate Mlle. de Blois, who had been haughtily rejected by the Prince of Orange. From time to time other spurious offshoots of royalty had been thrust upon the Condés.

"I am happy to congratulate Monsieur de la Salle upon his exploits," murmured Victor, wondering vaguely what they were, still hoping that the Prince would let him go. Instead, De Conti laid a hand on his shoulder, anchoring him to the spot. "This boy has come a long way since I first saw him, eight years ago. The court was making a tour through the North, stopping for three days at Rouen, where the principal families were presented. Dull affairs, presentations, and these rascally twins of the Marquis de Lorennes were a diversion."

"Twins?" asked La Salle.

"Oh, yes, there are two. They were in military school then. They had been sent to the Jesuit school first, with some idea of making priests of them. Marc was scholarly enough, but Victor here is about as unecclesiastical a soul as ever trod the soil of France." De Conti's laugh would have been called a bray in anyone but a prince.

Victor shrank in despair, but one does not shake off the hand of a prince of the blood.

"I was once a teacher and novice at that very school," said La Salle.

Surprised, Victor tried with little success to imagine a black soutane on the vigorous figure now splendidly clad in scarlet and gold.

"The Jesuits certainly don't like you now," commented the Prince.

"No." The explorer smiled briefly. "I realized after I took my first vows that I wanted to do more in New France than I could do as their missionary, and I left the order, though they had, and kept, my share of my father's estate. However, they dislike me not because I left them, but because my plans threaten their ideas of making a second Paraguay of New France."

"Imagine, Victor," interrupted the Prince, "when the Jesuits heard he was coming to court, one of them hurried to Monsieur Colbert and said that La Salle was really a madman who ought to be put in the Petites Maisons."

"He nearly succeeded," said La Salle. "If Your Highness had not persuaded Monsieur Colbert and His Majesty to give me a hearing——"

Under a polite mask, Victor writhed. "Perhaps I'll see you later, Monsieur de la Salle?"

"Yes," said the Prince comfortably. "He'll be at the palace all day. But I was going to tell him how you boys became guardsmen."

"I'm afraid," said La Salle, "we are detaining Monsieur le Capitaine."

Victor had become so restless that now even the Prince saw it. "Go on, go on, my boy. You'll see La Salle later when he has his audience."

The explorer glanced up the stairs, and his reserved mask dropped, revealing pure dread, almost panic. For an instant Victor saw a shy

22

man, already overcome by the magnificence of Versailles, dreading the ordeal of a royal audience.

"Your Highness, monsieur." Victor bowed, and quickly escaping, tried to make his way up the remaining steps. Yet as he reached the colonnaded vestibule above, he stopped of his own accord, and his plume swept twice toward the parquet with the particular grace and precision of salutes meant for royalty or ladies. For here, before a marble-framed window stood the Dauphin amid a cluster of ladies in waiting to Madame, wife of the King's brother. Before attending Madame at her levee, they were putting the final touches to their coiffures and to the latest gossip about their eccentric mistress: such a strange wife for the effeminate Monsieur, and so persistently German amid the delicacy of the French court. And since the dumpy, carelessly dressed Dauphin was never good company, the girls turned welcoming smiles toward Victor.

"By our Lady!" he said gaily. "Such good fortune, to meet the prettiest flowers of the court bouquet. Your pardon, if I borrow just one bud—" Expertly he detached and drew into a window embrasure the only one he really saw, the radiant Marie-Angélique de Scorailles, Demoiselle de Fontanges, recently come to court from her studies. "What good luck to see you! If only I weren't in such a hurry." But he made no move to go. "What did our fat friend want?"

"You silly!" She smiled. "You're jealous."

"Violently, and often. But not of that great imbecile."

She tossed her blond curls. "He'll be King some day."

"Unfortunately." It was hard to imagine the slothful Dauphin as the ruler of France.

"I couldn't send the King's son away," protested Angélique. When Victor scowled, she retreated behind a light laugh. "I'm teasing. I like to see what's under your debonair guardsman's manner."

"You'll see when we're married. I'll beat you every Wednesday and Saturday, just to keep you obedient." He smiled down at her, impatient to possess this tantalizing perfection. Before she came, he had flirted with numerous court beauties. But the morning he met Madame's new maid of honor on the Marble Staircase, he had fallen for her head over heels. Fallen literally, in fact; for he had stopped so suddenly at sight of her that some wine-befuddled count had knocked him off his feet. With her laughter in his ears, he had recovered his poise quickly enough to tell her that the bump on his head was less

23

important than the one on his heart. From that day on he had laid siege to her affections. Now they spent every second they could together, and he was impatient to have their bethrothal settled.

"It's wonderful, your being Captain! Father will surely be impressed."

"If it were only permanent. But even if the captaincy were for sale, I couldn't get ten thousand livres without becoming a highway bandit."

She laughed. "Something will turn up." Still in that exalted frame of mind of all who came newly to the splendors of this palace, she expected miracles at every turn. She would learn soon enough, thought Victor, that under the glitter and gaiety lay hard unpleasant facts. Still, his luck had been good so far.

"Let's hope so. . . . But I must go."

Aware of curious eyes, he bowed formally over her hand, but she murmured, "Here comes your friend La Rochefoucauld. And a distinguished gentleman with him."

Victor whirled around. "It's Father!" And he ran to embrace a handsome, gray-haired man whose bearing proclaimed him a true nobleman, not one of the mere courtiers who spent their lives defending the last petty privileges left to them.

"I am in time then, Monsieur le Capitaine." The Marquis could not quite conceal his pride in his son.

"I'm about to go to my post—after one errand." Victor hurried on, for no breath of that errand must come near his father. "You're looking splendid. How is everyone at home?"

"Quite well. Auguste sends his congratulations, and little Charles, who is, I fear, too young to understand the honor, sends his love. Your mother would have been proud of you."

The young hand sought and clasped the wrinkled one.

"I'm sorry Auguste and Charles couldn't come with you."

"Auguste is never happy far from his plants. He has contracted the tulip mania now, and would ruin himself for a rare bulb. And as only I could be of service to you——"

Victor started at a slight touch on his sleeve.

"Oh! Father, may I present Mademoiselle Marie-Angélique de Fontanges?"

The Marquis's bow was deep. Angélique sank slowly to the floor, holding the curtsy long enough for his rank. But as she rose, she darted a calculated, seductive glance upward at the Marquis and Victor, not even excluding the sad-eyed Duc de la Rochefoucauld.

24

The Marquis had not missed Victor's gesture in presenting her, saying without words that beneath the heavens existed nothing so lovely. But this girl with *le nom de la sainte vierge,* Marie, was no *sainte,* nor was she *angélique.* He felt most uneasy at his son's choice. What was her father thinking of to send her here? She should have been shut up in a convent until the day of her marriage. Sheer, unalloyed female, with a sensual charm: he knew the type well: here were all the makings of a court coquette. Well, if her dowry to her husband included horns, at least they would be gilded ones. "I am charmed, my dear," he said. "Perhaps after I see His Majesty we can celebrate the addition of so much beauty to our family."

"I hope so, sir." She gazed modestly at the floor. "I will do as my father arranges for me."

"Very pretty and dutiful," said the Marquis, with only a slight edge of irony. But she caught it, flushed, bowed, and sweeping up the train of her overdress, sauntered away with an easy grace.

A lackey in the Marquise de Montespan's dark blue livery approached Victor. "Madame de Montespan wants to see you immediately, Monsieur le Capitaine."

"Tell her I'm coming," said Victor impatiently.

The Marquis lifted his eyebrows after the departing lackey, but characteristically asked for no explanation.

"Did you bring a marriage contract for the King to sign?" whispered Victor.

"No. Her father still hesitates and wishes to postpone his decision. I can only sound out the King on his wishes for you. La Rochefoucauld and I will go on to the anteroom now. Don't be late."

Victor had absently drawn the violet packet from his coat, so eager was he to get rid of it, when a voice spoke behind him: "De Lorennes, may I have the honor to be presented to your father? I have wanted to meet him. Our names are so similar."

Victor turned, carefully masking his distaste. "Father, may I present Monsieur le Chevalier de Lorraine?"

After the exchange of bows the Marquis shot a stern glance at his son. The Chevalier symbolized everything that made him uneasy about sons at court. Handsome, brilliant, with a bearing that made most princes look like peasants, he was as rotten inside as he was fair on the surface. First among the perverted courtiers of Monsieur's circle, he was completely unscrupulous. Monsieur's first wife, Henrietta of England, had tried to get rid of him and had promptly died of what appeared to be poison.

"Our history makes honorable mention of both our ancestors," said the Marquis coldly. "Let us hope to be fortunate enough to add luster to it. We will excuse you, Victor."

"Thank you, Father. Your pardon, Monsieur de Lorraine."

Victor was about to pass, when the Chevalier flicked a lace handkerchief toward the packet. It was too late for Victor to conceal it. "I see," said the Chevalier lightly, "that I was not mistaken. You visited a most questionable mansion this dawn."

Bad luck this time, thought Victor. He hadn't recognized anyone at La Voisin's, but it had been dark in the solitary fields of Bonne-Nouvelle, where her house, behind a dense hedge, awaited mysterious clients in coaches with closed curtains and covered crests.

"I was there myself to get some perfumes for Monsieur," added the Chevalier. "She makes excellent ones."

"At dawn?"

"Oh, that's part of the game of going to La Voisin's." He flicked an imaginary speck of dust from his coat. "At dawn or dusk, and always with a mask. You should have been more careful. On horseback, openly like that—fie, you should know better. Your presence might make one wonder which of her famous *poudres* you needed, knowing you are paying court to the beautiful and rich Madamoiselle Fontanges. And then here is your father. You might need both La Voisin's famous aids."

Victor's fingers tightened on the packet. Everyone knew that under cover of dealings in essences and perfumes, La Voisin dispensed love powders and the far more sinister ones called *poudres de succession,* for those over-eager to come into their inheritance.

"Don't become the concern of 'Monsieur de Paris,'" taunted the Chevalier.

Victor's rising anger boiled over beyond the limits of what he called his patience. "When I am insulted, I am capable of being an executioner myself!"

"*Pas de drame, s'il vous plait.* Do take your hand off your sword, Monsieur le Capitaine." He laughed loudly, as if the whole thing were a huge joke, but he was looking narrowly at the mended tear in the blue sleeve. Victor's eyes widened. The Chevalier was about the build of the man he had thrown over the hedge. "Is that the suit you have worn all morning?" he asked abruptly.

26

"But of course. Don't you like it?" the Chevalier asked, as of a connoisseur.

"It's perfect. But I dreamed I saw you in violet."

"My dear Captain, I never wear violet, except as mourning." He bowed and turned away.

"By the Mass!" protested the Marquis. "I was waiting to offer my services as second, as soon as you challenged him."

"I couldn't, Father, and he knew it. The new law against dueling——"

"I know the law," said his father crossly. "But even the King thinks differently as a man than as a lawgiver. He would certainly wish an officer to resent flagrant insults."

I shall take care of the Chevalier, thought Victor grimly. He tried to kill me this morning! "But it must look like an accidental encounter," he said.

"It was better in my day: formalities properly taken care of, above board."

Another of Montespan's lackeys was hurrying toward them. "Please excuse me, Father," murmured Victor. "I'll see you at His Majesty's levee."

3

IT was fortunate for Victor, as late as it was, that La Montespan's apartments were so near. In the drawing room the usual crowd of hangers-on, hoping for crumbs of the royal favor La Montespan had in such plenty, was milling about. Pink draperies and pink lamp shades, to flatter an aging complexion, bathed in a rosy glow rooms that were unusually luxurious even for so ostentatious a palace, for Montespan lived in almost open recognition and in the style and prominence of Louis's second—and favorite—wife.

Though a small fire burned in the grate, the room, like all the vast palace rooms, was chilly. Yet the shiver that went over Victor as he made his way through it was not from cold. Nor was it fear, though Montespan was noted for being as explosive as saltpeter. It was a shiver of discomfort, of foreboding. This violet packet resting uneasily in his hand was unsavory and dangerous business. In the rich soil of Paris, where the strangest things were easily naturalized, thrived a host of magicians, soothsayers, and sorcerers. Their predictions were often sound because they also supplied the means to carry them out. To eliminate someone who stood in a client's way, clever hands could infuse death into a bouquet of flowers, a handkerchief, a drinking cup—and could even make the effects of crime look like natural illness.

Of all the sorcerers, the most sought-after, Victor knew, was La Voisin, who, under cover of selling essences and perfumed toys, had acquired enough secrets to send to the gallows half of Paris and the court. Strange tales were afloat of the dreadful incantations, aphrodisiac powders, and Black Masses Madame de Montespan had employed to secure and hold the King's affections.

Yet Victor had become involved in this business innocently enough. At the *appartements* on Monday night he had lost heavily to Madame de Montespan at lansquenet; and before everyone, including the King, she had refused payment, saying gaily that she would claim instead a little of his time for an errand, and his sworn oath that he would never tell anyone what it was. His Majesty had laughed and said, "You are lucky, De Lorennes, to get off so easily." Victor could only stammer, "At your pleasure, Madame la Marquise."

Pleasure was a peculiar word for it. Victor drew a deep breath, scratched at a gold and white door, and as it opened, stepped through as if about to face Spanish cannon. Crossing the pink and gold bedroom, he paused at the encrusted ivory balustrade, behind which, upon a platform, rose the sculptured and gilded bed, so placed that its occupant, reclining behind partly drawn curtains, could see everyone who arrived. As Victor saluted, he flushed. Ladies of the court commonly received their callers in bed, but none so scantily clad as the Marquise. As she harangued her steward, a bare leg dangled out of a lace and muslin negligee.

Diabolically beautiful, Montespan had increased her charms by every known artifice. Her bleached red-gold hair made a striking frame for her rosy white skin, her full curving lips and her deep blue eyes that reflected few emotions other than triumph or greed. This was the woman who had dominated the King's heart for more than half Victor's lifetime, and who had founded a line of seven bastard princes and princesses. Louis had loaded her with gifts beyond belief. Yet as she turned with a smile after dismissing her steward, Victor could see that she was not above impressing a guardsman young enough to be her son.

"A thousand compliments, Madame la Marquise," he stammered, and turned to look for one of her ladies to whom he might hand the packet. But Montespan beckoned Victor into the ruelle, the enclosed space around the bed, conferring this honor on him as if she were indeed the Queen.

When they were alone, she held out her hand for his kiss. A wave of the heavy scent she always wore in lieu of bathing rose to his nostrils. Hastily he bent his lips over the beringed fingers and pressed the violet packet into them.

"*Merci,* Monsieur le Capitaine," she said archly.

"I pay my debts, Madame." Victor retreated and tried to bow his way out of this ruelle in which so many court intrigues had been hatched.

But Madame de Montespan cried, "Wait! I want you to see what you brought." She drew out of the packet a small vial and a folded white parchment. "A new perfume, created just for me. With this and my new gown—well, we'll see, And here—" she unfolded the parchment—"the horoscope. Oh, very good!" She read with increasing good humor, sniffing the vial, which she would scarcely do if it were anything lethal. Victor breathed more easily until he noticed she had laid the wrappings aside with great care. Accompanying the horoscope might still be something to help fulfill the prophecies. "Perhaps I can do you a favor in return," she said. "A word to the King about your marriage?"

"If you choose, Madame la Marquise." He bowed and tried again to withdraw.

"Where was the King yesterday? I waited all afternoon."

"I'm sorry. I could not reveal any movements of His Majesty that he wished to keep secret."

"Secret!" she burst out. "He goes to her room openly. A poor widow that I brought here as governess—and to read to him and relieve me of having to amuse him all the time." Red spots now disfigured the Montespan cheeks.

Odd, thought Victor, that she seemed so afraid of the one woman whose friendship with the King was assumed to be platonic, though she had watched almost with unconcern when the Princesse de Soubise, Mme. de Ludrès and others had had their brief days in the sun. Unlike the gentle La Vallière, who, at Louis's first indifferent glance, had faded away to a convent, this one was fighting to hold him—not for love of him but of her position.

With an effort, she controlled herself, and put honey into her voice. "You and I are going to be the best of friends." The violet wrappings rustled between her fingers. "This is a secret between us?"

He gave her a stock gallant answer. "For a lady's secret, my mind is a coffer of brass, the key to which I have lost."

"What did La Voisin say?"

"Nothing much. At first she insisted on assuming I had come on my own account. She talked about an unusual future—full of travel, violence, then happiness in a place I have never yet seen."

"But how incredibly fascinating!"

"The travel and violence are easy enough, since I'll probably go back to the army with His Majesty. The rest——?"

Montespan waved a lace-draped hand. "The book of the stars holds the truth. But I can tell you something even La Voisin may not know. The Duc de Luxembourg may be removed from his post."

"I cannot believe that," protested Victor, "of our most distinguished soldier. He has brought back so many enemy flags to adorn the Cathedral of Paris that he's called 'Upholsterer of Notre Dame.'"

"The Minister of War hates him. For years Monsieur Louvois has tried to blacken the Duc in the King's eyes. And now he has something to work on. It seems the Duc went to one of La Voisin's associates, the priest Le Sage, for help in recovering some papers. They were found in the hands of a Mlle. Dupin, who has since been cut into quarters and thrown into the river. Her brother has been poisoned. When the time is ripe, Luxembourg will be accused and thrown into the Bastille. Then, if you are popular with the right people——"

"No—no, Madame," stammered Victor.

"Oh, yes!" she said firmly. "Remember, all the evidence against Luxembourg is that he went to see Le Sage once. It may have been as innocent as this trip of yours to La Voisin. But there were witnesses—in both cases. *Mais,* don't look so black." With the smile that had conquered many a foreign ambassador, she held out her hand. "You needn't worry, as long as you and I are friends. Did La Voisin say when my other vial will be ready?"

"In a week, Madame. And now I must——"

"You will get that one for me, too." She flung both feet over the side of the bed and sat up, very close to him, exerting all her seductive power.

"No, Madame. I must ask to be excused."

"You are joking." Her laughter had a little of an adder's hiss.

He stepped backward. "I have fulfilled the conditions you laid down at the lansquenet table. I must ask you to send one of your lackeys next time." He bowed and tried to retreat, but she seized his sword belt.

"I can't trust a lackey with something that involves His Majesty's happiness. He could give me the wrong package, or add something to the right one."

In a flash Victor saw in what ship he had embarked. If the love potion, or worse, still hidden in the wrappings, should have a harmful effect on the King, and blame were traced to her, she had a scapegoat all ready to serve up, and the Chevalier de Lorraine would support her. She may even have sent him to dispose of me this morning, he thought. Her wrath at the threat of being supplanted by Madame de Maintenon had grown so intense that the whole court feared she might poison her rival, or even the King himself. And His Majesty could not even be warned. Poison was a forbidden word in his presence since the Princess Henrietta's death.

Victor hesitated and then stepped back, so that she had to release his sword belt or be dragged after him. Instantly her face changed from coquettish wheedling to that mask of wrath before which the King himself had often quailed.

"Then I will ruin you, you precious little Captain . . ." She rose and came toward him, her rose negligee falling away in unheeded exposure as her mouth, no longer lovely, poured forth a stream of vile abuse. In a flash Victor remembered the night when he and Marc had followed Montespan's carriage and watched from hiding as she took part in a Black Mass, her voluptuous body naked across an altar in a dark, reddish mist, while a priest in white thrust a long needle into the throat of a new-born child and collected its blood in a chalice for her to drink. Now her torrent of words was so horrifying that Victor could only lower his head and retreat toward the door.

"You have been at court long enough to know better than to make an enemy of me," she concluded. "Now get out!" She seized a pair of precious statuettes unfortunate enough to be within reach and held them in raised, tense hands.

Victor lost no time. As he pulled the outer door shut behind him, he heard two crashes, one after the other.

31

4

ALLOWING his spurs to jingle in true military fashion, Victor passed through the Hall of the Guards and pushed his way into the Chambre des Bassons, where like a swarm of multicolored butterflies the most favored of the courtiers were gathered, as they must every morning, to wait—to wait days, years, entire lifetimes—upon the caprice of their master.

At his approach, the silver and blue guardsmen straightened like lances and brought their halberds to attention. Victor returned the salute, passed critically down the line, and, finding nothing amiss, stepped smartly to the double gilt and white doors of the King's bed-chamber and turned, with only seconds remaining, to savor this great moment. His father waved from a high-arched window embrasure, where he and La Rochefoucauld stood with the Prince de Conti and his protégé, La Salle, while their swords were being unbuckled by lackeys. Victor smiled inwardly at this reminder that only the Captain of the Guards went armed into the King's presence.

Silence crept over the anteroom as all eyes turned reverently toward that gold and white door. When the outer door opened, two men came through and approached Victor, while bewigged heads bowed low before them. The elder, the King's brother, called Monsieur, was short, despite his immensely high-heeled shoes. His pampered, fair complexion, his overlong curling black wig, brought forward profusely on each side of the narrow face, would have suited a princess rather than a prince.

Monsieur was plainly out of sorts. "I'm so upset I don't know how I got dressed." He fussed irritably at his ribbons. "Just as I was putting on my rouge—firecrackers under my window! Nearly startled me into a fit. Some guardsman did it, and you must get rid of him, Captain, when I find out which one it was."

Victor saluted, inwardly uneasy. "Yes, Your Highness." At least he hadn't been recognized. He wasn't afraid of dismissal, but if Monsieur irritated the King with complaints, His Majesty wouldn't be in the best mood for the Marquis's audience.

32

The younger man, the Dauphin, merely stared at the door, boredly awaiting its opening. As lackeys relieved the two of their swords, Monsieur added, "De Lorennes, I appoint you to help me get up a victory ball, if I can pry enough money out of Colbert's tight fists." Monsieur arranged all the social affairs; he liked the endless fussing over details, and had all the facts of lineage and precedence in his head.

"I shall be honored, Your Highness." Inwardly Victor cursed. Chimes denoting the half-hour came faintly from the Hall of the Guards, and the anteroom fell into complete, almost breathless silence.

The door opened, and Bontems, the head *valet de chambre,* with a brusque but respectful signal, beckoned Victor inside. Trembling with excitement, the youthful captain doffed his plumed hat and saluted the handsome, imperious face of Louis XIV, encased in the satins and laces of the bed.

"Good morning, Victor. And put your hat on. The Captain has the unique privilege of remaining covered in my presence." Louis spoke in slow, precise accents, a manner he cultivated to lend gravity to everything he said, for he reigned with the solemnity of a devout and dedicated priest. *"Mordieux!* I declare you're one of the finest figures of a man at court! But your color appears to be a little heightened this morning. You have not taken up the fashion of rouge?"

"Oh, no, sire. It must be the excitement of this overwhelming honor. Also, I have been hurrying to get here on time."

"You overslept? Fie!"

"Oh, no, sire. I awoke at dawn. I have just returned from a long ride. Madame de Montespan chose this morning for the errand she exacted from me at the card game, you remember."

"So?" the King was interested in even the smallest detail concerning his court. "And what was the errand?"

Though Victor had chosen this way of reminding the King of Montespan's demand, he shrank from what might be stirred up if he divulged the full details, quite aside from his oath of secrecy. "She asked me to bring her a small package from Paris."

"Vrai dieu, it must have been valuable, to need my Captain of Guards to escort it," grumbled the King. "So you've been to Paris and back already. I will recommend the practice to the ladies of the court. It would put better roses in their cheeks than they get from boxes."

Victor suppressed a smile. The ladies already suffered from the King's enthusiasm for outdoor exercise. Besides the almost daily hunts,

33

he was given to long, suddenly-decided-upon excursions which included everyone at court, even the indisposed and the pregnant.

"This is the day your father is to be here, I believe."

"Yes, sire, he has arrived and is waiting to pay his respects."

"And how is Marc?"

"He walks with no limp now, sire."

"Good." The King was fond of his guardsmen, and Victor knew it had particularly amused him to have two who looked exactly alike. He liked to place one on each side of his throne, to confuse visiting dignitaries.

"Did you see anyone of the court?"

"The Duc de Maine, outside the palace."

Louis's face lit with affection. "What was he doing?"

Victor, more at ease now, described the firecracker episode, and the King smiled with his usual delight when one of his brood of illegitimates scored off a member of the royal family.

"I'll wager Philip gave a fine display of hysterics. *Eh bien,* we must get on with the levee. Bontems, you may give the word."

As the valet stepped into the Chambre des Bassons to announce that the King no longer slept, Victor saluted and backed smartly to his place beside the door. First to enter were Monsieur and the Dauphin, hats in hand, to make their morning obeisance. At once Monsieur burst out fretfully: "I have a complaint. I won't be tormented! Firecrackers! Tricks on your brother!" He ranted with the voluble rage of all weaklings. "It has put me out of humor for the whole day. My tailor is bringing a dozen new suits, and now I'm in no mood to try them on."

"You are forgetting yourself, Philip," said the King coldly.

Victor, desperate to curb the ominous drooping of the Bourbon lip, interrupted solicitously, "Shall I get some Schaffhausen water for Monsieur, sire?"

At the mention of this emetic remedy for apoplexy, Monsieur clapped his hands to his face, and ran to the nearest mirror to see whether his looks were impaired. The King flicked Victor an appreciative glance, Victor lifted his eyes to heaven in gratitude, and Monsieur came back visibly sulking. But already the King had turned to the Dauphin. "Good morning, Louis. Have you any requests?"

"No."

"At least stand up straight. You look more like a German every day."

The Dauphin's face changed little; he was used to being treated as a subject rather than as a son. All the King's parental affection went to his illegitimate children.

Now the royal eyes traveled on toward the door, which, at that signal, opened to admit a string of splendidly garbed men: the Duc de la Rochefoucauld, First Lord of the Bedchamber, followed by numerous other officers, each carrying a piece of the royal clothing. The King's old nurse was followed by the black-robed Père la Chaise, the King's confessor, a Jesuit, for Louis took care not to incur the enmity of that order. As Victor announced the First Surgeon and Daquin, the king's physician, he had a disturbing thought: Daquin was Montespan's creature. He watched tensely as the aged nurse kissed the royal cheek and the physician and surgeon made their daily examination. If they gave the King a tonic, might it contain something from that violet packet? He gasped almost visibly with relief as they stepped down, consulted briefly, solemnly pronounced His Majesty in perfect health, and turned back to give their patient his massage. Père la Chaise approached the head of the bed, and began murmuring earnestly. Victor let his attention wander until he heard the name La Salle.

"We of the Order of Jesus do not consider him a reliable person, and we who have done so much for New France have a right to be heard. We are eager to keep Your Majesty's power unthreatened——"

"Yes, yes, you have told me all that," dismissed the king, turning to Bontems, who aided him in hasty ablutions, after which he was clothed, piece by piece, by his courtiers.

Victor gazed with adoration upon the regal figure who paused for an instant in a shaft of sunlight that seemed to rest with especial friendliness upon proud features inherited from Bourbon, Medici, and Hapsburg. By virtue of wigs and high heels, every man in the room had raised his height, but nature had raised the King a good three inches above the rest; just as she had given him grace, beauty, and a natural charm. Well might the sunlight, thought Victor, feel at home on the broad brow framed by the *perruque majestueuse,* for Louis had adopted the sun and the god Apollo as the symbols of his glittering reign, and he stood now at the zenith of power and success. He felt himself a worthy successor to Charlemagne, and with reason, Victor exulted. From the very day when the bishop placed on his finger the coronation ring that wed him to France, he had furthered the trend toward absolute monarchy, until he was its culmination.

35

Now, crossing to the fireplace and seating himself in the carved arm-chair, he composed his expression as if he were on the stage, about to play the part of a king.

"The first entree!" he said.

"The first entree!" repeated La Rochefoucauld loudly, and the Prince de Conti entered, followed by a line of others, among them the Marquis de Lorennes. Each advanced, bowed three times deeply, and murmured a few words of inquiry and compliment. They formed a semicircle at a distance, after which the barber came, surrounded by attendants with towels and a steaming silver bowl. In silence he soaped and shaved the royal chin, and Bontems held a mirror while the King wiped his face. The Master of the Robes approached, and the King announced,

"The grand entree!"

Immediately a cluster of attendants took positions at the gold and white doors to assist Victor. Admission to the levee was a favor which even those of highest rank might spend their lives sighing in vain to achieve. As each individual scratched at the door with his nails or his wig comb, Victor in a low, clipped voice, repeated the name, which passed along the row of attendants until it reached La Rochefoucauld, who whispered it to the King. If His Majesty made no reply, the visitor was admitted, and was marshaled to his place. Only three in the procession were exempt from this tedious procedure: Racine, the writer, Boileau, the critic, and Mansard, the architect. Louis XIV hated to read, but in his love for *les beaux arts* he was a true son of the Medicis.

Victor was busy every instant, for now came bishops and cardinals, officers of the household, and M. Colbert, the surly but brilliant Minister of Finance. At the very end of this procession came M. de la Salle. Victor stopped him politely, half expecting the King to reject the name. But Louis gave him a gracious nod, whereupon everyone turned to mark the handsome man in red who must here-after be treated with courtesy in anterooms and galleries. As La Salle approached, the Prince de Conti stepped forward one pace, and bowed. Only by a certain blankness did the King show his regret at the respect he must pay this prince. "Sire, it is my honor to present again to Your Majesty my friend, Monsieur Robert Cavelier, Sieur de la Salle, of Montreal and Fort Frontenac, in New France. He presents himself also as a representative of the Governor-General, Count Frontenac."

The King nodded as La Salle made the prescribed three bows. To Victor, his bows seemed to have the special integrity of one who lays at his sovereign's feet deeds accomplished in his name.

Louis was also staring at the bronzed explorer. "You were here four years ago."

"Yes, sire." The voice was low, with the proper hint of being overwhelmed by a dazzling presence.

"In consideration of your services in exploration we gave you at that time a patent of nobility. We also granted you the seigneury of Fort Frontenac. You were to pay back the ten thousand francs it had cost me, maintain it at your own expense with a garrison as large as that of Montreal, form a French colony around it, build a church and maintain two Recollet friars." The King spoke as if he had kept all these details in his head, though he may have been refreshed about them the day before by M. Colbert.

"It has all been done as Your Majesty stipulated."

"The richest seigneury in New France. You could make a fortune in the fur trade."

"Yes, sire. But now I wish to serve Your Majesty in extending the colony." The low voice grew stronger and more confident.

"The Governor-General speaks highly of you and your plans."

"Count Frontenac has been very kind."

"Monsieur Colbert, too, waxes lyrical. A good partisan to have, the Minister of Finance." The King smiled, and an answering wave of amusement went obediently through the salon. "I have asked him to be present at your audience. At ten, then."

La Salle bowed, backed away, and the levee was resumed.

"Ah, Sully," said the King, looking around the semicircle before him, so like a bed of brilliant flowers. "So you are back from Vichy? You look well."

Victor felt the wave of pity, diluted with indifference, that went toward the Duc. Being a favorite was an active position and its duties must be done regularly. If Louis gave a man permission to go take the waters, his favor must be nearing the end.

The little Duc bowed so deeply he was almost kneeling. "A thousand thanks, Your Majesty," he babbled eagerly. "I look well not from the Vichy waters but because I am again so close to the sun, the creator of light. As one of the tiniest of stars, I receive gratefully the reflection of Your Majesty's rays."

Though Louis XIV disliked perfume, the incense of flattery could never be too heavy for him. With a gracious nod, he continued his penetrating gaze down the tensely waiting line.

"Ah, De Lorennes." Victor started forward, but it was his father who was being addressed. A flush of pride went over him as the handsome Marquis bowed before his monarch; his bearing marked him as one of the proud *noblesse d'épée,* the families who had won their titles by military service. "It is a long time since you have been at court, Marquis. I almost do not know you."

Victor shivered. That was close to what the king said to dispose of a man utterly and finally: I do not know him. Louis XIV could never understand why one who might have the honor of being near him could wish to be anywhere else.

"Your Majesty, the imperfection of my health and the pressure of other duties keep me upon my estates. Both Your Majesty and your father have had many proofs of my devotion, and I hope my two sons in your service represent me worthily."

"Your sons at home, Auguste and Charles, is it? They are well? Charles will soon be old enough to consider his career. We might take him as a page in the Ecurie."

Victor kept his face modestly composed at this honor. The King's stables were the elite training school in horsemanship and fencing.

The Marquis bowed. "Your Majesty is very kind. But I shall keep him at home as long as I can. Two sons at court are enough—" the King raised his eyebrows and the Marquis added smoothly—"enough honor for one modest family."

"I hope you yourself will be here more often in future." At the friendly tone the whole room relaxed. "I do not forget your long service."

"I envy the young who can follow you to war now," said the Marquis.

"Anyone who has made a name like yours is entitled to rest on his laurels."

"Fresh laurels are excellent, but older ones often seem of little use."

Victor's spirits soared at this interchange. Surely after such skillful reminders the King could deny the Marquis nothing. But now the ceremony was nearing an end. When the King rose, the courtiers grew alert for his announcement of the day's plans. Then for the first time they would know their own.

"This afternoon we shall walk in the gardens while I inspect the work. There will be no hunt. I shall soon return to the chase of a

38

bigger fox, an Orange one. Tonight you will attend the *appartements*. On Sunday we will go to St. Germain-en-Laye. Monday, I shall rejoin the army of Flanders. Those whose duties require it will attend me."

From his listeners arose an almost audible sigh, expressing all shades of emotion from despair to elation. Victor was at first elated, thinking how he would march off to war in the most magnificent army Europe had seen since the Crusades. But then he came to earth with a thud. How would he ever pay his way on such a costly trip?

The King, with a few favorites, was already passing from his chamber to his cabinet, leaving the door slightly ajar. Bontems reappeared, holding before Victor a sheet of paper bearing the names of those granted the privilege of a royal audience on that twenty-seventh of May of the year 1678. Swiftly Victor memorized the brief list and its order: M. Colbert, the Marquis de Lorennes, M. de la Salle. He nodded, dismissing Bontems, and sat down on a bench just outside the cabinet, his only duty now to prevent intruders. Within, M. Mansard was presenting plans for the grand gallery that was to be the masterpiece of Versailles.

Victor, watching the courtiers disperse for the two hours before the King's lunch, wondered idly where Marc was. He had hoped to see him before this and, he admitted, smiling to himself, to have Marc see him in his new position. Quickly he changed the smile to one of welcome, as he saw his father making his way through the crowd, followed by the scarlet-coated La Salle bearing a roll of papers under his arm. Victor rose and returned the salutes. "Father, and Monsieur. You are early."

"It doesn't matter. We expect to wait." The Marquis listened to the discussion of subjects for gallery paintings still going on inside. "Such attention to trifles sometimes breeds inability to deal with momentous matters."

"But the King loves going over these details of building and decoration," said Victor. "He should be in a good mood for your audience. And yours, Monsieur de la Salle," he added. But the scarlet-clad figure had withdrawn to a window embrasure, where he stood like a man accustomed to being alone, not only in this palace but in the world.

5

PROMPTLY on the stroke of ten, M. Mansard departed, and M. Colbert appeared and was admitted to the cabinet. Victor sat on the bench, reconciled to the passing of more than one bad quarter hour before he would know whether he and Angélique could plan their wedding. Through the half-open door, the abrupt voice of Colbert alternated with the deliberate one of the King.

While Victor waited for the signal to announce his father, the outer doors of the anteroom were flung open, and Monsieur burst in, his ribbons aflutter. "I want to see my brother," he said imperiously, "and I shall not wait a half hour while lesser people are in there as I did yesterday."

Victor rose and bowed, and turned toward the cabinet door.

"Attendez, un petit moment, Victor," said Monsieur. "I'll tell you what I want."

"That is not necessary, Your Royal Highness."

"I know it isn't." Monsieur was pettishly fingering his curls. "But I choose to tell you. I intend to ask if I can head an army again. And I want a detachment of guards to head it, with you and your brother as my lieutenants."

"That will be as His Majesty wishes. But may I be allowed a small wager?"

"Yes, of course."

"Ten pistoles that he will not give you the command."

Monsieur stared. "Why not?"

Before Victor had to answer, Colbert stood in the doorway. "His Majesty is ready."

Monsieur advanced. Colbert scowled but stood aside to let him pass. In a few minutes it was over: a request, a refusal, a few protestations cut short. Almost brutally the King thrust Monsieur back into his proper niche: "You may plan a fête to celebrate our victory."

The flustered prince burst into the anteroom and dashed his hat to the floor. Silently Victor retrieved the hat, presented it with a bow,

40

and Monsieur, seizing it, glared at him and pulled out of his pocket ten pistoles, at the same time scattering sweetmeats all over the parquet. As the beribboned coattails flew out the door, Victor dropped the coins into his pocket.

"Easy money, with no risk," said the Marquis with a faint smile.

La Salle turned from the window and approached like a man returning from a far place. "Certainly a command couldn't be given to one so ill-fitted for it."

"Not exactly for that reason," said the Marquis. He settled back on the bench, his eyes half closed. "Tell him, Victor."

Father is very tired, thought Victor in concern, but he turned obediently to La Salle. "At court Monsieur constantly bestirs himself on affairs of no consequence, like a child chasing a butterfly. But when he was in command at Montcassel, he showed that he, too, was a grandson of Henry IV, and defeated the Prince of Orange in open battle, which His Majesty has never done. Monsieur also received a bullet in his cuirass with an indifference everyone took for heroism, and he was very popular afterward. So he'll never again be allowed to lead an army."

"All the same," said La Salle, "I would not choose him to stalk Iroquois with me."

"What manner of animals are they?"

But Colbert was in the doorway, signaling. Quickly Victor stepped inside and announced M. le Marquis de Lorennes. *"Bonne chance, mon père,"* he whispered. To his disappointment the door closed behind his father.

La Salle stood quietly, his face showing the strain of the approaching audience, which would determine the course of his life. Victor felt he could match the man's impatience with his own.

Both halves of the outer door burst open and Monsieur came rushing in again. "About the victory fête, De Lorennes—"

Victor rose with a sigh. "I appreciate the honor, but I shall be going back to the army. You had better choose someone else. Le Comte d'Artois?"

"Nom de dieu, non!" giggled Monsieur. "He's so ignorant he thinks Henry IV was the son of Henry III. And your name will look better in the *Mercure*. We'll plan it before you go. I thought we might have a play, out in the Marble Court . . ."

Victor could have strangled him. Now there was no chance of hearing fragments of the conference inside.

". . . or we might have a water party on the canal. No, a ballet. You plan the theme and get Lulli to compose the music and direct the dances. I'll choose costumes, and dance the feminine lead. You'll dance in it, of course."

"Why not get professionals? They dance better."

Monsieur ignored the suggestion. "What about a historical theme?"

"Very suitable. But I'm still not the man for you. Even at school I was no good at history."

"Then get Marc to help you." He fluttered through the door, popping a bonbon into his mouth.

Victor's irritation evaporated. Being the younger brother of a King was no enviable destiny.

"So you dance in ballet?" La Salle eyed him appraisingly.

Victor stared. "Everyone does, age and figure permitting. Lustily, if not well. If we have a marriage, a birth, a peace treaty, or an important foreign visitor—anything is an excuse for a ballet. His Majesty used to dance in them himself as Jupiter or Apollo . . ." He broke off abruptly, for the Marquis was coming out.

La Salle drew a deep breath, as if summoning all his reserves. Victor announced him, and then, back in the anteroom, changed instantly from guardsman to anxious son. "What did His Majesty say?"

"I'm afraid the pear is not yet ripe," the Marquis said softly. "He thought you needn't be in such haste to marry for money. I hinted that this damsel had other attractions. He would only say he would have her presented to him this evening, and then—'We will see.'"

Victor threw out his hands in despair. "His usual way of postponing a decision indefinitely."

"Since he neither permits nor forbids, we are none the worse off." The Marquis picked up his hat and cloak. "I shall walk in the Orangerie for a while."

"The Orangerie? But Father, only the royal family and those the King himself invites may go there."

"I know." The Marquis smiled. "His Majesty suggested I might like it."

Victor brightened. "Then that's a sign you are in favor!"

The Marquis flashed a peculiar glance at him. "Perhaps so. I prefer another favor: following his dinner at one, you are to post another guard and be at my disposal until supper."

Victor dismissed a brief regret at leaving his post on this first day. Anyway, since the King would spend the afternoon walking in the gardens and visiting Montespan or Maintenon, nothing interesting would happen before evening. So he answered heartily, *"A la bonne heure!* He almost never releases anyone from duty!"

"Oh, yes—Marc asked me to tell you that he had a chance to ride into Paris. We can meet him at Villette's and come back together. The Prince de Conti has offered me his carriage. I'll wait for you in the forecourt. And don't be discouraged, my son. Have patience until the King meets your intended. He is very . . . susceptible to beauty."

Alone in the anteroom, Victor settled back on the narrow bench, feeling disquieted and empty. Still, he tried to tell himself, everything must wait until after this campaign. But he had hoped to go away definitely betrothed. Trying to obey his father's suggestion of patience, he turned to another of his worries. How could he get some money? Unless the cards were with him this evening, he would have to visit a moneylender. With the room quiet, the voices came distinctly through the open door. Victor moved closer. Was M. de la Salle having any luck? Despite his own problems, he was deeply curious about this explorer, whose rough life had apparently not diminished his good breeding.

The King was speaking. "Do Count Frontenac and my Intendant Monsieur Duchesneau show any signs of greater harmony?"

"Occasions of difference and friction still exist, I believe."

"Your Majesty," Colbert put in, "the intendant and governor of every province in France have similar conflicts. It is because Your Majesty gives neither one definite authority, and each is answerable only to the crown."

"At least dissension keeps them from conspiring against that crown," said Louis dryly. "Continue, La Salle."

"You will see by Count Frontenac's report, which I have delivered to Monsieur Colbert, that in New France the Bishop claims authority over both—and the Bishop is the creature of the Jesuits."

"We shall consider the report. Tell me now of your own requests."

"Thank you, Your Majesty. Twelve years ago, when I first went to New France, I continued upriver from Quebec to the island of Montreal."

"A dangerous place," interposed Colbert. "Lots of trouble with the Iroquois."

"Yes. It's often said that its town, Ville Marie, 'exists only by a continuous miracle.' Its owners, the St. Sulpice priests, sold me a large

43

tract of land, about three leagues up the river. I called my property the Seigneury de St. Sulpice, but I'm afraid it's better known as La Chine, Chinatown, in mockery of my hopes of finding a western route to China."

"At least," said Colbert, "it indicates your vision does not stop at the end of your nose."

"I had long believed, it is true, as others have, that there is a passage to the South Sea. Indians bringing their furs east have talked with me repeatedly of a great river rising in their country. It does flow into the sea, they say, but far away, a journey of eight or nine months." La Salle paused, evidently at a royal gesture, for the next words were in the deliberate tones of the sovereign: "Do you have interpreters to talk with all these savages?"

"No. I have myself mastered Iroquois and seven other languages and dialects." La Salle paused. "I hope these will be sufficient for the task I ask Your Majesty's permission to do for France." He hesitated again.

How skillful, or well coached, is this La Salle, thought Victor. The King liked confidence in a man, but liked more to see himself feared. Nothing advanced a petitioner's interests better than to grow suddenly embarrassed, as if overcome by majesty. "Go on," said the royal voice.

"I believed at first that this river they spoke of must flow into the Vermilion Sea, the Gulf of California. Like others, I assumed the savage term 'great water' referred to the sea, but I believe now that it means this river itself, which they call Mississippi. Upon studying the reports of Monsieur Joliet and Father Marquette, who explored a part of it, I feel certain that it must flow into the gulf near Spanish Mexico. That might be just as desirable for France. To be brief, I want to explore the Mississippi to its mouth."

"Are there reports," the King interposed, "of silver mines near this river?"

"No, sire. I have heard of none except the Spanish mines in Mexico."

"Too bad." It vexed Louis greatly that what most appealed to him in the New World was in the hands of Spain.

"I sold my land and buildings back to the seminary," La Salle resumed, "and with the money spent two years in preliminary exploration of the West. I found a portage route from the Lake of the Illinois to a river that flows into the Mississippi; so I am ready to proceed when I have men and supplies. If Your Majesty will be kind enough to glance at this map——?"

44

Apparently there was a nod of consent, for a rustling of paper followed. Victor glanced through the door and saw that on the King's table lay a long map, one end held down by the explorer's brown hand, the other by a gold inkstand set with jewels.

"Here, Your Majesty can observe how the St. Lawrence strikes into the heart of the continent to Lake Ontario, where Fort Frontenac is located. Beyond Ontario are the short, narrow straits called Niagara, where one must portage around a great waterfall. I have not seen this cataract, but I have heard a continuous distant thunder as I passed over the portage around it."

What a chance, thought Victor, for an obsequious man to add: "Even as the report of your greatness reaches many who have never seen Your Majesty." But La Salle was in another world.

". . . one then traverses Lake Erie. From it a short river trip to the Lake of the Hurons, which one traverses to Michilimackinac, here—where the Great Lakes come together. Thus far we French can control the waters, by adding a fort at the mouth of the Niagara strait."

The voice had deepened with intense emotion. How can this mean so much to him? wondered Victor.

"What I propose," said La Salle earnestly, "is to explore the Mississippi and build a chain of forts from the Great Lakes to the Gulf of Mexico and, at the Mississippi's mouth, a fort that will be the key to the entire continent. This great river will be open then only to the ships of France. England will be confined to the seacoast, and Spain to its colonies in Florida and Mexico. This vast interior will be a great new empire for Your Majesty, for these western lands appear infinitely more desirable than those along the St. Lawrence. They are reported to have a temperate climate, fertile soil, with forests, prairies, rivers, fish and game. The trade in furs alone will enrich France beyond all imagining. Wild oxen are numerous, and their fine wool can be used for making cloth and hats. Their hides are better than those of French oxen. I brought one of them to Monsieur Colbert."

"They seem to have excellent possibilities in manufacturing," added Colbert.

"It is a bulky fur," said La Salle, "and expensive to transport all the way to Quebec in canoes, over so many portages. But with an opening to the gulf, this trade can become a rich one."

Colbert interrupted again. "Tell His Majesty of the obstacles to your plan."

"There are five. The first is the difficulty of navigation, because of

45

rapids and the great cataract, and the portage between the Lake of the Illinois and the Mississippi. The second will be that of maintaining a supply route so far from French settlements. The third is the expense of supporting enough men to build these forts and defend them. The fourth problem is the Iroquois, who might destroy our settlements or cut off our communication. The fifth is the nearness of the English colonies: at any time they might seize the entrance to Lake Ontario or Lake Erie. We must hasten to forestall them."

"France's domain lies more properly in Europe," said the King.

"But you, sire, have already made France the greatest power on this continent. Now you can make her dominant over the new one."

Louis bent over the map. "I don't like my people spread out too much."

"Yet the sun can shine on more than one field at a time," urged La Salle. "And this vast region can be of great service to France. The forests can build your ships. There are certain to be mines of copper and iron, even perhaps of gold and silver. The colonists can supply materials, and buy manufactured goods from France."

Victor glanced in again. Colbert was nodding his head repeatedly. Victor knew that most of the projects Colbert encouraged, especially art and letters, the Minister cared little for, but since they should flourish under a great ruler, they must flourish under Louis. What really touched his heart was the country's trade.

The King smiled at his enthusiasm. "Yes, Colbert, a nation should have colonies, but I doubt the wisdom of scattering our people through a wilderness. Better for them to stay near Quebec, under the eye of my Governor. Later, we will see."

"But England and Spain will not wait," La Salle urged desperately. "If we do not take this river valley, they will."

"Spain!" Into the word Louis put a lifetime of hatred, aggravated by the insolence of the grandees when he married their Infanta. "And the English! That island of heretics abandoned by God since they defied the divine right of kings and beheaded one."

In the silence following this explosion Victor peered in to make sure nothing was amiss. But the three were still bent over the map. Colbert's sunken eyes were agleam. "You have omitted one obstacle. The Jesuits have their missions on the first part of your route, and they have asked for the territory along the Mississippi. Monsieur Joliet, one of their lay brothers, has asked for a trading center there."

46

La Salle sighed. "One has to respect what some Jesuits have done in New France, suffering as they did even torture and death. But greater than their efforts 'for the greater glory of God,' are those they make for the power and wealth of the Order of Jesus." He turned to the King, with an apologetic gesture. "They will allow no priests but their own, wherever they have missions, and expect even the authority of the crown to be subservient. They are determined to rule the lakes and the Mississippi, not to benefit the Indians or France, but to add to the vast possessions of their order. They would exclude all other white men, and monopolize the fur trade. That is why I prefer Recollets, who ask nothing but an opportunity to bring the savages into the fold of Christ. That is why you have heard so much against me from the Jesuits, sire. If I am permitted to expand New France, they cannot increase their hold on it."

The King glanced around uneasily as if someone might be standing behind him. But there was only the Protestant Colbert, who commented tonelessly, "The Jesuits are tireless."

Louis XIV scowled. "But they shall not dictate to the crown of France. I'll show you something. Colbert, bring me the plans for completing Versailles." The minister crossed to a chest, opened a drawer and returned. Amid a crackling of paper, the King resumed, "See on this drawing where I am putting the new chapel—at one side of the main building. The Queen's Spanish relatives are shocked; they say it should be the center. My symbolism is deliberate. It will be prominent, but not joined to the palace. I allow no interference from the Church in affairs of state. While all France should be Christian, I will not have it run like a religious order—heaven should not weigh so heavily upon earth. So, Monsieur de la Salle, I approve your choice of Recollets." He bent again over the explorer's map, but with less interest than he had devoted to the great gallery plans an hour earlier. "A fort on the gulf," he mused. "Yes, we might make good use of it. What exactly do you propose?" He glanced at a gold and ormolu clock.

La Salle bent forward, tense, a gambler staking everything he owned. "I propose to lead France into the valley of the Mississippi, which, with your permission, I shall rename the River Colbert, and the entire territory it waters, Louisiana. I wish to build enough forts to hold this valley. I ask no money or supplies, but only the lordship of such lands as I shall explore, on the condition that I give up those for which I do not obtain settlers within twenty years, and I ask the rank of governor in these new countries. On my part I bind myself not to trade with any tribes that take their furs to our present settlements."

Victor was listening now with such absorbed interest that a scratching at the outer door penetrated his awareness only when it became thoroughly irritated. He hastened to open it, taken aback to see Madame de Montespan herself, holding a sealed envelope. "Give this to His Majesty," she said, as to a lackey, with no sign of recognition, and swept majestically away.

In a few minutes La Salle at last came out, showing signs of great strain, and Victor scratched lightly at the cabinet door. At the King's "Come," he stepped through with the note and waited tensely to see whether the King were any less friendly since hearing of his request to marry. But Louis only glanced at him and continued to Colbert, ". . . I agree, but certain reservations occur to me. He may be an honest man, as you say, but I can see that he might become a dangerous one."

"With Your Majesty's great intellect and farseeing judgment, you perceive many things that are missed by my duller brain. To me, this La Salle seems a most valuable man."

"But a man with such large projects may rise too far. What he has sketched this morning is an empire."

"I believe," said Colbert, "he has no plans that would not be held by a loyal subject. And they will cost the treasury nothing at all. Count Frontenac speaks highly of his integrity, his nobility, his patriotism. Let me read his latest letter." He hastily extracted a sheet from the folio under his arm.

"I cannot but recommend to you, Monseigneur, the Sieur de la Salle. He is a man of sense and intelligence, and is the most capable I know here for all the enterprises and explorations which it may be desired to entrust to him, for he has a most complete knowledge of the condition of this country, as will be apparent to you——"

The King cut him off with a gesture. "Spare me the rest. I intend to make use of the young man. But 'integrity,' 'nobility,' 'patriotism,'— I would put my hand in the flame that no one has such grand schemes without expecting to get something for himself. We shall clip his wings. I shall approve his plan for a string of forts, but we shall

48

shorten the time he wants, from twenty years to five. Do you think he can really pay for the forts?"

"We might give him a monopoly of the trade in these wild oxen hides."

"Very good. No one at Quebec could object to that. Draw up a suitable patent."

"Of course we can watch him closely," said Colbert. "Your Intendant at Quebec, on your orders, already requires every explorer to keep a journal and undergo a written examination upon his return."

"We shall do better than that. He shall have plenty of rope, but our hand will be firmly on the end of it."

"I suppose the Governor could send someone to watch him."

The royal fingers played over the jeweled inkstand. "Not good enough. I must be sure of loyalty to me alone. I'll send someone from my own court."

"He told me," said Colbert thoughtfully, "something about recruiting associates here in Paris. You might introduce your spy among them."

"I must think of the right man." The King dropped into silence, while his gaze roamed over the paintings and tapestries, and came to rest at last on Victor, waiting with the note. He looked at him thoughtfully. Victor's flesh began to tighten. Even when one is in favor, there is a chill in being looked at too long by a king. "Oh, yes. Come here." He read the note, frowned, and tossed it carelessly on the table.

Soon the other ministers began arriving for a meeting of the Council of State. Victor watched for a smile or word from the King, and receiving none, followed dejectedly three paces behind as the monarch was joined by Monsieur and passed between the double line of courtiers waiting to accompany him to Mass. His Majesty seemed somewhat preoccupied all the way to the gallery where he commonly met the Queen and her retinue. Confronting no one there, he stopped. "Is Her Majesty not ready?"

"Her Majesty begs to be excused this morning," La Rochefoucauld offered uncomfortably.

The King frowned, nodded curtly, and the procession moved on, Victor alertly scanning the crowd on both sides. Anyone, high or low, was allowed to make a request or hand a petition to the King at this time, but must first obtain permission from the Captain of the Guards.

49

There were several this morning, of the usual kinds: a farmer whose grain had been trampled by the hunt, another complaining of tyranny from his lord. The widow of a workman killed on the scaffoldings at Versailles was given a pension on the spot, but most who approached were told only, "We shall see."

The last petitioner, awaiting them in the Salon of Abundance, was a graceful, slight man in his late twenties, in the uniform of a French *garde-marine,* though the cast of his handsome dark features was Italian. The Italian had been in French uniform ten years, since he was eighteen, he told the King, stepping backward meanwhile as nimbly as a dancer before the procession's inexorable progress. He had taken part in several naval campaigns, three in warships and four in the galleys. Now that the war was nearly over, and his part of the forces was being disbanded, he lacked employment. He asked a small pension or some work to support himself and his parents.

"A great many soldiers and sailors will be out of employment." said the King. The *garde-marine* waited. *"Eh bien,* we shall see."

"But sire, if I had said that to my captain when he sent me into battle, I would still have my hand and would not need to ask for anything." He held up briefly a stiff, unnatural glove.

The King, struck by his ready answer, observed him more intently. "Don't I know you?"

"I was here before, just after I lost my hand. Your Majesty granted me three hundred livres. I had an artificial hand made, and re-enlisted in the galleys. I was in the campaign against Sicily and took part in all the victories over Spain's fleet in the Mediterranean. I hope you can now find a way for me to serve France once more."

"I remember now. Your father was the one who invented that insurance scheme."

"It is most gracious of Your Majesty to remember. And I am grateful that he was finally released from the Bastille last year. But after his eight years in prison he and my mother need help from their sons."

The royal hand stroked the Bourbon nose. "It escapes me for the moment why he was put in."

"Only because the insurance plan did not seem to work at first, and Cardinal Mazarin became angry with its inventor. But the French government has now been making money on the Tontine for many years."

"Your name?"

"Henri de Tonti, sire."

50

Louis had reached the opposite door of the Salon of Abundance. "You have had three hundred livres. That is all we can do for you."

His disappointment showing only in his eyes, the Italian bowed and stepped aside. As Victor passed him, on an impulse he smiled. He wished he might make some suggestion. But what could he say?

Organ music drew the procession to the King's daily hour of devotion in the chapel.

6

WHEN Louis was ready to tour the gardens, Victor summoned a lieutenant as his relief and set off on a run for the guards' mess hall, where he bolted a hurried meal, and then to the wrought-iron gate, where he found the Marquis waiting in the superb, ornate carriage bearing the Condé arms, attended by a swarm of outriders in the Prince de Conti's peach-colored liveries.

As they rolled along the Cours-la-Reine, Victor lolled back against the velvet cushions, reveling in the pomp of traveling as a prince. The carriage was one of the new kind, slung on springs and fitted in velvet, with glass windows that could be raised and lowered. If luck stays with me, he thought, Angélique and I might live almost as well as this sometime. If only I knew what trouble La Montespan is brewing.

At the rumble of approaching wheels, he turned to look back and saw a furiously driven carriage. Its driver hailed theirs, asking permission to pass. As they pulled to one side, a flock of outriders dashed past and then a calèche with six horses, bearing Madame de Montespan and her favorite lady in waiting. Behind came another coach with six more of her women.

"Phew!" The Marquis recoiled from the dust. "The lady can scarcely be said to move calmly along the road."

Victor fumbled with the catch that closed the windows. "She often boasts that no carriage cleaves the air like hers." He counted the attendants as they vanished into the dust. "At least forty persons! She always travels that way, and utterly breakneck."

"That seems the whole tone of the court these days."

"You don't like it, Father?"

The Marquis answered carefully, aware of the readiness of youth to consider its elders out of date. "Some things I like very much—the delight in beauty, and the desire for a full life. But I can't like its carelessness as to means, and its arrogant selfishness. . . ." He lapsed into silence, unwilling to cast any blot on the boy's day of triumph. True, on the surface, the reign of Louis XIV seemed ideal—so full of glory, amusement, and happiness. And in the growth of literature, art, and sculpture, it was an age to compare with that of Pericles in Greece. But everything that shone had its shadow. This dark side lay in the nature of the King. The young Louis XIV, forced into a marriage of policy with Marie-Thérèse of Spain, had from the very marriage day rejected his stodgy bride and set foot on the path of dalliance, and thus set the tone for the court.

As a father, the Marquis had regretted the King's taking a fancy to Victor and Marc and bringing them so young into this pageantry stained with every vice. Ducs and princes were here as often enamoured of page boys as of ladies in waiting; and young men of the highest families were living at the expense of rich old crones. The twins had no lack of friends; that there were two so alike and so handsome was diverting, and this century loved diversion.

The Marquis stole a glance at Victor, now smiling at some inner thought. This unexpected show of the King's favor would make Victor a target. This Fontanges girl, too, altered the picture. He knew from the teasing of Dreux that neither twin had before been involved beyond light flirtations. Of course, many De Lorennes men had made their choice late in life. Auguste, a stolid Norman, more like a Dutchman, had not yet married at twenty-three, and apparently had given his heart to his horses, orchards, and fields.

He wished he felt better about this marriage Victor was set on. "Manuring your fields" was the current term for marrying a rich commoner's daughter. Of course, it would make no difference in the coming generations, since a nobleman's children were noble, no matter how plebeian the mother. Money and position were the important considerations in founding a new family, but he himself had been lucky enough to marry for love. Thinking that he wished a similar happiness for his sons, he sighed.

Victor roused himself from daydreaming. "Aren't you well, Father? You said something to the King about your health."

"Not quite as well as usual. A little stomach trouble. It's worse

52

after a nervous strain, like an audience with His Majesty. It's not easy to face anyone who can say, as master, *Je le veux* or *Je ne le veux pas*. Withholding his consent may have been punishment for my evading the question of returning to court. Then too—letting you marry money would restore our family. He prefers to have the nobility dependent on him, preferably at Versailles, where they must imitate his own splendor, which impoverishes them, makes them more dependent, and so his power grows. To create this brilliance of a sun king he has dimmed the luster of all the old houses."

"Even if His Majesty consents," Victor pursued his own thought, "we still have Angélique's father to persuade. She thinks he would be impressed by a Captain of the Guards. It was hinted to me this morning that if I could get the money—"

"You may hold the post for some time, anyway. De Luxembourg will probably continue in the field."

Victor decided to say nothing about the other hints. "But the war is about over!"

"Sooner or later it will be renewed. There will be no end to Louis's expansion of his glory until he is forced to stop. I don't see how the country can pay for all these wars, besides all the extravagant building. And I'm afraid," added the Marquis, "you've been imitating the manner of kings and scattering your money in all directions."

Victor grinned. *"Touché.* This uniform isn't even paid for. But everyone owes his tailor. Except Marc. He's almost bourgeois about paying on time."

"If you marry, that will be the first break between you. But perhaps Marc has a lady in mind, too?"

Victor laughed. "No lady interests him for more than one evening, unless she is between the covers of a book."

The coach was rattling over the road now as if racing for a prize, until finally it had to slow at the outskirts of Paris. The morning's rain, augmented by slops, had converted the narrow streets into streams of black mud. It took all the driver's skill to make his way through with the enormous coach. Pedestrians had to flatten themselves against doorways to avoid being spattered, yet they smiled with respect and affection at the Condé arms and liveries.

"I'll wager they didn't smile if Montespan came this way," said Victor. "If you're slow on your feet she'll run you down."

The Rue St. Denis was crowded with small tradesmen's shops whose huge signs swung low over the street. There was little travel in this region, but within a hundred paces of Villette's shop another coach, small and shabby, blocked their passage.

"Make way for the carriage of the Prince de Conti!" bawled their coachman.

Victor leaned out. Two ladies were alone in the other carriage. "Wait. He is having trouble making the turn."

"Let the Prince's carriage be held up by a plain hired hack?" the coachman grumbled. "I'll be despised by every coachman in Paris." But he drew up the horses.

Victor could see that the two ladies in long, capelike traveling cloaks were strangers, with no masks, and with bonnets several years behind the style. As he watched, a shabbily dressed fellow rushed to their coach window. "Stop, ma'am!" he called. "Your coach beam is broken."

Their driver stopped and leaned over to examine the beam, while the older lady stuck her head out of the window. Instantly the fellow seized her brooch, ripping it from her laces. But as he turned to escape he found Victor almost upon him with drawn sword. Screaming in terror, he threw the brooch to the ground. Victor snatched it up and, unable to pursue the thief through the crowd, returned to the shabby carriage.

"My compliments, ladies," he said, bowing. "May I be of any further help to you?"

The older lady was clutching her throat, moaning. "Oh, thank you, sir. Paris is a dreadful place! I've never been so frightened."

"My aunt gets overwrought easily," said the younger in a surprisingly pleasant voice. "We've been driving all day and she is tired."

"Of course. May I introduce myself? I am Victor de Lorennes, Lieutenant—I mean, Captain of His Majesty's Guards."

"We are happy to meet you. This is my aunt, Madame Arronte, and I am Michelle Mornay."

Victor bowed low.

"We were trying to find our way to the Carmelite convent," said the girl sadly.

"Then you are on the wrong street. May I direct your coachman to the Rue St. Jacques?"

The Marquis leaned from his coach window. "I think you should accompany them. I'll go on to Villette's and send the coach to bring you back."

"Very well, sir." Victor gave the necessary instructions to both coachmen, and, asking permission, entered the ladies' coach, careful not to show how bored he was at this unwelcome task. Still, if His Majesty could take time to be courteous to maidservants, his Captain could do no less.

Victor had given the niece one glance that revealed her as no beauty, though not exactly repulsive. She had nice hands, rather good eyes and ankles, and a figure that was not flattered by the worn black dress made apparently for someone else. Not to embarrass her, he divided his further attention between the older woman and the coach window. But it grew upon him that the girl was now regarding him with admiration, and he tried to revive the conversation.

Before the girl's clear, unblinking gaze he dropped his eyes. He tried again. "Do you have friends at the convent?"

"No. We know no one," said the aunt.

His curiosity, being so little fed, grew apace. Of course many ladies of the court, after a round of dissipation, put aside their jewelry, rouge, and patches, and went to some fashionable convent. After a few days of retreat, confession, and absolution, they returned to go through the same round again. Though these scarcely seemed the type, he asked: "Are you going to spend a few days *en retraite?*"

"No. My niece is going to prepare herself to become one of the sisters."

Victor glanced at the girl again. Her face was smooth and white; and though the contour was not faultless, it was framed by a wealth of chestnut hair and given distinction by dark lustrous eyes.

"Have I seen you before—in a carriage on the Boulevard—or perhaps at the Théâtre?" He flattered them by speaking as if they were of Paris, though from their accent and their clothes, he knew better.

"No," answered Mme. Arronte. "We have just come from Provence."

"Of course, from Provence! It is noted for lovely women."

"It is good to be near the end of our journey, is it not, Michelle?" sighed the aunt.

"Yes." The girl spoke as meekly as a child, but she was tying hard knots in a black-bordered handkerchief.

"We have been living with a wealthy relative, Monsieur," said Madame Arronte. "She has just died after a long illness. She made no provision for us, except to recommend me to a place in the household of the Princess de Conti, and arrange for the Carmelites to take Michelle. Her father is a Huguenot, and she was taken from him to be educated in the Catholic faith, as the law provides. Since she has no dowry, she will have to stay and become a nun. She has no money to give the convent, either, of course, but she was well educated until her mother died, when she was fourteen. It's just as well, I tell her," the old lady rambled on, "for a woman without beauty can't succeed in the world. I did write to the Comtesse de Soissons, a distant relative of hers, but I received no answer."

Victor regarded the girl now with both pity and interest. He and Marc had lost their mother at the same age. And he saw now that she resembled the Comtesse de Soisson's sister, Marie de Mancini, now the Princesse de Colonna of Italy. She had the same elfin face that seemed all eyes. Slight rings around them spoke of nights of weeping. A pity, he thought, that so many girls, in default of a dowry, could not escape the cloister. To encourage her, he said lightly, "They tried once to make a priest of me, but as you see, I attained garments that become me more."

She raised her eyes with a gleam of interest, but the carriage was slowing; they were at the pillared entrance of the convent. Victor helped both ladies to alight, and escorted them to the door. While the aunt was parleying with the portress, he turned to the girl. "I wish I could do something for you."

"Will you, then?" she asked with sudden intensity. "Will you come to see me?"

So she had spirit, after all, and was trying to cling to something outside these walls. "I doubt if they would admit a man who is not a relative." Dismayed, as her face fell, he added hastily, "But I'll try to think of something. I'd be delighted to call——"

The portress departed to announce them. "This place must have a back gate," whispered Michelle hastily. "I'll find a way to get out there, tomorrow night, as soon as it is dark."

The aunt was looking at them.

"You'll come?" Michelle whispered urgently.

He could not resist lightening so great an unhappiness by a trifle. The hope of such an escapade might help her through these next hours, even if he only agreed now, and later sent a note of regret. He nodded to her.

The peach-colored Conti liveries were coming around the corner, and the shabby coach quickly pulled ahead to make room. As the carriage jerked and started, Victor settled back in it with a sigh of pleasure.

* * *

56

In the back room of M. Villette's shop, the Marquis de Lorennes sat with his elbows on the large central table. The place was in the happy disorder of research, with papers, books, pamphlets, and apparatus spilled over every horizontal surface. Marc stood at a small furnace, holding with black tongs a small smoke-stained vessel directly over the glowing coals. He turned at a question.

"This is a crucible. I'm melting several substances together."

"What sort of substances? And what are all these—?" The Marquis waved at the shelves loaded with odd-shaped phials and flasks.

"The usual materials—gold, silver, mercury, sulphur, salt, tin, lead, alum, quicklime, saltpeter, sal ammoniac, oil of vitriol, blue vitriol, aqua vitae . . ."

A narrow door opened to the empty shop in front, where on other shelves multicolored liquids and crystals caught the light, giving something of the effect of a stained-glass window. It was a place dedicated, thought the Marquis, but the dedication was to the care of the body rather than the spirit. Yet, judging by Marc's concentration, the spirit was involved. Though there was no future for the son of a nobleman in crucibles and retorts, the Marquis was tolerant, seeing Marc happy. As Marc withdrew the crucible and set it aside to cool, the bell of the outer door tinkled.

"It's Victor, at last," he called to the Marquis.

"I trust you delivered the ladies to their destination," the Marquis laughed in greeting.

"And one of them into misery." Victor explained briefly, and added, "I felt so sorry for her I even promised to see her again—tomorrow night at the back gate. It would be an adventure, at that." He picked up a dish of quicksilver and toyed with it, tipping it back and forth.

"It is too bad the Comtesse de Soissons couldn't find a place for her," said the Marquis.

"She has left Paris," said Marc, "suspected of having poisoned her late husband."

"Poison! Poison!" Victor burst out. "The gossips don't let anyone die a natural death any more."

"During the last reign," said the Marquis, "we settled our antagonism with our swords. Poison is the weapon of a slave, not a gentleman."

"It had a good fling in Italy, in the train of the Medicis," Marc offered.

57

The Marquis shuddered. "Dealing with people's lives like cards in a game—some to be kept and others discarded, according to one's whim. It's good that all of us get on well together." He smiled. "With Marc spending so much time in an apothecary's shop, someone might suspect him of sinister designs. I'm glad that he'll soon be back in the Guards."

"As to that, Father," said Marc, soberly, "I don't want to go back."

A glass tube crashed in Victor's hand, and then the room was so still one could hear a tiny flame puffing under a retort.

"With your permission and His Majesty's, of course." Marc appealed to his father, "I can sell my place in the Guards for enough to live on for a while. I want to learn more about what I'm trying to do. Maybe at the Sorbonne. Some workers now are not trying to turn base metals into gold, but to find out what properties and uses the metals have in themselves. There is a Monsieur Boyle in England, for instance." He selected a pamphlet from the heap on the table.

The Marquis took it and glanced over the first pages. "Hmm, I see Monsieur Boyle is of the nobility, too. But son, your plans sound so indefinite."

"If Victor marries, we won't be together so much, anyway. I might as well find my own place in the world, and it does not lie in the Guards."

The Marquis and Victor stared. Never before had Marc made such a decision of his own.

"And when your money is gone?" asked the Marquis gently.

"I can always go back in the army and work with Monsieur Vauban. It is better than guard duty."

Victor held at arm's length a glass tube in which some material had burned to a black crisp. "This stuff is more attractive to you than people of quality?"

"It's cleaner than some." Marc took the tube and replaced it in a rack.

The Marquis said lightly, to appease their discord, "Actually Victor is not so remote from this kind of thing."

"What—what do you mean?" Victor stammered, his mind on the violet package.

The Marquis raised his eyebrows. "I was about to make a bad joke: that your hand is a sort of crucible—it melts money in an instant."

Victor smiled feebly. "I know too many agreeable ways of spending it."

The Marquis smiled. "It's good that you aren't like some courtiers. If you poisoned me and then Auguste, you'd have the estate."

"*Nom de dieu!* Don't even joke about it!"

"You're upset today." Marc's eyes narrowed. "And it isn't just the strain of being Captain."

Victor fought for calm. "It's nothing, nothing. Oh, let's get out of here and find something more amusing."

"Good," agreed the Marquis. "But when had you thought of speaking to the King about this, Marc?"

"Tonight at the *appartements.*"

7

WHILE lesser arrivals were pouring in through the Court of the Ministers, the Marquis and his sons were admitted to the Royal Court and the marble and bronze Stairway of the Ambassadors. Victor walked quickly in anticipation of seeing Angélique. He planned to ask Madame to present her just as the King was ready to go to supper. Surely when His Majesty saw her charm he would consent at once.

At the top of the stairs the Marquis leaned against the balustrade, breathing heavily. "I do believe I'll go to La Rochefoucauld's apartment for a glass of wine. Will you not come, too?"

"Not unless you need us. I should make the rounds of the Guards," said Victor. "Marc can come with me. But you go, Father, and rest for a while. There's plenty of time."

"Shouldn't he have a doctor?" asked Marc, as they walked on alone.

"He says it's only indigestion and fatigue. A little rest and some wine will set him right."

Victor's uneventful inspection ended outside the apartment of Madame de Maintenon, where the lieutenant on duty saluted. "His Majesty has been in there three hours. I can't imagine why. He's sitting in an armchair beside the fireplace, and she's in the opposite one, embroidering."

Victor opened his eyes wide. "In an armchair? Everyone below the rank of duchess sits on a stool in his presence."

"Non, it is Monsieur Racine who occupies the stool as he reads to them. His voice must be cracking by now. Maintenon must be freezing. His Majesty threw open the window, and she has a terror of drafts. They say he likes her brains—it's a change, if that's the part of a woman he's interested in now," sniggered the guardsman. "He went to Montespan earlier, but they quarreled. Just as he left in a fury I heard him say, 'The crowned heads of Europe do not dictate to me in my kingdom and you shall not dictate to me in my palace.' "

Victor remembered uneasily his morning's sight of Montespan disheveled and furious. Could their quarrel have been about him?

The door opened, and M. Racine, in a black, ill-cut suit, backed out, pausing anxiously at some royal gesture, "Sire?"

"I'm sorry you were not on the last campaign," came the deliberate voice. "You might have written something about our victory."

"Sire," said Racine, "I had no proper clothes. I ordered a suit, but the places you attacked were taken before it was finished."

The King chuckled in delight. "Then you can wear it now. Accompany me Monday."

"I shall be honored. *Au revoir,* Your Majesty. *Au revoir,* Madame la Marquise."

The poet bowed again and closed the door, to bend then in humble salute to the twins. As one man, they gravely returned the salute. They had known him for a long time, at first merely as a friend of M. Molière. One would never take M. Racine for a poet. He had the air of a modest, well-bred bourgeois. As he stuffed a manuscript into a flat leather case, he said apologetically, "My new drama, *Phèdre.* Madame de Maintenon seemed to like it."

"We'll look forward to seeing it played," said Marc.

He needn't bother being kind, thought Victor. The court was saying that coffee drinking and M. Racine's tragedies were introduced to society at the same time, and neither would go far.

As M. Racine hastily took his departure, Victor and Marc went on up two flights of stairs into the stinking, airless corridors connecting a labyrinth of low, dark rooms, staircases, kitchens and entresols where the lesser fry lived.

Marc, following Victor into the dark cell-like room that went with his captaincy, said, "We were better off in the barracks."

"Better men than we spend their lives conniving for one of these little cubbyholes."

As the brothers dressed for the evening, they tucked small bags of coins into their belts, for no counters were used for card playing at court. One wagered with coin.

Downstairs, they made their way through salons so densely crowded that they could progress only inches at a time to where their father, in a black velvet habit embroidered in gold, awaited them with La Rochefoucauld.

"I feel quite all right now," he answered in response to their inquiry. "Where should we go first?"

"We should be in the Salon of Mars when His Majesty enters," said Victor. "These *appartements* are informal, but the King does appear there before he goes to the card table."

In the war god's salon, the King's orchestra of twenty-four violins was playing, and the Queen was just entering, followed by her ladies and escorted by her Captain of the Guards in his red tunic. Trailing many yards of gold brocade, she walked with an ungainly bending of the knees, managing with difficulty the three-inch heels intended to give her more of an air of importance. In the brilliant court that bowed before her, she was a cipher. Like all the Spanish infantas, she had been reared in solid virtue and stupidity. But she had been taught to rule; and dumpy though she was, she did wear with dignity the fleur-de-lis mantle on state occasions, even if her crown rested upon an unhappy brow.

Victor, though he liked the Queen, gave her only the briefest of glances; for now Madame, the stalwart German wife of Monsieur, was making her entrance, swinging along among her maids of honor like a Swiss Guard in court dress. Yes, Angélique was with her, he saw with delight, though so dense was the crowd that he could only glimpse her bright hair. He ached to rush to her side, but at this moment Lulli led his orchestra off on a composition in honor of the King, and the room grew alert. When the doors were flung open, Louis XIV stood revealed in brilliant purple with gold and silver lace.

With an eager, hopelessly admiring look, the Queen awaited his approach. He bowed and kissed her jeweled fingers. "My compliments, Your Majesty."

"*Gracias,* sir. You are so handsome this evening, as always," she gushed, unfortunately revealing teeth black and decayed from eating too much chocolate.

"The luster of a clear conscience, my dear. You see, I went to Mass."

61

The Queen looked stricken. "Oh, sir, I forgot." She put her hand to trembling lips; then mindful of the eyes upon her, lowered it. "It will not occur again."

"*Et plus,* I hear you were at the card tables at that time, and that you lost at *hoca.*"

The Queen had not learned much French, but she understood this reproof, and bent her head meekly.

"Twenty thousand francs," he continued inexorably. "Let us calculate how much that would be in a year."

As always at his slightest criticism, the Queen began to cry. Then, gaining control of herself, she said, "I had a bad morning, sir. I shall not offend again." Nearby courtiers and ladies repressed contemptuous smiles. Cards had become a mania with the Queen, and yet she could not learn to play even the simplest game well.

Louis bowed, and turned away. "Oh, sir," she urged quickly, "this morning Madame de Noailles told a witty story . . ." She babbled desperately in broken French, trying to hold him, but he stood waiting for the end with the air of an absent-minded man listening to a fountain.

Though courtiers were not free to converse until the King made the rounds, converse they did, statue-like, without turning their heads. In this fashion, Marc said to Victor, "I'm going to ask him when he comes this way."

"He'll think you're out of your mind."

Louis finally broke away with an almost curt "Another time, my dear," and began to move down the long salon, addressing a word to each lady and courtier. As he acknowledged the four salutes from the Marquis's party, his eyes singled out Marc. "And how is your wound now?"

Marc's bow was deep and appreciative: "Much better, sire, thank you."

"Good. You have been an excellent officer. I am pleased with you." Many a man present would have died to receive such praise from those lips. "I trust you'll be able to ride to the campaign on Monday."

Marc blushed, for one could not contradict the King or even speak to anyone else in his presence. Glancing at his father, he was relieved to see a slight nod. This was the time. "Would Your Majesty be much displeased if I did not go? Though I am very proud to have been in the Guards, I should like to sell my post and go on with my studies for a time, and then perhaps go back with Monsieur Vauban."

62

The King frowned. "This is a surprise. And what of your brother?"

"He does not wish to change."

"Um. Do you have your father's approval for this strange idea?"

"Only, of course, sire," said the Marquis, "if he can obtain yours."

"What's the matter with your family? First you choose to stay away from court, and now your son wants to leave. Victor, is anything on your mind besides your wish to marry with doubtful suitability?" He spoke smilingly, avoiding the irony that wounds so cruelly from lips no one may answer.

"As always, I would rather die, sire, than fail in my duty to you in the slightest matter. I am sorry no better opportunity presents itself for my serving you, that I might give proof of my esteem."

"Very well said," the King answered thoughtfully. "Let us not be precipitate. We will talk about this again. Now I must release you all to your pleasure by completing my rounds."

"Thank you, sire," said Marc evenly. "I shall await Your Majesty's pleasure."

Victor was puzzled. The king was taking Marc's request too mildly, as if it were no affront, but might well fit into some plan of his own.

Slowly Louis toured the remainder of the room and returned to the Queen, as M. Lulli, raising the tall pole he used as a baton, led his musicians into the first notes of a pavane. The younger maids of honor would dance with each other when their gallants had gone to the card tables, for at the *appartements* the men were not allowed to dance; but at the moment the music was only a background for flirtation. Louis offered his arm to his Queen, and with a train of followers, began a slow progress toward the game room. The instant he had passed, each courtier hastened to the lady of his choice. Victor reached Angélique just in time to cut off the handsome Marquis de Seignelay, Colbert's son, so faultlessly and strikingly dressed in white satin that Victor grew acutely conscious of the mended tear in his own sleeve. De Seignelay saluted laughingly and turned to another lady.

Etiquette forbade Angélique to leave her place. "Tell me quickly," she whispered behind her fan, "what did His Majesty say?"

"Nothing, really. But you are to be presented. Madame might do it just before supper."

"Oh! I shall faint with excitement." Her eyes followed the King, whose arrival at the door coincided with the end of the pavane. Then, before Lulli could begin the next tune, the attendant called out, "Madame La Marquise de Montespan."

63

Silence fell instantly, and the King's party halted as Françoise de Montespan, graceful and haughty, stepped through, followed by her ladies. She was gowned in transparent black lace with jewels blazing from arms, throat, and ears. She hesitated in the doorway until all had seen her; then, between rows of bowed heads, swept forward regally. With a deep curtsy she kissed the hem of the Queen's robe, and smiled at the King. "I trust I am in time to go to the tables with you. Do you like my flowers?" She thrust under his nose a bouquet of Bengal roses, surrounding a new Haarlem tulip of delicate gray and violet which, Victor heard, had taken a gardener five years to develop and had cost five thousand livres of the King's money. Victor started, remembering La Voisin's *aqua tofana,* which could be shaken on flowers like dew, and, while not harming them, could breath death from every petal at the approach of one's nostrils. But the King did not bend to them, and when Montespan brought them up to her own face, Victor relaxed, scolding himself again for a feverish imagination.

Louis replied carefully to her first remark. "Yes. You are in time." He turned then to speak more generally. "This evening, aside from playing for your own money as much as you please, there will be the added inducement of prizes—brocades for the gentlemen, and ribbons, fans, and other trinkets for the ladies. And, if you will present yourselves in this room again at a quarter of ten, you will have a chance to enrich yourselves in a lottery given by Madame de Montespan."

Montespan herself added, "The first prize will be one hundred thousand francs, the second, twenty thousand francs, and there will be a hundred others of two hundred francs each. The tickets are twenty francs each, and can be had from any of my people." She nodded toward a row of lackeys in her blue and gold livery ranged beside the door. Sweeping up her train, she took the King's arm, only to have him hand her deftly to another gentleman in his party, and give his arm again to the Queen.

The royal party departed and the orchestra resumed its playing. As Madame's ladies began dancing the pavane, Victor pressed Angélique's fingers to his lips, whispering that he would see her again at ten. Since Marc had disappeared, and their father had been claimed by Madame de Sévigné, he followed the procession toward the card rooms. His fingers were itching for cards, but his purse was thin and he must be careful whose table he joined.

From the lansquenet table next to the King's came a hail from M. Colbert, alone with his son. "Victor! We need two more."

64

"I'll do as ill here as anywhere." Victor pulled out a stool and sat down. "Luck has been acting like a jade to me lately."

"She's an expensive mistress," laughed De Seignelay.

"There are no cheap ones, they tell me."

"Where's Marc?" Colbert asked. "Won't he make our fourth?"

"He seldom plays. Cards won't be the rocks that wreck his career."

Louis called gaily, "Here is my Colbert scowling as usual!"

Colbert grunted. "I am trying to think how to find the fifty millions of livres the Dutch war has cost. Neither in war nor peace do you consult your finances to determine your expenditures."

Louis laughed as he would have at a devoted old servant whose grumblings need not be taken seriously. "The King gives alms in spending largely."

"In the provinces the peasants are already living on boiled herbs, and we've buried everyone under an avalanche of salt to collect the *gabelle.*"

"Well, don't oppress the people," said Louis gaily.

Hearty laughter rose from the tables near by, amid which the King said, "Here's a fourth for you." He indicated an approaching figure in scarlet and gold.

M. de la Salle hesitated. "I care little for cards."

The King frowned, and La Salle added quickly, 'I abuse gambling, sire, out of pure revenge, as Montaigne says of youth."

Very neat, thought Victor, very neat. This explorer knows enough to take each step here with as much care as in the worst wilderness. The King was smiling again. "Perhaps tonight you can earn some of the expenses of your expedition."

La Salle surveyed the heaps of gold and silver on every table as far as he could see, but he said nothing, as with obvious reluctance he yielded to the implied royal command, and took a stool at Colbert's left, nodding to the others.

"Are you familiar with lansquenet?" Colbert asked.

"No. It was being played when I was here before, but I was not invited to the *appartements.*"

"A good sign, your being invited this time," said Colbert.

"I hope so. I need his favor. And yours."

Colbert's gloomy features lighted. *"Eh bien,* what I do is part of my work. Colonies are in my department. But remember"—his forehead wrinkled under the black skull cap—"I am no Richelieu, and Louis XIV is not Louis XIII." His small, piercing eyes glanced at the table

65

where the King was deeply engrossed, Montespan leaning against him, holding the cards for both.

"Well. With your permission, gentlemen, I'll go through one hand to show Monsieur de la Salle. It's a simple gambling game, harmless when played by honest souls like ourselves."

"A polite way of picking pockets, as La Rochefoucauld remarked this morning," said Victor.

"Then I'll act as master thief. The people call me worse than that." Colbert's lips twitched in rough good-humor. "It was an army game to begin with, the name coming from the old German foot-soldiers who carried lances—*landsknecht*. First, we spread out the cards and draw for bank . . ."

"It seems simple enough," said La Salle finally. "If one's pistoles hold out."

"Well, here's to financing your expedition," answered De Seignelay.

As the stakes grew higher at nearby tables, the noise increased. Someone was weeping, someone else banging on a table with his fist, another cursing, expertly keeping his voice too low to reach the King's ears. Faces became lined with despair. Victor mused that though gambling went on for twenty-four hours a day around the palace, no one ever seemed to have any joy in it.

No conversation could be carried on in such a clamor, so they concentrated on the game. M. Colbert gradually acquired a pile of winnings, and La Salle had a little. Victor was at the end of his purse, when a turn of luck came. He won three times in a row and then again. Looking at the size of the bank, M. Colbert said, "What will you do?"

Victor appraised the heap of gold. It would go a long way toward the captaincy, but if he let it go once more, doubled, it would be more than enough. With no perceptible hesitation, he said, "Let it go." As he turned the cards, he felt La Salle's eyes upon him. The explorer had dropped out three rounds before. No matching card had turned up for either side when a staff rapped for silence, and the King's voice rang out:

"As I am about to return to the Salon of Mars, I will now distribute the brocades and trinkets. Then you may continue to play for another half hour. The winner at each table at this moment will please rise to make his selection."

Hubbub rose all over the room, for until the King tired of cards, no courtier was permitted to stop.

66

"Eh bien, Victor, that's you," said Colbert.

"But the play isn't finished!"

"The King's word is law."

As Victor rose, uniformed lackeys were loading their arms with brocades and seeking out the winners. "You are to choose three pieces, sir," said the lackey who came to Victor. From among a tempting heap he selected one in soft green, another in silver, and one with white satin flowers upon a dull white background. Then he resumed turning cards, fingering them like the beads of a rosary, praying for a four. A knave, a ten, a deuce, a queen. He turned another, expelled his breath, and threw down the rest. A five, his opponents' card!

Ill as he felt, Victor laughed. "I told you Fortune is a jade to me." If he had only stopped in time—but there was no profit in regrets.

"Sell me the D'Artagnan sword," urged De Seignelay. "I'll raise my bid to eighty thousand francs."

"Confound you, no!"

"Make it one hundred thousand francs."

"Mille tonnerres, no!" snapped Victor. "Every time I lose a few sous at cards, I have to tell you again: *it is not for sale.* Anyway, I can recoup on the next deal."

But he hadn't another pistole. No use borrowing, for gambling debts had to be paid within twenty-four hours. He was searching feverishly for an excuse to leave the table, when someone jostled his arm. It was De Conti, accompanied by a slender stranger in naval uniform—the same *garde-marine* who had petitioned the King before Mass.

De Conti had obviously been at the punch bowl more than once. He leaned heavily on their table. No one rose; since at card tables one did not rise even for the King. "Gen'lemen, gen'lemen—I want you to meet a friend. An Italian. I don't like Italians. They all remind me of that damned Mazarin—God rest his soul. But I like this one. But it's so *condamné* noisy in here, you can't hear his name if I tell you." The Prince was as profane when drunk as he was circumspect when sober. "I want you to meet him, but *sacré sang de dieu,* it's so noisy."

"Yes, we couldn't hear a thunderbolt." Victor rose and tossed the brocades over his arm. Saved by the Prince and his *garde-marine* friend!

In the Salon of Diana, moderately deserted now, the Prince came to an unsteady halt, leaning on a sideboard loaded with silver. "Now, gen'lemen, may I present Monsieur Tonti? Monsieur Tonti, may I present Monsieur Colbert, Monsieur de Seignelay, Monsieur de Lorennes, and the man I told you about, Monsieur de la Salle."

M. Tonti bowed lithely to each in turn, while the Prince rested a heavy hand on La Salle's scarlet-covered back. "La Salle, this is an honest man, just like you."

Both men bowed before this ultimate praise. The Prince beamed happily. "And I want you to take him with you. Just the man for you. *Corps de dieu!* the very man."

La Salle's startled dark eyes went from the Prince to the *garde-marine,* who underwent the appraisal with quiet composure, as well he might. He was handsome, with a good figure and leg, and an amiable expression. His leather gloves were molded over delicate hands—no, one delicate hand. Victor saw that La Salle had observed also the one ungraceful member of this elegant figure.

"I would be much honored—" the Italian began gently, but the Prince cut him off: "Tell you a joke. The Papal Nuncio stinks of liquor!"

"No! Not the Nuncio!" laughed De Seignelay.

"Blind drunk," asserted De Conti earnestly.

"It could not be you who has been drinking?" suggested Colbert.

The Prince glared at him. "That's what he said, and the Dauphin, and the Queen. You are all making the same mistake. I'm going to ask the Nuncio where he got so befuddled. I need another glass myself." Passing his jeweled fingers through the heavy curls of his wig, he surged away, listing badly. M. Colbert hastened to take one arm, motioning De Seignelay to take the other. "Pray excuse us, Messieurs."

Left with La Salle and Tonti, Victor lingered with the brocades over his arm, feeling a curious urge to stay, yet knowing he ought to go.

"I hope you can make use of me, Monsieur de la Salle," said the soft Italian voice.

"Why should you want to go to New France?"

"For many reasons." Like the gestures of all Italians, Tonti's were profuse and expressive. "I like the sound of your project. And I would like to see something of New France. I have a cousin there—the Sieur du Luth."

"Du Luth—your cousin?" La Salle brightened. "He has covered more of that continent than anyone but myself."

Tonti laughed softly. "He once wrote me that whenever one of you other explorers come upon some tribe supposedly unknown to white men, you find him already beside the fire, married to the chief's daughter."

La Salle laughed. "That's close to the truth."

"Du Luth—?" asked Victor. "He used to be in the King's Guards."

"Yes. He was," said La Salle without taking appraising eyes from Tonti. "Now he wears quite a different garb, but it's no less picturesque in its way."

Tonti resumed. "I assure you, if you will accept me in your company, you will find that the family spirit is not exclusively my cousin's."

"It will be a strenuous life. What about—?" La Salle gestured delicately toward the stiff glove.

Tonti smiled without embarrassment. "If I were not sure I could do my share, Monsieur, I would not be asking to go."

"In that case, I shall be glad to have you," said La Salle quietly.

"Merci bien, monsieur."

"Come to my rooms, at 17 Rue de la Truanderie, to discuss arrangements. Tomorrow afternoon?"

"Gladly. But now we must beg the pardon of Monsieur de Lorennes. We are boring him."

"Not in the least," protested Victor. "But I must send a lackey to my room with these brocades, if you will excuse me."

As he left, he passed the Abbé Bernou, hastening toward La Salle with outstretched hands. "Monsieur, we have been talking about the New World," he called. "Would you join us, and put us straight on certain matters?"

8

WHEN Victor had disposed of the brocades and pushed his way into the crowded Salon of Mars, he could catch no sight of Angélique anywhere. Montespan's lackeys were selling the last of the lottery tickets, but Victor shook his head and worked his way farther into the room. He must find someone to borrow from. Where in the deuce was Marc? Montespan stood in the center of the room, cool and sure of herself, enough light flashing from her jewels to brighten a Paris street. Circling the walls to avoid her brought Victor to a cluster of courtiers surrounding La Salle, who, the Abbé Bernou at his side, seemed to be giving an informal lecture. Here Victor lingered, keeping an eye out for anyone who might lend him twenty francs.

"The richest fruits of that continent have not yet been found," the explorer was saying earnestly. "The way to them is through the Mississippi and not the St. Lawrence." He spoke of his hope to find that river's mouth and build a fort that would end Spain's monopoly of the Mexican gulf. Victor had heard all this before, and had little interest in it anyway, but he could not help watching the speaker. How in the world could a gentleman develop such enthusiasm over so remote and uncivilized a place?

"The greatest service anyone could do for France, I believe," La Salle was saying, "is to place thousands of her peasants and artisans in that great river valley."

The general atmosphere in the group was one of approval. Only the Jesuit Père la Chaise, who stood at one side listening, presented a discordant note, as his eyes flashed hatred. Next Louis himself approached, indicating that no one should call attention to his presence. But, at the first pause, the King came closer and gave La Salle his hand.

"Monsieur de la Salle, I am pleased with you." The explorer bowed low and the circle hushed. "Monsieur Colbert is preparing a suitable patent, which I will sign at St. Germain on Sunday. The crown will grant most of your petition. But the time allowed to complete your project will be shortened from twenty to five years."

"Five years!" La Salle paled.

"I trust the terms are satisfactory?" Louis's tone was ominous.

La Salle sought for control and achieved it. "Yes . . . of course, Your Majesty."

"Good. Then in five years, we shall expect you back with a complete report. And I have not finished conferring honors upon you. Monsieur Lulli—" the King beckoned to the orchestra leader "—you might find inspiration for a ballet on the theme of the new empire La Salle is to give us." He conferred a further accolade: "And I might dance in it myself."

Victor saw La Salle's blank astonishment and admired his quick recovery as he bent again. "Sire . . . you honor me too greatly."

A stir in the center of the room resolved itself into the imperious Montespan. "Sire, my lottery."

Victor shrugged. Too late now to get a ticket. But while he waited to see whom fortune would favor, he caught sight of Marc near the door waving two tickets in the air. Victor beamed, and beckoned him closer, when, at the King's nod, an officer clapped for attention. Two lackeys brought out a carved Chinese table and set upon it a silver bowl filled with numbered pieces of wood.

"Who is to have the honor of drawing?" asked the King.

"Oh, yes, I must choose." Madame de Montespan walked slowly down the open space, her gold train swishing softly on the marble, until she reached Madame, to whom she bowed as to an equal, not kissing her hem. Madame frigidly returned the salute.

"May I borrow one of your ladies, Madame?"

"It depends, Marquise, on what you intend to do with her."

"Only to ask her to be the instrument of fate." Montespan swung gaily about, inspecting the circle, and reached out a hand. "Come, my dear."

"Oh, no!" Victor gasped under his breath, then waited with foreboding as Montespan clasped Angélique's hand and led her formally down the room.

"Here's your ticket," said Marc's voice behind him, and Victor felt the pasteboard pressed into his palm.

"Your Majesty," Montespan was saying, "may I present a charming newcomer to court, Mlle. Marie-Angélique de Fontanges, new maid of honor to Her Royal Highness?"

Victor bit his lips, miserable to see the presentation from which he had hoped so much carried out in this manner. Angélique sank in her curtsy, looking terrified. Victor boiled with rage. Angélique was being deliberately paraded before the King as bait. Montespan had done it before. Rather than surrender him to a really feared rival, like Maintenon, she would prefer him to be attracted to an innocent young girl she could later push aside.

Angélique was almost swooning with excitement under the admiring gaze of the handsome King. "I am very happy, my child," said the King, "to make a gesture to fortune and salute rare beauty at the same time." He kissed her fingers, and held them, as the hushed room watched. Then he broke the spell with a wave toward the silver bowl. "We are waiting for our fate at your lovely hands, Mademoiselle."

Flustered, Angélique turned to Montespan, who tied her own lace handkerchief over her eyes, and guided her hand to the bowl.

"Number two," Montespan announced into the suspenseful silence.

71

A little gasp went up. Number two was always the Queen's, as number one was the King's whenever he entered the lottery as he had not done tonight, further evidence that he was paying for it. Montespan approached the Queen with a heavy little bag. The Queen's dignity warred with her cupidity and shame at receiving so much money from those hands.

"Now, the second prize, twenty thousand francs." Angélique reached into the bowl. "Deeper," said Montespan, laying her plump hand briefly over the younger one. The two hands came up again. "Number sixty four."

Marc jabbed Victor. "Look at your ticket!" Victor scanned the cardboard: 64 was his! Elated, he stepped forward and handed it with a bow to Madame de Montespan, expecting her to show dismay. Instead she struck him playfully with her fan, and with a peculiar smile, handed him the bag. "Don't spend it foolishly, Monsieur le Capitaine."

The crowd waited for his answer, and he made an effort to rise to the occasion. "Foolishly? Some follies are catching, like smallpox," he declaimed with an exaggerated sweep of his arm. "And there are people fitted to be fools, who not only do foolish things by choice, but are driven to them by their destiny. Yet, perhaps he who lives without folly is not so wise as he thinks." Bowing, he backed away.

Louis himself led the applause. "I should grant you a pension for those aphorisms."

"I am sorry they are not mine, sire. They are Monsieur de la Rochefoucauld's."

"All the better! They will then cost me nothing, since he already has a pension as First Lord of the Bedchamber."

Amid the obedient laughter, Victor turned away, and looked full into the eyes of M. de la Salle. They wore a peculiar questioning, as if he wondered whether pensions were really so lightly given.

The King had turned to face the stalwart Madame, who was now approaching him. "Have you come to congratulate one of your favorites?" He glanced at Victor.

"Yes," Madame replied bluntly. "And to claim another. Come, Angélique. I feel indisposed."

"I had hoped for the company of you both at dinner," said the King.

To anyone else, that would have been a command, but not to Madame. "You will not lack for company." She stalked away and

Angélique followed like a child being dragged away from a jar of sweetmeats.

Now Montespan beckoned to the nearest maid of honor, and the drawing for the smaller prizes was begun. Victor found Marc standing alone near the orchestra.

"Here—we've got something to divide." Victor held out the bag with a grin, letting his arm fall as if the weight were twice what it was.

"All right," said Marc. "But I have an idea. Let's divide half of it and invest the other ten thousand francs with Monsieur de la Salle."

"What? How do you mean?"

"While you've been basking in all your glory today, I've been listening in the back of the room. His expedition is going to cost money. He has to borrow it. And he promises an interest of from twenty-five to forty per cent."

"Why doesn't the King give it to him, if he can spare one hundred and forty thousand francs for Montespan's lottery?"

"La Salle is in no position to demand. Montespan is."

"It's a risk," Victor said dubiously. "The first time I've had such a sum, too."

"Of course. But aren't you a gambler? Somehow I believe in him. Colbert does, too, you notice."

"Well," said Victor, "If you want to take a chance."

"Good. You tell him. I'll go put the money in our strongbox and tell old Jacques to guard it. Then I must find Father. His Majesty will soon be going to supper."

When Victor found the explorer, La Salle said, "Monsieur le Capitaine, will you be good enough to tell me when I can take my leave? The Prince de Conti is quite beyond questioning."

"Wait until His Majesty goes to supper—unless you've been invited to dine?"

"No. I fear I am not that important."

"Dining with the King is an honor Louis XIV has never granted freely. But I'd like to speak with you. Would you care to walk on the terrace?"

"By all means."

Even on the terrace there was no privacy. But the air was fresh and cool. "I must not forget to congratulate you," La Salle began. "Fortune relented sooner than usual. I admired your wagering such a large sum

73

at lansquenet and losing with such coolness. I have seen few men so little afraid of risks."

"Such risks are of little consequence beside those you take, sir. I just plunged to see how far luck would stay with me."

"I've often done the same thing, though not at cards. You know, you are the kind of man I need in New France, if I am to finish in the time His Majesty sets—as I must, and will. I wish you were free to go with me."

The man was sober and perfectly serious. Could an experienced explorer actually choose men on so slight an acquaintance?

"Sir, I am greatly honored." He realized even as he spoke the trite phrase that it was perfectly true. "But of course my duties prevent my considering your invitation. I do wish, though, to tell you that my brother and I would like to have a share in your success. We'd like to invest half of our lottery winnings with you. Would you accept a loan of ten thousand francs?"

"*A la bonne heure!*" La Salle held out a vigorous hand to shake Victor's. "I am honored at your confidence. It is most unusual for money to be brought to me; I always have to go after it."

"Would you like it tonight? I suppose, though, there will be papers to sign."

"Yes, but I am not sure how I am to get back to Paris. Could you bring it to me there, as soon as it is convenient?"

"Of course."

"I'll have the contract drawn up. I wish you could go along to see your money grow. I need good men, but of course His Majesty needs them even more."

"He does, indeed." An unmistakable voice spoke behind them.

Both men whirled and bowed low: "Sire!"

"You two young men were in deep converse. Was it love or war?"

Victor was certain the King had heard exactly what it was. "Monsieur de la Salle flatters me, sire. He says I would make a good explorer."

"La Salle, you must not lure away important young men from my court," said the King.

"I am not planning to go, sire," Victor said hastily. "I'll invest money with him, but I don't intend to throw the handle after the hatchet and invest myself."

"I was not trying to lure him away," explained La Salle. "Though I

74

would be glad to have him. To be in Your Majesty's household speaks for his courage. I need men with that kind of training and discipline. When I came to France four years ago, everyone was praising the Guards for having remained eight hours under fire, when the Prince de Condé, won the battle of Seneffe. Incidentally, two men who took part in that victory are in New France now: Monsieur du Luth of the Guards, and a field chaplain, Father Louis Hennepin."

Louis XIV, always deaf to praise of the Condés, waited for La Salle to finish, and then, oblivious to anything he had said, laid a hand on Victor's shoulder. "Yes, he has courage. He is absolutely without fortune, but he has the rare gift of making friends. Marc is as pleasing, but he has too much fury for looking up the definitions of things. Victor, I must ask you to come with me into the anteroom. I have some special instructions."

Victor bowed. "Until later, then, Monsieur de la Salle."

Backing toward the door, La Salle turned and departed, his relief almost as visible upon his retreating back as his scarlet cloak.

In the anteroom, Victor stood waiting while the King paced up and down, pulling thoughtfully at the full Bourbon lower lip. Finally he stopped in front of Victor. "How would you like to go to New France?"

"New . . . France? To New—" Confusion tangled Victor's usually facile tongue. "Is Your Majesty thinking of going there?"

"Heaven for— well, no. But I want you to go."

Victor stood as if turned to stone, his mind shocked into blankness. Surely he wasn't to be sent away, and to such a remote spot, so soon after his promotion!

"Well?" Louis's voice had an impatient ring to it.

"Exile, sire?" Victor stammered. His hand twisted the lace of his ruffle until it tore. What could have brought this about? Or who? Madame de Montespan?

"Not exile," said the King. "A task to be done."

Victor fought to regain his breath.

"This La Salle," Louis explained, "has the reputation of being too secretive. But when I heard him speak to you, I saw in a flash that you might be the very one to keep me informed. The Jesuits make accusations against him. Of course they say anything that serves their purposes. But I must find out the truth. He may indeed want to be the ruler of that vast western region. He might even raise a savage army against our Canadian colonies. He must have some personal ambition. You will go with him as an associate, but actually you will still be a soldier under orders."

Victor stared in consternation. "I am—I am moved by the honor Your Majesty does me," he stammered, searching wildly in his thoughts for a way of escape. The King had spies everywhere: in court, in town, in the provinces, alert for the least remark that might be of interest. A small army of Swiss Guards did nothing but prowl around anterooms and passages, lurk in lavatories or in the bushes of the garden, listening to conversations, following suspects, marking where everyone went. They reported to the valet Bontems, who reported to the King. Letters were opened and extracts made. All France was a great spider web, with Louis XIV at the heart. But Victor had little respect for those content to spend their lives in such an occupation.

"You are precisely the man for this," continued the King. "Gay and lighthearted, the very kind who might go for adventure and money. He'll never suspect you. But don't look so downhearted. It will not be forever. And since it is so important to me, you have my word that there will be a suitable reward."

Victor felt the monarch's gaze upon him. He who had been served by the genius of a Turenne, a Condé, a Vauban, and a Colbert, was graciously implying that Victor's contribution would be the equal to theirs. The captaincy, even, was practically promised in that smile. To escape, Victor felt he must weigh his words as carefully as a goldsmith his metal.

"You do me too much honor, sire." He spoke like a prudent navigator sailing among rocks. "That Italian *garde-marine,* Monsieur Tonti, is going with La Salle. Could he not do what you wish?"

The King's smile froze. "Do you expect me to trust an Italian with such a mission?"

Victor straightened. Since he had to swallow the cup, it was better to do so with good grace. "I shall perform the task to the best of my ability. I hope Your Majesty will be pleased." But as Victor bent his knee and pressed the royal hand to his lips in token of obedience, he knew he would have felt no worse if condemned to the living death of La Trappe, there to fast and pray in eternal silence.

"Good. You will see La Salle tomorrow and volunteer your services. Of course he is not to know you are being sent by me. Nor is anyone else to know—" The King paused. "What of Marc?"

76

"Marc!" Thoughts raced through Victor's mind so fast they were blurted out almost without control. "Why, he—why, we've always been together. We can't—I can't——"

Louis held up a hand to dam the flow. "Then he must go along."

"But Marc couldn't act as a spy!"

"Why not?"

"There is nothing at court he wants that much." He blurted out the truth and then awaited the King's anger.

But Louis merely nodded. "These scholars are a little unpractical at times. Then tell him I merely wish you both to assist La Salle."

Marc! What would he think? Victor shrugged it off. At least this will be no worse for him than to leave the Guards and become a grubby scholar.

"To La Salle himself, and to everyone else," Louis was saying, "you will imply that you have lost your place in the Guards and that your interest has been fired by La Salle's plans. You can tell him you need to repair your fortune; I understand he is generous with his company and lets them trade with the savages. And you will see to it that, once in New France, you accompany him on every step he takes. Do not let him leave you in Quebec, or send you on some errand while he goes elsewhere. And don't fall under a spell and send me reports of how brilliant, how noble, how disinterested, how eager he is to serve France. I've had enough of that already in Le Comte de Frontenac's letters. There must be another side. Find out how much he wants for himself. Above all," the King concluded, "be sure never to incur any risk of his finding out why you are with him. I shall be disappointed if he dismisses you."

Victor knew what was implied by the King's disappointment.

"You might make your fortune, too, if you manage well. Your salary in the Guards will be placed to your credit with Monsieur Colbert, to be collected when you return. And when the task is done—well, we'll see."

"I might hope Your Majesty will then look favorably upon my marriage?"

A queer smile passed over Louis's face. "Yes, you may wed anyone then who accepts your proposal. Is that enough?"

"More than enough, sire."

"You will need time for arrangements, so you will be relieved of your duties tomorrow, before I rejoin the army. But remember, what

77

is delayed is not lost. Your new post will be no less important in the
service of the King!"

In the service of the King! Victor's spirits lifted a little at these
words, so full of glamour, of prestige. It was a distasteful path, but
perhaps he could yet make it a ladder of ascent.

9

VICTOR'S brief exultation vanished almost as soon as they were out
of the anteroom. Like a uniformed marionette, he followed the King
across the Salon of Mars where waited those invited to supper. Saluting his queen with the public respect he always paid her, Louis gave
her his arm.

Marie-Thérèse, long used to suffering, knew anguish when she saw
it. "What is wrong with your new captain?" she whispered. The King
answered her in a low tone.

"Can't you send someone else? Of all your Guards, those two boys
are kindest to me. And I don't believe he wants——"

He silenced her. *"Je le veux."*

Victor was touched. This was the nearest he had ever heard her come
to reproaching this living Jupiter. And even after the King's reproach,
she turned and pressed Victor's hand as they paused at the entrance of
the long apartment where the supper was laid *en grand couvert,* on
one large table with five places and on five smaller ones of sixteen
places each. On impulse Marie-Thérèse pulled a diamond ring from
her finger. "You will confer pleasure upon me by accepting this ring,"
she said formally.

Victor took it, overwhelmed. "Your Majesty! It is priceless!"

"I had hoped to give you a marriage gift. Perhaps the ring will
bring you more happiness than it has to me. Come back to us soon."

"As soon as I can." He kissed the chubby hand. "When you count
the hearts over which you reign, I beg you not to forget that of your
very humble, very obedient servant."

He tucked the ring into his waistcoat pocket just as the usher of
the hall knocked sharply three times on the door of the bodyguards'

78

room, crying, "To the King's *couvert!*" The elaborate supper routine had begun.

Victor tried to arouse himself, since what he had expected to be the first of many such occasions was actually to be his last. But not until the King leaned back in his chair, with signs that the enormous Bourbon appetite was sated, could he shake off his lethargy and remember his duties. Now they were only chores to be got through before he could talk to his brother and his father. His eyes sought out the Marquis, finding him at the same table with the bejeweled and triumphant Marquise de Montespan, who was evidently exerting her famous wit, for most of the gaiety seemed centered there. And then the Marquise, apparently in the middle of an anecdote, stopped speaking and her hand gripped the table's edge so hard that her fingers turned white. Victor glanced around to see what might have disturbed her. The cupbearer had just called "Drink for the King!" setting into action the ceremony of serving the King's wine.

The wine! A chill went over Victor. The two officers *du gobelet* were Duchesne, a former lackey whom Montespan had introduced into the King's service, and Gilot, a great believer in magic, who was said to consult Le Sage in her behalf. Of course! This was where she would use the contents of the violet packet, if she intended to poison the King or someone at his table. Victor, fully alert now, watched with heightening tension as Duchesne and Gilot went to the sideboard to get a salver and cup of gold and two crystal decanters of wine and water. Preceded by the chiefs of the goblet and the wine cellars, they returned to the King's table, where the Chief of the Goblet made the trial of the wine in a little silver cup, and with a deep bow presented the King with the golden cup and the decanters. Louis poured out his usual half Burgundy, half water, and held it up.

The cup was still aloft, Victor staring at it, frozen, as the King's eyes roamed the tables and came to rest. "Fill the cup of the Marquis de Lorennes with the same."

Faces at all tables were raised in congratulation and envy. It was a special honor to be sent anything from the King's table. Victor's heart beat wildly. He couldn't speak without accusing Montespan, which he dared not do even had he evidence instead of mere suspicion. The cupbearer had rounded the end of the King's table when Victor said desperately, "Wait!"

The King looked around, astonished. Victor bowed. "May I have the honor of bearing it to my father?"

79

The King's lips relaxed into a gracious smile and he gave a nod of approval.

Victor, conscious of all eyes upon him, rounded the tables. Since the crowd of servitors was so dense, it was easy for Victor to pretend, just before he reached his father, that someone had jostled him. The decanter dropped and the wine spilled across the floor.

The King frowned. The Marquis snatched up the decanter almost as soon as it touched the floor, and poured what remained of the wine into his cup. Rising quickly to cover his son's awkwardness, he lifted the cup toward the King's table.

"Father, don't drink it!" Victor's whispered warning was urgent. "Find some excuse. Present it to me!"

"Are you mad?" whispered the Marquis fiercely, and added aloud, "To Your Majesty's health and long reign!"

As the gathering rose to drink the toast, Victor stifled a groan. The Marquis raised the cup to eye level, as if he would enjoy it with all his senses, emptied it, and resumed his place. The King sipped briefly, set his own cup aside and turned to attack a large plate of fruit.

Under the confusion, as everyone resumed his seat, the Marquis demanded, with unmoving lips, *"Non de dieu,* what ails you?"

"Nothing, Father. I'm sorry." Victor was weak with anxiety, which began to lift, however, as the Marquis resumed his eating. Miserably he hastened back to his place, reaching it just as the King finished and rose, all his guests rising with him and following into the bedchamber. Victor remained on guard at the door, until time for the *petit coucher,* when he admitted a few others privileged to attend this counterpart in reverse of the levee; for Louis took off his clothes as ceremoniously as he had put them on.

Inside the chamber, his ceremonial disrobing over and almost alone at last, the King spoke to Bontems. "What have you there?"

"A letter I found on the floor. Unsigned."

Dropping an anonymous letter where it would be found was a common means of communication to the King. Louis read the note quickly and crushed it in an impatient hand. "Another complaint about my Captain of the Guards."

"He seems an excellent young man, too," declared Bontems. "Perhaps a little young."

"The problem is already solved. I am sending him to New France."

"As usual," said Bontems impassively, "Your Majesty's wisdom is unequaled."

80

The King yawned. "I have no desire for sleep."

Bontems came to the bed, awaiting orders. "Your Majesty possesses the convenient faculty of doing with little of it."

"If Madame de Montespan were not in such bad humor— If the other one would come—"

"Your Majesty's choice is not so limited," Bontems hinted.

"I am no Charles of England, to send for an admired beauty forthwith. I have enough respect for women to court them with proper preliminaries. By the way, that new beauty, Mademoiselle de Fontanges —remind me to send her a present tomorrow. Now I'd better think of the long ride to Flanders. Bring me the folder of battle plans, and Louvois's reports." In a few minutes the monarch was pondering aloud on ammunition and food. He always prepared these lists himself down to the least item: "A thousand grenades, two hundred sandbags, a hundred axes for the men attacking the counterscarp, fifteen hundred brush hooks and five hundred axes to clear the way for the artillery. . . ."

After a time Bontems closed the curtains, extinguished the tapers, and undressed himself to lie on the watch-bed. The room grew quiet; the monarch slept.

When Victor's relief came, he hurried to where his father and Marc waited in the Hall of the Guards.

"*Dame,* but you have received a blow of some kind," said Marc. "Your face could be one of those white plaster casts the Italians sell. Surely Monsieur le Capitaine is not so upset over a moment's awkwardness? Or did you lose our lottery money?"

"I'm not Monsieur le Capitaine. Tomorrow I'm to be relieved of my post."

The two faces became distorted with consternation. "Surely His Majesty didn't——" began the Marquis.

Victor drew out his handkerchief to mop his brow. "His Majesty told me to set out for New France!"

"What?" the Marquis exclaimed incredulously.

"It's true." Victor told them briefly of his orders, omitting the real reason, as the King had commanded. "I might as well go home and plant cabbages for Auguste! I'd as soon go with La Trappe as La Salle!"

"The brown robes wouldn't suit you," said Marc. "Or the silence."

"Might as well be silent in New France. There'll be no conversation there—save to exchange grunts with Indians or bears!"

"Some very civilized people live in other places than Paris."

"There are even Parisians in New France," said the Marquis. "Count Frontenac, the Governor General, is an old friend of mine. If you're really going, I must give you a letter to him."

"If the Count can stand it," said Marc, "New France can't be too wretched. When do we leave?"

"We? What do you mean?" asked the Marquis. "Are you going, too?"

"I am sure Victor managed it somehow."

Victor nodded absently. "Yes, you are to go."

"But your studies?" the Marquis asked quietly.

Marc shrugged, and grinned. "Time enough. And I, at least, don't want to stay attached to Versailles like an oyster to its bed. We may like it there. There is a proverb: One learns to howl with the wolves."

On the way to La Rochefoucauld's apartment, where the Marquis was to spend the night, he was unusually silent.

"Are you worried about us, Father?" Marc asked.

"No. I was impressed with this La Salle. I believe you'll be in good hands. I am surprised, naturally; and I wish His Majesty had discussed this with me first. Still—"

He ended with such a gasp that both boys stopped in their tracks. Violently trembling now, the father clutched his sons by the arms. Victor's earlier fears rushed back, but the Marquis said, "It's nothing. Indigestion, perhaps. I have had these spells often. Pain, dizziness, and a burning in my stomach. It will pass."

But he leaned more and more heavily on them until at last they almost carried him to his bed. Removing his wig to the wig stand, they loosened his waistcoat and shirt, and leaving him in the care of the worried Duc and his valet, they ran for two doctors: M. Daquin, the King's, and M. Fagon, the Queen's. They came in their dressing gowns, wigless, carrying bags. Fagon, thin, humpbacked, puffing with asthma, bowed deeply to the stricken Marquis.

"Rich food," Daquin said cheerfully. "I keep protesting to His Majesty's cooks about it, but they tell me it is their job to feed the King and mine to purge him." He bent over in examination; then wheeled his humped body about on thighs as thin as a bird's, to confer with Fagon.

"An enema," said Fagon, "and a heavy dose of Peruvian bark—*le quinquina.*" A devotee of both treatments, he had given as many as seventy enemas in one illness.

Daquin nodded. "And a bleeding from the foot. A dose of Lady Kent's powders, to make him sweat freely?"

"And English drops?" Fagon asked uncertainly. "No, the malady isn't in the chest."

Victor and Marc exchanged worried glances. Fagon was said to be better at foretelling death than saving life. Victor bent over the bed. "How do you feel now, Father?"

"A sharp pain here," gasped the Marquis, pointing to a spot below his temple.

While the doctors performed their ministrations, the Marquis grew steadily worse. Lethargy alternated with pain until three o'clock, when he seemed to be resting easily, doses of ass's milk and quinine having lowered his fever. At three quarters past four, seeing the boys half asleep on a divan, La Rochefoucauld packed them off to their own room, saying he and his valet would take turns at watching over the Marquis.

Late as it was, and dull as they were from fatigue, the boys sat listlessly on the edge of their cots. They dismissed old Jacques, who, pistol in hand, had been half-dozing on guard below their coffer of francs. Victor got the coffer down, opened it, and let coins cascade through his fingers. "The finest music I've heard in years, but the past few hours have dulled its sound."

Victor awoke in alarm soon after sunrise. He awakened Marc, and they got hastily into uniform and ran to the Duc's apartment. The valet reported that the Marquis, now asleep, had had feverish awakenings but seemed no worse.

The levee, audience, and council hours seemed to Victor interminably long. No courtiers sought him out now; and though Victor had seen it happen to others, it was his first personal taste of the bitter fact that a royal favorite dwells in crowds, while adversity is solitary. Only Dreux came to him, while he waited again on the anteroom bench. "I hear you're going to New France—what adventure! I want to go along. I shall ask Monsieur Colbert's permission to ask Monsieur de la Salle."

"You're crazy," said Victor affectionately. "But I hope you succeed."

Dreux's enthusiasm was cut short when M. Colbert came out. "Sorry, my boy. I'd do anything I could for you. But Huguenots are not allowed to go to New France. Thieves, jailbirds, prostitutes, murderers, yes. Huguenots, no."

83

The next hours Victor spent in his room, looking over his clothes and arms, and getting his boots oiled by the heavy-lidded Jacques, who had expressed little surprise at the news. "Will you go with us?"

Jacques lifted his hands to shoulder height and dropped them. "I might as well. A Breton serves his master until he sees him dead."

The familiar phrase made Victor shudder. "And then I suppose you'll let them bury you alive at our feet, like those old-time servants."

"It's good that I have two masters," said Jacques glumly. "Maybe one of you will live through this madness."

Victor began sorting out his books. In a place where there was no society, there would be time to read. From under his mattress he took the letters of Pascal, kept hidden against the advent of a visit from a mischievous priest. As he was about to hand it to Jacques, a knock sounded on the door and it swung open. He held the book behind him, for on the threshold, as if produced by a conjuror, stood the tall, black-clad Père la Chaise.

"Did I startle you?" The Jesuit smiled. "I came to say *au revoir*."

"Thank you, Father," Victor answered. "I'm sorry Marc is not here."

"I wonder," mused La Chaise, "why His Majesty lets two of his best young officers go to help this La Salle, when the worth of his plans is so doubtful."

Victor made a safe reply. "Undoubtedly His Majesty knows best."

"Of course." Père la Chaise picked up a Ronsard volume but leafed it through as if he were really not seeing it. "Many very wise people, who know New France, believe La Salle's plans impossible and dangerous. They would be grateful to anyone who— shall we say?—aided in bringing his schemes to an end."

So that's it, thought Victor. "Grateful?"

Père La Chaise returned the Ronsard to its place. "It is difficult to speak definitely here, you understand. But the General of our Order has much influence. Remember, too, one renders a service to society when one destroys the schemes of a madman."

Victor said, as naïvely as he could, "But I thought he seemed quite sane. Even brilliant."

The Jesuit sighed, then said in a brisker voice, "May I ask you to take a letter and a small gift to my good friend, the Superior of our order in Quebec?"

"Certainly, Father."

"I'll send it to you at once. God go with you." The black soutane whisked out the narrow doorway.

84

Victor shrugged, and handed the Pascal to Jacques. "Wrap an issue of the *Mercure* around this. It seems we're of interest to the Jesuits now. Let's take care not to be an object of their wrath. Whatever their quarrel with La Salle, it's his affair, not mine."

"They mix themselves in everything," said Jacques stolidly. "Do we take these?" He lifted the brocades won the night before.

"No. Yes. Do as you like."

"I beg your pardon, sir!" The startled voice came from a young, round-faced lackey in the livery of Orleans who stood in the doorway. "Her Royal Highness, Madame Royale, Elizabeth Charlotte of Bavaria, Princess of Palatine, Duchess of Orleans, would like to see you."

Victor lifted his eyebrows. This must be a new lackey, infatuated with the sound of titles. "I shall be honored to call upon Madame. But let me tell you something. Your mistress is called 'Madame,' her husband 'Monsieur.' If she hears you rolling forth all those titles, she'll box your ears."

"Thank you, sir. I'll remember, sir." The red-faced boy backed away and disappeared around the corner.

Victor had intended to visit Madame as soon as she could receive him, since she was one of his favorite court women. And there was a chance of seeing Angélique, too, at this time of day; so he abandoned the packing and hastened down to the Orleans wing, where the sturdy Madame, great-granddaughter of Mary, Queen of Scots, was making her toilette. Angélique, reading aloud, stopped and looked up at him with an adoration that nearly made him giddy.

"Come in!" Madame called heartily, offering her hand to kiss. "Your visits do me more good than quinine."

"You have recovered from your indisposition of last evening?" he asked, for Madame was dressed for hunting, in a brown coat that made her look even more mannish than usual. Madame's liking for the hunt was her chief tie with the King, to whom she was devoted for his kindness to her when she first came to Versailles from strict, sober Heidelberg. Genuine, impulsive, vigorously outspoken, she demanded every inch of the respect due her position. The gossips had found her a tough nut to crack and left her alone. Victor liked her. If she brought the odor of cabbage into the court, it was a better odor than some.

"I wasn't sick," she replied. "I was only, as they say in the dear Palatinate, as cross as a bug. I had had enough of Montespan's show. And the women all stink so, I can't stand a mass of them. Too much

85

powder and scent, too little soap. And the men—worse than stableboys. Not even as housebroken as my dogs. I wince every time I pass any of those places under the staircases where they—" She stopped just short of delineating some of the less pleasant habits of the palace crowd.

"It was unkind of you to deprive us of your company so early."

"You mean of the company of one of my ladies. Let me see—" She ignored Angélique's blushes. "Is your beloved the one with teeth like a horse about to bite?"

"Now, Madame. Is that what you think of my taste?"

"Love is a sauce that makes all dishes palatable, they say. But you look sick yourself. Attacked by the poetical malady? Or is your liver out of order?"

"Neither. I'm worried. My father has been ill since last evening."

"Oh, I am sorry." Her broad face sobered. "I hope no doctor got near him."

"Two of them."

She threw up her hands. "Then only Heaven can help him. But it's not just your father that makes you look like your own ghost. You are leaving us."

Victor was not surprised that she knew, for Madame, as well as the King, had paid spies to bring her information.

"Alle Tag was neues und selten was gutes!" Madame exclaimed. "I've said that so often here—'Every day something new happens, but hardly ever anything good.' However—" she opened a drawer and pulled out a handful of medals, only a sample of her big collection at her own residence, St. Cloud. "I hope the King will have one of these struck some day to celebrate the exploits of La Salle and the De Lorennes."

Angélique let her book fall with a whimper. "La Salle! I thought you were going back to the army with the King."

At Madame's gesture, Victor sat on a folding stool between them, and took a hand of each, while he told as much as he could of his journey.

"You don't have to go all that way," Angélique wailed, "for adventure and money!"

He forced a smile, caressing her hand. "I'll be back. Everything will be just as we hoped, but later."

"La Salle has only five years," said Madame.

"Five years!" Angélique wailed, letting her head fall into Madame's lap. "I'll be an old woman."

86

Madame smoothed the soft, gleaming curls. "Even at the advanced age of twenty, you'll have plenty of beauty to set off your wedding gown. And Victor's one of the few young men around here worth waiting for."

Victor pressed Madame's short, heavy fingers. "I'd be your slave forever, if you could influence the King to recall me sooner."

"If the opportunity arrives—" Madame smiled.

"*Bien*. And I hope to have the honor of receiving some of your famous letters."

"Of course. What's one letter more? I often write fifty sheets a day. *Donnerwetter*, what day can I give you? On Sunday I write to Lorraine and Hanover; on Monday to Savoy and Spain; Tuesday to Prussia; and so on. On Saturday I make up arrears. I'll write to you on the Saturdays when I have no arrears." She took up her quill, and gently raised Angélique from her lap. "Child, go look in my jewel cabinet. In the black case, you'll find a diamond-set locket the King gave me. Put a lock of your hair in it; then I'll be sure Victor will prize it." She cut off his thanks. "And then"—she stopped Angélique at the door—"go out in the labyrinth and see if you can find the comb I lost yesterday. Take Mademoiselle Esmant with you and set her to look for the comb, in case a young man should come to take his farewell in decent privacy."

When the door had closed behind her, Madame added, "Give her a minute to get your present ready and wipe her eyes. Now don't worry. I'll accept the office of dragon to watch over your treasure. I think it may be good to go and make a fortune, so you won't be dependent on what Angélique will have. As Monsieur Racine says, '*point d'argent, point de Suisse.*' No money, no Swiss Guards at your door."

"You'll look after her," asked Victor anxiously, "no matter how high the suitors?"

"I look after my maids as if they were my daughters," said Madame evenly, holding out her hand for him to kiss. "Now run along to your sweetheart."

Victor found Angélique sitting alone on a bench, while in the distance the skirts of Mlle. Esmant swept back and forth along the path. With a tearful smile, Angélique moved her skirt so he could sit down. He kissed her hand and buried his face for an instant in the lace at her throat. Its fragrance sharpened unbearably the pain of leaving her. "You *will* wait for me?"

"I swear it, *sur le dieu que j'adore*." She crossed herself. "I'll never marry anyone else, if I have to be an old maid and retire to a convent."

Thoughts of the girl Michelle inexplicably crossed his mind as he pressed Angélique's hand. "No, no. The King gave his word that we may be married as soon as I come back."

"His Majesty is so wonderful!" she sighed. "So handsome, so kind——"

Victor cut off her raptures. "Yes, all the superlatives fit him. But now pray concentrate on one of his subjects."

She pressed a lacy bit of nothing to her eyes. "All at once, I'm afraid—and I don't know what I'm afraid of. . . ."

"If we could only be married now——" Desire hoarsened his voice. "We could spend some weeks in Rouen, and then you could wait there with Father and our brothers."

"The King won't let us!" she said hastily. "Nor would my father. I must stay here. But come back soon. With lots of money. Do you know the first thing I want? A carriage of my own." She glowed. "Do you know the one of the Comtesse de Soissons? A gilt frame, with a white body rising from it, shaped like a lily! Six white horses, and coachmen and outriders in gold and purple!"

Victor felt embarrassed by her vehemence. "I'll try to get you one just as fine. I've invested money with La Salle that should bring a good return. And the King may give me a pension——" He stopped short of revealing what it might be given for.

"Oh, that will be *merveilleux*. And could I have——"

Victor got up, drew her to her feet and stopped her with a long kiss. They clung together desperately, murmuring incoherent reassurances and promises between kisses, until they heard a warning cough from Mlle. Esmant. "I must go," said Angélique woefully. "I hate hunting. I get so tired, and my clothes so mussed. Oh, here's the locket. It has a curl from here." She indicated her coiffure just above her right ear. He pressed the bit of jewelry to his lips and dropped it into his pocket. "That curl will travel to places you'll never see."

She threw her arms around him and gave him a long, passionate kiss. "You mustn't—you just mustn't stay away long. Oh, I'm afraid——"

"Not an instant longer than I have to," he said huskily.

In La Rochefoucauld's apartment, the Marquis was awake now, almost as pale as his pillow. Marc had been reading aloud, but put down his book when Victor came in, and, at a sign from his father, dismissed the valet hovering about. Victor drew up a stool opposite Marc, and lifted one of the pale hands on the bed. "How do you feel?"

"Much better. You boys must not stay here on my account. Go to Paris, conclude your business with Monsieur de la Salle, and order the clothes you'll need. Don't spare expense. I'll manage the bills."

"That's not necessary, Father," said Marc. "We have money from the lottery."

"Take the evening, too. It may be your last in Paris for some time. If I keep very quiet today and go to sleep early, we may be able to start home tomorrow. But now, before you see La Salle . . ." The Marquis slowly clasped and unclasped his hands on the silk coverlet, hesitating as if weakness forced him to arrange his ideas into the fewest possible words. "I just want to tell you I have complete faith that you can take care of yourselves anywhere. Try to serve France well. And remember that a wellbred person will do anything reasonably required of him. After all, it's good to have adventure in youth. Time enough later for glory in the anterooms."

He held up his hands. "Put yours in mine."

They obeyed, and as he clasped theirs he began speaking again, gravely now. Both boys fell startled to their knees, for he was repeating the solemn ceremony which released a son from parental authority, except for the demands of honor, respect and affection. In token, as he finished speaking, the Marquis took away his own hands, releasing those of his sons and giving them liberty to do what they would with their own lives. For an instant he let his fingers pass lovingly over the emerald-set hilt of D'Artagnan's sword. There were tears in the young eyes as the older ones slowly closed in weariness. The two boys rose and went softly from the room.

10

IN the midst of the cumbersome exodus of King and court to St. Germain, the twins rode to Paris to see La Salle. They felt worldly and rich as never before, with the lottery winnings in their saddlebags and each wearing a priceless ring, for the Queen had given Marc a fine emerald to balance her gift to Victor.

As they approached La Salle's house at No. 17 Rue de la Truanderie, a modest street of narrow, prim houses, they saw that a carriage, capacious and highly ornamented but without a coat of arms, stood before the door. In it sat a girl in a blue dress, her head down as if she were asleep, a veil and a blue satin bonnet concealing her face.

"I hope La Salle will take both of us," Victor mused uneasily as they waited. "The King wants us to persuade him without mentioning the royal orders."

"I wonder why?"

Victor avoided his eyes. " '*Je le veux,*' " he quoted.

Victor rapped sharply on the door again, impatient to get this interview over; and at last the door swung open to reveal a porter with gray touseled hair whose scowl, at sight of their uniforms, changed quickly to an ingratiating deep bow. Answering their inquiry, he said, "Go up the stairs, and turn—*mais attendez,* here comes that heathen. You can follow him."

The boys spun around. Although Paris drew persons from all parts of the world, they were not prepared for the figure that seemed to float up the steps. Bare except for a loincloth and a square of scarlet material draped carelessly upon his back, the heathen had a skin the color of ripe chestnuts and an extremely wiry body. His hair, thick and black, hung straight to his shoulders, restrained only by a headband of bright striped cloth; and, strangest of all, the lower part of his ear rim had been long ago cut loose so it hung low and was decorated with earrings and beads. Beads and shellwork decorated a soft foot covering that explained why they had not heard him coming. Since they blocked the doorway, this queer creature stopped, but instead of saluting, he stood examining them from their fine riding boots to the plumed hats upon their bright hair, seeming to find them as noteworthy as they found him. An amused glance passing between them, they wondered in what language they would hear the usual comment on their resemblance. Surprisingly it came in gutturally accented French: "Bad!"

They were startled, amused, and more than a little indignant. A ripple of laughter came from the carriage.

"Bad medicine." The brown one made signs that appeared to be for himself, not for communication. "My tribe kill one when born."

"That's you, Marc," laughed Victor. "I was born first."

"Most primitive peoples think twins are bad luck," said Marc.

"Some not so primitive, too." Victor was thinking of the perennially whispered story that the famous prisoner in the iron mask was a twin of Louis XIV, kept from the public since birth that he might never become a menace to the throne. "But I hope this Iroquois, or whatever he is, doesn't intend to remedy things by despatching one of us now."

"Not Iroquois!" The savage face took on such animation that their hands went to their sword hilts. "Shawano." His keen eyes looked at them as if he were waiting for an apology.

Uncertainly, Victor shrugged: "Forgive me, pray." The savage's features relaxed. He fingered the gold lacings on Victor's uniform, as a child might have done, and then made repeated motions toward the plumed hat.

"I think he wants you to take it off, sir. He's crazy," said the porter.

"Nonsense." Victor was amused. "I can—or could yesterday—remain covered before the King himself!"

"Why not humor him?" asked Marc, at another vigorous gesture of the brown hand. "Let's see what he'll do."

Victor lifted his hat. The brown fellow snatched it, stroked the white plumes, clapped it on his own head, and disappeared through the door as soundless as a ghost.

Marc's mouth hung open. "The winged step of Mercury!"

Laughter was coming from the carriage again, and the boys turned to see that the blue bonnet now framed a comely face with sparkling eyes as blue as her dress. Victor bowed hastily, and pulled Marc's sleeve. "Quick, after my hat!"

Inside, they plunged up the stairs in time to see the savage gliding toward the far end of the hall. He passed through a doorway without knocking, almost bowling over a gentleman in gold-trimmed glasses, who was just leaving. Victor rapped at the door, and received a prompt, "Entrez."

They found themselves in a small, dim room with one mediocre tapestry on the wall, a bed, a mirror, a portrait of Louis XIV, and a table spread with maps, near which La Salle stood with the *garde-marine* and a short man in the garb of a wealthy merchant.

"So you're the brother who 'has a passion for looking up the defini-tion of things,' to quote His Majesty." La Salle smiled. "May I present Monsieur Tonti, and my cousin, Monsieur Francois Plet."

Before M. Plet lay several piles of louis d'or, for which he had ap-parently just received a receipt. "We were wondering where Nika got the hat." M. Plet glanced at Victor's uncovered head. The savage was now sitting on the floor, the hat in his lap, while he stroked the plume.

"Your strange servant makes himself a bit free with other's property," commented Victor dryly.

"Nika is more than a servant. He is a sort of *fidus Achates.*"

"Even for an original like you," said M. Plet, "it seems an unusual choice."

"I didn't choose him. I am very fortunate that he chose me."

"What do you mean, fortunate?" M. Plet persisted.

"Well," said La Salle reluctantly, "it is common for an Indian to choose another man about his own age to be his most intimate friend. The two will brave any danger and run any risk to aid each other. Even death has no terrors, for they believe they will meet in the other world and need each other's assistance there. So it is with Nika and me. Nika, incidentally, means friend, or brother. His name is really White Beaver."

Victor stood amazed, wondering if La Salle's devotion to this heathen included letting him keep his hat. As if he had said it aloud, La Salle retrieved the hat and restored it to Victor. "I sometimes have difficulty with his manners. According to his customs, he had a right to try on anything of yours he admired. In fact, he really thought you had given it to him. He'd give you anything he has."

Victor surveyed the scantily covered figure and shuddered.

"I rather admire those things on his feet," said Marc.

La Salle gave him an approving glance. "An excellent choice. Moccasins are the most comfortable foot covering in the world."

Nika started to take them off. "No, the gentleman doesn't want them just now," said La Salle, adding a few words in a strange tongue which sent the savage gliding silently out of the room.

"Now to business," said La Salle. "François, will you affix the amount of your loan to this list of my other debts?"

"Quite a list, Robert." M. Plet ran his quill down the margin. "Four hundred livres, six thousand livres, twenty-four thousand, four thousand, thirteen thousand six hundred and twenty-three—that's owed to Count Frontenac, I see. And there are nine other sums. Have you no doubts of paying?"

La Salle smiled. "Not the slightest. The valley of the Mississippi should yield more than a thousand times that total. And for the ten thousand livres so weighty in the hands of you young gentlemen, will forty per cent interest, the whole sum payable in five years, be satisfactory?"

Victor wanted to protest the length of time, but he was in no position to argue. He signed a contract, handed the quill to Marc, and tossed the moneybags upon the table. Assisted by M. Tonti, M. Plet counted out the 10,000 livres.

"Then may I thank you again?" La Salle's polite words had a hint of dismissal.

Victor hesitated, as before a height to be taken with one quick lunge. "Monsieur de la Salle, since I talked with you at Versailles, I have been thinking of your invitation." He rushed to get the lie past his lips. "I would like to join your expedition."

La Salle's eyes flashed. "Why?"

"His Majesty has just relieved me of my duty in the Guards."

"Why?"

Victor hesitated.

"You'd rather not say?"

"I'd rather not."

"It must have been a duel," offered the *garde-marine,* with a glance at Victor's mended sleeve.

"I am perhaps too quick with my sword," admitted Victor. "And so my brother and I would like to seek our fortune in the New World."

"And I, monsieur, add my prayers that we be allowed to go," said Marc. "I, too, was impressed by what I heard of your plans. I would —we would—consider it an honor to be permitted to help you."

Marc's sincerity was unmistakable, and a little warmth crept into La Salle's eyes. "I fear I have nearly completed my company. The gentlemen you must have passed in the hall, Monsieur la Motte de Lussière, was the last associate I intend to take. I need now only some workers in wood and iron, and a secretary. Letters, contracts, reports— I must not have my time cluttered with them. And a journal has to be kept on every expedition, a day-by-day account, for the Intendant at Quebec."

Consternation seized Victor's throat. The King would expect him to overcome any objections, yet he couldn't force his way into the company. His mind raced, trying to think of the right argument, and found only one. "I should be glad to serve as your secretary."

Meeting La Salle's stern gaze, Victor cursed himself for being so precipitous. The man surely smelled a rat.

"You see, sir," interposed Marc, "we want to do our share, and will gladly take any part you care to assign us. My brother does have a certain facility with the pen. As for myself, besides some knowledge of drugs and medicine, I have a little experience with maps and fortification. I worked with Monsieur Vauban for nearly a year."

"A year with Vauban!" La Salle was obviously impressed. "I can indeed use you well." And to Victor he added evenly, "You'll do as well as another. We leave the first of July, I hope. From La Rochelle. I suggest you arrive there at least the day before."

"And what clothing should we take?"

"I cannot imagine anything better than that uniform to impress savages."

"Monsieur! I have never found it necessary to impress savages."

"I am afraid you will if you go with me. But you won't need much. In Quebec society your uniform will be your best passport. Beyond Quebec, we can't carry much baggage. Your uniform, one other suit, and a warm jacket and some other woods clothing you can get in Quebec."

"What about our horses, sir?" asked Marc.

"Leave them here. And you won't be wearing swords except for dress occasions."

"But, monsieur!" exclaimed Victor. "Surely, even there, a sword is the mark of the gentleman?"

La Salle leaned forward, his hands on the table. "Where I am going, you will be whatever you are—without swords. July first, then, at La Rochelle."

M. Plet folded his receipt and inserted it in a waistcoat pocket. "Well, Robert, I'd better go along now, too, or my daughter will be coming to get me. Come, you must meet Susette," he insisted to the twins as the three of them headed for the stairs.

Susette proved to be as susceptible as any other woman to their uniforms. "Won't you come home with us for tea?" she begged.

"I am deeply sorry, mademoiselle, but we have other errands."

"They are going to New France with La Salle," added her father.

"How wonderful! I wish we could go there. *Mon père,* couldn't we?"

M. Plet climbed heavily into the carriage. "Maybe sometime, pet," he said indulgently. He spoke to his coachman, and they were off in a clatter of hoofs and wheels.

At the Rue St. Denis the brothers left their horses in the stables of the nearest inn. "Shall we go to Monsieur Tourneau's first?" Victor asked.

94

"No, you pick out something for us both, as usual. I have some books to sort at Monsieur Villette's."

"Then I'll meet you there later." Victor had been uneasily silent for most of the ride. Did La Salle suspect anything?

Even M. Tourneau's shop did not cheer him. Briefly, avoiding the tailor's curiosity, he settled past debts and paid in advance for two dark green traveling suits. Usually he spent a leisurely time examining materials, but today he selected quickly and gave indifferent orders about embroidery and lace.

With the same coolness toward tasks he usually delighted in, he visited other fashionable shops, ordering boots and traveling hats, shirts and undergarments. For Angélique, he selected at a jeweler's a handsome sweetmeat box, to be ornamented with his crest and portrait. An exquisite antique gold cross and chain caught his eye, and he asked its price, only to reject it. Angélique would think it too old-fashioned. But as he was leaving the shop he thought of the girl at the convent, and on impulse went back and gave directions to have it sent to her with no card. Certainly they would let her keep it, and she deserved one piece of beauty in that dull place.

His purse much lightened, he sought out Marc. "Almost ready?"

Marc had brought something resembling neatness to the cluttered back room. "Almost. But Monsieur Villette wants to send Father a new tonic. He has gone across the city for one of the rare ingredients. It may be late evening before he has it made up."

"That's all right. Father said for us to spend the evening here." Victor was not eager to return. Their father would be asleep, and with the King and court at St. Germain, Versailles would be empty. Yet he didn't want to wait in the shop, and he wondered, when he was in the street again, what to do. Ordinarily it was no problem. He would be welcome at Ninon de Lenclos's salon and at any number of other resorts or cafés, but he felt no desire to talk to anyone. A passing peddler thrust a piece of paper into his hand, and he accepted this kind message from the fates. *Le Bourgeois Gentilhomme* was playing. He ran back to tell Marc, and then engaged a sedan chair to take him to the Theâtre.

When the hour grew late and M. Villette had not returned, Mme. Villette came down to take over the shop and Marc strolled outside. It was too late to follow Victor to the Theâtre, but he hoped M. Molière's comedy would relieve Victor's depression. Odd that yesterday Victor had felt sorry for the girl he had taken to the convent; now he himself had been sentenced to something he dreaded as much.

The girl! Victor had promised to see her. Was she waiting? Marc glanced at his watch. He still had time, and she wouldn't know the difference between them.

He strode down the street, dodging the low-hung signs, and made his way toward the spacious Pont Neuf that spanned the Seine where the two arms united. As usual, the bridge was like a perpetual fair, so crowded he could scarcely get through, holding his purse with one hand, for this was a favorite rendezvous for thieves. All day and far into the night streetwalkers plied their trade here, charlatans sold balsams, players presented farces in little open-air theaters, song sellers sang their wares accompanied by violin or guitar.

At a book stall Marc purchased a thin volume of verse, and then plunged into the Rue St. Jacques, so dark that he could hardly see where to put his foot. He could just make out that on one side was a high stone wall, lined by a row of chestnut trees. He was at the end of his quest: this was the wall about the Carmelite grounds. If the girl had managed to get out she would go to the gate farthest from the buildings.

As he peered for the gate he heard a slight whimper from inside; and stopped so sharply that a bird above him fluttered away.

The sound was repeated. *Mille diables,* he thought, someone is crying! He pulled himself up on a low-growing branch of a chestnut tree and scanned the grounds beyond the wall, lit faintly by a distant lantern at the convent door. There was a scrambling below, and a hushed voice came drifting up. "It *is* you! You did come!"

"Yes, I came," he answered softly from his perch on the tree branch. "How did you get out?"

"I believe *le bon dieu* intended I should. I was in the garden after vespers with Sister Anne and Sister Emilie. As we were going in, Sister Anne turned her ankle and Sister Emilie helped her inside. So I slipped into the garden again and hid behind St. Joseph's statue until it got dark. Of course they'll miss me before long."

"Will you be punished?"

"What could they do to make me more miserable than I am already?"

"Is that why you were crying?"

"No. It was because I thought you had forgotten Michelle already."

So that was her name. "I wish I could help you."

A light appeared across the garden and she shrank back. "It's the portress." The light wavered and disappeared as if behind a closing door. "Wait!" She ran to a tree on her side of the wall, and to his surprise, shinnied up the trunk like a boy and scrambled out on a limb as agilely as a sailor. Now she was only a few feet away.

"Well!" he said admiringly, "nobody but a devil or a cat can get you now."

She laughed in delight. As his eyes grew more accustomed to the dimness he could see a pleasant little face with a smile that was warm but not in the least coquettish. "Tell me about yourself," she demanded. "What exactly does a guardsman have to do?"

In cautious whispers he told her something of the routine of guard duty, adding: "But I'm about to have a change. I'm going to New France."

"Oh! *quelle bonne chance!* I've read a lot about our colonies."

"You have?"

"Yes. I've always been alone so much, I read everything I could find. I know about Champlain and Nicolet and the Jesuit fathers. Oh, I wish I were a man. I'd go, too!"

She sounded more fit to wear a soldier's tunic than a skirt. "An old friend of my father's is Governor-General. I don't know him very well, but Madame Frontenac is often at court. She's one of the ladies in waiting."

"But, what is she doing here if her husband is in Quebec?"

"It may not be a place for a fine lady."

"Nonsense," said Michelle firmly.

Marc abandoned the argument. "Monsieur de la Salle, with whom I am going, doesn't plan to stay in Quebec himself. We're going west into unexplored wilderness."

"Why?" she leaned forward eagerly.

"Well, it seems there is a river with a strange name. . . ." As he spoke of La Salle's plans, he found enthusiasm growing in his voice, and Michelle recklessly let go of the limb to clap her hands. "But how exciting! How lucky you are!"

The moon was rising now, and he could see her more clearly. Victor had given the impression that she was being banished to a convent because she was ugly. But her features were good; a little happiness might make her a lovely woman.

"By the way, I brought you something." Taking the little book from his pocket, he tossed it toward her. She caught it expertly and tried to make out the title.

97

"Just some verses from the Pont Neuf. You'll probably have to hide them, though."

"I'll manage. Oh, you've been so kind. I love your other gift."

"Other—?" He caught himself. She was gazing down at her chest. Victor must have sent her the handsome cross gleaming against her drab gown.

"It came just before vespers. I love it," she said simply.

"I'm glad he didn't forget. I mean . . . the shopkeeper did deliver it."

"No one but you cares anything about me." She made it a simple statement of fact, with no overtones of self-pity.

"Try not to be unhappy," he urged. "One never knows what's going to happen."

"Will you come to see me, as soon as you are back?"

"The first thing I do," he said promptly, smiling to see the quick leap of joy in her eyes. Whether he could come or not, the hope would be one little thought for her to hold between herself and this life she hated. And with time her dislike of it might wear away, and she would become reconciled.

They sat in companionable silence for a time. "I suppose I must go," he said reluctantly. "I have to ride back to Versailles tonight. I'll try to send you something from New France. I won't put my name on it. You can tell the sisters whatever you like. Now, good-bye!" He descended quickly, feeling it more merciful than a prolonged farewell. As he struck off toward the center of town again, he began to whistle, both for her ears and because of the unaccountable lift the episode had given his own spirits.

M. Villette gave Marc a small leather case holding a row of vials— the new tonic and various potions and healing agents for fevers or accidents they might encounter in New France. "This last one is an antidote," he said. "In case they poison people over there, too."

When the boys ascended the hollowly echoing staircases to La Rochefoucauld's apartment, the Duc's valet met them at the door. "My master presents his deep regrets. His Majesty would not permit him to stay behind with his sick friend."

They were staring past him. The bed curtains were wide open, telling the news even before the servant's words: "I'm sorry, Messieurs. Your father died an hour ago."

PART II

PART II

11

AT dawn on the following September 15, Victor and Marc came up on the deck of the *St. Honoré*, in full uniform as La Salle had requested, for the merchant ship was already far inside the American continent and today would end their two months' journey. The air was crisp, and the boys sat down in the sun near the bow, where Victor took out a quill to write letters to go back with the ship. Giving the ink to Marc to hold, he rested the paper on the book whose blank pages were to hold the official journal of the expedition.

Marc, holding the inkstand on one knee, gazed at the passing scenery. Curiosity had long since changed into amazement and deepened into awe, for even now he could not get used to league after league of forest grandeur with never a sign of human life. From the time the ship had entered this broad shining river, so like a sea at its mouth, he had waited incredulously for it to narrow to some semblance of the rivers he knew, but it was never less than a mile wide. The ship had to veer, night and day, between wooded islands, and a moment's laxness would have left her on one of their banks. The north shore, a mountainous, rugged bulk looming on their right, was now and then cut by smaller tributary rivers, gliding smoothly through evergreen forests or tumbling over rocky ledges.

From Tadoussac, a small trading and fishing post, they had closely followed the northern coast, sailing by night into endless mystery, with the dark shimmering river below and the path of stars above. The Frenchmen who had come before had here and there set a name upon this land of mist and mountains, for the sailors greeted certain beetling rocks at a river's mouth as Malbaie and a wild romantic gorge with foaming waterfalls as the ravine of the Eboulements.

Marc wondered whether those earlier ones had come here by any more strange sequence of events than he and Victor. On guard duty at the palace he had often stared at a mosaic until with closed eyes he could still see its arrangement of gay or somber triangles, diamonds, and squares. So it was with the days since their father's death had shattered the framework of their lives.

One bit of the mosaic was the sad trip to Rouen and the funeral. Had Montespan tried to poison the King rather than lose him to her rival? Whatever the plot, she and the Chevalier had certainly taken care to involve Victor, in case he proved unmanageable. Victor had alternately grieved and reproached himself. Lonesome for the court and for Angélique, he had wandered about in stunned apathy through their days with Auguste and Charles in the isolated Château de Lorennes.

Marc sighed, turning the inkstand sidewise so Victor could get the last drops. Other bits of the mosaic had been put into the pattern at La Rochelle. Thanks to the lottery, they had ample means for getting across France, but their purses were much depleted by costs of bed and supper and hay by the time they entered the gate of that bright, clean city, spread in a horseshoe-shaped embrace about a bay. Marc had been interested to see how well it was fortified; Victor fretted because he had just remembered leaving Marie-Thérèse's ring at home.

Finding none of La Salle's party at the principal inn, they had exchanged boots and spurs for shoes and hose and gone to the quay, lined with commercial houses. Just beyond the tall ribs of a ship under construction they had found La Salle, in a brown traveling suit, checking boxes and bales and casks. On one side of him was the Italian, his naval uniform now exchanged for neat gray; on the other side, La Motte de Lussière, of the gold-rimmed glasses. La Salle greeted them with quiet cordiality, turned his lists over to Tonti and Marc, and bade Victor go with him to see the Secretary of Commerce, since a record of this interview would be his first journal entry. When they had gone, La Motte wandered off to a tavern while Tonti told Marc that La Salle was very much worried. Most of his goods were on ship board and stowed away, supplies and trading goods, and the rigging and anchors for two ships he intended to build—everything except about 22,000 francs' worth that another ship was to bring the following summer. Twenty men were to come with the later ship, and thirty were to go on this one.

"The *St. Honoré* should be sailing now, with us aboard." Tonti waved toward the staid procession of ships moving through the narrow passage into the outer harbor. "A loaded ship cannot move out except with the tide of the new or full moon; otherwise there is not enough depth. So the delay will mean a fortnight of waiting." And the cause of this delay? The

Secretary of Commerce, Sieur Bellinzani, wouldn't give La Salle his commission for sailing.

Unable to afford loss of time for legal protests, La Salle finally had had to bribe Bellinzani heavily. The fortnight of waiting was tedious, as delay always is when one is poised for action, but at last, on a Sunday when bells were ringing, the tide came again, and providence also sent the favor of a light easterly wind. The *St. Honoré* was the first to pass out between the two towers when the massive iron chain was lifted. With a last glance back, Victor had faced with the others toward the New World.

The ocean voyage had made them no better acquainted with La Salle, who had used the time to learn navigation from the ship's captain. As studiously as an apprentice he bent over charts or compass or practiced with an astrolabe. Marc watched enviously, but hesitated to intrude in face of La Salle's absorption and aloofness.

Victor finished his letter and handed quill and inkstand to Jacques, waiting near by. "Your baggage is all ready to take off," said Jacques glumly. "The sailors say we are almost there." A small knot of men was gathering, staring up the river. Here the *St. Honoré* was passing south of a long, wooded island someone spoke of as Orleans, whose forests were broken by cabanes and cleared fields. Rounding the western end, they caught a glimpse at the right of a high, foamy cataract and someone murmured the name of another of France's great families, Montmorency.

Directly ahead the river narrowed between two cliffs, and ships were anchored at the base of the higher one, on the right, which was crowned by numerous walls and towers. They had reached the capital of New France: Quebec. Its strange name went round among the voyagers, each savoring it as if to taste what it held for him.

12

THE great cliff, rising in the angle between another sizable river and the St. Lawrence, had the steepness of those heights on which the ancients built their holy places. Marc perceived that a cathedral's cross

shared eminence with the Bourbon lilies flying above a wooden structure that must be the Governor's palace, its square flanking towers,
walls, and bastions resting like a crown upon the brink of the precipice. At the foot of the cliff sprawled a lower town: crude wooden
taverns, shops, and warehouses, in Norman style, with wide chimneys,
dormer windows, and steep roofs curving upward at the eaves.

Marc and Victor worked their way forward to the *St. Honoré's* bow
to join La Salle, Nika, Tonti, and La Motte. La Salle was gazing
silently up at the towering rock, and the concentration in that bronze
profile told Marc that this explorer was a true descendant of the North-
men who ravaged the coast of France a thousand years ago and settled
there.

"It reminds me of Gibraltar," said Tonti.

"A good place for a fort," said Marc. "High, and protected on two
sides by water."

"So this is where the ships that we used to watch being unloaded
at Le Havre came from," mused Victor.

La Salle's intensity relaxed into a smile. "Yes. In fact, as you see,
some are loading now."

Nika was watching every movement in the harbor, but with less
attention to the ships' boats plying back and forth to the shore than to
the stranger craft going up and down the river, some like hollowed-out
logs, some made of a framework covered with thin bark, propelled by
a kind of oar.

"How many kinds of 'canoes' are there?" Marc asked, recalling their
name.

Nika held up two fingers. La Salle slightly expanded the statement:
"The elmbark ones are Iroquois. Most tribes—and we French—use the
birch ones, because they are light enough to carry overland."

"If they are so light," said the naval-minded Tonti, "it must take
considerable skill to manage them."

"It does," said La Salle. "Nika here is the best boatman I have seen
in any water, salt or fresh."

"I wouldn't care to ride in even the best of them," commented
Victor.

"Au contraire," said La Salle, "you'll ride many a league in that
fashion. And while we are in Quebec, you newcomers must learn to
paddle one."

"Fichtre!" exploded Victor. "Don't you employ regular boatmen?"

La Salle stiffened. "Here we do not travel as if we were in a carriage.

Gentlemen and priests take their turns at the paddles. In fact, canoe-men refuse to be burdened with anyone who will not."

With a boom of her cannon, the *St. Honoré* now moved in and came to rest among the anchored ships. As they were disembarking in the ship's boat, Marc looked eagerly toward the great rock of Quebec. To him it's an adventure, thought Victor, realizing that he himself felt rather like a soldier on a campaign, wanting only to get it over and go home. Absently he touched the hilt of D'Artagnan's sword, seeking the clasp of a faithful companion.

"Look at the crowd at the water's edge!" Marc gestured excitedly.

"Not a very distinguished reception committee," said Victor.

"Peasants." La Motte, smoothing his ruffles, dismissed the rows of men in coarse blue trousers and wide-skirted coats tied in at the waist with blue scarves.

"Just like Honfleur, Dieppe, or Havre," said Victor. "Let a ship approach and the whole town runs to the waterside."

"After all that wildness," added Marc, "the St. Lawrence turns into a river as Norman as the Seine. But then, wasn't New France settled by Norman fishermen, sailors, and the carpenters and masons from Champlain's fleet?"

La Salle, in the bow, turned around. "I must warn you not to say 'peasants' here. They don't like it. They call themselves 'habitants.'"

As the rhythmical dip and splash of the oars brought them closer to shore, they could see other groups, like islands, among the gaily dressed "habitants." A few, obviously sober merchants, were waiting with carts to claim goods from the ship. Soldiers with slouch hats, plumes, and bandoliers chatted with figures in leather tunics and fringed leggings. Aloof from the rest stood lithe brown savages. Mingling with all classes were gray-hooded Recollets and black-soutaned, broad-hatted Jesuits. And as the boat pulled up to the dock, the twins heard in the distance a rhythmic clatter that could only be a squad of soldiers marching on cobblestones. As if on cue, the close-pressed crowd parted, allowing ten pairs of bodyguards to pass through and form smartly into two lines at attention. Between them advanced a green-and-gold-clad nobleman of obvious military bearing.

"Distinguished enough for you?" asked Marc dryly.

Victor stared at the tall man with his high aquiline nose and fierce gray eyes beneath tufted brows. It was a face lined and marked by weather, age, or worry since it had last been seen at court.

"Count Frontenac himself!" Never in France had they seen the Count show such personal warmth as he did in his embrace of La Salle when the explorer stepped ashore.

"*A la bonne heure*! I had nearly given you up for this year. I got your message about the infuriating delay at La Rochelle! What news from France?"

"The King is well, as is the Dauphin and the Queen. And Madame Frontenac is her usual vivacious self."

"Tempestous, you mean. And your affairs?"

"On the whole, they went very well."

"We must have a long talk. But now you may present your associates." The Count gestured with his left hand, his right arm having been useless since it was broken at the seige of Orbitello more than thirty years before. "*Mais, c'est impossible! Mon dieu,* have you raided the very King's Guard? Two . . . or am I seeing double?"

La Salle presented them: "Victor and Marc de Lorennes, late of the Guards. And here is——"

"De Lorennes! But I know them! I often used to visit your home in Paris, and also your château. You were infants then. Your father and I were very close in our army days. How is the good Marquis?"

Victor replied, "I regret to inform you that he died last May. But he knew we were coming, and intended to write you."

"You have my sympathy," said the Count softly. "La Salle, if all your company is made of as good stuff, it augurs well for the expedition."

"That will decide itself later," said La Salle. "May I also present De Lussière? And Monsieur Tonti, formerly of Naples and of the French navy? He's a cousin of Du Luth."

The Count extended his hand. "By this fortnight of delay, you have just missed a reunion with him."

Tonti was visibly disappointed. "Will he be back soon, sir?"

"I fear not. He never stays long in Quebec. Up and down the rivers —daring, restless—I have to hold him on a long, loose leash. Now he has gone, with only six men, three of them savages, where few men will go—west of the lakes, among the fierce Sioux—the Iroquois of the West. But now—" he added with a gesture toward the cliff, "I welcome all of you to our capital. Did you ever see a more superb site?"

He led the way through the lower town, the little party following with the halting steps of feet that have long known only a moving deck. In this street of crude wooden buildings roofed with bark, the largest were warehouses, for through their open doors sunlight fell upon the sheen of furs. Men with soft moccasined feet and quick voices speaking a French patois mixed with something even less understandable, were loading packs on their backs and carrying them toward the wharf. Those furs are going on the *St. Honoré,* thought Victor. Some of them may be worn at court. But it'll be a long time before I see them.

"A little climb now, messieurs," said the Count. Beyond the last warehouse loomed a steep, well-worn mountain path, the only ascent to the upper town. "You are following in historic footsteps. Champlain and his men ascended here to plant the lilies of France on what was then a naked rock."

Stony and uneven, the long winding path seemed more fitting for goats than for men. It was bounded on one side by a picket fence and lined on the other by taverns and shops, set one above the other as on stairs. Just now a crowd filled its length, streaming downward. At first Victor observed only externals: the cheerful robustness of the habitants, the businesslike carriage of Jesuits, the ageless pallor of nuns, and the vigorous bodies of the half-naked savages. Unsmiling and strange, they passed by on their uncannily silent feet, and no one but the newcomers gave them more than a passing glance.

"Where do you suppose they ever came from?" murmured Victor.

"From Adam, even as you and I," said Marc. "But look at these!" Saluting the Governor was a cluster of men who seemed neither savage, habitant, nor gentlemen. They were thin, long-faced, lean, like Indians, yet with the features of white men above soft leather jackets with fringed-seam trousers and beaded moccasins. A knife hung at every belt, and a few carried muskets as casually as a gentlemen a pair of gloves. "M'sieu La Salle, welcome back," said one.

"Jean Michel!" said La Salle warmly. "What are you doing here?"

"I came all the way from Fort Frontenac to ask you not to hire a surgeon for your expedition. I'd like to go with you."

"Good, Jean! Then I'll hire someone else for the fort."

"Thank you, m'sieu." He beckoned his companions forward. "My friends want to sign up, too. You know them all—they were at Lachine with you."

"Of course." La Salle shook the hand of each. "Quesnel, the gunsmith. Glad to have you. And Lavigne, Le Bourbonnais, La Douceur, Prud'homme, Ptolmee. It is good to have all of you."

"We sign as canoemen, or whatever you need," said the one called Prud'homme. "You're a good seigneur, fair to everybody. When you hiring?"

"Tomorrow morning. At the Lion d'Or. I'll have the crier make the rounds. And Jean, bring me a list of supplies you'll need."

"At the castle," added Count Frontenac. "La Salle is to be my guest."

"*Merci bien,*" said La Salle, "but I hope not to impose on your hospitality more than a few days. Then I'll be off to the West."

"Not that soon, I'm afraid. There are some matters here—but I'll tell you later."

As they started on up the hill, Victor commented, "That man didn't look like much like a doctor."

Frontenac turned, smiling. "You'll have many such surprises. Here we don't judge either a man's rank or occupation by his dress."

The climb was steeper now. Frontenac seemed to enjoy the deference paid him by this assorted crowd, and returned all the salutes as paternally as would Louis XIV himself. Victor had expected more melancholy from one who, born and bred at the very center of civilization, and, as the godson of Louis XIII, accustomed to the splendors of St. Germain and Fontainebleau. The Count had also been so prominent a military figure that the great Turenne, the first soldier of Europe, had chosen him out of the entire French army when the Venetians asked for a French officer to lead them against the Turks. When he had disappeared from society upon being sent to New France, rumors had flitted about Paris: his fortunes were ruined, he and his wife could not get along, he had been smiled upon by Madame de Montespan and a jealous King had sent him away.

Victor's thoughts were brought back to the colorful scene about him by an exuberant shout from above. Coming down, his arms outstretched, was a monk with gray garments flying out behind his portly figure. Beneath the thrown-back hood a round face radiated joy as he came to sliding stop and seized La Salle's hand. "I've been waiting for you for a month, and then my duties kept me from meeting the ship!"

"Father Hennepin!" La Salle was cordial, but cool, as if to restrain some of the other's exuberance. "It's good to see you, of course. Why aren't you at Fort Frontenac?"

"I came to meet you. But you're weeks overdue."

"I'm sorry we kept you waiting." La Salle half turned as if to present those behind him, but the Governor took his arm. "You can talk with La Salle later, Father," he said firmly.

But the Recollet struck with the tenacity of a fat but agile leech. "All is well? You have the permission? And you will take Recollets with you?"

"Perhaps this will ease your mind." From an inner pocket La Salle brought out a folded paper and handed it to the friar, who seized it, read it avidly, and lifted his face in ecstasy. "My provincial, Father le Fevre, gives me permission to undertake this journey! Oh, what an experience, what an adventure! For all these unknown tribes, I mean, to learn of our Lord," he added hastily. His round face sobered abruptly. "But now I must go down to the sailors and offer myself as confessor. Can't let the Jesuits have them all." His eyes twinkling, he scurried on down the rough path like a fat gray squirrel.

"He wants to hear some sailor yarns, he means," Count Frontenac chuckled. "He's been so afraid he'd miss the big adventure. I hope he's a good choice for you."

"At least he is strong, energetic, and gets along with savages," said La Salle, "I can't use the meek, timid kind of priest. I have authority to select two others. I should consult the Bishop, I suppose."

"Yes, but don't count on his being helpful," said Frontenac sourly.

At the top of the path they passed through the arched stone gate of the city wall and emerged upon an uneven summit. The upper town seemed to be all spired, slate-roofed palaces, mostly ecclesiastical heavy gray buildings, steep-pitched and dormered like those in the north of France. There were a few scattered log houses, no two on the same level. The party halted in an open square, lying between a cathedral and a much larger stone structure where black-soutaned men were going in and out in pairs, according to Jesuit rules. On the far side, on the highest ground, in contrast to the massive stone ecclesiastical buildings, the shabby wooden Château St. Louis formed one side of a palisaded fort within the city walls. Its high-arched gate was surmounted by a shield where the crown and fleur-de-lis flashed in the sun above the muskets and bayonets of sentries.

Frontenac and La Salle paused before the cathedral, conversing in low tones. In the square, as on Mountain Hill, savages and gaily dressed habitants mingled with gorgeously appareled civil and military functionaries, ecclesiastics and, occasionally, a gentleman with plumed chapeau, dress sword, and cloak. One of these, in a two-wheeled *calèche,* with a pretty brown-haired young lady by his side, slowed to salute the Governor, only to whip up his horse when he saw who was with him, to the lady's visible regret. Her delicate face had lighted as she leaned forward to speak to La Salle.

"Lucie!" La Salle stepped forward with an unconscious gesture toward her with both hands. His habitual cool reserve quite fallen away, he was visibly shaken with joy and longing. She smiled at him tearfully, but whatever she wanted to say was cut off by a word from the man beside her, and the touch of the whip to the horse threw her roughly back in the seat as the carriage rattled away over the stones.

Count Frontenac raised his eyebrows. "So Monsieur le Ber is up from Montreal. And I'll swear it's no coincidence that he's here when you arrive."

"Apparently he didn't come to enable his daughter to see me," said La Salle, gazing after the carriage.

"He's an ambitious man," said Frontenac. "Did you notice that plume? He just bought himself a patent of nobility—untitled, of course—for six thousand livres. But in spite of her father, the lovely Lucie likes you as much as ever. God, man, why aren't you more aggressive? It's not the first time a man has fallen in love with his enemy's daughter."

La Salle firmly cut him short. "I have promised my older brother to take on no more obligations until I finish this expedition and repay my family and other creditors."

"Oh. But just because Jean Cavalier is a priest, he may not know best."

"He is right this time. I could not take her with me, nor even set her up in a proper establishment in Montreal. I can only hope she'll wait for me."

"When you are Governor of our western colonies, you will be a real catch, and by that time shopkeepers like Le Ber will have learned you aren't going to ruin them." Becoming aware that La Salle's party was all ears to this unexpected touch of romance, the Count broke off and waved toward the Château. "My castle. It's a poor structure with crumbling walls, and I hope to rebuild it in stone, as soon as I can get money from the King. Meanwhile, I expect to be buried under it every time the wind blows. But until then you are always welcome. The view from my terrace is one of the world's finest."

With a signal to his guards, he turned and strode away at their head.

La Salle gave Victor and Marc the address of a rooming house and another address to La Motte and Tonti. "And Victor, I'll want your services when I hire at nine tomorrow." Making no other appointment with any of them, he set off across the Place d'Armes toward the Château.

"Anyway, I'm glad to learn that he's in love," said Victor, when he and Marc were alone.

"In Heaven's name, why?"

"Because he'll finish his expedition the sooner. Nothing like a woman to put quicksilver in a man's shoes."

They waited at the head of the Mountain Hill ascent until Jacques, scowling suspiciously at everything, came struggling up with the first of their bags and boxes.

The house they had been directed to lay along a slope rising to the highest point on the cliff, Cape Diamond. As they knocked at the open door a broad dumpy woman waddled toward them out of a dark hall, changing her suspicious look to one of respect at the sight of the uniforms and the servant. *"Oui, Messieurs?"*

"Monsieur de la Salle sent us to see if you have a room."

"Oh, yes. I am Madame Dumont."

Every detail of her dress proclaimed her a Breton: the winged white cap, the greenish-blue homespun apron and skirt of darker hue, the black bodice laced with blue. Fat, awkward, and with a set, professional smile, there was nothing genial about her. Yet the smell of fresh bread was in the air, a tantalizing smell to one who had been long on shipboard. They climbed stone steps, leaping over a yellow cat and a scrubbing pail. At the end of a long upstairs hallway, Madame Dumont threw open a door to a room that was sizable if only moderately clean.

"Where's the bed?" asked Victor.

She pointed to a dim corner, where a striped paillasse was spilling some very ancient straw. "You don't mean we are to sleep on that, like animals!" exclaimed Victor.

"Of course. Everyone does here. There are no regular beds except in the homes of the Governor and Intendant and the seigneurs."

"Surely a beautiful woman like you doesn't sleep like that?"

She preened herself and nodded.

"No bedclothes, either?"

Marc tried to keep Victor's disgust from rising to the boiling point.

"One would think that you'd never been a soldier in a tent with a bundle of grass for a pillow. Pretend you're still in the service of the king."

Victor started, stared at him, quickly lowered his eyes, and muttered. "But I want a bed."

The landlady smiled placatingly. Very fine gentlemen they must be; willing to pay the highest prices for everything. "Jean Landelle, my husband's brother-in-law, is down below at the market. He has a little woodworking shop and he can make you a fine one."

"Then we'll go order it right now. And at least get some fresh straw in here for tonight. How much for the room?" At her answer, he yelped. "I could get the best lodgings in Paris for that!"

Mme. Dumont shrugged. "The livre is worth only fifteen sols here instead of twenty as in Paris. And we have to pay the church high rent for our sites, and tithes, too. And supplies cost a lot. The goods from the ships disappear into those big warehouses down below, and the price doubles before they come out. It's the same with the furs that come in. It's the merchants who are getting rich. Them and the tax-farmers." She sniffed. "Supposed to collect twenty-five per cent for the King, but they take enough to fatten their own pockets. . . ."

"All right!" Victor cut off the flow. "It won't be for long, anyway."

The market place in the lower town was a clutter of dogcarts and stalls. Walking along the cobbled square, the twins felt as if they were in a market in Normandy: the same pretty flowers, great heads of lettuce and cabbage, baskets with chickens, geese, and ducks. The air rang with shouts in nipped provincial French, as habitants and their wives and maidservants proclaimed the quality and cheapness of their apples, pears, and grapes, their butter and sacks of meal. Hunters displayed dressed game; fishermen, slightly aloof, had dripping, slimy carts of fish and eels. At the moment, the whole market had been overrun by sailors from the *St. Honoré*, especially the stalls with fresh milk, butter and Breton pancakes.

Marc and Victor bought grapes and pears, and sauntered along eating them. Upon inquiry they found Monsieur Landelle behind a cart piled high with long black bunches of tobacco leaves. Making a purchase was the strangely dressed surgeon Jean Michel, some queer meaty shapes hanging over his arm. He recognized them and nodded.

"Bonjour. And what is that you're carrying?" asked Victor.

The surgeon grinned. "Pig bladders. To fill with hot water when someone has a pain." He stood aside and waited while Victor bargained for a double bed. When an agreement had been reached, and the bed ordered, the surgeon added, "I'm paddling over to the Ile d'Orleans to visit my parents. If you'd like to meet me at the Lion d'Or this evening, right after the sunset gun, we might drink to the success of our trip. May it be a quick and profitable one for us all!"

13

"NOW that you have prospects of sleeping as befits your station," said Marc, "what next?"

They were again in the upper town, passing the Jesuit college, where a lay brother was picking purple clusters from grapevines espaliered against the stone walls. Victor paused. "While we're here, we might deliver that note and package from Père la Chaise. I have them in my pocket."

"I don't know why he couldn't send them by regular post."

Outside the Superior's office, they had to wait for a party of habitants just emerging, led by a rough character with a red beard and a hooded sailor's cap, who turned boldly to stare at the twins. Inside the office they forgot him at once as the aged Superior, informed of their errand, greeted them cordially.

"I am glad the good La Chaise hasn't forgotten me while I have been in the wilds. But come. I was just going to dinner, and you must join us. Nearly everyone here dines at midday."

The black soutane swept them, protesting, along to the dining hall, where a dozen or more in the same black awaited, making Victor and Marc feel like gay birds of plumage among ravens. Grace over, they were served a fish better than they had ever had at court, for fish in Paris was usually "high" after it had come all the way from the sea. Dessert consisted of pancakes with honey and preserves.

Only when the meal was over did the Superior inform the others at the table: "These gentlemen are of Monsieur de la Salle's company."

"Ah. So . . ." In the air was a tightening, a marshaling of forces, a lining-up as if a bugle had sounded.

"It is one of our sorrows that Monsieur de la Salle will not work with us," said the Superior. "A man of ability who is using his talents badly."

"He is a fur trader, and when one says that, one has said enough," croaked a wrinkled old priest. "These traders have an evil influence at all our missions. We plant the seed of faith, and the trader uproots it with liquor and lewdness. Not that La Salle is a bad man himself, but all traders should be excluded from the woods."

"His motives are purely selfish, purely mercenary . . ." began another.

"Let us leave his private life to his confessor," the Superior chided smoothly.

"Who, unfortunately, is never one of us," blurted out a young priest.

The Superior shot him a look of warning. "Let us say that he is in need of wise counsel, for his ill-conceived plans endanger the lives of those who go with him."

"He will surely fail. Indeed, he must," said another priest heatedly, and a murmur of agreement passed around the table.

This has gone far enough, thought Marc, remembering Victor's report on Père la Chaise's proposals. "We certainly hope not. We have been personally assigned by His Majesty to aid him—and we have invested money with him."

The black-clad figures frowned as one man. "Do you know how much money La Salle raised?" asked the withered one.

"That is not our affair," said Marc brusquely, and the boys rose, murmuring thanks for the excellent dinner.

Outside, they shivered, though the air was not cold.

"So La Salle's plans are insane," mused Marc, "and can't succeed. Yet they're afraid of him—it showed on every face."

"They're a lot more subtle than La Salle. They could put him into a sack and sell him without his noticing, as the proverb says."

"I'm not so sure."

"Well, fie on them, anyway." Victor sighed. "I'm glad we have no reason to come here again."

They emerged from the tree-shaded path, and there before them was La Salle, his eyes like cold steel. "I have been looking for you. I planned to take you to dinner, but I see you found a place to dine. They tell me the Jesuits eat very well."

"Yes, we . . ." Seeing how angry La Salle was, Marc stopped. There

114

was no use giving explanations to one in no state to understand them.

"I will have Nika bring you a sample contract and a quire of paper," the explorer went on to Victor. "Make thirty copies for use tomorrow." He turned abruptly away and crossed the square.

"What's the matter with him?" exploded Victor. "It was a perfectly innocent errand."

"True, but I suspect he's surprised that our first act in this city was to go to the Jesuits.—He knows they're bad enemies."

Victor's lips tightened. "If I thought Père la Chaise sent us there on purpose to get us in trouble, I believe I'd . . . I'd turn Huguenot. At least it's a good way to get sent home—no heretics allowed."

As they climbed the slope toward Mme. Dumont's, a Jesuit was taking leave of their landlady. When he saw them, he departed hastily. Mme. Dumont waited in the doorway, her color heightened. "Have you had dinner?"

"An excellent one. At the Jesuit college."

For some reason the news seemed to strike her forcibly. "Oh, I didn't know—" she stammered, and with a whirl of her skirts was gone into the remote regions of the house. Victor and Marc looked at each other, puzzled.

At their room they found in astonishment that their effects were scattered in tangled confusion. The over neat Jacques couldn't have left them so. Lifting a pile of things on the paillasse, Marc swore as he found their Pascal on its face with jagged edges where pages had been torn out. Simultaneously a howl of rage came from Victor, who was lifting from a trash basket a deck of cards and Mlle. de Scudéry's novel. Jacques appeared in the doorway with two more of their bags, and stood amazed equally at the sight and the reproaches hurled at him. "But I didn't do it. Everything was all right when I went back to the ship to fetch these."

Headlong, Victor dashed down to the kitchen, two steps at a time. "Who has been in our room?"

"Monsieur de la Salle called, but he didn't go in," evaded Mme. Dumont.

"That priest!" exploded Victor. "Did you let him in? Throwing our cards in the trash, mutilating our books——"

The piglike eyes were evasive. "You can't read romances here—or plays or any books they don't approve of. And if you gamble, they call you by name right from the pulpit. So we are all devout."

"I'll do worse than call names!" He rushed back to their room, stopping short at sight of Marc kneeling beside the straw paillasse. "*Nom de dieu,* are you praying about it?"

Marc turned a flushed face. "*Mille tonnerres,* no! I'm unpacking the books he missed and putting them under the bed." He rose, dusting his hands.

After an hour of fencing to keep their hands in, they returned to their straw mattress for a long rest; then rose and dressed in their violet suits. As twilight closed in upon the Rock, loneliness assailed them and a sort of panic at being so distant from any familiar place. "Let's go get some wine," Victor ventured at last in a strained voice.

"The surgeon!" Marc remembered. "Come on."

They crossed the Place d'Armes as the sunset gun boomed and the passing of another hour was being struck by the clock of the Recollets. Drums and bugles signaled the closing of the fort gates and the setting of the watch for the night. Under the long tattoo, soldiers hastened to their quarters and merchants closed their shop doors. The Place d'Armes was almost empty save for themselves and the shadowy sentries pacing up and down before the Château. As they descended Mountain Hill it seemed that all life had drained down the cliff into the lower town. The sounds from below—laughter, violins, and feet beating out a jig with heavy clogs—might have resounded in any French port.

At the sign of the Lion d'Or, the heavy wooden door stood open. Beyond the nearest tables, where villagers sat over their wine, Jean Michel awaited them with a bottle of *vin supérieur.* After they had clicked glasses once with a "*Vive le Roi!*", Victor related what had happened in their room. "But how did they know about our books and cards? Do they inspect the belongings of every newcomer to Quebec?'

"Your worthy landlady"—the surgeon lowered his voice—"is probably a member of the organization called the Sainte Famille. They spy on everyone for the Jesuits, and report any irregular conduct. They meet in the cathedral every Thursday, behind closed doors, and relate all they have learned about other people during the week. It is a sort of female Inquisition. But they keep the secrets of the Jesuits' friends."

"That's why she was so flustered," said Marc.

"Yes, since you had dined with the Superior, she assumed she had made a mistake to inform on you."

116

"Well, let's forget it," said Victor. "We won't be here long. What do you think this expedition will be like? Have you traveled much here?"

"Only to Fort Frontenac, where I have been stationed." As Jean Michel told them about the river journey to the fort, every corner of the tavern filled with gaiety. At one table a sailor was telling his adventures on the high seas; at another a Carignan-Salières captain was riotously comparing his encounters with Iroquois to those with the Turks.

Six men wearing blue tunics and deerskins sat at the next table. Coarsely familiar with the stout barmaid, they downed round after round from thick mugs. Conspicuous among them was the big fellow with the red beard they had seen at the Jesuits'. His hood now thrown back to reveal tousled red hair, he was haranguing his companions drunkenly, as they shuffled a deck of cards. At another table sat a group of men dressed like prosperous merchants, one of whom the twins recognized as Le Ber, father of the pretty Lucie.

"Bring another for Guillaume here, the stubborn fool," Le Ber was saying. "One more drink might bring him to his senses."

Guillaume scowled. "I have more sense than you."

"Sense he calls it," Le Ber was derisive, "to push into a deal with an adventurer."

Guillaume pounded the table. "I don't like him, either. The monopoly at Fort Frontenac was bad enough, but now he's aiming at half a continent—and with the King's permission, don't forget! But I say our best hope is to keep a finger in the pie, as he's offering us a chance to do."

"I want no alliance with him," said Le Ber angrily, "and I speak for every merchant at Ville Marie.'

"But how could we lose?" asked another. "We can make him give us a claim on his property. If he doesn't keep his agreements, or doesn't come back . . ."

Lowering their voices they talked on, like hornets seeking every vulnerable spot to sting. Well trained in court eavesdropping, the boys gave no hint of their interest, as they and the surgeon bent over the wine. Le Ber at last looked over at the table of men in deerskins, and beckoned. "Come here, Luc—and the rest of you."

Cards paused in mid air and dropped to the table. The redhead rose deliberately and sauntered over, hands thrust into his pea jacket, as Le Ber added to his cronies: ". . . if they hire out to La Salle—"

Belatedly cautious, he motioned Luc closer, and whatever he said to him was lost in the tavern noise.

"Let's go now," suggested Jean Michel. They rose and walked up Mountain Hill in silence. As they reached the upper town, the great clock of the Recollets struck nine with an appropriate solemn resonance to distinguish the night hours from those of the day. No one else was in sight but the sentries pacing before the Château.

"I'm not in La Salle's confidence," said Jean Michel worriedly. "No one is. But I think he should know what's going on, before he hires. Let's go see him now. He and the Governor will be up talking most of the night."

Victor drew back. I can't spy both for and against him, he thought. "No," he added aloud, "I have all those contracts to copy. I'll go on to our room."

"I'll go with Monsieur Michel, then," Marc offered. "I'll try to explain about our dinner, too. And then I'll come and help you." And before the ships leave, he thought, I want to write to Michelle at the convent that we have arrived safely.

And I must write to His Majesty, thought Victor. But what can I tell him? Only that many people here think La Salle is out to ruin them. What I'd like to write is a plea to let me come back to court, in any capacity at all. He strode away, once more morose at finding himself on the wrong side of the Atlantic.

14

IN the morning they were awakened by a crier at the corner below, announcing that the Sieur de la Salle was at the Lion d'Or to hire men for his expedition. Hastily putting on their uniforms, they bolted some excellent fresh rolls and cool milk, and with the pile of contracts, crossed the upper town and clambered down the steep pathway. A few men in habitant dress chatted in fluid patois outside the tavern. Inside, except for the tavernkeeper polishing glasses at the bar, were only La Salle and Tonti at a corner table, while Nika sat cross-legged on the floor. La Salle gave them a brief *bonjour,* adding, "Good. You have the contracts." He motioned Victor to a chair before which lay two piles of paper, a quill pen, ink, and a box of sand. "Fill in the name and salary as I give them to you, and read the contract to the man being hired. He will sign it, or make his mark. The smaller pile of contracts I have already filled in for the surgeon and a few others."

Victor dropped into the chair, and pushed back his cuffs. As he did so, Nika leaned over and touched the lace and braid. "No good in woods," he grunted. "No good in canoe."

"I'm glad His Majesty can't hear you criticize his favorite uniform," said Victor.

"Too much clothes, too tight." Nika flapped his arms at his side, like an agitated chicken. "Must have arms free. Some French things very good, but not French shoes. Hard shoes break through canoe." He rose in one fluid motion, like a cat. "I go now, find you something."

Victor appealed to La Salle in alarm. "Surely we should oversee his selections?"

"One of you should go, for the measurements. Nika knows a woman who makes excellent moccasins, but since you'll need several pairs, you can start with whatever fits you from one of the shops. You can find woodsman's clothing ready-made, too. Marc isn't busy—he can go with Nika."

Victor opened his mouth, saw Marc's look of amusement, shrugged, and turned away to sharpen his quill. Now that a savage was to be their style mentor, what difference who went?

Tonti rose. "I'll get mine, too, if you don't need me."

La Salle nodded. "Send in some of the men as you go out."

The first to appear in the doorway was a short, homely, grinning fellow. "Ah, *bonjou', m'sieu!*"

"Well, Accau!" said La Salle. "Come in."

The little man's nose had been permanently turned to one side by some accident or fight, and his teeth grew at seemingly impossible angles, but his clothes, though frayed, were as clean as care could make them. "I got word you wanted to see me, m'sieu."

"Yes, Accau. You have heard about my expedition?"

"Couldn't help it. Quebec been talkin' 'bout nothin' else."

"I hope you can go along. The Indian languages you know will be useful."

"I can get 'round 'mongst the common ones. 'Course there's things a man don't need language for. Signs work mighty well. Them Indian women——"

"No, Accau. Not on this trip."

"Goin' to be kinda dull, then." Accau winked at Victor. "But I obey orders, you know that. How much you payin' for canoemen?"

"Two hundred livres a year."

Accau twisted his cap in his hand, making a careful circuit of his fingers. Then, as if his mind had also made full turn, he said with decision, "I'll go. I been to Michilimackinac twice. I'd as soon see what's beyond."

La Salle gestured to Victor. "Michel Accau, two hundred livres."

When Accau had signed, La Salle added, "I'll put you in one of the big canoes. Where can we find you?"

Accau grinned impudently. "There's times you can't. But when you want me, just tell anybody in the lower town."

Next a swarthy, good-natured fellow who had been listening at the door came in for a job as canoeman, his action releasing a flow of others that nearly filled the taproom with short, cheerful and carefree Frenchmen, dark of skin and colorful of dress.

"Where do they come from?" asked Victor when the room had finally been cleared.

"Where there is money there are people to be had. Some of them have been with me before."

"You must have treated them well."

La Salle glanced up. "I always treat my men at least as well as they deserve."

"I didn't mean—" Victor broke off as a man shaped like a pair of bellows came through the door and sauntered over to the table. Of a different mold from the others, short, pear-shaped, with straggling blond hair framing sullen, heavy features, he was plainly of Netherlands ancestry.

"Well, Moyse Hillaret!" said La Salle cordially as the Dutchman spun a chair around and sat down. "Why aren't you at Fort Frontenac?"

"Nothing to do, and Father Hennepin's too bossy. I look for other work, maybe."

"But I need you on this expedition. You're the best shipbuilder on this side of the ocean."

"So?" Moyse asked stolidly. "I built you four good ships at the fort. How many more you need?"

"One on the Niagara River, to sail on the upper lakes. Then another to descend the Mississippi, from a base among the Illinois Indians."

"You got rigging, anchors, wire for nails?"

"Yes, everything. Part of it came on the *St. Honoré*. The rest will come next summer and follow us into the interior. Master shipbuilder, two hundred and forty livres a year—how does that sound?"

The carpenter gazed at his stubby fingers. "I don't know," he mumbled. "I owe twelve hundred livres here."

A shadow passed over La Salle's face, but he said, tersely, "I'll advance you enough for the debt."

"Then I'll build your ships."

"Good," said La Salle with relief. Moyse scratched his name on the contract, and pointed toward the door. "If I go, I got men outside I want as helpers. I got to have carpenters that know what they're doing."

"By all means." And so Jean le Mire, a ship carpenter, and "La Forge," a smith and nailmaker, were promptly hired. After their departure, a man came in who had so many names Victor waited to see which should go on the contract. "My real name is Antoine Auguel, but they call me Picard du Gay, or le Pickard. I hear you need good paddling arms?"

"The greatest need ever."

"I'd like to go, m'sieu. The only trouble is, I owe a hundred livres here."

"I'll advance it to you."

"Merci bien, m'sieu. A la bonne heure! Where do I put my mark!" Le Picard grasped the quill as if it were a paddle.

The tavern was again empty for a time, although a good pile of contracts still lay before Victor. "We'll pick up a few workmen from Fort Frontenac," said La Salle, "but I must have five more canoemen here."

At the sound of singing outside, Victor followed La Salle to the window. Four laughing young Frenchmen touched their caps as they passed.

"Won't you enter?" invited La Salle. "I'd like to talk to you."

They turned, grinning, and filed in the door.

"Do you know who I am?" asked La Salle. They nodded. "Had you thought of signing with me?"

They exchanged glances, shook their heads, and one said, "We're doing well enough here."

'I am paying two hundred livres. High wages."

The youths raised their eyebrows, withdrew for a prolonged whispered conference, and then, as one man, presented themselves at the table, giving their names as Chapelle, Le Blanc, Messier, and Laurent. Contracts signed, they went on down the hill, resuming their song as if their lives had not been changed between two of its verses.

Throughout the rest of the forenoon, other contracts flowed through Victor's hands: canoemen, ship carpenters, housewrights. If a man needed money, La Salle gave him a liberal sum in advance, or promised to pay his debts in Quebec. As the great clock of the Recollets struck eleven, La Salle stood up in relief. "A good morning's work." But as Victor rose, he stared over La Salle's shoulder at the doorway. Two men were standing there that he had seen twice before—at the Jesuits' and again last night at the tavern. They came in, followed by the big red-bearded Luc. Victor watched uneasily while La Salle signed up the first two as canoemen, and Luc shambled forward. "You need a pilot?"

La Salle looked him over with great interest. "I do. I have a good one at the fort, but I'll need another for a new ship on the lakes."

"With fifteen years ocean experience, I'm as good as you'll find."

"*Tout bien.* I am glad to have you."

Victor hesitated, contract in hand. Hadn't Jean Michel and Marc described these men to La Salle? Should he accuse them now? But he had no real proof. Their errand with the Jesuits might have been as innocent as his own, and he didn't know what had come of their conference with Le Ber. While he hesitated, Luc seized the contract and made his mark.

When they were alone again, Victor ran his hand along the edge of the contracts. "This is a varied lot of men," he said slowly. "Some of them will make strange companions."

"You'll have to get used to a different breed of men here." La Salle abruptly gathered up the papers. "They're not snuffbox-tapping courtiers."

Victor felt a flush rise to his cheeks. "I didn't imply that they should be," he said angrily. "I was only wondering whether you consider the loyalty of the men you hire." At once he wished he had kept his mouth shut. He had reasons for being cautious about touching upon that string, having himself been bought by the King's promises.

"I hire all kinds, because I must," said La Salle evenly. "Men with special skills are very scarce here. To bring them all from France would be expensive and would load the expedition with men not used to the rigors of traveling in a wilderness. Loyalty is indeed important; my very life may depend upon it. But just how *could* I make sure?

I've found loyalty a dubious and shifting thing. Probably every man I hire could be bought by the Jesuits and their associates, if the price were high enough. A few pistoles have a wonderful effect when put into hands not much accustomed to gold."

The lean silent figure of Nika appeared in the doorway.

"Here is one at least," said La Salle, "whose loyalty I am sure of."

"Well, White Beaver, where is my brother?" asked Victor.

"He here, with Tonti. They dressed for the woods now. You see."

As the two made an elaborate stage entrance through the doorway, Victor burst out laughing and put his hand over his eyes. *"Mais, c'est beau, ça!* It is painful, too, such brilliance! What masquerade are you going to?"

Marc and Tonti laid some packages on the table, grinned, and stood back, striking a pose in their elkskin trousers ornamented with fringes, topped by blue shirts and elkskin jackets. Wool sashes at their waists matched the jaunty red caps. Their feet were encased in moccasins trimmed with beadwork. Marc lifted one foot and waggled it. "Aren't they handsome? And comfortable, too. I've been wanting to try a pair since I saw them in Paris."

"It's the perfect footgear," agreed La Salle.

Victor sniffed. "What's so good about them?"

"In swamps, for instance, where heavy boots would make deep holes, moccasins will carry you from hummock to grass tuft." La Salle smiled reminiscently. "They're porous and allow the feet to perspire, yet protect them from slight wounds. If wet, they dry quickly on the foot. They follow every movement, like a second skin. And, in dire need, many a man has roasted and eaten his moccasins."

Marc indicated the packages. "Here is your new winter wardrobe, Victor. Just like mine."

"I assure you I am in no hurry to put it on."

"Au contraire," said Tonti, "better put it on now. White Beaver is to give us our first canoe lesson today, down on the St. Charles."

"Good," pronounced La Salle. "You both look fine. Only one item missing." He turned to Nika. "Run up and bring the green box on the chest in my room." Nika was away, silent and swift.

"The gentleman can step back in the kitchen if he wants to change," said the tavernkeeper.

Victor, under the challenge of all eyes, picked up the bundles and followed the man to a back room, where he put on the strange garments. Returning with his uniform and sword in his hands, he mused:

123

"I feel naked. First time I've appeared in public without a sword since I was a child."

"You can't wear one in a canoe," said La Salle. "But take it and your French clothing for ceremonial occasions."

Reluctantly Victor laid sword and baldric on his clothes on the bar and took a few steps to get used to the feel of these strange leathers. One had a good deal of freedom in them, he had to admit.

When the Indian reappeared as silently as he had left, La Salle opened the green box to reveal an assortment of leather-sheathed hunting knives. "Perhaps not the finest workmanship, but of good temper. Pray accept them them as my gift." He handed one to each of them. "Wear it thrust through your sash, within easy reach. You'll find it more useful than a sword."

Curving his hand about the hilt of the strange knife, Victor looked down at himself. "Behold the erstwhile Captain of the Guards. I wonder what D'Artagnan would think."

Nika slid close to Victor and lightly touched the soft leather of the jacket. "Too plain? I find someone to embroider it. Any pattern."

Victor laughed. "What would you suggest?"

"Band of beads all around. And here"—he laid his hand on the left breast—"you have a totem?"

"No, I don't think so. Must I have one of those, too?"

"The mark of your family," explained Nika. "Mine, turtle!" He bared his chest to reveal an unmistakable turtle tattooed on his bare skin. "Frenchman sometimes put mark on clothes and papers."

"Oh, a coat of arms!" said Victor. "By all means, let's have the De Lorennes crest put on these things."

"You may," said Marc. "You're nearer the succession. Just plain bands on mine."

"Good," said Nika. "You give me coats after lesson today. I have them fixed. Now we go learn canoe paddling."

"Well, come on, Victor," said Marc. "You've worn stranger costumes in many a drama or masque."

Victor started. If he knew what a giant masquerade I'm in right now, he thought. To cover the moment, he bowed mockingly to Nika, as to a dancing teacher. "My sword has shrunk to a knife. Let's go shrink the guardsman to a canoeman."

But Nika held back. "Something troubling you?" La Salle asked him.

"You get enough men? The black robes spread stories that kept some away."

La Salle looked harassed, but he said only, "There is nothing I can do about lies."

"Nothing," agreed Nika. "My people say, 'If a skunk walks in your trail and leaves odor, do not go out of your way to prove it is not yours.'"

15

ON swift feet Nika lead the way down past the Hôtel-Dieu to the brink of the St. Charles, a river neither so swift nor so deep as the St. Lawrence. The three followed more gingerly, in this footwear that let one feel the shape of every cobblestone. "Where's La Motte?" asked Victor. "Doesn't he have to take lessons, too?"

Tonti sighed. "I couldn't rouse him this morning. I'm afraid he celebrated too thoroughly last night."

"What do you think of him?" asked Marc.

"Not much," said Tonti reluctantly. "But La Salle must see something in him I don't."

They joined Nika beside a long row of canoes inverted on the riverbank.

"La Salle has already bought these for our journey?" asked Tonti.

Nika nodded. "Good Algonquin canoes. Chief use no others."

Victor laid his uniform on the bank, his sword on top, and doubtfully examined one of the awkward-looking craft. "We are actually to trust our lives in things like this?"

Nika grunted, swung a twenty-foot canoe up over his head, carried it to the water, and set it down right side up, all in one quick motion.

"Why can't we travel by ship?" asked Victor. "I've seen them go on upriver."

"Like the tide, ships can go about six hundred miles more, they say," explained Tonti. "The river is deep that far. But above Montreal Island are rapids that will not allow a ship to pass. Canoes can be carried around them."

"I would still prefer to go on horseback," said Victor dubiously.

"Oh, I don't know," said Marc. "Watch me." He stepped to the side of a small canoe, and, lifting it, tried to swing it over his head as Nika had done. There was a grunt, a crash, and Marc was on the ground, the canoe bouncing on top of him. Amid the laughter, Nika came running, but let Marc wriggle out alone, his whole attention on the canoe. "Only one tear. I fix later."

"You mean they break that easily?" demanded Victor.

"Must take hold here," Nika instructed, demonstrating. "But they very strong." The Indian ran his hands over the outside. "Bark of birch tree. Light and strong." He went on, pointing out the parts of the structure as his listeners might have indicated the good points of a horse.

"Where is the rudder?" asked Marc. Nika stared. "To steer it," Marc explained.

"Steer with paddles. When there is wind, use sails a little." Nika pointed to a hole in a square piece of wood between the ribs and the bark, near the bottom. "Mast goes in here. Now. Which one try first?"

Tonti nodded to Victor. "Monsieur here is of the highest rank. He should have first chance."

"For once, I'll gladly yield to the gentleman from Italy." Victor made a low bow.

"Oh, no, monsieur," said Tonti with mock solemnity. "I would not think of taking precedence over you."

"Then you, Marc."

Marc bowed. "I would not venture to take the *pas* of you, either. Your rank carries with it obligations as well as privileges."

"Merci bien! I appreciate your yielding to me. Do not forget to do so on more auspicious occasions as well." Victor bowed first to the one and then the other, and marched to the side of the canoe as if proceeding to his post of duty. "Why didn't His Majesty condemn me to the galleys and be done with it? What do I do first, *mon vieux?"*

Nika, who had watched impassively, now shoved the canoe into the river so that one end rested on shore, the other bobbing gently in the pull of waves and current. "First, just ride." He held the canoe while Victor climbed gingerly in.

"Where do I sit?"

Nika pointed to a piece of bearskin a little forward of center. "On knees."

Victor knelt, and lifted a shaky hand to wave to Marc and Tonti. *"Allez-y!"*

"Stay in middle," commanded Nika, climbing in. With the paddle he pushed away from the shore.

"En avant! Vive le Roi!" said Victor, a little uncertainly, as they bounded out upon the river, literally upon it, for the craft drew so little water Victor felt as if he were riding a chip. He was sure he could feel the shape of the waves beneath as he had felt cobbles through his moccasins. "This thin shell wouldn't even make a decent coffin!"

"Very light, canoe is," said Nika. "Frenchmen say good one travel on heavy dew."

"How is it?" called Marc from shore.

"Fine. Only the thickness of five sheets of paper between me and death. Is the river very deep here?" Victor leaned out to look. Nika shouted and threw himself to the other side, but the canoe went over and they were plunged into the coldest water Victor had ever felt. He choked and flailed blindly for agonizing seconds until he felt himself lifted by the scruff by Nika.

"Hang on!" Nika brought Victor close enough to grasp the canoe, and began swimming and drawing it to shore, where Marc and Tonti were dancing with mirth.

"You don't look quite so fine as you did," gasped Marc.

"What kind of infernal contraption tips over that easily?" Victor sputtered.

Nika came up the beach. "Learning and wisdom are hard moose to trail."

"Now I can see a reason for such clothes." Victor shivered. "A wet ting can't make them look much worse than they did in the first place. At least they saved me from ruining my uniform."

"This not last time you get wet," predicted Nika calmly. "Why didn't you swim?"

"I can't swim," protested Victor. "Gentlemen have no occasion to, in France."

"Here gentleman die from not knowing. I teach you that, too."

"Well, thanks very much!" Victor's irony was ruined by his chattering teeth. "But not today. I've done enough toward atonement for my sins. You two take your turns at the devilish business. I'm off for some blankets and brandy. *Fichtre!* What a noble animal a horse is!"

Succeeding days were a little better. Nika started them using a paddle in the front of the canoe, while he controlled it with one in the rear, teaching them not to dip the paddle too far ahead or too deep, and with an easy swing to put back and shoulder into the stroke, letting the right hand take the paddle forward while the left one brought it back. They marveled that men so well trained in the skills of a gentleman and a soldier were yet awkward at this one. Gradually, and with some pride, they began to master it. Surprisingly Tonti kept pace with them with only one good hand. Nika was hard to please and sparing with praise, determined that they should become equal to the best canoemen of New France. In time the craft came to seem even safe and steady, and they dared an occasional race against the canoemen also waiting for La Salle's departure. But however they exerted themselves they never came close to Nika's skill, and concluded his body must be better adapted to such labors.

As one crisp autumn day followed another while La Salle lingered in Quebec, the boys underwent a training that would have done credit to D'Artagnan or Martinet. Nika taught them to swim, in a little bay of the St. Charles. He took them hunting, and they marveled at the many acres where anyone could hunt as he pleased. They spent most of their time on river or in woods, and gladly, for they found that, in town, under the vigilance of the church, there was little entertainment and there was an uncomfortable sense of being spied upon. In the woods as they struggled through the underbrush, evading stinging branches above and logs below, they understood why horses were of little use for travel here, why swords would be an encumbrance. They began to appreciate the practical moccasins and the jaunty red wool caps. Victor had the De Lorennes crest embroidered on his jacket, and ordered another suit of the same kind for himself and Marc, with green shirts and green fringes.

When Nika let them have their first day off, being absent on some errand of his own, they went to the carpenter's shop to watch their bed being finished. Victor began to experiment with woodcarving tools, until he could finally turn out a creditable plaque with the De Lorennes crest. In one of the lower-town shops, where they found their French gold very popular, Nika helped them select blankets, ribbons, beads, tobacco and cloth to add to their stock, red powder horns that held four pounds of powder, and heavy, hand-knitted woolen socks. Most business was done by bills of exchange given by the company for furs which the traders gave in turn to merchants for goods and the merchants could send to France for new stock.

One day Marc turned to Nika in the shop and said: "What about you, Nika? Is there anything here you like? I—we wish to buy you a present for helping us."

Nika looked at him appraisingly, and laid his hand on a musket. "This?"

Marc glanced at Victor. "But I thought you had a gun," said Victor. "Not like this."

Victor made the purchase, and laid the musket in the sinewy brown hands.

"You have a good heart," Nika said, and his quiet dignity made a strange alteration in the act. Victor had thought of it as a gesture to an inferior, as one would give a handful of coins to a peasant who stopped one's runaway horse. But Nika's manner had somehow reversed their positions, making him a schoolboy giving a present to his teacher.

If La Salle gave no indication of how much longer he would tarry, it was not for lack of Father Hennepin's plucking at his sleeve, in the square, on the cathedral steps, at the gate of the Château. One Sunday he blocked the way, his face set in Flemish stubbornness. "I am all ready to go. I have finished my retreat, I have my portable chapel, and a year's supply of sacramental wine." With such momentous matters settled, his tone implied, La Salle must be a trifler in details.

Count Frontenac stepped forward with a vehemence that made the fat priest back away. "Then why haven't you gone back to the fort? Your place is there until the expedition begins! By all means, set off at once. Go on!"

The rushing stream of the Governor's orders quite overwhelmed the fat gadfly, and he stammered agreement.

"Good!" said Frontenac. Aware that listening Jesuits might relish his impatience with a Recollet, he added cordially, "We'll have a farewell dinner at the Château. Next Sunday, when the seigneurs present their homage. There'll be a banquet afterwards in honor of La Salle's company. Damme," he added under his breath, "I'll have to ask the Bishop, too." He started forward as if leading a charge, and Father Hennepin stepped aside with dignity.

"Thank you, Your Excellency," he said, once more articulate, "and perhaps my example in setting out in advance will oblige the rest to expedite their affairs."

16

THE farewell dinner was preceded by High Mass at the cathedral, to which the lords of the outlying seigneuries came in their carriages, each followed by his tenants. Marc, in a group with Victor, La Salle, Tonti, and a sulky La Motte, let the opening phrases of the Jesuit sermon pass absently over his head, but the next words jerked him to attention.

"In this matter Louis XIV has gone too far. He had no right to license the trade in brandy with the Indians, after our esteemed Bishop had declared it to be a sin."

More heads were turned to the Governor's pew than toward the pulpit. Count Frontenac's eyes snapped with fury as he sat forward. The priest saw the movement and instantly veered into other topics, but Frontenac's wrath mounted, modified not one whit by the sermon's end or the harmonies of organ and choir. The Governor and his guards filed out, followed by the ecclesiastics, an order of precedence over which many a fierce battle had been fought. In the porch, the Count waited for two of the churchmen, the Superior of the Jesuits, and the Bishop, M. de Laval, lean, long-faced and imposing in mien and attire.

"I never expected to hear such seditious remarks uttered anywhere in His Majesty's realm," the Count began angrily. "On his behalf, I demand an apology."

Faced with such fury and authority, the Bishop grew conciliatory, as did the Jesuit Superior, murmuring apologies, ". . . deeply regret, I assure you . . . too much zeal . . . it will not happen again." The apology was accepted, but neither side lowered the banners of hatred from its eyes, and the Count departed with a curt warning: "Next time anything like it happens, I shall myself put the preacher in jail until he learns to speak properly of his King."

Followed by his guards, the Governor strode across the Place d'Armes, and through the castle gate, but since the dinner was to be preceded by an official ceremony, the guests waited for a signal to enter: a boom, a flash, and a puff of smoke from the battery. And then through the sally port, below the shield of golden fleur-de-lis, moved the entire landed aristocracy of New France, augmented by La Salle's associates and a few churchmen, among them the solid Father Hennepin wearing his gray cowl and robe as if they were the velvet and satin of a man of the world.

Just inside the Hall of Audience and Council, La Salle laid aside his hat and sword on a broad carved table, waving the rest of his party on. "Only the seigneurs must divest themselves of swords, and only until after the oath." Marc and Victor went to a window embrasure where they could observe the gathering crowd. Their own uniforms, while the finest, were not so conspicuous as one would expect in so remote an outpost. Here was plenty of gold lace and embroidery, of glittering stars and crosses. Framed as the scene was by lofty carved ceiling, polished pillars and panels, it reflected not too faintly the glories of Louis XIV's court.

With a second boom of the cannon and the sound of marching feet, silence fell in the hall. The doors were flung open and the Captain of the Guards announced: "His Excellency, the Governor General of New France, and representative of His Majesty Louis XIV, Louis de Buade, Comte de Frontenac!"

In dress uniform the Count appeared in the doorway, and followed by a crowd of officers, marched to the vice-regal chair, every inch the nobleman and King's representative. When his bodyguards had spread to the right and left, each seigneur present, in the order of the age of his seigneury, knelt on one knee facing the Governor, and in a repetition of the ceremony in which he had received his grant, repeated a short oath of allegiance for himself and his tenants to His Majesty, afterward placing upon the table a symbolic piece of gold. When the last one had passed, M. Duchesneau, the Intendant, took charge of these funds, and the Governor rose and led the way to the dining hall.

Two great tables were set up to seat the company of nearly seventy. Victor and Marc were directed to the Governor's own table, directly across from Frontenac's high-backed chair which was flanked on one side by Duchesneau's and on the other by Bishop Laval's. Next to the Bishop was Father Hennepin; and while his plumpness and beaming face were in contrast to the dour asceticism of his superior, his air of importance was scarcely less. At Duchesneau's left sat La Salle, and the other seigneurs filled the remaining places.

While the soup was being passed around, the Count introduced Victor and Marc, La Motte and Tonti, and then commanded the twins, "Now tell us the choice news from the court. Is Montespan really holding her place?"

"Yes," said Victor, "but she has rivals." Bewigged heads nodded. At least that hadn't changed since their own days in the homeland. They plied Victor with questions about everything from the ascendance of Maintenon to the recent news of the war or the peace, whichever it was now. Marc smiled to see Victor hold the company fascinated in his role as gossip.

At last Count Frontenac seized the conversational reins and kept them firmly in his hands, while dispensing hospitality that suffered little for being remote from Paris. The tables were set with heavy silver and fine china, and Bohemian goblets held excellent French and Spanish wines. The main dish was a huge pasty, which the Count praised as if he had invented it, and recited its ingredients, which Marc memorized to send to Dreux: a turkey, two chickens, two partridges, two pigeons, two rabbits, slices of fat pork, two hams seasoned with onions, and the whole flavored with spices.

When only their ruby glasses were left on the table, a silver box of tobacco was brought in, along with a rack of pipes and a lighted candle. A pungent smoke began ascending above the polished board. Count Frontenac leaned forward to address Father Hennepin, sulking beyond Bishop Laval. "Since you, Father, are the first to depart, I am pleased as the King's representative to wish you success in your mission."

"And as your superior," Bishop Laval added smoothly, "I am glad to make public my approval of your energy and devotion to duty, and shall give you my blessing when you are ready to depart." Laval's words had no warmth, nor had his face. His drooping portentous nose, his well-formed forehead, his thin lips, were features that seemed to have been carved for a soldier rather than a Bishop.

"Yes, I am burning with eagerness to reach the poor souls in these unknown parts." Father Hennepin, sulkiness gone, quickly seized the center of attention. "During my retreat I thought of the difficulties of this mission, and it seemed a rash attempt. But I looked up to God, and was inspired with courage and resolution." He beamed, scarcely

132

able to keep the cassock of religious duty pulled over his intense love of adventure.

As the priest babbled on, Marc stifled a yawn, and saw more than one doing the same. Laval finally raised a thin imperious hand. "Though I had no part in selecting you, Father Hennepin, I am glad you feel ready for the responsibility."

Father Hennepin, ignoring the Bishop's sourness, plunged headlong into a most ticklish subject. "It pleases me that His Majesty recognized the Recollets' fine work in this colony by selecting them for this new mission."

The Bishop looked at him as if the sight scarce repaid the effort.

"Isn't it fortunate," said Count Frontenac, "that we have a few men of character who dare take a stand against Jesuit ambitions?"

"Monsieur de la Salle," said the Bishop coldly, "has brought upon himself the enmity of a powerful body of the church, and all for nothing, for the Recollets, worthy as they are, will have to ask help of the Jesuits in these western lands—if any of them are actually colonized."

"But there was a reason for our asking their aid here in the North," interposed Father Hennepin. "You see"—he turned to address the whole gathering—"our saintly founder, St. Francis, imposed on his followers a vow of absolute poverty that prevents us from owning property and collecting rents, and the Recollets prefer to keep to this original austerity. We own no real estate, no land yielding revenue, and do not congregate in sumptuous monasteries." He drew a long breath. "We have succeeded as well as the Jesuits in Brazil and India, for in hot climates the natives can subsist on the products of the soil. But to reach the heart of the North American savage, you must relieve his temporal wants. This we cannot do, and we can't erect and maintain colleges for Indians and French. Unlike St. Francis, Loyola preferred to use the tremendous power that resides in great wealth. The Jesuits can own property and collect rents to maintain their schools. So, not without misgiving, the Recollets invited their aid. We were warned that they would drive us out, and that has already happened once."

"Surely they have done important things for the colony," protested the Bishop. "Even you, Monsieur de la Salle, must admit it."

"Gladly, Your Grace," said La Salle. "But they also already own one million acres of the choicest land. I would sum up their record as

133

one of personal self-abnegation to the height of martyrdom, coupled with corporate selfishness in acquiring and managing a vast estate."

"Very well put," said Count Frontenac. "Remember, Monsieur de Laval, it was the strictness of their rule and the heavy tithes they imposed that made our citizens petition to have back the good Recollet friars who worked among them without asking for tithes. Naturally Your Grace is annoyed when you are trying to persuade the King a village curé needs six hundred livres a year, and the Recollets offer to do the work for nothing."

"I think it is most unbecoming," said Laval sternly, "for the King's representative to voice such enmity toward a branch of the Church!"

"You tell your Jesuits what is becoming!" exploded Count Frontenac. "And that a little humility is supposed to go with the work of God! In confession they demand not only the nature of the offense, but the names of accomplices and all the details—information they then use as a source of pressure. They carry tales, telling a husband what his wife does, a mother about her daughter. Matters revealed in the confessional become public property. And you, supposedly the impartial head of the Church here, are completely subservient to them. You have made them masters in spiritual matters, thus giving them a powerful lever for moving everything else. You even encourage their meddling in state affairs."

Laval's features had been growing darker. "How dare you criticize your bishop! The Church is the voice of God, and the arbiter of all things human. Naturally we take cognizance of a man's private life, and of the still more important concentration of human interests and duties that are involved in state affairs, no matter how much the statesmen dislike it." In his agitation he rose, gathered his cassock about him, and walked indignantly to and fro. "The princes and rulers of this world must be subject to guidance at the hands of the Pope, the vicar of Christ on earth. I am the Pope's vicar, and in New France's bounds, the Holy Father has cloaked me with his own authority. I would be guilty before heaven if I did not uphold the supremacy of the Church over the powers both of earth and of hell."

One could not doubt his sincerity, but Victor mouthed silently the word "Montmorency" and Marc nodded. Laval was driven not only by a conviction of his duty to the Church, but also by a nature that loved to rule and could not endure yielding. Count Frontenac was now trembling with anger.

"In the early days," shouted the Count, "Champlain and Montmagny

134

were little else than chiefs of police under the missionaries. But the very presence of a governor, an intendant, a regiment of soldiers should show you, Monsieur de Laval, that domination by the missions is past, and any hope of a theocracy has vanished. This is a royal colony, controlled by the sword and the law."

Laval snorted. "The hosts of the world are beleaguering the sanctuary, and I am called by Heaven to defend it!"

"The Holy Scriptures," retorted Frontenac, "command us to obey our sovereign. The duty of you priests is to convert the Indians. As for me, I shall consecrate all my efforts, and if need be, my life itself, to extending the empire of Jesus Christ and the supremacy of the King throughout this land." He struck the table and the goblets jumped. "But I shall strive to my dying hour against seeing the Great Lakes and the entire valley of the Mississippi added to the vast possessions of the Jesuit order!" He leaned back, red-faced. "Tell your Jesuits to stop thinking so much about beaver skins and more about souls."

"Be careful of accusations without proof." Bishop Laval stopped pacing.

"I have plenty of reliable reports that the Jesuits are dealing in beaver. That is why they are so eager to go among the Indians and neglect our French parishes. No wonder I approve of the Recollets' taking care of spiritual matters in the empire Monsieur de la Salle is going to add to France!"

"Because," thundered Laval, "you are counting on this 'empire' to make your fortune as well as La Salle's!"

A gleam in Frontenac's eye showed that the shot had gone home, but that it did no damage. "Jealousy! Jealousy! This whole colony is shot through with it. Religious orders jealous of each other, and of the royal authority. Quebec is jealous of Montreal and Montreal of Quebec, and both of them of the men with enough courage and ambition to go into the interior." He settled back, sought for control, and raised his hand to signal for more wine. "And I'm tired of the eternal conflict between traders and priests."

Laval turned on him. "The traders undo the work of the Church. Why should we tolerate their debauching the Indians? I wrote to Monsieur Colbert that brandy would ruin all the religion in New France."

The Governor chuckled. "I know. He sent me a copy of his answer: that brandy hadn't yet overcome the Church in older lands. A smart

135

man, Colbert. It's perfectly legal to sell brandy, as you might remind that insolent pup in the pulpit this morning. If he isn't careful, he'll go to the dungeon like all other traitors."

The Intendant, Duchesneau, had been silent, letting the storm rage. But now he cleared his throat. "About the brandy trade . . ."

"What about it?" challenged Frontenac.

"While the principal men of the colony are here, I should like to make known the contents of a letter from His Majesty I received on the *St. Honoré*. He has taken note of complaints from Quebec about the brandy trade." He drew a paper from his pocket, unfolded it, and laid it on the table so that the great seal of yellow wax, the heading "Saint-Germain-en-Laye, 22nd Mai," the signature "Colbert," the mandate signed "Louis" and further, "By the king, Colbert," were easily visible. "He commands herein," stated Duchesneau, "that the Governor and I meet with twenty of the most important seigneurs to receive their opinions as to whether the trade should be prohibited. You gentlemen will receive notices when I have set a date for the meeting. It will be early enough to include the Sieur de la Salle."

M. de Laval, resuming his chair, interposed, "Do I understand that none of the clergy is invited to this council?"

"Such are His Majesty's commands," admitted Duchesneau.

"But that is an outrage!"

"How wise His Majesty is, as always," said Count Frontenac smoothly. "It is for the laity to decide what is good or bad for trade, not ecclesiastics."

Laval's thin face became a study in rage, but His Majesty's name was enough to keep his tongue in check. Frontenac was now enjoying himself. Glancing around the table, he said, "Let us hear some opinions on the matter."

No one was eager to be the first to enter the conflict, until, prodded by Frontenac's glance, a seigneur near him said, "To keep the Indians sober is a worthy Christian idea. But to prohibit them entirely from strong liquors smells of the Turks."

Other opinions, supporting and dissenting, followed quickly and sour tempers began to flare.

"I should like," at last said M. Berthier, a former army captain, "to hear from Monsieur de la Salle. He has traveled more among Indians than any of us other seigneurs."

"By all means!" Duchesneau's patronage was almost sneering. "He knows all about Indians."

"No one knows all about Indians," said La Salle quietly. "But my opinion is that the welfare of the colony depends upon selling brandy to them." The Bishop's lips tensed, but La Salle went on calmly, "I would personally rather see an Indian trade his furs for blankets or kettles, but we have to take him what he wants. The crux of the matter is this: our refusal to sell them brandy will not prevent them from getting it. They'll go to the English and Dutch. Too many furs are already going in that direction, because we can't compete with the English prices. At Albany a savage can get a musket for two beavers; we have to charge him five. He can get eight pounds of powder there for one beaver; we have to charge him four. Everything he wants costs him from two to four times as much to get from us. Now if we drive him to the English in order to get rum—and he can commit crimes on English liquor as well as on any—we have gained nothing but harm for our trade."

There was a murmur of agreement, and the Sieur Berthier, glancing placatingly at the frowning Laval, said, "And if they betake themselves to the English and Dutch, they will be exposed to their heresy, instead of the true gospel they learn from us."

Victor and Marc stole an amused glance at each other. That statement had more than a trace of hypocrisy about it, but it was a hard one for Laval to answer.

"And they can get arms to make war on us," added the Sieur Romain.

La Salle nodded. "I firmly believe if we were to refuse brandy to the Iroquois, we would not long remain at peace with them. It's a tragedy that of all the savages on this continent, those in whose hands firearms are the most dangerous are the ones who can most readily procure them."

A shudder went around the table. In the pause, Marc asked, "Why that difference in prices?"

"My brother's aim in life," said Victor, "is to find out all there is to know about everything."

Count Frontenac smiled benignly. "There are worse traits for a young man. There are several reasons for our prices. Blankets, kettles, cloth, can be bought more cheaply in England than in France. Then freight costs twice as much from France to Quebec, because of the difficult navigation on the St. Lawrence, as from London to Boston or New York. Rum from the British West Indies is cheaper than French brandy. Also we have to pay duties on all furs shipped from the colony—and then the King has set the prices high enough to assure our merchants a large profit."

"Then," said Marc, "if Monsieur de la Salle found a better shipping route, open for a longer season, he could sell goods cheaper—" He stopped, aware from numerous frowns that he had touched on one note that made La Salle's plans unpopular.

Duchesneau rescued him. "Since we have differences of opinion on the brandy trade, I shall ask each of you to put your opinions in writing, and bring these statements to the council."

"But if this council is to be composed of the principal seigneurs," said Laval, "you cannot leave out the Church. The Reverend Jesuit Fathers are seigneurs of a part of Quebec, of part of Beauport, and the manors of Petite Rivière, Notre Dame des Anges, Sillery, St. Charles, Petite Auvergne, Charlebourg, St. François Xavier, St. Francis, St. Ignace, to the best part of the coast of Lauzon, all the coast from Ste. Anne to above Trois Rivières, seven leagues frontage by thirty deep——"

"*Mon dieu!*" Frontenac interrupted this recital. "They do have a stranglehold. But this is a matter for the seigneurs concerned in trade, and the Jesuits are forbidden to trade. Even though, as we all know, they do it."

"So is it forbidden for the Governor to trade," snapped Laval. "Equally, we all know he does it."

Frontenac turned in a rage, his hand creeping halfway to his sword hilt, as if only the opponent's cloth kept him from a challenge.

"Let us leave further discussion," Duchesneau said quickly, "until the council. You will have at least a fortnight to prepare your statements."

Frontenac turned his anger upon the Intendant. "I shall call the council when it pleases me."

"On September 3, 1675, His Majesty ordered that the Intendant be president of council."

"I have a letter dated 12 Mai, 1678, in which I am given that title. You are to preside only in the absence of the Governor."

"I shall not yield," said Duchesneau haughtily.

"You will, by Heaven! If I have to shut you up in a dungeon until you come to your senses."

"You know you dare nothing of the sort."

At this, the room became a furore of shouts and recriminations. At last the Sieur Auteil tried to interpose in favor of the Intendant, and

Frontenac struck the table with his fist. "While I am Governor, His Majesty's wishes are going to be obeyed."

Duchesneau snorted. "You ignore the royal edicts yourself, when it suits you. What of the illegal traders—the *coureurs de bois,* that you are supposed to arrest? His Majesty wants some people to cultivate the land instead of having everyone chase after beaver, so he has strictly regulated the trade, allowing only twenty-five licenses a year, but the woods are full of traders. These outlaws even carry their furs to the English when they please."

"How can I arrest them all?" asked Frontenac. "I have few soldiers at my disposal and none in the forest to gather evidence to convict them."

"You never try to punish them. Over four hundred of our small population of young men have vanished into the wilderness. They're not helping with the work of the colony, they're not increasing the population as the King wishes, though they probably increase it in Indian villages. You are not only not punishing them, you are in league with them. Knowing that Du Luth is the very head of these *coureurs de bois,* why did you permit him to make this journey he just departed upon?"

Frontenac, trembling with rage, tried to answer calmly. "Because he is the only one who has been in that region beyond the lakes, and he has a genius for making friends with savages. He is a courageous and able gentleman, and the only man who has any influence with these *coureurs,* who after all are Frenchmen and citizens, some of them sons of gentlemen seated at this table, and all of them men of spirit. Too much severity will send them to the English or convert them permanently into lawless banditti. Any governor who didn't make use of such a man as Du Luth would be a fool, and whatever else I may be, I am not that." He rose to his feet. "And I never give way to anger except when attacks are made on the authority I represent." He turned to Laval. "You are constantly trying to undermine that authority, and in view of the poverty of the country, you are collecting enormous revenues. In short, your object is mastery, and you use all means to obtain it."

Laval replied coldly, "Actually and rightfully, I have the greater power. Your appointment is for three years, and can be recalled at any time. I am appointed by His Holiness the Pope, and can be recalled only by him. I am beyond the reach of royal authority. And let me remind you that I have already made and unmade governors. I went

139

to court in 1662 and procured the removal of Avagour, and was invited to select a governor to take his place. I can do it again if need arises. And I can excommunicate even a governor, if I choose."

Laval rose with great dignity. "I see no further reason for remaining here. Count Frontenac, my compliments on your hospitality. Father Hennepin, let me again wish you every success."

Duchesneau made stiff farewells and departed after him, upon which a few seigneurs made excuses of various other appointments and followed.

"*Eh bien,* birds of a feather flock together, as the Devil said to the charcoal burner," laughed Frontenac grimly. When the wineglasses had been refilled, the gathering visibly relaxed, since all who had sided with the Intendant or the Bishop had gone.

"Well," commented M. Berthier, "the Bishop will set all the artillery of the Church against you. He'll refuse to let you dip your finger in the holy water and make you go back to being sprinkled like common folk."

Frontenac laughed. "I'll take even that chance. But I'm sorry this farewell party was the scene of a quarrel."

"It will not in the least affect my mission," said Father Hennepin serenely.

M. Berthier turned to La Salle, "Have you set the date for your departure?"

"Not yet. A project of this kind takes much preparation at one's bases."

Still more delay? thought Victor resentfully, and Father Hennepin sniffed. Frontenac wiped his lips and laid his napkin on the table. "Have you decided on your lieutenants, the next in command?"

"Yes, I have," said La Salle. "I hope none of the others will think I consider them less worthy, but for my own reasons I have selected Monsieur Tonti, and Monsieur de la Motte de Lussière as next in command. Monsieur Marc de Lorennes will help me on fortification, and Monsieur Victor has the post he asked for as my secretary and keeper of the official record."

Tonti cast his eyes down to cover his pleasure. Farther down the table La Motte, his face flushed from wine, was polishing his gold-rimmed spectacles. His fingers jerked to a surprised stop, and he nodded grave thanks toward La Salle.

No one need be surprised at the choice of Tonti, thought Marc, for he and La Salle had been constantly together. But second place might have gone to Victor. He himself had expected nothing; but he saw eyebrows rise about the table and speculative glances cast at Victor, whose possession of the D'Artagnan sword had set high in their estimation. And Victor was not the man to let his toes be trodden on without protest. For once Marc could not tell what his brother was thinking.

La Salle's announcement had, at first, shaken Victor with hot resentment. But he had recovered quickly, knowing that whatever the reason he had been passed over, it was better this way. In his peculiar position as spy for the King, he wouldn't want it reported at court that he was La Salle's lieutenant. Easily he smiled his congratulations to Tonti and La Motte, as Frontenac lifted his glass.

"To Monsieur de La Salle and his lieutenants, and the success of their venture!" When the glasses were drained, he added, "We shall have another party before you go, with no disturbing elements. A ball. All of you and your ladies will receive notes."

Father Hennepin frowned. "I protest against indulgence in a venial sin like dancing, and balls are forbidden by the Bishop."

"Not to me they aren't," Frontenac said firmly, "any more than I allow him to forbid cards to my soldiers. I'm a religious man, but in spite of the Bishop I uphold one military tradition: dancing is the best training for marching."

Father Hennepin rose. "Will you excuse me now? I must say good-by to my brother Recollets."

Amid a general chorus of farewells and good wishes, La Salle said, "Your canoe will be on the *batture* an hour after sunrise. I'll send two men with you."

"That won't be necessary," said Father Hennepin stiffly. "I've made my own arrangements."

After the priest had gone, the talk lazed on through the afternoon, though gradually seigneurs from distant settlements left to make the journey home by daylight. A few had been privately asked to remain for supper, the De Lorennes and La Salle among them. Now the conversation turned from France to the colony, in reminiscence of the early days. Every story emphasized the enmity of the Iroquois. For the history of New France was practically a story of hand-to-hand struggle against this confederation of five Indian nations, lying chiefly south of the great inland lake, Ontario, and spreading from there east and west. Horrible tales were told of their forays into Montreal and Quebec; of their near extermination of the Christianized Hurons.

141

"Why did they never wipe out the French entirely, if they're so numerous?" asked Marc.

"They don't fight in an organized way," said Frontenac. "A few come out of the woods in a surprise raid, harass and burn, and then retire to the woods again. And then they like to trade with us, when it is more convenient than going to the Dutch or English."

"Well, I hope they leave us alone from now on," said the Sieur Berthier. "We have enough problems in creating civilized estates out of a wilderness. . . ."

That night the boys wrote additional letters to go with a packet of trinkets from Quebec shops for their brothers, Auguste and Charles. Victor also wrote to Angélique, Madame, and the King, though even much chewing on his quill had produced little to report, except that the expedition had not yet begun because La Salle was trying to raise more money and make peace with his enemies. This letter he kept hidden from Marc, who also had his own secret—another letter and a package with samples of Indian crafts for the girl at the convent.

The following morning when they took their packets down to the ship, they joined a considerable company on the shore: the Governor, the Intendant, and the Bishop had all brought numerous well-stuffed envelopes they wanted to see personally on board.

"I don't know how His Majesty and Colbert can really evaluate these quarrels," said Marc. "They have us puzzled, and we're on the spot."

"Of course," said Victor, "we don't have His Majesty's wisdom."

"That," said Marc drily, "is incontestable."

La Salle came down, too, with a packet of letters, and when the mail was safely on board, he and the Governor waited to bid godspeed to Father Hennepin, at that moment on the way down Mountain Hill. Vigor shook from every fold of the flying gray robe as the rotund figure came leaping down in the moccasins he had exchanged for his sandals. The pointed hood was thrown back, tossing from one shoulder to the other, while the crucifix and rosary danced from the rude girdle. On his back was a portable altar and behind him came two fellow Recollets with blankets and a rolled rush mat. Beside a small canoe, two *voyageurs,* stolidly waiting, touched their caps briefly to the friar and stowed away his possessions.

"I need little for myself," said Father Hennepin cheerfully. "In New France you learn to desire only God. Now, Monsieur de la Salle, you must follow me closely."

"I hope to," said La Salle.

Having bade farewell to Count Frontenac and his fellow Recollets, Father Hennepin stepped expertly into the canoe, wedging his bulk down into its narrow confine. As the light craft skipped out upon the current and turned its nose to the west, the crowd cheered. The paddles dipped and rose, the bright sunshine turning the spray to a shower of diamonds. The canoe, light on the blue water, darted along until it vanished like the shadow of a cloud in the distance.

17

WHEN the last merchantman had departed for France, Victor sighed. "Now we shall have to stay in this wilderness at least a year. I wish we could be through by next October. You and La Salle put up those forts in a hurry, will you?"

"It isn't just the forts," said Marc. "He has to have flourishing colonies around them within five years, and make enough money in the fur trade to pay all his debts."

"You're not in such a hurry as I am," Victor replied. "You don't have a girl like Angélique waiting for you."

"No. I certainly don't."

"Well, let's hope the year will at least fatten our purses."

But their only profit continued to be at cards with the officers of the Carignan-Salières regiment, from whom they also learned that the rift in the colony was widening. On the very day the last sail disappeared beyond the Ile d'Orleans, Frontenac had called for a showdown. Seigneurs and merchants under Jesuit influence supported the Intendant, and Duchesneau became abusive to the Governor. Merchants, traders, and even their clerks were split into two factions; and as quarrels ranged up and down the cliff, canes and sticks came into play, even swords.

Predisposed toward Frontenac as a family friend, the more the twins saw of him the more they liked him. Unquestionably he was remarkably fit for his office. Whenever he stopped to talk to visiting Indians, it was as good as a show on the Pont Neuf. He conformed to their ways, borrowed their figures of speech, and flattered them smoothly, yet always maintained an air of fatherly superiority. Even the arrogant Iroquois accepted this status.

The first biting winds of autumn began to buffet Quebec. The boys, marking impatient time, watched with amazement as the forests broke out in a riot of red and gold, the like of which they had never seen in France. On the morning of the first break in this seemingly endless wait, it was so cold that they had gone to the lower town to buy the popular blanket coats. Crossing the Place d'Armes on the way back, they encountered La Salle and La Motte emerging from the Château. La Motte hailed them in a voice of authority. "I have orders for you. Monsieur de la Salle has decided not to keep so many men idle and waste what little good weather remains. So the main party is to go ahead with me, and he will join us later at Fort Frontenac."

Victor recovered first. *"Eh bien!* Let's be off. But I thought Tonti was second in command."

La Salle cleared his throat. "Monsieur Tonti will wait here with me, as will you, Victor. Your brother will proceed with La Motte." Oblivious of their astonishment, he turned to his lieutenant. "I shall also keep Nika, of course, and canoemen for three canoes. Have everyone else ready to leave on the morning tide. You will take all of our goods your canoes can hold."

"I'll be glad," said La Motte, "to get away from all these priests and their eternal tinkling and tolling of bells."

"Why must you separate my brother and me?" demanded Victor. "Our army captains never did."

"In my service," La Salle said coldly, "every man must work where he's needed. Your place is here, to draw up my statement on the sale of brandy, and other papers. Marc meanwhile can be studying the fortifications used in this country—adapted from Vauban's—of which Fort Frontenac is an excellent example."

As La Salle began giving detailed orders to Marc and La Motte, Victor strode angrily away along the fort palisade.

"After a few days' rest at the fort," La Salle resumed, "you will ask Captain la Forest, my commandant, to help you select fifteen men, supply them with trading goods and send them west in canoes. They can save us time by establishing trade relations with the Indians ahead of us along the route, and collecting provisions. Tell them to go as far as the Illinois, if we do not come up with them sooner."

"Very good, sir," said La Motte. "An excellent plan."

144

It was an almost automatic reply, but it held so strange a note that Marc glanced at the dissipated face. He was startled to see that the man was desperately afraid. But La Salle missed it entirely. He was staring after the obviously disgruntled Victor. "I, too," he said, smiling faintly, "have lived under the thumb of an older brother."

"It's damned highhanded of him, whatever his reason," growled Victor, as Marc caught up with him near their hillside lodgings.

"It's only for a short time," said Marc.

"I wonder if Tonti could change his mind, if we asked him."

"I don't think even the Governor could."

Mention of the King's representative reminded Victor of his orders not to allow himself to be separated from La Salle. "No, I guess there's no use."

After dinner, they divided their possessions. The new things acquired here—the four pairs of moccasins Nika had insisted upon, the trading goods, the woods clothing—made a sizable pile, to which Marc added his uniform, his lute, a few books, and a blank journal for sketching fortifications.

"What about Jacques?" asked Victor.

"You keep him. Where is he, anyway?"

"Working in the landlady's garden, of all things."

"He always did like that kind of work. Remember how he was always helping Auguste when we went home for a visit?" Marc kicked the bundle of brocades Victor had won in the card game. "What will you do with those, when you leave?"

"They can stay here. I'll offer Mme. Dumont a few livres to keep our room for us until we come back. She has others empty, and not much chance to rent them in winter. We'd have to store the bed somewhere."

The next morning they went down early to the river, where the row of twenty-foot canoes was being loaded. La Salle and Tonti were helping La Motte stow each one with eight or nine hundred pounds of baggage, distributed to leave space for three or four men. "Here," called Tonti, "put your things in this one, Marc. These are your men— Messier and Laurent. I've already put in your rush mat and two blankets."

Marc acknowledged the cheerful salutes of the two voyageurs:

Laurent, short and wiry, with sandy hair and twinkling eyes; Messier, a broad giant whose smile revealed gaps in his square white teeth.

La Salle looked at his watch, and then to the east. "You may as well start. The tide will be coming up within the half hour." He shook hands with Marc and La Motte. "You'll be in good hands. These are experienced men."

"Ah, *oui, m'sieu,*" laughingly interposed Laurent. *"Nous sommes les hommes choisis, les plus beaux chanteurs du monde!"*

"So 'the choicest men' means the best singers," said Marc.

"Yes," said La Salle, "and only partly because the best singers are the best paddlers. A smooth voyage to you. When Brossard comes, put him in charge of camping for the night. You can trust his judgment. And he is an excellent interpreter, if you encounter any savages."

"Merci, m'sieu, I will take care of everything." The voice was softer, the words slower than was usual among these lively *voyageurs.* The speaker, tall and lean, came down the slope with his packs and loped to the canoe beside Marc's with a litheness that had been borrowed from the Indians.

"I hope they all know their jobs." La Motte's forehead crinkled into worried lines above his spectacles. "This is all new to me, you know."

When the little fleet was out on the river, Marc felt a queer pang as he saw the distance grow between him and Victor. It was as if he were leaving a part of himself behind. But as the quays receded the excitement of the journey seized him and left little room for regrets.

Marc helped Messier set the sail, about four ells of linen cloth on a little mast. With the weight of men and baggage, the canoe did not ride as high upon the waves as when Marc had shared one with Nika or Victor, but still it skimmed along with the tide and the wind, while the men, using their paddles now only for steering, settled back and took out their pipes for a smoke. Besides their fleet, other canoes had also taken advantage of the tide, forming a kind of carefree procession. Greetings flew back and forth, some teasing and challenging: "Don't leave that fine head of hair on some Iroquois belt!" Others were serious: "Good voyage! Clear weather! Short portages and long rests!"

The incoming tide carried them upstream for the six hours. Then the paddling began. As Marc took his turn at the paddles he began to have a new feeling for the canoe as a good tool for its job, exactly as one would value the right sword.

At the first portage one of the canoemen handed Marc a *paqueton,*

146

a carrying-strap, and helped him lift one of the bales, fastening the *paqueton's* broad band around his head so that the load was shared equally by forehead and back. It was a strain, for he was unused to walking at all, having always had a horse at his disposal; and he felt like an ox dragging a load with its head. But the voyageurs were kind. *"Très bien! Très bien!* You will yet be as good a man as Messier." And Messier would laugh, confident that he could carry a heavier pack than any of them. Marc learned to carry his pack high and not let it sway; and he imitated the voyageurs' light, elastic step as they wound about rocks and climbed ascents, following broad paths over a soft cushion of leaves. Afterward it was a relief to get back into the canoe.

It was a hard life, even for one used to army campaigns. At night, usually spent on an island, Marc was so tired he could hardly wait until the canoe was unloaded and turned over, and camp was made, though by the time the fire flared he was ravenous for the pound of pork alloted to each man and served with a biscuit, sometimes varied by cornmeal porridge seasoned with fish. He marveled that in spite of incredible fatigue, the voyageurs' gaiety never failed. Like most unlettered men they found their keenest pleasures in noise and energetic movement. They needed no salon in which to discuss for a whole evening the difference between *la joie* and *l'enjouement;* they had both. As soon as their meal was finished and they had smoked their short clay pipes, they went fishing or organized some game. Marc wanted only to roll up in his blanket on his mat, underlaid with evergreen branches where they could be had. He always fell asleep instantly and soundly.

With the first dim light they were up and away again. It would have been a gay trip under a different leader. But La Motte resented the hardships, and alternately endured them in silence and broke out into bitter complaint. Though he looked well and was not drinking now, he was in poor condition for such exertions and he grew increasingly irritable, quarreling over details with Brossard, revealing such ignorance that behind his back the men began to snicker at everything he said. Such ridicule of La Motte was usually led, Marc noticed, either by the sullen, red-bearded Luc, or by a canoeman named Duplessis, older than the rest and more quarrelsome. Every night of the six days to Trois Rivières, La Motte chafed at having to stay with the men, instead of finding hospitality at some seigneury as he and

147

Marc could have done if traveling alone. "The only good thing about this trip," he said once, "is that we didn't have to go with Father Hennepin. For once we are free of priests."

Above Trois Rivières the river widened into Lac St. Pierre. Here the current pushed against them even more strongly. But the muscles of youth have a way of adapting to what they must do, and for Marc the utter exhaustion of the earliest days dwindled to a mere fatigue, dissipated by a night's rest. Aside from his concern for La Motte, he began once more to enjoy the journey through the brilliant autumn color. Sometimes the only event of the day might be the sight of the flat, catlike head and arrow-shaped track of an otter swimming for shore, or sliding clownlike down a muddy bank. Sometimes they met Indian canoes, or pirogues hollowed out of an elm tree, too heavy for portage. Since these latter were manned by Iroquois, there was a certain excitement in these encounters, but the savages were few and peaceful.

18

VILLE MARIE, below the two-peaked dome of Mount Royal, long the outpost of the settlements, stretched in a thin line along the island of Montreal, beginning with a fortified and loopholed stone windmill and completed at the far end by a square wooden fort. On the one long street, compact wooden houses were connected by footpaths. Two enclosures held more stately buildings of freestone, one the Hôtel-Dieu and the other the Seminary of St. Sulpice, built, Marc noticed, somewhat after the model of St. Sulpice in Paris.

Without walls or palisades, the village lay open toward the surrounding fields, and coming and going was a crowd much like the one at Quebec, except that the habitants wore red hats—the *bonnet rouge*—and the visible priests were all in Sulpitian black.

As the canoes turned in toward the beach, the solid door of the seminary was flung open and down the wide path to the river came a priest so striking in appearance that Marc uttered an exclamation.

Here was one of the most massive human beings he had ever seen; and he did not merely walk toward them, he marched as if thousands marched with him, his bearing giving the illusion that his loose black robes must be a disguise worn over a uniform. Sweeping toward them like a tide of benevolence as they landed, he sent a questioning glance over the group. La Motte stepped forward, to have his hand seized in a grip that sent a visible tremor through his frame. "Welcome to Ville Marie." The vigor of the priest's tones matched that of his body. "I am Dollier de Casson, Superior of the Seminary."

La Motte bowed with more respect than he usually showed to a cassock. "May I present my companion Monsieur Marc de Lorennes. We are associates of Monsieur de la Salle."

Marc had his turn at a grip to make the very Devil wince.

"I know the name," said Father de Casson. "When I was a cavalry officer under Turenne, your father, if I am not mistaken, was an officer in the musketeers?"

Marc nodded. "I have heard of you, too, I think, Father. Were you not the man who could extend his arms and hold up a man seated in each hand?"

De Casson roared. "I sometimes think that was my only distinction in the army. But let me tell you, I can still do it. So you're one of La Salle's men now!"

"In your footsteps, Father, I think. Weren't you with him on one of his earlier journeys?"

"True. Brilliant man, La Salle. A little headstrong, though." He grinned. "We started together but disagreed about the route and went our own ways. Of course I'm not headstrong—just determined to have my own way." He roared with laughter again. "But come, you must share our simple meal."

"It will be a treat, after a fortnight on the river," said La Motte.

"We have forgotten how to sit on chairs and benches," added Marc.

De Casson regarded them with amusement. "But from Quebec to Montreal is not much of a trip as we deal in distance here. Our Abbé Fenelon and the mayor of Ville Marie once walked it on ice in winter."

"Walked?" La Motte's voice squeaked. "One hundred eighty miles, isn't it?"

The Superior regarded him thoughtfully. "In New France one needs a taste for the strenuous life."

"So I'm beginning to see." La Motte polished his glasses nervously.

149

"I intend to make my fortune and get out as fast as I can. *Eh bien,* we are pleased to accept your hospitality. Brossard, take charge of everything."

The wiry canoeman nodded, assigned three men to watch the goods, and dismissed the rest, who raced to the nearest tavern like hounds after game.

The Superior watched them tolerantly. "At Ville Marie we are half religious, half devoted to Mammon. As the center of the fur trade, we're the center of the devil-may-care spirit that trade engenders. Or perhaps it attracts that kind."

"You have a beautiful spot for your seminary," said Marc, as the three of them started up the path. Back of Ville Marie the forest lined the side of Mount Royal with gold and red, framing a rush of white water in the rapids to the west, where ship navigation ended with the ocean tide.

"We certainly have," De Casson said exuberantly, slapping an oak trunk as he passed it. "You must climb the mountain sometime. The view is superb. We have two rivers, you know. The Ottawa comes in at the end of the island. That is the most traveled route to Michili-mackinac and the other northern posts, because it avoids the Iroquois. When Cartier came here in 1535, the Iroquois were living on this very island. But by the time M. Maisonneuve came to establish Ville Marie, thirty-six years ago, the Hurons and Algonquins had driven them out. Maisonneuve's friendship with those tribes incurred the hatred of the Iroquois, and those first years were filled with their attacks. At one time they pressed us so hard we didn't dare till the earth even beneath the cannons of the fort."

Under the current of talk, Marc had been wondering how such a man endured monastic life. He suspected that the celibacy, the uncomfortable bed, the unearthly rising hours, the one suit of clothes, were not as bad as being deprived of the simple pleasure of sitting with carefree soldiers.

"The whole island belongs to you?" asked La Motte.

"Yes. Various companies and individuals before us tried to meet the King's conditions—supporting missionaries and colonists to spread the faith and clear the land. Finally it was given to our order, and we Sulpitians are doing quite well, which of course irks the Quebec Jesuits worse than a hair shirt."

As they reached the seminary door, it opened and a group of priests came out. One of them lingered, appraising them with cool eyes. In his early forties, of medium height and spare, his face had a familiar cast. Before Marc had time to place the resemblance, De Casson said, "Oh, yes, Father Jean. Here is part of your brother's expedition. Gentlemen, this is Abbé Jean Cavelier, brother of your La Salle."

The Abbé bowed coldly. "Is my brother not with you?"

"No," said La Motte. "He was detained at Quebec, and sent most of his party ahead in my charge."

The Abbé scowled, but whether La Motte or La Salle was the cause no one could tell. He lifted an apparently bloodless hand to wave toward the shore. "You have his supplies and equipment in those canoes?"

"Some of it," said La Motte curtly. "He will bring the rest when he joins us."

"When does he expect that to be?" asked the Abbé as if he were putting a backward child through the catechism.

La Motte's dislike of priests came to the surface. "That's his business."

De Casson interposed. "Father Jean is interested in this expedition because the family has invested in it heavily, and as the oldest member he feels responsible."

"He owes me personally ten thousand nineteen livres sixteen sols, acknowledged before a notary in Rouen," said the Abbé bleakly.

"Perhaps you'd better bring the canoes and supplies within our stockade for the night," suggested De Casson.

"Yes, and keep your canoemen under your eye," ordered the Abbé, "or you'll lose them as Father Hennepin did. My brother should have enough sense to keep his party together." He turned impatiently toward the shore. "Where is the canoeman I ordered?"

"You are going on a journey?" asked De Casson mildly, but with a reminder of authority.

The Abbé waved to the west. "To Lachine." His lips were a thin line. "I have obtained a court order to seize and sell Pierre Cavelier's house and property for what he owes me." He flung himself around them in a wide detour as if afraid they might detain him, and pursued his way in long uneven strides.

"Between that greedy one and Father Hennepin," said La Motte grimly, "I'd take the fat father."

Marc silently agreed. The touch of asceticism in La Salle had in this

151

man deepened and twisted until it had become fanaticism; and La Salle's fondness for solitude and independence had in this brother become a dislike for all other humans.

"I think La Salle would, too," said De Casson. "Father Jean keeps a tight rein on him. Indeed I'm afraid it's the only reason Father Jean stays in New France. He is little suited to missionary work."

"What's this about Father Hennepin losing his men?" asked Marc.

"Oh, yes. The good father arrived here full of his usual enthusiasm, leaving behind him a spiritual trail of masses, marriages, and baptisms in all those isolated homes along the St. Lawrence. But when he was ready to leave, neither his canoe nor his men could be found. I'm afraid the men were bribed to leave him, by someone who wants to hinder La Salle. Father Hennepin was very justifiably annoyed. He didn't want to wait here for La Salle to pick him up, for he considered himself the advance guard and the most important part of the expedition." De Casson rumbled with laughter. "He wasn't a bit discouraged. He harangued every resident of the island, and finally persuaded two men to take him, in probably the most decrepit canoe Ville Marie has ever seen, but he got into it with as much confidence as if it were one of the King's best vessels. I'll be relieved to hear that he reached Fort Frontenac safely. And, while I don't wish to seem inhospitable, I think you should proceed there at once, and get your men out of reach of La Salle's enemies. They're numerous here, and powerful."

"I had hoped to rest awhile," said La Motte. "But we'll leave again at dawn."

They did not leave at dawn. When Marc came out of the seminary enclosure after a good breakfast, he found about half of the *voyageurs* waiting for him, including Brossard, Messier, and Laurent. "What's wrong?" asked Marc. "And where's La Motte?"

"Last time I saw 'the boss,'" said Brossard, with an edge of contempt on his tone, "he was asleep with his head on a table in the tavern. *Mais oui,* he got very drunk last night."

"Some of the men were keeping him company," said Laurent, "but Duplessis and that Luc went out to the Indian village to find women. They're not back yet."

Alarm had seized Marc, but he made himself speak calmly, since the voyageurs apparently expected him to take charge. "I'll find Monsieur de Lussière. He'll want to leave at once. Maybe one or two of you'd better go to the Indian village."

"That's three miles out there," grumbled one canoeman.

"What of it?" asked Brossard. "You heard Monsieur de Lorennes." He pulled a deck of cards from his pocket. "Cut for it—the two low men go."

Marc found La Motte still sprawled over a tavern table, and set to work sobering him up. It was noon before the last of the men had been brought to the shore, half-drunk, and surly at being snatched from their pleasures. Reluctantly they brought out goods and canoes from the seminary stockade, but at last they were all launched upriver, to follow the afternoon westward, paddling now against a strong current. About nine miles above the village they came to the rapids whose sound had been increasing since they left Ville Marie.

"We portage here, of course," Marc said to Laurent.

"*Non, monsieur.* The Saut St. Louis is violent, but short and shallow. Sit tight, m'sieu." With the words he was over the side, waist-deep in the tumbling water, and Messier followed. Glancing around, Marc saw that the other canoemen were doing the same, dragging the canoes against the turbulent stream, making slow but definite progress. In the icy water it was hard for the men to keep their feet, but the challenge brought a quick rebound to their spirits. Laurent grinned back at Marc. "Easier than unloading and portaging. Enough of that not far ahead."

They met one canoe coming down, riding the rapids, in danger of capsizing every instant. But its gay voyageur yelped at them as he tossed and bounced. "I think," said Marc, "one has to be a little crazy to get along in this country."

Messier grunted. "It makes you happier at least. It is well, also, to keep one's soul always ready to face its Creator."

The canoe was brought at length into smooth water; the voyageurs climbed in carefully, paddling feverishly for a few yards to keep from being carried back into the rapids, and then drew into shore beside a seigneury. "Lachine," said Brossard. "We pick up some men here."

The seigneury, a neat palisaded village containing at least one sizable Norman house, faced a wide strip of river called Lac St. Louis. Through this lake paddled the little fleet, augmented by half a dozen Lachine habitants and their canoes. At the end of the lake they encountered another chain of rapids. Here began days of such fatigue and discomfort as Marc had never dreamed of. Portage followed portage; and when they were paddling, strong currents dragged at their arms. Marc's shoulders grew lame, his back and forehead sore from the heavy packs. He was always wet and cold from dragging canoes in water up to his knees or even to the armpits; and his feet were cut by stones that slashed his moccasins. Every night the voyageurs had to inspect the canoes, gumming anew each chink and broken seam.

Miserable as he was, Marc knew La Motte was suffering even more. The thin leader did far less than his share, but he had passed beyond all complaints into dull silence. Just as Marc became sure that La Motte would have to order a day's rest, they came to a pass called La Galète, beyond which spread water as still as a pool.

"That's the last of the rapids." Laurent's teeth flashed with his delight. "Only sixty miles of calm water. Islands all the way—must be a thousand—and then the lake and Fort Frontenac."

Though sore of body, Marc was able to appreciate such beauty as he had never seen. In a long file they glided in and out among rocky islets, green as only islands can be, some with tall crags to remind one of castles on the Rhine, others so tiny they seemed to exist only to hold a lone pine against the sky. Toward evening of the 8th of November, the river seemed suddenly to end; and before them lay a great boundless sea, an expanse of water that reached to the very horizon.

"*Voilà* Ontario!" exclaimed Laurent. "*Hé!*" he added in alarm, for Marc in his astonishment nearly stood up in the canoe. "You need not jump into the lake just because there is plenty of room."

Marc sank to his knees, a not unsuitable posture, he thought, for he felt as if confronted by a miracle. "Lake! This is no lake. It is an ocean!" He leaned over the side, cupped water in his hands and brought it to his lips. "It's fresh!" Astonished, he tasted another handful. "It really is! No salt!"

"*Non, m'sieu.* And there are four more lakes like it."

"Surely not this size?"

"*Ah, oui, m'sieu,* even larger, they say."

"Ontario," Marc murmured its Indian name, and then the French one, "Frontenac. Nowhere in Europe or Asia have I heard of such a thing."

"You'll have plenty of time to look at this one, m'sieu," said Laurent. "For we have arrived." He lifted his paddle in a brief gesture to a point of land some distance to the west, where a stone wall, blockhouses, and a few bark roofs emerged faintly from the autumn haze. "*Voilà* Fort Frontenac!"

19

IF it be true, as Montaigne says, that ambition seeks nothing so much as elbow room, thought Marc a week later, Fort Frontenac must be one of her favorite stamping grounds. Sitting in a deep window ledge of the *maison principale* which shared the enclosure with a smithy, a guard-house, a barracks, a magazine, a cow shed and a well, he had been reading Montaigne's "Of Solitude." Low voices came from an adjoining office where the Commandant, the Sieur de la Forest, was holding his daily conference with Jacques Dautray, the middle-aged son of the Attorney General, who managed the seigneury finances and kept the trading records. With them had formerly sat André Hinaut who had supervised the actual trading, his peculiar long-jawed, v-shaped face bent over the records, but he was now somewhere in the west in charge of the fifteen-man party that was to start trading with the natives along the route. It had been easy to find that many men—like Duplessis—who preferred action to waiting, and the freedom of the woods to strict fort discipline.

On the window sill beside Marc lay a journal of notes on the construction of Fort Frontenac, and a record of observations influenced by Boyle's *The Sceptical Chymist*. Unlike other scientists, who explained Nature by reasoning from accepted religious and philosophical ideas, M. Boyle believed in experimenting first and formulating laws from the results. Not that Marc had spent all this time of waiting for La Salle and Victor in reading or writing. Among other things he had made himself useful to La Forest at the trading post, learning the different furs and their values—for all goods in the trading post were priced in beavers, not in French currency. A silver or black fox was counted as thirty beavers; an otter as four; while ten muskrats or two red foxes were one beaver.

Fort Frontenac was a comfortable enough place to wait. The thick stone walls formed a good protection against the cold; the huge fireplaces were constantly replenished; and in the ovens and kettles pork and fowls alternated with fish and game. Loopholes in the walls, not yet stuffed against the approach of winter, were a reminder that this was a fortress, yet beside them were good prints above graceful French chairs and sofas.

Here were French classics, a few religious books, several of mathematics and geography, a treatise on navigation, the voyages of Columbus and the rambles of De Soto. Most carefully read and underlined, with copious marginal questions and notations, was a manuscript, a copy of Père Marquette's account of his voyage with Joliet. Marc had already read it and studied its map, astonished at the great distance yet to go to follow the route of these explorers, considering that from Quebec to Fort Frontenac was as far as from the north coast of France to the Mediterranean—and Fort Frontenac was only a starting place.

Beside the manuscript was a small pamphlet. Marc, flicking open its plain cover, found a summary of a habitant's obligations to his seigneur. As he read, from idle curiosity, an idea began to take shape. A tenant had only to do yearly homage, pay a rental of one or two sous an acre and half a bushel of oats; he had to grind his corn at the seigneur's mill, paying one-fourteenth of the yield for the service; he had to work for the seigneur certain days in the year, to give him one fish out of eleven caught. . . . Jacques, Marc was thinking, will loathe the rigors of canoe travel, but he likes to grow things. If Victor would give up having a personal servant, Jacques could stay here and work under a good seigneur and commandant, until we go home.

Marc wondered if Victor and La Salle might be in sight now. Picking up his journal, he put on his blanket coat and strolled out through the fort enclosure, as busy a place as a Versailles courtyard. Masons were at work along the water side of the enclosure, replacing a wooden palisade with stone. The land side was already finished, with a wall three feet thick and twelve feet high, its expanse broken only by the powder magazine against it, where Messier, Laurent, and Brossard were packing arms and ammunition for the expedition.

Marc leaned against an elm, opened his journal, and began adding to his carefully sketched plan of the fort. Inside moats fifteen feet wide, it was a square with four bastions, measuring 300 fathoms around, originally enclosed only by palisades of logs set on end in earth and pointed at the top. He sketched the buildings inside the walls, added stables, barns, and a lime kiln outside, and indicated that beyond was a small French village of twelve habitant families, dwelling under protection of the seigneur's château. He had observed in these habitants an independence and self-confidence not seen in the peasants of France; perhaps because most of them were soldiers and sailors turned farmer, or perhaps because there was so much rich land here that a man could raise as much as he could plant. It was a country fit for good living, if not to drive one's coach through.

He sketched in the other village, on a little rise back from the water, like nothing to be seen in France: one hundred Iroquois living in dome-shaped huts, scattered as irregularly as the trees of their sheltering grove. Quiet, orderly, the Indians worked in the fields and on fortifications beside the Frenchmen, and sent their children daily to the Recollet school.

Marc could understand why La Salle had been called foolish to give this up for the unknown. Here he was feudal lord of a twelve-mile strip of land along the water, commander of a garrison of eighty men, and a merchant prince with a brisk Indian trade. Yet he had mortgaged it all because his nature, Marc suspected, was ill-suited to the routine mercantile duties. For evidence of where La Salle's heart lay, Marc had only to swing to the left. There, in a cove, he could see a fleet of twenty-foot bark canoes like so many turtles in the sun; and beyond them, a shipyard, the first on this continent. Four decked vessels, hewn from the forest behind them, rode at anchor, fully rigged, mounting one or more cannon. From where he sat he could even read three of the names: the *General,* ten tons, the *Cataraqui,* ten, and the larger flagship, the *Frontenac,* upon which the Dutchman, Moyse Hillaret, and his workmen were making repairs. At the blacksmith's quarters near by, the stocky Jean Meilleur, nicknamed La Forge, was leaning over his coal pit, bellows in hand. Here as inside the fort, there was no idleness because the seigneur was away.

Marc closed his journal, walked out to the tip of the peninsula, and sat staring toward the opening of the St. Lawrence. There was no sign of canoes bearing Victor and La Salle.

As the sun dropped lower, Marc drowsed to the endless swish of waves upon pebbles. Approaching footsteps roused him.

"Asleep at your post! To the guardhouse!" La Forest snapped, but his gray eyes twinkled as he dropped on the beach beside Marc. "On second thought, I sentence you to accompany me to the Iroquois village."

"A fair punishment, *mon capitaine.*" Marc glanced at La Forest, surprised to see him scowl. "Trouble?"

"Minor, I hope," answered La Forest. "But a nuisance. La Motte was drunk again last night, followed the cook's Indian helper home and got into a brawl with her husband. The fellow is behaving in ways La Salle won't tolerate in the least canoeman. I wonder why La Salle picked him as lieutenant? He had other choices."

"I'm afraid he doesn't trust my brother and me. He misunderstood our delivering a message from Père la Chaise to the Jesuit Superior."

"He has ample reason to be wary." La Forest plucked a weed and began pulling it apart slowly as he talked. "A favorite Jesuit trick is to place men in his service with instructions to desert him later and take refuge in their missions. They have done it even here at the fort."

"What good would it do here?"

"La Salle is obliged to maintain a certain garrison, and if they can reduce it, he might forfeit possession. Many of the Jesuits' friends would like to have this place. Then, too, we are along the route to their missions and it is embarrassing for them to pass here with their canoes full of forbidden furs. Also our Indian settlement annoys them. It's too well administered by Recollets." He glanced over the water as if yearning for sight of the canoe that would lift responsibility from him, but the wind-swept water remained stubbornly empty. Marc rose, brushing his deerskins. "This trouble at the Indian village, is it serious?" he asked as they started back. "They seem so tame."

"One never knows, with Indians. Especially Iroquois. One incident that struck them as unforgivable, and pouf! they'd be gone in a day. You know, one danger in La Salle's plans is that he's going directly to the western tribes who trade most of their furs now to Iroquois, who in turn trade mostly with the Dutch and English. There's not much beaver left in Iroquois country, and they won't like La Salle's diverting what has been going through their hands."

"It's important to keep them at peace," said Marc. "Even the best fort of Monsieur Vauban would be vulnerable, so far from any other garrisons. This spot could easily be taken by siege."

"We know," said La Forest grimly. "And La Salle's western forts will be even more defenseless. He shouldn't take a single man who doesn't understand the importance of peace with the savages," La Forest went on earnestly. "And I'm worried about this long delay. It's getting late now for a trip on the lakes."

"Do they freeze over?"

La Forest laughed. "Hardly. But the channels do, and the lakes are given to severe storms in late fall and winter. I wish he'd get started. And I wish I were going with him."

"So do I." Marc had grown fond of this man, uncomplicated and perhaps uninteresting, but so honest and direct. One of the most valuable military types; not a man to plan strategy, but one who does his duty conscientiously.

"I can help him more here, he tells me, at his base of supplies. Did you know that Jacques Dautray wants to go? I don't know how I"ll replace him. One of the habitants has been trained in bookkeeping, but he can't do it and tend his acres, too."

"Oh! Would this man be willing to turn his land over to someone else? I have an idea that our man, Jacques, who loves to farm, would be only too pleased to stay here."

La Forest brightened. "He might, with a small sum for the improvements he has put on it. We'll ask him." Now arrived at the stockade, he turned for another look over Ontario where the last flaming colors of day were fading, and the islands were sinking into a soft purple dusk. *"Mon dieu, look!"*

"A canoe!" Marc raced to the shore.

"It's one of La Salle's!" said La Forest, close behind him. "I know those men—Accau and Le Picard. He must be close behind them."

But no other canoes appeared. The fatigued voyageurs came straight to the sand and pulled up their canoe. Accau touched his blue cap, his crooked teeth gleaming in an apologetic smile as he handed two envelopes and a long narrow package to La Forest. "I am sorry, m'sieu, to bring only these, instead of the Sieur himself."

One letter was addressed to La Forest, the other and the package to La Motte. La Forest tore his open. "He is still in Quebec, still delayed," he said unhappily. "He sends orders for La Motte, you, Father Hennepin, and the rest of the men to embark on the *Cataraqui* and proceed to the other end of the lake, to the strait of Niagara."

"Par le sang dieu!" exclaimed Marc. "What are we supposed to do there?"

"Build a fort at the river entrance, and find a place to build a ship above the cataract. He'll bring a sergeant and men to garrison the fort."

Marc's spirits sank at the prospect of going further into the wilderness without Victor, accompanied by the unsteady La Motte and the officious Father Hennepin. While he silently helped the messengers unload their canoe and turn it over, his gloom was interrupted by shouts, muffled thumps, and running feet from within the fort. A soldier burst out of the gate and looked wildly around. "Captain! A fight! La Salle's men!"

As La Forest and Marc rushed into the barracks, La Motte, struggling with a carpenter, Noel le Blanc, turned, panting and wavering, a bloody knife in one hand. "I was trying to stop them," he mumbled. The red-bearded Luc stood close by, blood streaming from his shoulder.

La Forest seized the knife, and ignoring La Motte, turned steely eyes on Luc. "What happened?"

"What does it look like?" Luc answered insolently. "What do you expect when La Salle leaves us rotting in this dull hole? I'm going to quit and go back to Quebec."

"No, you aren't," said La Forest sternly. "You know the penalty for military desertion." He turned to La Motte. "New orders have just come. You're going on ahead, by ship. But Jacques Cochois will go as your pilot. Luc and Noel here will wait for La Salle. In the guardhouse."

20

THE next morning, when La Motte was sobered, he worked quite cheerfully with La Forest, getting the *Cataraqui* loaded with the carpenters' tools and materials for shipbuilding, and as many supplies as the small vessel could carry. Marc made an inventory of the cargo, including biscuits, corn, and pork, to last until they could get food from the Indians, and boxes of goods to be used for trading.

"This will be easier than traveling in canoes," La Motte exulted. "No more sleeping on the ground and worrying about being scalped by savages. Speaking of savages, La Salle says here"—he tapped the letter in his jacket pocket—"that we may have to take gifts to the Senecas near the Niagara, in case they object to our building a fort. I suppose Brossard'll know what to do. La Salle says they're not dangerous. The package was one of those pipes trimmed with feathers, that's supposed to be some kind of magic safe-conduct. I'll show it to you later." Adjusting his glasses firmly on his nose, he climbed into a canoe and was paddled out to the ship.

Behind Marc the surly but efficient Moyse Hillaret and the other artisans were busily packing their tools. "So I'm to build a ship on the Niagara," Moyse growled, "without enough anchors and cables?"

"La Salle knows what you need," said La Forest patiently. "He'll bring everything in the *Frontenac.*"

By the evening of the 17th of November, the last kegs and bales were packed into the little ten-ton brigantine. Marc finished his letters to Auguste and Charles, to Michelle at the convent, and one he would leave for Victor. On the dawn of the 18th, he rose to hear a high wind howling around the fort. Below he found La Forest and La Motte staring out at high waves breaking in from the lake.

"Too bad," said La Forest. "You could postpone your sailing; but at this time of the year you might have a long wait for better weather."

La Motte shook his head helplessly. "La Salle ought to be here to make these decisions himself!"

"After breakfast let's talk with Cochois," said La Forest. "He's an experienced pilot."

When they descended to the shipyard, followed by most of the soldiers, habitants, and even a few Iroquois, they found Jacques Cochois surrounded by a group of sailors protesting that so small a ship could never weather such waves. Cochois, clearly worried himself, turned with relief at the appearance of his superiors. "I think we can make it, Messieurs. But you must decide."

"You'd have to hug the north side, just as if you were in canoes," said La Forest, "or this northwest wind would blow you right onto the southern shore."

"The *Cataraqui* can take more of a storm than this," snapped Moyse. "I know. I built her. Let's go now and get his ship and fort built. The sooner we go, the sooner we get back."

"Of course we can go," said Father Hennepin pompously. "The divine hand will uphold us——"

"Marc, what do you say?" La Motte interrupted.

"I'm willing, if Moyse and Cochois believe it can be done."

"Then we'll sail in half an hour."

With dubious glances toward the tossing lake, crew and passengers scattered to get their baggage, and soon were on their way in canoeloads out to the ship. La Forest clasped the hands of La Motte and Marc. "The best of luck."

"Everyone has a supply of that commodity," said Marc, mostly for La Motte's ears. "And I'm sure ours isn't all gone."

Father Hennepin embraced Fathers Buisset and Ribourde of the fort mission and knelt for the elderly Father Ribourde's blessing. "This storm will do us no harm," he announced confidently as he rose. "St. Anthony of Padua knows I am from his province, and he is the patron saint of mariners."

The anchor was raised and the *Cataraqui* sailed easily out of the comparative calm of the cove. But when the brigantine struck open water, the wind billowed her sails, and she began to pitch alarmingly. Pilot and crew were hard put to keep her near to shore, yet clear of rocks and sand bars. Farther out the storm turned to a blizzard; and, amid whirlwinds of snow, the prow crashed into a huge billows that threatened to engulf the ship. Below deck the passengers clung to anything stable they could find. Even Cochois showed strain when he came down for short reliefs. *"Mal·à such sailing!"* he complained wearily. "No charts, no lights, no buoys—nothing but skill and guesswork to keep us off the rocks. I'd like to see how Luc would make out, with all his boasting about his salt water piloting."

Keeping close in, they crossed slowly and perilously from headland to headland. Sometimes they were blown away to the south; and laboriously the crew worked the ship back, hands and faces freezing in the cold gale. At night no one got more than fitful sleep. Eight days later, on the 26th, when they were exhausted by interminable high seas, a new storm arose, blowing them far from the shore. "Take the sounding," Cochois ordered. They were in over sixty fathoms of water, but he had the anchor let down. "Nothing we can do until morning."

To add to other discomforts, the crossing had already taken longer than expected and the biscuits had grown so hard they had to be swallowed in pieces like pills. Besides, they were almost gone. But morning brought a slight clearing in the weather, and the first sight of other human beings. From out of the mists of the southern shore a canoe approached slowly, rising and falling on the waves. In it were three savages and a dog, his forepaws on the canoe's edge.

As the Indians came closer, Brossard hailed them, and a long conversation in Iroquois ensued across the tossing waves. Then the canoe turned back, and Brossard explained, "He says there is a river over there, and he invites us into its shelter."

La Motte pulled a manuscript map out of his pocket, and spread it in a sheltered spot on the deck. "That must be this Seneca village of Taiaiagon. We'll pull the ship in there, and get some rest. Also, maybe some corn."

It was not easy to reach even this temporary haven. Near the opening of the river, they ran aground. They cast off ballast, and the ship floated free; but in a new approach, it ran aground again. This time, even after all ballast had gone overboard, the *Cataraqui* stayed aground. Now some Iroquois who had been watching from the shore came out in canoes, and after Father Hennepin and Brossard explained the difficulty, the savages paddled ashore all fourteen men not needed on the ship. A great shout of relief went up when the ship was finally freed and anchored in the river. Immediately the Iroquois crowded about the Frenchmen, eager to trade corn for one of the boxes of goods.

Expecting this to be an overnight camp at most, they slept on the ship. But a fiercely cold spell set in; ice formed on the edge of the lake; and then the river froze, forcing the whole company, in shifts, to keep the brigantine free by chipping ice with axes. Constantly La Motte gazed out over the water. "According to this map, it's only about forty-five miles from here to the Niagara. These savages told Brossard that river is so swift it never freezes. The instant the wind changes, we'll try to get across."

On the morning of December 5, the wind seemed favorable for the crossing, but the Iroquois tried to discourage them. La Motte shrugged off their protests. "They just want to keep us here to trade." But once out in the middle of the lake they found the savages had been right. The wind changed, a storm blew up, and after struggling till dark, they lowered canvas and anchored some fifteen miles from shore. All night the storm raged about them; but on the morning of the sixth, St. Nicolas's Day, the wind abated. On the only sunny, calm day since they had set sail, the weary crew cheered at sight of the mouth of the Niagara, free of ice save for drifting chunks. A small Indian village on one shore offered further prospect of food. Cheerfully they sailed into the river between high snow-covered banks, coming to rest in a natural haven.

"We made it!" exulted Marc, as the anchor went down. "This must be where La Salle wants his first fort." He raised his eyes to the heights. A long row of savages stood peering over at them amidst grunts and gestures of amazement. Father Hennepin waved at them enthusiastically. "Senecas—one of the Five Nations of Iroquois. No

163

wonder they're excited. We"—he turned impressively to the little crowd on deck—"are the first ever to sail a ship into this river."

Once on land, they knelt in deep, sparkling snow, while Father Hennepin offered prayers. Then, while the Senecas listened in wonder, they raised their voice in a rousing *Te Deum,* the first ever heard on these shores.

With cautious glances now and then toward the Senecas' bark lodges, the canoemen scraped away the snow and built a fire. When it flared high in the wintry air, two Senecas in deerskins and fur robes came bearing reed baskets.

"*Poissons blancs!*" cried Father Hennepin, as they set down the baskets filled with fish larger than carp. "Whitefish—the best fish in the world!"

La Motte, motioning Brossard to his side, went to speak to the savages. They talked for some time, and as the two Senecas went back to their lodges, Brossard handed the fish to two canoemen, who quickly began to prepare them for cooking. "What did they say, Brossard?" asked Marc. "I caught a few words, but I guess I need more of your lessons."

Brossard smiled. "They said they had a very big catch today, so our ship brought them luck. They came to offer us a share."

"Good of them," grunted La Motte. "But they weren't so friendly after Brossard told them for me that we would have presents for them, too, and some trading goods as soon as we unloaded. In a flash they asked why we were unloading here. I told them we came from the Governor to build a fort. They might as well know it at once," he added defensively.

"They don't want a fort here," said Brossard. "They say this is their fishing place."

"This fishing party has no authority," said Father Hennepin crisply. "You'll have to do as La Salle said—take some presents to the chiefs at the main village on the Genessee River."

"How far is it?" La Motte consulted his map. "Eighty miles! We can't go one hundred sixty miles on foot!" He glared at the priest. "Stop telling me what to do! I'm in charge!"

To forestall a clash, Marc said quickly, "What a spot this is for a fort!" Talking fast to give La Motte's temper time to cool, he went on to point out that this triangular promontory dominated both lake and river and presented only one face to land attack.

164

"It will be a master stroke," Father Hennepin pointed out. "Niagara is the outlet of the four Great Lakes beyond, and can command the fur trade of the whole Northwest. Of course, it is an excellent place for a mission."

"And if La Salle didn't fortify it, and the English did, he couldn't maintain forts and colonies beyond," said Marc.

"We'd have to drag the logs from way over there." La Motte gloomily pointed to the woods beyond the clearing. "But that's your problem, not mine."

"It would be suicide to start any building before we have the Senecas' permission," warned Father Hennepin. "We'll camp here and explore the river for a shipbuilding site."

La Motte scowled. "Suppose you let *me* give the orders?"

"What you must decide, La Motte," said Marc, "is whether La Salle is more eager to have the fort or the new ship. We are too few to course two hares at the same time."

La Motte seized this chance to capitulate gracefully. "The ship, I suppose. But I intend to take a few days' rest. We'll sleep on the *Cataraqui* for the time being."

"Tomorrow I'll take a few men and explore the river," said Father Hennepin. "I'll find a good place for shipbuilding."

La Motte was both angry and baffled, not only at such officiousness, but at such energy. "The pleasure is yours. Marc, you take charge of the party. Let the gray robe go if you want him, but take someone useful, too."

Father Hennepin swallowed any further remarks, afraid he might be left out of the trip entirely.

The morning of the seventh dawned cold, but with the snow sparkling in sunshine that promised greater comfort by midday. One canoe could carry six and their provisions, so Marc chose Messier and Laurent, his favorites; Moyse, who would do the actual building of the ship; and, since La Motte wished to keep Brossard, he took along Accau as interpreter.

As they paddled up the river, the current grew ever swifter and they had to avoid huge cakes of ice floating down like ghostly canoes. Some nine miles of hard paddling brought them to the foot of rapids so violent they could go no farther. Here also there was a sharp change in the river banks. Although the water kept its same level, the land at this point rose abruptly on each side to a height of about four hundred feet, as if the river's bed from here on had been slashed out by a giant blade. Even if the current had allowed the party to go on, the sheer cliffs on each side of this gorge offered little hope of a landing higher up.

"We might try this side first." Father Hennepin pointed to the right-hand shore. Since they knew nothing about either side, Marc nodded to Laurent, who swung the canoe into relatively calm water behind a boulder. "Must be a great rapids above here," he panted, when they were safely ashore.

"It's a cataract, halfway between the lakes," grunted Father Hennepin, rearranging his cassock after the scramble of landing. " 'Taller than the tallest pine trees,' is the way the Indians describe it."

With provisions divided into six packs, and their muskets in hand, they slowly climbed the steep escarpment, seeking foot and hand holds as on a mountainside. At the top they stopped to rest, marveling at the forest-covered plateau spread before them, and below, the deep gorge with its swift river flowing between sheer cliffs of reddish brown rock.

"Never can launch a ship from this place," grumbled Moyse. "What am I to do? Build one and throw it over the cliff?"

"Let's wait and see what it's like above the cataract," said Marc.

Mile after mile they followed a snow-covered trail along the edge of the bluff. The snow softened as the sun rose higher, making difficult footing, and Marc called for frequent rests.

As they trudged ahead, the water far below became ever swifter, raging through the chasm. The course was just winding enough that one could not see far upstream, and it took one sharp turn where the swift current churned into a whirlpool, a veritable devil's cauldron. Above this the gorge narrowed, and the compressed river threw itself into violent, roaring fury. As they filed around another turn, the roar filled all the air, and they stopped, gasping in amazement. In the distance, spreading in a sweeping curve from one side of a vastly widened chasm to the other, was the greatest waterfall their eyes had ever seen. Father Hennepin fell to his knees; the rest pulled off their caps and sank beside him.

In the roar of the falling river, the priest's thin voice in prayer seemed to Marc like the twittering of a sparrow above cathedral organ tones. They rose, and in a trance, followed the brink until they were above the cataract, once more standing at water's level, with the falls beginning its furious descent at their very feet. A rainbow appeared below them, bright-hued in the tossing mist.

"*Jamais, mes amis,* never will you see the like!" exclaimed Father Hennepin. "A divine benediction!" He began to point out what they could see for themselves. Marc, irritated into action, indicated a deepening of the shadows on the side of the gorge. "Come along. It will soon be dark." He took up his pack and started slowly on upriver, the others pulling themselves away with many a backward look. The upper river raced alongside them among great boulders, churning and boiling toward the precipice in rapids that were a marvel in themselves. Some three miles upstream they found themselves on the bank of a smaller river entering the Niagara and blocking their way. "No use going farther anyway," said Marc. "What do you think, Moyse? You couldn't launch any kind of craft in this current—it would be carried down and over the falls."

Moyse tapped his big pipe against a tree. "No place on this side. Maybe over there." He pointed his pipe toward the opposite shore, where a long, wooded island broke the rushing stream. "Some place like that, where the main current would pass us by."

"Let's camp here tonight," suggested Father Hennepin. "We can go back, and then try it the next day on the other side." Marc nodded and the men put down their packs. Wearily they scraped away the snow until they had a place for a fire. Beside it they opened their packs and ate cold whitefish and corn cakes; after which they lay down with feet to the fire and slept.

In the morning they were startled by weird cries from a nearby oak. "Turkeys!" shouted Laurent. He led the rest to stand cautiously beneath the branches where the great birds roosted. Marc studied them with interest. They were larger than those of Europe. "At night they go up in the highest tree," whispered Laurent. "Just before they fly down in the morning they make those noises. If we all fire at once, we might get more than one." Five muskets roared as one and three of the birds fell to be added to their packs. On the long walk back, they stopped to rest once more opposite the cataract. This time Father Hennepin took out his journal and wrote at length. But Marc could only stare enthralled, wishing that those who so admired the artificial cascades of Versailles might stand upon this spot.

When they had returned to the *Cataraqui,* Marc reported to La Motte, describing the giant waterfall and explaining why they couldn't build a ship on that side of the river.

La Motte sighed, rubbing his face in perplexity. "I don't know what to do now. Brossard has been talking to the savages while you were gone, and he reached a complete impasse. They not only won't let us build a fort here; they won't let us carry our goods above the cataract to build a ship. They don't want anyone interfering with the furs that come out here, by way of portage."

"The portage must be on the other side," said Marc. "We saw no well-traveled path."

La Motte peered out over the lake. "Right now I'd like to see the sails of the *Frontenac*. Why must La Salle stay behind and leave these problems to me?"

But in the next few days, in spite of uncertainties ahead, the spirits of the company rose, as they rested, made repairs on the ship, and ate their fill of fish and turkey. At the end of the week La Motte himself made a trip by canoe to the foot of the escarpment, with Marc, Father Hennepin, Messier, and Laurent, and found a well-trodden portage path up the cliff on the east side. "All the ship materials, tools, and supplies will have to be portaged from this spot," said Marc. "If we could build a storehouse here, and fortify it a little, we could unload our ship, and later La Salle's, and take our time in carrying stuff over the portage."

"Good!" La Motte brightened. "The savages ought not object to our building a simple shelter here."

"What about the *Cataraqui,* though?" asked Marc. "We can't sail her up here, and we can't leave her down there unguarded."

"We might pull her up this far by cables," suggested Laurent. "But it'd be damn hard work."

"With the help of God," said Father Hennepin, "we can do anything we have to."

Fortunately the Senecas consented to the proposal to build a storehouse upriver; and by a morning in mid-December all was in readiness to take the brigantine up to the foot of the rapids, but then a southwest wind blew directly against them, and not for three days did it veer far enough to the north to be of some help. Moyse attached a cable so that three men on shore could help pull the ship along, and with Father Hennepin at the helm and a small crew manning the sails, the rest took turns hauling the ship laboriously upstream. Through gruelling days of fatigue and cold, they worked until the *Cataraqui* rested behind a great rock near the escarpment, made fast by a cable to a tree since the current was too swift and the river too deep for anchors.

With only a brief rest, they began felling and trimming trees for storehouse walls. It was hard work in the bitter cold, with the ground so frozen they had to heat kettles of boiling water to soften it so they could set the stakes in. It was uneasy work, too, for the Indians were keeping watch over every movement. Not an hour passed without a Seneca warrior or two appearing in the grove, observing them with as little expression as the trees themselves. If approached, they said nothing; but they now refused to trade, a serious blow, for corn was urgently needed. And then one day they were gone, the woods as empty as if the earth had been deserted. Messier and Laurent came back from a hunting trip downriver and reported that the whole camp had disappeared from the lake, even their direction of departure covered by a fresh fall of snow. And yet on the day the storehouse was completed and a palisade begun, four braves appeared, this time objecting to a palisade, for they had consented only to a house, not to a fortified place.

La Motte stopped work on the palisade, and paced the riverbank, staring angrily toward the lake for signs of La Salle's approach. "All hands are needed on another job," Cochois called to him. "The drifting ice is getting worse. The *Cataraqui* may be crushed in at any minute."

La Motte sighed. "We can't beach her like a canoe. *Sacré bleu*, I wish I'd never got into such a mess. La Salle's head ought to be aching, not mine."

Father Hennepin bustled out of the storehouse. "Canoe or not, we'll have to get her up on shore," he said sharply.

"Any fool can order the impossible," said La Motte bitterly. "Look at the height of these banks!"

Marc interrupted quickly, "There's a ravine just below where she's tied. Do you suppose we might get her in there?"

The ravine seemed the only hope; it was level and not far above the water. Quickly Moyse and his helpers made a capstan in the bow, and ran a rope from it to a sturdy tree in the ravine. Even then, turning the capstan to wind up the rope and thus pull the ship out of the water was such severe exertion that the men had to be relieved every few minutes. Only six or eight feet had been gained when the cable broke where it rubbed the side of the ship, and when tied together, broke again. "No use wasting any more cable," said Moyse flatly. "She won't move."

The exhausted men sat along the bank, as La Motte rubbed his arm over his chapped and reddened cheeks. "We've got to save her. She's our only chance of getting back if La Salle never comes."

Seeing worried scowls on the row of faces, Marc said, "He'll come. But he won't be happy if we've lost one of his ships. Any ideas, Moyse?"

"Hell, no. I can build ships, but I can't drag 'em around on land." Moyse spat disgustedly, but he rose and walked around the ship, studying her position. "One more thing we can try. Put a cable all the way 'round her, fasten some ropes to it, and all of us pull until our arms come out of their damned sockets."

"We'll try it," said La Motte. "I want to see every man pulling, too." He shot a glance at Father Hennepin. "That weight of yours will be more useful than prayers."

The cable and ropes were fastened, all hands fell to, and after much heartbreaking effort the *Cataraqui* moved slowly into the ravine.

Marc approached La Motte. "Shouldn't we unload the ship right away and put the goods in the storehouse?"

"I suppose so, or those murdering thieves—" La Motte turned to glare at two Senecas who had been watching them from the woods, but had now suddenly vanished. "Cursed snakes! How in hell do they disappear like that?"

With the unloading completed, a fresh quarrel broke out between Father Hennepin and La Motte, when the priest detached a group of men and ordered them to start building a chapel, stoutly maintaining his rights to have a mission wherever they established a headquarters. "Instead of arguing with me," he advised La Motte, "you'd do well to plan your trip to the Seneca village."

In the morning, while Father Hennepin was directing his workers, Marc drew the wrathful La Motte away to explore the deeply worn path up the side of the escarpment, the portage around the cataract and its rapids. They had just clambered to the top when there was a whizzing in the air and La Motte gave a startled yelp. When Marc reached him he was unhurt, staring stupidly at an arrow quivering in the ground before his feet. On the path, less than a stone's throw ahead, stood six Seneca warriors, hideously painted in black and white, fully armed with bows, arrows, tomahawks—and Dutch guns. The two men froze. The Senecas waited. Finally Marc recovered his voice. "Come back," he said quietly. "Make them think this is as far as we intended to go." He forced a smile and turned La Motte to one side as if they had come to view the snow-covered plain and river below.

Then leisurely they started down the steep path, their backs tense with fear.

"That settles it," gasped La Motte miserably. "We can't risk an attack. They could wipe us out in ten minutes. We'd better go to that village. Damn it, why doesn't La Salle come!"

"We must have food, too," said Brossard. "We can't even go back without it."

La Motte called the men together and announced his decision. "Seven men will go, and nine will remain to guard the ship and storehouse. I must go myself—and you, Marc. And Brossard, of course. Who else will go?"

Moyse and a few others avoided his eye, but from those who murmured that they'd just as soon be on the move as sit here and wait, La Motte picked three. "That makes six, then. The seventh will be Father Hennepin."

The priest looked up in consternation. "No. I must finish my chapel."

"But of course you will go," said La Motte smoothly. "You have so often told us how well you understand savages, and how much the glory of God is concerned in this undertaking. You wanted to visit strange tribes—well, here's one. And if you have any influence with savages, you'd better come along and use it. If we can't make these Senecas listen to reason, the expedition ends right here. And so do we—from murder or starvation."

21

IT was shortly after dawn on Christmas Day when the seven men set out on the long, dreaded journey, guns in hand, knives at their belts, and on their backs as much food and trade goods as could be spared. Besides his map, La Motte also carried the calumet, which he unwrapped and showed them at their first pause for rest. It was a pipe with a bowl of dark red, finely polished stone, and a two-foot stem of a strong reed, the Norman-French name of which gave the pipe its name. Around this stem had been tied the neck feathers of a loon. In a crude way, it was

Mercury's wand, Marc thought, or the staff of an ambassador seeking peace. *"A la bonne heure!"* Brossard exclaimed. "We are safe among all the allies of the nation that gave it to Monsieur de la Salle."

"We would be, anyway," said Father Hennepin sharply. "I offered special prayers to St. Christopher."

"Safe or not, we'll never make it," said La Motte unhappily as they resumed the trail. "These *raquettes* make my ankles ache."

"Don't lift the toes with every step," advised Father Hennepin. "Move along in an easy shuffle. I've gone hundreds of miles on snow-shoes."

The way at first led directly east along a succession of Indian trails that finally intercepted a broad, well-traveled one. Here came the first test of the calumet, for they encountered without warning a hunting party of Senecas, black squirrels dangling from their waists. La Motte, jumping back in alarm, almost went sprawling. A flicker passed through the savage eyes, but Brossard's greeting was answered warmly. La Motte steadied himself and held out the calumet, and to everyone's relief the warriors accepted their mission as one of negotiation. They told Brossard that this was indeed the trail to the main village, and gave him some black squirrels in exchange for a knife and a few beads.

Refreshed by squirrel stew, they plodded on through cold and snow. At night they piled snow in a bank around them, built a fire in the middle, and lay wrapped in their blankets. Seven days of walking seemed as many ages; for the unfamiliar snowshoes, the heavy pack, and fear of the well-known treachery of Iroquois of whom the Senecas were one tribe, turned the march into a purgatory. But at the end of the seventh day, they crossed the Genessee River in an elm-bark pirogue apparently left there by the Indians, and they knew they must be close to the Seneca village.

La Motte was visibly trembling. "I can't—no, I can't do it." He turned, but Brossard caught his arm. "Steady," he said sternly. "Don't show fear. I'll help. Now you and Marc must put on your French clothes."

They changed in a willow grove, after which they climbed the hill on which the palisaded village lay. Near the gate of the stockade, half a dozen old men loafed in deerskins and fur robes, their shaved heads and scalp locks framing dark ugly faces. From inside the stockade the barking of dogs ended in sharp yelps as if they had been kicked.

"Approach and lay down your guns, in token of friendship," said

172

Father Hennepin, and La Motte for once did his bidding without protest.

The oldest of the Indians rose, his strings of beads and shells rattling against his deerskin tunic, and in a surprisingly firm voice, harangued them at length. Brossard translated more tersely: "He says the Senecas are our brothers. We were expected, and a call to council will be sent to all the huts. We are to follow him." He added quietly, "Pick up your guns, but carry them loosely and smile."

As they entered the simple stockade, men, women, children, and dogs came pouring out to watch. The old man conducted the visitors to an open-ended house of bark, bare inside except for a few mats scattered on the hard-packed earth. This was the council house, the old man told Brossard; it had been prepared for them to sleep in.

"I understood most of what he said that time," commented Marc. "But I didn't get more than a dozen words of that harangue outside."

Brossard chuckled. "Maybe you weren't in the best state of mind for studying language."

The seven were glad enough to put down their packs and drop to the mats for rest. The crowd outside scattered and after a little the women began coming back a few at a time, with torches, kettles of cornmeal porridge, and meat in wooden bowls. Two women built a small fire in the center, lighting it from a firebrand. Young men came in and washed the visitors' tired feet, rubbing the soles with soothing unguents Brossard said were made of bear oil and deer grease. When they had gone, Father Hennepin examined the food in the bowls. Sniffing the first, he said, "Dog-meat stew," and hurried on to the next. "You'll like this better. Boiled maize, cooked with oil pressed from nuts and sunflower seeds. Also these little corn cakes are good, and the dried fruits."

"So far the cursed savages are friendly," said La Motte gloomily. I hope they'll be as agreeable in council."

"Hospitality doesn't mean they'll agree to what you want," said Father Hennepin. "But we can hope. The best thing now is to eat and then get a good sleep. We are in no danger."

"Just the same, one of us will keep watch," ordered La Motte.

"The father is right," said Brossard, "but if you will sleep better, I'll take the first watch."

"Wake me for the second," said Marc.

When Brossard woke him in the late evening, he whispered, "You'll find more provisions at the door, if you're hungry. We're quite a curiosity. The children kept coming for an hour or so, bringing a handful of dried fruits or an ear of corn as an excuse to get a close look at us."

Nibbling a handful of dried berries, Marc walked up and down before the door. The huts were all in shadow now, but fires were still burning inside and out. As he strolled about he could observe the nearest huts quite clearly. Saplings had been planted in a double row to form the sides, and then bent and lashed together at the top. Over this framework lay sheets of bark, overlapping like shingles to shed the rain. Totems were painted crudely above each doorway, draped with a skin or blanket.

Near one fire a circle of men squatted, playing some kind of game. At another two women were working over a dead dog: scorching it to remove the hair, scraping it well, cutting it into pieces dropped into a steaming kettle. I hope that isn't for our breakfast, thought Marc.

The next instant he started in surprise, for out of the gloom beyond the square two figures approached in flapping Jesuit cassocks!

"Bon soir," he said as they came up. "I was just thinking there were no other Frenchmen nearer than the Niagara."

"Bon soir, my son," said the taller. "We were tending a sick child when you came. He is sleeping now, so we hastened to welcome you to our mission. I am Father Julien Garnier and this is Father Pierre Raffeix. How was your journey?"

"Fairly difficult, Father. But let me call our leader——"

"By all means, no," said Father Garnier. "He is more in need of sleep than of company. He will have to be at his best to win permission to build a fort on the Niagara." A peculiar smile flitted over the priest's countenance as he went on, "Please give our regards to Father Hennepin when he wakes, and tell him we invite him to say Mass in our chapel tomorrow. It is the Jour de l'An, you know." With gestures of farewell they were gone into the dusk beyond the square.

So this is New Year's Eve, thought Marc. A more peculiar one I never expect to see.

When La Motte heard of the callers the next morning, he exploded with anger. "They probably ran all the way from Quebec, just to make trouble for us."

"You're showing your usual ignorance," retorted Father Hennepin. "Their errand is to instruct these barbarians in the gospel. Both have been missionaries among the Iroquois for eight or ten years. I will go at once and accept their invitation."

174

La Motte watched his brisk progress across the square. "Priests!" he snorted. "Meddlers, every one of them."

Marc stepped to the doorway from which he could see several new kettles being guarded by a small boy who was using a stick to keep the dogs away. Four women stood at one side, watching. "Some of those kettles are heavy. Why don't the men carry them over?"

"Because," said Brossard, "the women do everything but the smoking and fighting."

"Well, you'd better thank them for their hospitality."

Brossard looked up from putting on fresh moccasins, and grinned. "Why not try your own Iroquois?"

Rather shyly, Marc called out a few words of thanks. The women broke into laughter and scurried toward their lodges. Brossard chuckled, and joining Marc in the doorway, translated their ribald remarks, as coarse as the jokes at a Norman peasant's wedding. "You've made a hit with the ladies."

Marc laughed. "I don't see any that make a hit with me."

"I don't know. What's wrong with her, for instance?" Brossard pointed to a young woman carrying an armful of wood. She let it fall near a fire in front of a small lodge, and turned to go for another, passing the council house on her return. She was comely and neatly dressed, and her soft brown eyes cast side glances at the Frenchmen. Inspired by some imp or by the teasing of Brossard, Marc stepped out and made a motion as if to ask if he might carry her wood. She seemed to think he wanted it for himself, and watched him wide-eyed when he took it to her lodge. Saying nothing, she crouched to stir up the fire, smiling to show him his presence did not displease her.

"You—live alone?" asked Marc, trying his Iroquois.

"Alone. I am not a maiden. My husband was killed. I live alone until I get new one."

"That is bad."

She smiled and lowered her eyes. "Better to be a widow than a maiden. A maiden could not talk to you. I like you." Marc blushed as he had never done at the more subtle advances of court beauties.

"I am medicine woman." She cast her eyes down to the many strings of beads about her neck. "I have good dreams. I will dream for you."

Well, you're at least the prettiest prophet I've ever seen, thought Marc. If one had a taste for savage women, she was attractive as she stood there in the sun, in her long dress of pale soft skins, fringed and beaded, her hair neatly pulled back and dressed with discs of copper.

175

He backed away, confused by the frankly amorous look she sent after him.

"Come here, Marc," called La Motte. "I need help to open these packs and get ready for this damned council."

While they were sorting knives, cloth, and other oddments into various piles, an old woman appeared in the doorway with a roll of mats she added to those already on the dirt floor. Then she brought wood and replenished the fire until the Frenchmen choked in the acrid blue atmosphere.

"*Vrai dieu,* I wish this was over." La Motte sat back on his haunches. Fatigue strove with dissipation in the lines of his face. Exposure to the wind had reddened his thin cheeks. "This damned smoke." He rubbed his eyes.

He's a sick man, Marc realized. "You'd better rest and let Brossard and me finish."

La Motte willingly let himself be persuaded and reclined on the mat placed at the head of the lodge, obviously for the chief of the council. "Better tell me again the important things to remember, Brossard. Why can't we just talk to the chief and settle everything with him? Why all this bother of a council?"

Brossard went on calmly sorting and folding some lengths of cloth. "Because they don't do things that way. No Indian chief has absolute authority. Everything important is settled in council where every grown person has a voice."

"A strange system," grunted La Motte.

"Seems untidy to a Frenchman," said Brossard serenely. "But they like it. Remember not to expect an answer today. They'll hear you out and give their answers in another council tomorrow. By their rules, hasty decision is bad form. And remember for every point in your talk you must give them a present, or the point is not made. They won't remember it without a gift."

"Greedy devils," said La Motte.

"It's not entirely greediness," resumed Brossard calmly. "Among people with no writing, the gift remains to witness your words when the sound has died away."

La Motte sat up, rubbed his eyes, and looked apprehensively at the circle of mats. "Where's Father Hennepin?"

"He went to preach in the Jesuits' chapel," Brossard reminded him. "A sermon for the Jour de l'An. Our three men went along, but Monsieur Marc and I decided to stay with you."

176

"So it is New Year's!" La Motte's mouth twisted wryly. *"Heureuse Année!"*

"I doubt," said Marc, "that many of our friends will call to pay their respects."

"All I can say is that the beginning of this year is worse than the end of the last," said La Motte.

The first day of the year 1679, thought Marc, and seven months have already gone of La Salle's five years. At the moment I ask of this Jour de l'An only that I come through it with a whole skin. I hope La Motte says the right things. These people have the power of life or death over us.

He whispered something of his thought to Brossard, who nodded. "La Salle's letter told him what arguments to use, and I'll try to put them into the kind of language they like. It's really simple. There are only two reasons why savages suffer white men among them at all. One is fear—and we are in no position to instill that. The other is trading for goods they want. We'll have to make them see that what we want to do is going to be an advantage to them, not just to us."

"A good system for persuading anyone, red or white."

La Motte sat up again, shaking his head as if to clear it. "If I'd only known what was ahead! I thought from the way La Salle talked in Paris we had only to come to this country, travel down that Mississippi, and gather enough gold to buy all Paris. If we get safely out of this mess, I'm for going back to Quebec."

"I am under contract to Monsieur de la Salle," said Brossard coldly.

"My brother and I will stay with him, too," said Marc.

From across the square came four measured drumbeats. "The call to council!" Brossard peered out the door. "They are coming now," he warned. "Look dignified and imperious, m'sieu. They must be impressed with your manner."

La Motte drew himself up rigidly on the mat, while Marc sat erect, watching the old men come in, one after another, in their beaver and otter robes, their beads and bear-claw necklaces. They were tall, well-shaped and erect as few Europeans would be at their age. Their chief, impressive in beaver and an extraordinary crest of bright feathers, took his place to the right of La Motte, waiting silently until the lodge was filled. Marc was struck by their bearing. In the air was a strong tribal unity, yet every one held his head up in pride, with no obeisance, quite different from the way the council of Louis XIV assembled. Father Hennepin appeared, bold and assured, followed hesitantly by

177

the men who had attended Mass; and together they made their way through the circle to places near La Motte.

The chief filled the calumet with tobacco from a pouch at his waist, lighted it with a coal from the fire, and held it reverently toward the roof, down to the earth, in the four directions. Next he presented it to La Motte who, as he had been coached, took a puff, handed it to Marc, who touched it briefly to his lips and passed it to Brossard. From him it was passed around the circle, deliberately and ceremoniously. Midway of its progress, the doorway was darkened by a black robe, and Father Garnier appeared. Instantly La Motte jumped to his feet, cursing. One savage froze with the calumet in mid-air, as if someone had uttered an oath in the midst of a Mass.

"You have not been invited here!" snapped La Motte, and turned to Brossard. "Tell them that raven can't come in."

Brossard reluctantly repeated what he had said. The chief glanced at the Jesuit, at La Motte's angry flush, and at the pile of goods. Apparently French cloth and iron outweighed the priestly influence, for he grunted and the Jesuit withdrew. Brossard shook his head regretfully, and Father Hennepin's eyes narrowed. Rising, he said, "Then I, too, must leave, and bear part of the affront put upon him."

"As you please," said La Motte shortly.

When the pipe had returned to the chief, Brossard knelt to spread out the goods in the first pile. The dignity of the savages was not proof against curiosity, for every eye in the lodge was evaluating the knives, porcelain belts and collars, and scarlet cloth. La Motte began to speak,.looking down at a paper in his lap, pausing often to let Brossard translate: "We have come to pay you a visit on behalf of Onontio, the Governor, and smoke a pipe of peace with you." La Motte's voice shook, but grew a little more confident as he went on. "We give you this"—he looked to see what Brossard had selected—"porcelain belt, as a symbol of peace and friendship. We will soon be able to bring you many goods like these. To do that, we want to build a great ship of wood above the cataract in the Niagara River so we can bring goods from our country to you by a better route than through the long dangerous rapids of the St. Lawrence. Then we can let you have the goods cheaper. We wish you to tell all your people not to interfere with our building this ship, because it is for their own good." At a reminding nudge from Brossard, he took a bolt of scarlet cloth from the pile and laid it before the chief. "By using this ship we can get cloth like this to you cheaper than you get it from the English and Dutch."

178

The circle waited, changeless and quiet, the chief's feather crest as still as a stuffed bird.

La Motte continued. "At Niagara we will have a blacksmith and a gunsmith, who will mend your guns and axes." He threw onto the chief's pile a coat and more lengths of cloth, laying them out with deliberation as if with them he were also trying to buy time to think. On and on he went, using other arguments, pointing out the advantages of having the French close to them, and added a heap of goods to prevent their giving ear to any black-clad men who might say evil things.

When he finished speaking, a wave of emotion went over the circle inside, but whether it was of belief or disbelief Marc couldn't even guess. After a long pause the chief said, *"Niaoua!"* and the word was repeated in varying tones around the circle. La Motte looked at Brossard, but received only a signal to wait. Deliberately the chief rose. The others followed suit and filed outside, where more villagers awaited them. Marc watched from the doorway. The chief was moving about from group to group, consulting everyone above the age of childhood, apparently giving as much time and weight to the words of one as another.

"What did they say?" La Motte asked Brossard.

" *'Niaoua'* means 'You are right, brother.' "

"Then we did it! They are willing!" exclaimed La Motte.

"No. We won't know until tomorrow. They always hear a man out, no matter how absurd his statements, and then say, 'That is right.' Then they go out and think what they please—laugh at him, disagree, or never think of it again. That's why the priests never know whether they are making any impression."

In the morning, the same Senecas filed again into the hut and took their places on the mats. A few youths laid armfuls of dressed skins and porcelain belts before the chief and then glided out to sit in the open sunlight of the square. After the pipe ceremony the chief began speaking, with one of the belts and a bundle of sticks in his hand. Brossard translated: "Messenger of Onontio, give ear. I am the mouth of the Senecas; when you listen to me, you listen to all the Senecas. There is no evil in my heart. My song is a song of peace. We have thrown away our war songs." He laid the belt at La Motte's feet. "You are welcome among us." Another porcelain belt followed the first. "We are resolved to maintain peace with the French; our men

179

do not want to make war on the French." And then the chief began repeating what had been said the day before. Marc sat listening, amazed at his memory, for this savage was repeating word for word, with no aid but sticks, everything La Motte had said. After each point he made vague and general protestations of friendship and peace, acting always as if the point had been answered, though nothing definite was said.

Finally the chief laid one by one fourteen dressed deerskins at La Motte's feet. Rising, he spoke again, and Brossard repeated, "He says they do not think they need a fortified place on the Niagara or a ship on the lakes. But he wants us to wait until a large war party returns. He wants to get their voices on this matter." When Brossard finished, the chief exclaimed aloud three times, echoed in chorus by all the others, "It is well. We thank you." Brossard interpreted.

A messenger came in and whispered excitedly; whereupon the savages rose and slipped out of the door like so many animals. *"Koué! Koué!"* came shouts from beyond the palisade. The chief lingered to explain. "Our war party returning now"—he waved to the south and east—"from going against the Shawano and Kanawhas."

"They are victorious?" Brossard inquired politely.

The chief smiled. "Of course. The Five Nations have made every other tribe wear the clothes of women. We may have some entertainment for you, when the sun goes down." He departed into the square, and the Frenchmen were alone.

La Motte sighed. "What do we do now?"

"Nothing," said Brossard. "They won't have ears for anything now but this war party and its news. Tomorrow we can talk with the chief again." But there was no hope in his voice. "Why not ask Father Hennepin to try persuading them?"

La Motte rose and stretched. "I wouldn't bet a pistole on either his willingness or his ability. What can we do the rest of the day?"

"Wait until the excitement dies down, and then trade for corn. We have about four hundred francs worth of goods left."

Later the Senecas readily brought corn. While Brossard and La Motte took charge of the bargaining, Marc sat in the lodge doorway. Gradually he became aware that someone was at his side, and turned, startled, to see that the young widow he had spoken to before had noiselessly come up and was sitting there, composed and smiling. He smiled uncertainly and waited for her to speak first.

180

For a long time she watched the comings and goings in the square. But at last she turned her eyes to the Queen's emerald ring on Marc's finger. He turned his hand so she could see it better.

"I like." When she smiled like that, her looks were really striking. She'd be a sensation at court. It would be interesting to take her back to the Queen. Marie-Thérèse had been so pleased and diverted by the little Nubian slave boy someone had once given her.

"White warrior has great thoughts?"

Laughing, he tried to explain in his halting Iroquois. She was silent for a time and he began to wonder what she had made of his crude discourse. At last she looked up, her luminous eyes full of emotion. "It is good. I go with you." She moved closer and made it clear on what terms she thought he wanted her.

God! thought Marc. What do I do now? "It was just an idea—" He tried to explain, but she snuggled closer against him. "Yes, I go."

"How—how many beavers do you think the ring is worth?" he blurted out to distract her.

"Beaver robe, like chief."

Marc had noticed during council the beauty and softness of that robe. It must be warm, too. It was hard to remember when he had been really warm all over. And one couldn't get much comfort out of an emerald. "Could you get me two such robes for it?"

She nodded eagerly. "I bring nice new ones."

"No, no. Not new. Worn long time." He had learned at Fort Frontenac that the beaver that had been worn was the softest and most valuable, the oil the savages used on their skin making the pelts more supple. "The oldest you can find."

The girl looked pained, but glided to her feet and was away. When she did not return for a long time, he decided he must have offended her, or she had not been able to bargain for the robes. But when the shadows of the square were long, and the women setting fire once more under the kettles, she came back, breathless, with two beaver robes which she laid at his feet. Brossard and La Motte had returned, and Brossard came out to examine the furs. "Very fine. Better than one I got at Michilimackinac."

Marc picked up one and put it around his shoulders. The girl laughed at his awkwardness. "Like this." She arranged it over his left shoulder and under the other arm, drawing the lower part closely about his waist.

181

"That's comfortable." He took a few steps up and down.

"That's the way to wear a blanket, too," said Brossard. "What are you giving her?"

Marc drew the emerald from his finger. "No!" said Brossard. "Are you crazy? Wait a minute."

He went back in the lodge and from the now greatly diminished packs of trading goods selected a long string of gaudy blue beads, and tossed them to Marc. "See what you can do with these."

"But I promised her the ring."

"Let her choose, then."

Hesitantly Marc held out the beads in one hand, the ring in the other. The girl looked carefully at both, then smiled and reached for the beads. Looping them about her neck she waited, her eyes on Marc, but as two women approached with kettles, she departed abruptly toward her own lodge. Marc watched her go, wondering whether he felt more guilty or relieved that he had given her a worthless trinket for it instead of the Queen's ring.

"One robe for your brother, *n'est-ce pas?*" La Motte came out of the lodge. "They'll be a help on our eighty-mile walk. It's getting colder all the time."

"You wear one of them until we get back," offered Marc.

"With my thanks. Well, let's eat what we can of this pig's fare, and then pack up our corn and the other gifts. We'll start back in the morning right after I see the chief."

When the square was in shadows once more save for its scattered fires, Father Hennepin returned from eating with the Jesuits. La Motte, sitting outside the lodge with Marc, did not even glance at him.

"What are the Jesuits up to now?" Marc pointed to the far side of the square, where the two black robes were surrounded by painted warriors. An argument was in progress, apparently over a tied-up captive toward whom Father Garnier kept gesturing as he talked.

Father Hennepin sat down, sighing. "Probably they are trying to buy him—to set him free. I tried myself."

A chill gripped Marc. "Then—then they are going to torture him! Is that the entertainment they promised us?"

Father Hennepin nodded sadly.

"I thought it would be some kind of victory dance!" La Motte exclaimed. "You don't mean we have to sit here and watch torture!"

"I'm afraid so. It won't be pleasant. But when it begins, we must on

182

no account interfere. The excitement will be so great that they'd kill us."

All during the evening meal of the returned warriors a keg of Dutch rum made its rounds, each one tipping it up and drinking from the bunghole. As soon as the sun had gone down, the drums began to beat and a wild dance erupted all over the square. Painted and ornamented with beads and feathers, the Seneca warriors threw themselves into a shrieking, leaping frenzy, their feet striking the ground to the beat of rude drums. At the height of the dance, a brave approached the captive with a red-hot gun barrel. Marc sickened to watch the captive writhe as the Seneca stolidly applied the glowing iron to his feet and legs.

The French had fallen into kind of paralysis, but now panic rose among them, a fear for their own safety. What was to prevent this frenzied, drunken crowd from realizing they had other potential victims in their midst?

"I can't stand it another second!" screamed La Motte. "Let's get out of here!"

Not a voice was heard in disagreement, even though to leave now meant certain failure for their mission. With their packs and corn, their guns and snowshoes, they slipped behind the lodge to the palisade, following it to the gate. Beside it stood the young widow.

"I will go with you to see this Queen," the girl said. Marc gasped in consternation. There was no time to argue with her.

"I do not go to France for a long time," he said desperately.

"I will wait with you."

"No! Our leader does not permit women in our camp. Anyway, I already have a woman in my own country."

"You can have more than one wife," she urged stubbornly.

"No. We French don't do that." Marc laughed ruefully. "This is getting nowhere," he said to Brossard. "How can we get away from her?"

"Later," said Brossard to the girl. "Not now. Wait here with your people. Make moccasins for long, long journey."

At this she yielded, drooping in disappointment. "Then you take marriage coat with you," she said sadly to Marc. "You wear it when you come back for me." From under her arm she unfolded a fine deerskin jacket, bleached pale and soft, the finest Marc had seen.

"Take it," said Brossard.

183

Marc bowed. "I will never forget your kindness." As she laid the soft garment across his arm, he added, "Will you tell me something? Why did La Motte fail to get what we wanted?"

She made a gesture that conveyed inadequacy. "He does not make good talk. It takes very good talk when someone has spoken against you before you came. I go now," she said. "You come back soon."

She disappeared into the shadows, and Marc and Brossard ran down the trail to catch up with the others at the river. Silently they crossed, put on their snowshoes, and hastened along the slippery path. The air was sharp with cold, but as they sped along Marc was oblivious of the weather. The scenes in the square kept flooding back into his mind.

After three hours, La Motte came to a stop, exhausted. In a sheltered place beneath closely entangled cedars they put down their packs and wrapped blankets about them. As they bent over their packs, one by one their hands fell away with the realization that they had nothing to eat except ears of corn—and no hand mill for grinding it.

"We can't break our teeth on that," complained one.

La Motte shrugged wearily. "Even if we starve, I'm glad to be here and not back with those devils." He turned on Father Hennepin. "What good is it to preach to people like that?"

Father Hennepin's voice was calm. "I don't expect them to be different until their children get a civilized education." He sighed and drew his blanket closer about him. "Sometimes their tortures are even worse. They keep a victim just barely alive for months."

"I never heard of such barbarity!" exclaimed La Motte.

Marc curled up on the ground, adjusting his body as best he could to the contour of the earth. "Only among civilized men in Europe."

"You must be crazy!" said La Motte.

"Did you never see an accused put to the question, both ordinary and extraordinary, before being executed? And how about a prisoner condemned to the galleys for life, chained to the oar? And the beheadings, tortures, burnings on the Place de Grève? And did you never hear of the Inquisition, or the treatment of Huguenots in the last century?"

"Ah, but the Inquisition is run by priests," snorted La Motte. "What can you expect?"

For once Father Hennepin failed to enter the argument. Snores were already arising from his corpulent form.

The urge to get back among their own kind was so strong that at first they pushed on without food. Then realizing their growing weakness they took time out to hunt. Game was scarce; they brought down only an occasional squirrel. Corn crushed between two wayside rocks was barely edible. Fresh snow kept falling, and the sun shone day after day upon it with unrelenting glare. La Motte's eyes grew so inflamed he could scarcely open them; at last he was completely snowblind and had to be led. Father Hennepin stood the rigors better than the rest, perhaps because of his good constitution and his experience, perhaps from greater reserves in body and mind. When they dropped down in a grove one night, he said, "In truth I am so weary my body can do no more, but since my suffering is in God's service, my soul is at peace."

It was not until the 14th of January that, weary, haggard, and emaciated, they emerged into the clearing about the fragmentary palisades on the Niagara.

"*Vrai dieu!*" Marc stopped in his tracks and then began running weakly toward the storehouse.

"What is it?" demanded La Motte, stumbling along behind, leaning heavily on Brossard. "Take these bandages off my eyes!"

"A soldier in uniform, on guard," said Brossard happily. "Monsieur de la Salle must be here!"

As they neared the storehouse, they heard laughter and French talk. "*Mordieux!*" shouted someone, and Marc yipped with joy. Only one other person on this continent used that expression. He flung the door open. The long room was full of men in deerskins and soldiers' uniforms, their startled faces a mere blur to Marc, half-blinded by snow. And then, clasping his hand, Tonti was there, his handsome oval face lined with fatigue, but his large black eyes sparkling. Two others he recognized as his eyes grew accustomed to the dimness, as Dautray and Jean Michel the surgeon. As La Motte and the others came through the door, Michel took La Motte's arm, asking about the bandages.

"We failed," said La Motte bitterly. "You may as well know."

Marc was frantically searching the crowd with his eyes. "*Mordieux! Let me through!*" came a shout.

"Victor!" Marc pressed through an opening in the crowd. The familiar face had changed in some subtle way. It was thinner, but apparently Victor had stood the rigorous trip well. Here he stood, graceful and elegant as usual in spite of soiled deerskins.

"You look well, I must say." Victor inspected his ragged and dirty twin from head to foot.

"You look a bit strange yourself," retorted Marc.

Victor struck a pose. "It is the duty of an envoy to transform himself into all sorts of things to carry out his duties."

"But I don't see La Salle," Father Hennepin interrupted. "Where is he?"

"He'll be here soon," said Tonti. "It's a long story. After we make you travelers comfortable, we'll tell you the news."

No king of France was ever more tenderly cared for. They were seated on benches on each side of the fire, where Jean Michel put ointment on blisters and cuts. Dry moccasins, shirts and trousers were brought and put on them almost as if they were infants. Bowls were handed them brimming with whitefish and a fine sauce made of the broth. Gradually they began to feel alive again. They were fed; they were warm; and with their own kind. For the moment this was happiness enough.

Marc began to notice a kind of excitement through the storehouse that went beyond joy over the travelers' return. There were mysterious whisperings and glances and a sense of anticipation as the men came and went. It was even in Victor's gaiety. It was everywhere—except in Tonti, who was unusually silent. At last he came to sit on the bench opposite Victor and Marc, and regarded the twins, smiling, "I can tell you apart now. But we'll soon have one as fat as the other."

"Marc is lucky to be alive at all," said La Motte faintly. Jean Michel had settled him on a bench away from the brightness of the fire. "He'd better use the rest of his luck to get back to France."

"We *are* going back!" shouted La Forge, the blacksmith. The words released the pent-up excitement and were repeated in a ragged chorus. "We're all going home!"

Marc looked a startled question at Victor, but Tonti was on his feet. "No!" he said decisively. "We do not go back until Monsieur de la Salle says so."

Moyse, squatting against the log wall, took his pipe from his mouth. "There ain't no other sensible order he can give. We can't go ahead with nothing to eat or work with."

A few murmurs of agreement died under Tonti's severe glance. "It is not for us to make a decision." He turned to La Motte. "You were gone so long we were worried. Do you want to tell us about your trip?"

La Motte emitted a stream of words he had never learned in a spelling book. "Nothing to tell," he concluded. "No fort, no ship."

186

"That doesn't matter now," said Tonti. "We've fixed all that." But La Motte went on muttering oaths and obscenities.

Tonti said mildly, but with authority, "La Salle gave orders against blasphemy."

"He's not here to enforce his orders," said La Motte rudely.

"But I am," said Tonti firmly. La Motte scowled beneath his bandages, but subsided.

Marc was puzzled, too, waiting for Tonti to explain, but as he didn't begin, addressed a question to Victor. "Jacques?"

"At Fort Fontenac," said Victor. "I could see by that time that I'd be taking care of him on this expedition, not he of me. When I read your letter to him, he raised his arms and let them fall and said, 'Might as well.' But he was grinning like a courtier who has just received a million-franc pension, and I swear twenty years dropped off him in that many seconds." Victor chuckled.

"The D'Artagnan sword—you brought it?"

"It's in my pack. I wouldn't trust it in any other hands."

"But where in hell is La Salle?" demanded La Motte.

Tonti roused from his reverie. "We've been having our adventures, too. We had quite a difficult time on the lake. Our ship was larger but crowded with all these soldiers and our own party. And Luc was unskillful, or else he deliberately—well, that's for La Salle to decide. Anyway, he nearly had us on the rocks several times. But on Christmas we got across to the mouth of the Genesee River."

La Motte interrupted, "Then you weren't far from that Seneca village we just came from. The Genesee flows past it."

"We were *in* it," said Tonti. "We needed corn, so La Salle decided to take the two ship's canoes up the river to see the Senecas. We arrived the day after your departure. If you hadn't gone in the middle of the night, you could have returned with us."

Marc and La Motte groaned. Coming back by canoe and ship would have been, by comparison, paradise.

"What did the savages say to you?" demanded La Motte.

"They were a little standoffish at first, but they agreed to a council, and La Salle talked with them—such talk as I have never heard!" Tonti's voice was almost a rhapsody of admiration. "The language was so flattering and so figurative I could hardly follow it at times."

"They'd seen him before," said Victor, "but it wasn't old acquaintance that made them respond. It was the way he handled them. He was as persuasive as when he stood before Louis XIV, even more so, for he seemed completely at home here. He made them believe he was doing them a favor by building a fort and a ship. The next day they granted everything he had asked, and gave him all the corn we could carry. He does know how to handle savages," he added thoughtfully, "and I begin to see that's important in this business."

"So we needn't have taken that wretched trip at all." La Motte fumbled wearily at his bandage.

"But then what's this talk about going back?" asked Marc.

"It was later," said Tonti, "that we had such bad luck. When we got back to the brigantine and embarked for the Niagara, contrary winds slowed our progress. La Salle got so impatient he had himself, me, and Victor set ashore, after ordering Luc to bring the ship to the Niagara's mouth when he could.

"The three of us walked along the shore westward. In the evening we reached the Niagara and ate whitefish and corn porridge with some fishing Senecas. But La Salle couldn't wait—he insisted that we set off by moonlight and walk up here. He was worried to find you weren't back. The next day Victor and I stayed here to rest, but La Salle made a trip farther upriver, following the portage path to where it comes out above the upper rapids. Right there, he says, is a good place to build a ship."

Victor groaned. "I can't get over the walking people do in this country!"

"When he got back here," Tonti resumed, "he set out again for the mouth of the Niagara, to meet the *Frontenac*. And this is the blow: the Senecas told him the *Frontenac* had been wrecked!"

Amid their startled exclamations, he continued, "It seems that after we came ashore, Luc and the sailors left the ship at anchor one night and went to sleep on land. The wind rose so they couldn't get back to her in the morning, and she dragged her anchor, struck on the rocks, and broke up. After hearing this, La Salle set off to the spot, walking another thirty miles. But he could save nothing but some cables and anchors for the new ships. Everything else—our bark canoes, food, supplies, trading goods—everything for the enterprise on the Mississippi, except what you brought, had gone to the bottom."

Marc groaned. "What La Salle must have said to that Luc! But where is La Salle now?"

"We had some dogs on board that were saved, too," said Tonti, "and he and Luc and a few others made sledges and went to bring whatever could be salvaged."

188

"He will have to give up now," said La Motte.

"It may be," said Tonti, "but we won't plan on it until he says so."

After a few days of rest and good food, the seven began to feel more like themselves. Father Hennepin held regular services in his chapel and wrote endlessly in his journal. Tonti asked him about it one day.

"The Jesuits are not the only ones to have adventures in New France," the priest gloated. "This"—he tapped his journal—"will be more widely read some day than their *Relations.*" Tonti smiled and walked away, the priest looking after him in annoyance. With the presence of Tonti, the position of the bossy priest had changed. Tonti, ever mild, made it nevertheless clear that he was in command. But the priest was useful in helping keep the men in order while waiting for La Salle, for with inaction and uncertainty their tempers grew short and their quarrels were frequent.

The weather, so ruthless during the long overland trip, now relented, and a few days later it grew so springlike that Victor and Marc, the beaver robes over their shoulders, went to walk on the riverbank, watching the large blocks of ice sail down.

"I wonder how soon we'll be back in Quebec," said Victor. "The *Cataraqui* is our only way to get there now and it'll take several trips to carry everyone."

"You're happy to be going back?"

"On the first ship that sails!" Victor rejoiced. "Back to a civilized life!" And to Angélique, he thought.

"Well, I'm sorry," said Marc. "I've really enjoyed myself, though it hasn't been easy. I want to go on and build those forts. And I'm sorry for La Salle. All that time and effort and money!"

"I'll admit I've never seen his like," agreed Victor seriously. "I wonder about our money—will he ever pay it back?"

"I don't know. You remember he has more goods and men coming on a ship from France next summer. Maybe he'll keep us all in Quebec until then, and make a new start."

Victor's heart sank, and he walked in gloomy silence for a while. "By the way, how did you get all this beaver?" he asked finally.

"I'm not so proud of that purchase." Marc related the details of his trade, and Victor burst into chuckles. "In driving a bargain, a Norman is without a rival."

"I still think I should have given her the ring."

"*Pas du tout!* She had her choice. The beads certainly were more suited to her costume than poor Marie-Thérèse's emerald. And you're not the first man to take advantage of a girl's infatuation."

Marc changed the subject abruptly by trying to describe the cataract he had seen up the river, knowing that, no matter how many words he used, it would be a shock and a thrill to Victor when he saw it. "If we do go back, we must go up there first. You musn't miss it."

They sat down on rocks close to the rushing water and ice, and Victor filled in the details of his own journey. He had arrived at Fort Frontenac with La Salle the second week in December, and La Salle had been most severe with Luc and Noel, who were still in the guard-house. Still, he had taken them along. He would need every man, he told La Forest, and particularly the two pilots for his ships."

"Do you think Luc deliberately wrecked the *Frontenac?*" asked Marc. "Strange that it happened when everyone was safe on shore."

"I don't know," said Victor soberly. "He tried to recover what he could, even going out in a canoe in dangerous water to do it. If it hadn't been for that, I think La Salle would have skinned him alive. As it is, he can't prove it was anything worse than carelessness."

"But why would La Salle go ashore and set off on foot like that?"

"He hates delay," said Victor, "and he's impatient with details. He can make sound general plans, but he doesn't choose men carefully or supervise them properly. And he dislikes the actual trading for supplies or furs. Tonti took on that part of the job at the Seneca village. He's good at it. Well, anyway, La Salle acted as if he couldn't wait to tell you to start building the fort. Of course he expected Luc to wait for favorable winds and then bring the ship on to an anchorage."

"Understanding a nature like La Salle's might be a long process." Marc rose and adjusted his beaver robe. "Let's go back. He and Luc should arrive sometime today."

"*Eh bien, en avant!*" Victor set off briskly down the path. "The sooner we get out of this wilderness, the better."

22

THE shadows were long in the *Cataraqui's* ravine when La Salle returned, his arrival announced by the yelping of dogs hitched to a crude sledge. Close behind it, bent under heavy packs, came La Salle, Nika, two new Indians with the same Shawano loops on their ears, and a surly Luc.

"The remains of all I had on the *Frontenac.*" La Salle dropped his pack and looked around. "Marc! Father Hennepin! You travelers are back! All is well?"

Father Hennepin pushed forward. "Safe and well, thanks to the good God."

La Salle hastened to welcome La Motte as he was led out of the storehouse, and asked about his bandaged eyes. He included Marc in a warm smile. "I appreciate your attempt to conciliate the Senecas."

"I hear you got everything you asked for," said La Motte unhappily.

"Fortunately, yes. They even gave me permission to carry arms and ammunition over the portage. And I bring further good news: it is now the hunting season and nearly all of them have gone to their hunting grounds below Lake Erie. So we won't see them again till spring."

"*Mille tonnerres!*" exclaimed La Motte. "You talk as if you were going right on, in spite of the shipwreck!"

"But of course I am."

Silence fell over the hillside. Victor, glancing around, saw only disappointment, resentment, and sullenness. But the chagrin was most naked on Luc's face. One needed only to look at him to know he had wrecked the ship on purpose.

An angry murmur grew in the silence as Moyse, his unlit pipe for once forgotten, strode forward as spokesman. "How am I to build a ship, with nothing but cables and anchors, and not enough of those?"

"According to our inventory," said La Salle calmly, "you had on the *Cataraqui* enough sailcloth and ropes for one ship, as well as nailrods, bolts, and tools. All the timbers can be cut on the spot. You can begin work with what you have, while I go back to Fort Frontenac and get whatever else is needed."

After a startled silence, Tonti exclaimed, "Go back? How can you, in all this ice and snow?"

"Through the forest, and over the ice where it's thick enough." La Salle turned to bid Laurent release the dogs and take care of them.

"Two hundred fifty miles!" protested Tonti.

"So it is," said La Salle. "I should be back about the time you have the ship ready to launch."

Victor regarded him with appraising eyes. He can't do it—two hundred and fifty miles in mid-winter!

"Even if you can do the impossible, what will we use for food?" insisted Moyse.

Tonti scowled at him. "We have plenty of corn from the Senecas, and we can hunt."

Moyse scowled. "Well," he said, "I don't think I'll stay——"

La Salle interrupted him. "It's not for you to decide. I stated my terms at Quebec, and you accepted them. I even gave you an advance to pay your debts. You have not yet earned the amount you owe me."

Angrily Moyse turned on his heel and strode off toward the store-house, while the rest of the men melted away. Supper that evening was a glum meal. La Salle himself ate in silence, absently, and Marc could not but wonder why he had made no attempt to improve the morale of his men. Instead of bluntly announcing his decision, why hadn't he talked to them as he had to the Senecas?

In all the room only Father Hennepin's face was serene. After the meal he invited them to a special service in the chapel, and in his sermon tried to compensate for La Salle's omission, exhorting the men to do their duty, promising that God would reward them.

In the middle of the night Victor awoke at the sound of crunching snow. Even before he saw whose blankets were empty, he knew it was La Salle. Maybe he is not so confident after all, he thought. Who would be, faced with such a journey! *Par le sang dieu!* Victor started upright, wide awake. I've got to go with him! The King's orders—not to let him out of my sight! He lay down again, groaning as if in pain. Then he threw off his blanket and went outside.

A faint moonlight revealed the trail along the frozen edge of the river, and La Salle standing by it, staring downstream toward the lake. He turned as Victor approached. "Pretty out here," said Victor, "but, *mon dieu,* how cold!"

"I'm afraid I haven't been appreciating the view."

Victor leaned against the palisade as if to brace himself for the preposterous offer he must make. "Would you like me to go along on that little jaunt?"

La Salle gazed at him so searchingly that Victor grew cold from more than the biting air. "No," he said at last. "You are needed here to help Tonti."

A vast relief swept over Victor. His Majesty wouldn't expect him to insist against a command. "I guess I wouldn't be much use, anyway. I probably couldn't even make it."

"It is well to know one's limitations," said La Salle coolly. "I like your candor about them."

"My only virtue," said Victor sardonically.

"By no means. You are astute, and have more than a little courage, among other things."

"I thank you for that." Victor turned away. He had done his best to follow orders. And nothing about this trip would be of interest to His Majesty.

"Tell me!" La Salle's voice came from the shadows. "You didn't offer to go with the intention of not returning?"

"On my word of honor, sir," said Victor truthfully, "that thought had not entered my head."

The next morning it became clear that the strain of waiting and inaction was over. Victor and Marc helped La Salle sort the cargo of the *Cataraqui* according to what was to go over the portage to the new shipyard and what was to be left at the storehouse, where La Motte would remain with Sergeant le Fleur and his men. These efforts were probably wasted, Victor thought; but if all these men must stay behind while La Salle tries to walk to Fort Frontenac and back, they needed some occupation, and building a ship would do as well as any.

Early in the dawn of January 22, about thirty men, packs on their backs and carrying snowshoes, started climbing the steep incline of the escarpment. La Salle went first, followed by Father Hennepin, his portable altar on his back. The heaviest and most awkward burdens were the anchors. Tonti insisted on helping with them, so he and Marc carried the first between them, while Victor and Dautray brought the other, followed by Nika with a cask of brandy on his shoulders, the blacksmith with his forge and tools, and a line of men bearing other awkward burdens. At the top, they all set their packs down for a rest. Looking back and down, they could see the sheen of Ontario in the distance, and at the left, the heights across the river.

"Beautiful," Victor said to Marc who had come up beside him. "If one has taste for the wild and lonely. But that's a taste I find hard to develop when every step spells danger."

La Salle, overhearing, asked sternly, "Surely you are not really afraid."

Victor grinned. "I've been scared to death ever since we left the soil of France."

La Salle relaxed. "You haven't shown it."

Victor shrugged. "I'm getting used to it. *Enfin, haut le pied!* Let's be off!"

"Did you call us *haut-le-pieds,* homeless wanderers?" asked Tonti. "Sometimes I feel like one. But then I have no place to go back to, as you have."

"Usually absence from court means degenerating into a turnip," said Victor, "but it looks as if we'll never stay in one place long enough to become even a decent vegetable. We ought to have some good stories to tell when we get back—at least we'll make them good!"

The men were laughing as they rose to lace on snowshoes and resume their loads, and La Salle smiled as he went ahead. It was easier going now, on the level trail, and soon Father Hennepin began to sing, joyously and loud, a true disciple of St. Francis rejoicing in the brotherhood of nature.

"What's that noise?" asked Victor, when a dull roar came through the forest from their right.

"The cataract," Father Hennepin called back; and Marc added, "This path must cut across that sharp bend in the river where it falls."

As they plodded on, Father Hennepin began extolling in his pointless rhetoric the wonders of the great fall of water.

"Is it really so great?" La Salle asked Marc.

Marc answered simply, "You must see it, sir. It's worth the trouble." He rather admired his understatement.

La Salle nodded. "I shall visit it, then, but not until we get the ship started."

Marc shook his head. How single-minded he is! I would never pass over this trail as many times as he has without going to see what made that noise.

About six miles above the cataract they crossed a frozen creek, following a trail between tall bare oaks, until La Salle led them to a willow-hung bank.

"What do you think of this, Moyse?"

Even the ship carpenter could find nothing wrong with the site. They were standing at the edge of a narrow channel that had been diverted from the Niagara by an island. Though its current was swift, it had none of the speed and turbulence of the main river rushing down toward the cataract.

"It might have been made for us," exulted La Salle. "At the end of a good, broad portage path and in a sheltered place."

Moyse wandered about thoughtfully, his eternal pipe in his mouth, studying the terrain and the river, and finally nodded approval. "It's a good place. If you can get her out into the river afterward."

"You build her, Moyse." La Salle was exuberant. "We'll get her out."

23

NIKA and the other Shawanos had left on a turkey hunt, and La Salle was already out on the slope, marking for Moyse the best place for the ship's stocks. The early morning light followed La Salle up to the level ground above, where he scratched in snow and earth the outlines of four cabins, a chapel, and a dwelling for Father Hennepin. He gave every man an assignment. Tonti was given workmen to clear the slope; Dautray and Jean Michel with four others were sent back over the portage path to bring more goods from the storehouse; and Victor and Marc went with Moyse and his helpers to the nearest grove, where, hatchet in hand, Moyse stolidly appraised the trees and blazed the ones he wanted.

Away from the fire the air was bitterly cold. At first the twins were awkward at this strenuous work; yet it was exciting as the axes sank again and again into the living wood and the cut deepened until at the tree's heart one last stroke sent the great trunk crashing to the earth. With blistered hands and aching backs, the workers returned at midday to the kettles steaming with turkey and squirrel stew from the morning's hunt. Now that there was enough to eat and work to do, discontent gradually disappeared. Voices echoed cheerfully back and forth across the slope, laced with snatches of song.

But the gaiety was abruptly checked when, on the fourth day, Moyse stopped in his tracks, grunted, and called back to La Salle, "Thought you said they had all gone away!"

Some distance up the portage path stood four Seneca warriors, their black eyes taking in everything that was going on. "Go back to your jobs," La Salle ordered quietly. "They are just curious." After cautious activity had been resumed, the Senecas watched for perhaps an hour and vanished. Afterward they came once or twice a day, and the workmen grew nervous, constantly aware of jet-black eyes watching from the thickets. Once a carpenter who had laid down his hatchet found it gone when he reached for it. But the work itself was actually spurred. More white oaks fell and were sawed into planks and ribs; a particularly fine one was trimmed and shaped for the keel. The blacksmith assembled his forge; and with a helper at the bellows, began making square spikes from nailrods. The portage path was incessantly tramped up and down, all taking turns carrying goods from the storehouse. A magazine was built and their ammunition stored in it. Axes rang from morning to night, the woods resounding with their strokes. The young surgeon was constantly in demand to treat cuts, bruises and blisters. To augment the Norwegian pitch they had brought from La Rochelle the voyageurs gathered gum from the fir trees, melted and purified it.

La Salle appeared to be everywhere at once, always ready to give a hand where one was needed. But it was Tonti who took over the details, issuing the tools and checking them in at night, making lists of what was needed, looking after injuries and complaints, supervising the building of the cabins that took shape slowly because Father Hennepin was constantly removing carpenters to work on his chapel. While its walls were rising, the busy Recollet set up his altar in the open air. A black cloth stretched over two supports became a confessional closet, while the priest's stool was a foot-length of log set on end. Another such log made a stool for the basin of holy water. The boys saw that, despite his human frailty, he was dignified, sincere, and devout before his altar, and his influence was strong, for these simple Frenchmen were accustomed to the authority of a curé. Even the

Senecas began appearing at vespers, staring in open admiration at the splendid priestly vestments.

On January 26, the keel of the ship was laid, and Moyse came to La Salle, his broad face shining with pride. "Ready for the first bolt, m'sieu!"

"*A la bonne heure!* Let's do it with ceremony. Call the men together, Moyse."

Enthusiastically he rounded up his associates himself, and in their log cabin, the first one made habitable, they put on their dress clothes or uniforms while he donned his scarlet and gold. Nika disappeared to put on his best deerskins, heavily embroidered with beads and porcupine quills. When he reappeared, flanked by the other two Indians, he looked like the chief's son he was.

Outside, Marc, Victor, Tonti, and Dautray, waited with La Salle while the workmen came from woods and slope to form a half circle about the stocks. After days of intense cold the air was milder.

"Where are our Seneca friends?" murmured Jean Michel as he came up, strange in plain blue homespun. "Don't tell me they are going to miss this!"

Victor grimaced. "I wish they *would* appear. The invisible ones worry me more than those I can see."

The circle was complete. La Salle stepped forward, and stood facing them beside the keel. "I shall not make a long speech, but I called you together to remind you that it is our privilege to stand here at a place and a moment that will have meaning in the history of this new land, this new empire of our beloved France. We are laying the keel of the first ship to sail these great inland seas. Many more will follow this one, and they may be larger. But none of them can be the first. Our ship has that honor and privilege, and no one can ever take that distinction from us. Let us be both proud and humble that God has so honored us." He paused, and the silence deepened, broken only when a glistening crow passed above, uttered one raucous cry, and winged swiftly toward the island elms. La Salle's eyes roamed the circle until they lighted on the portly friar. "Father Hennepin, will you accept the honor of driving the first bolt?" he asked courteously.

But strangely the friar, usually so eager to be the center of interest, held back, his round face dully inscrutable. "Thank you, Monsieur, but I do not feel it is suitable to my calling. My turn will come in the blessing of the ship, if—I mean, when it is completed."

"As you wish, Father."

Marc wondered why the priest had refused. Mere resentment toward La Salle? Or could it be that he was convinced the ship would never sail and, as in the Seneca village when he walked out of La Motte's council, he refused to be associated with failure?

Tonti cleared his throat. "I think, Monsieur de la Salle, you should drive the bolt yourself. Without your vision and your effort there would have been no ship."

A murmur of agreement went around the circle. La Salle bowed and took the bolt and hammer from La Forge's hands. Moyse brought the first rib and held it in position, and La Salle drove the bolt straight and true.

"*Vive la France! Vive le Roi! Vive La Salle!*" When the cheers died away, La Salle smilingly raised his hand. "I think a drink is next in order: bring out a cask of brandy!"

With shouts of delight, the workmen broke up the circle and a cask was rolled out. Toasts were drunk, both gay and solemn.

"The name of the ship?" asked Tonti.

"Yes, she must be named," said La Salle thoughtfully. "I should like to honor the Governor for his help and support. But we had a ship named the *Frontenac*. The Buade, perhaps. Or something from his coat of arms might be a subtle compliment. Eagle's claws, a griffin——"

"The griffin, sir," Marc offered respectfully, "is an important symbol in alchemy: a combination of the lion and the eagle, that is, of the fixed and the volatile."

La Salle beamed at him warmly. "The fixed and the volatile! Then it's the perfect name for a ship! And may the *Griffin* ever fly above the ravens!"

The boys glanced at each other in a new recognition of how much this ship meant to La Salle, how intense was his anticipation that she would lead him to success in spite of his persistent black-robed enemies. "I'm glad to drink to that," murmured Victor.

The cups were filled once more, and the toast was drunk. "Vive le *Griffin!*"

La Salle turned to Moyse. "Can you make a griffin figurehead for her?"

"I am not familiar with the animal," said the sturdy Dutchman. La Salle looked from one to the other, but all faces were dubious.

"Victor could do it," said Marc. "He carved a good plaque in Quebec."

He got the expected startled glance from his brother, but the hazel eyes filled almost at once with thoughtful interest. "I might try it," said Victor slowly.

"Good!" La Salle swung around to face the whole circle. "Then let us be proud that the *Griffin* is a French ship, and build her accordingly. Monsieur Tonti," he added formally, "you will be in command here after I leave for Fort Frontenac."

"Oh, by the way, I'm going with you," said Father Hennepin. "I ought to see about getting more priests for the missions we'll establish."

"I can attend to that. Your work is here," said La Salle, plainly not intending to be burdened by the fat priest just because he was too restless to stay in one place. "Nika will go with me; the other two Shawanos will stay here to hunt. Monsieur la Motte and Marc will go as far as the mouth of the Niagara, to remain there in charge of building a fort. Perhaps Monsieur Tonti should accompany me that far, to acquaint himself with the general fort plan, and then return here to the shipyard."

Tonti nodded. "What shall we call the new fort?"

This time La Salle was ready. "Fort Conti. In honor of your benefactor and mine at court."

La Salle was determined to set off, *bon gré mal gré;* so he and Nika made a new dog sledge to drag provisions and baggage over the ice. He selected a canoeman and the baggage of the three was strapped on the sledge, with one small bag of parched corn, all La Salle would consent to take from their small store of provisions.

"That pigheaded Luc!" said Tonti. "If he did wreck the *Frontenac* on purpose he ought to be hanged! Two hundred fifty miles ahead of you on his account, through forests full of snow and Iroquois!"

"I don't doubt he ought to be hanged," agreed La Salle. "But we'll need him to pilot the *Griffin.*"

As the little pilgrimage set out for the mouth of the Niagara, an early morning rain that froze as it fell had turned the portage path to sleet. La Salle, Nika, and the canoeman were followed by Marc, Tonti, and a dozen men not needed in shipbuilding. At the storehouse they were joined by Sergeant le Fleur, his soldiers, and La Motte de Lussière. La Motte, still complaining about his eyes, was despondent and at first insisted on going along to Fort Frontenac. "And I want my money now, too," he said.

"You are in no condition for a long trip," La Salle pointed out. "And as for your pay, you agreed to wait until the expedition is over."

Muttering rebelliously, La Motte went with them to the bluff at the Niagara's mouth. Here La Salle and Marc laid out the positions of two blockhouses and the stockade, and Marc started to draw up detailed plans for the fort and its buildings.

As La Salle was giving his final instructions, Tonti asked, "What about the fifteen men that went ahead? They'll be waiting much longer than they expected."

"Hinaut is a capable man," said La Salle confidently. "And he has two of my best voyageurs, Chapelle and Leblanc—no relation to the carpenter, Noel. They can all maintain themselves in the woods indefinitely. Now if you have any trouble with the men here, just remind them of the alternative: punishment for a servant's desertion is to be set in the pillory for the first offense and whipped and branded for the second. Or if I wish I can invoke the penalty for military desertion: death."

After La Salle's party had disappeared beyond a distant curve of the shore and the fort was well started, Tonti went back on the long trek to take up his duties at the shipyard.

La Motte, though he did work, was so apathetic that nothing would have been done if the men had not, fortunately, taken their pace from Marc, who was enthusiastic about the site and eager to put into practice what he had learned from M. Vauban. But when Senecas began watching from the woods, the workmen grew uneasy. Marc kept a steady procession of logs moving toward the fort site only by pointing out that the sooner they built an enclosure, the safer they'd be. Father Hennepin visited them occasionally, tramping cheerfully back and forth on the twenty-one-mile trail from shipyard to fort, carrying messages and news of progress. He reported that the Senecas came also to the shipyard every day to gaze at the ribs of the strange monster with fear and jealousy, and that they had formally protested at such an elaborate fort being built on the lake. Finally he brought a letter from Tonti, recommending that Marc build only a single stockade and one house inside it for the soldiers, and leave the planned outer stockades, pits, and ramparts until La Salle came back. Marc was disappointed, but pressed the work forward. The cold and snow continued, and February seemed the dreariest month of the year. Marc was lonely and missed Victor. La Motte was worse company than no one at all and his complaints were keeping the men in a state of further unrest.

Finally he announced that he couldn't endure such a life, and was going to set out for the east to return to France. Despite Marc's arguments, he went, taking half the workmen with him, including the crew of the *Cataraqui*. Marc nevertheless finished the house and stockade, lettered FORT CONTI on a board over the entrance, installed the sergeant and his men, and started back to the shipyard.

On the little rise of land above the half-finished ship, Victor worked on his most personal contribution, a fairly credible lion with extended eagles' wings. He had been supplied by Moyse with the paint he was now putting on it: bronze for its body, red for the wings. March's mild breezes blew off the water, lifting his hair and stirring the fringes of his jacket. Beside him, next to the D'Artagnan sword he kept constantly with him, was a half-drained mug of a new drink made by the Indian hunters from the sweet sap of certain trees. Victor regarded the ship thoughtfully. In spite of Moyse's eternal grumbling at the lack of proper supplies and tools, he had pride in his craft. Knowing that these lakes were no place for a weak vessel, he had continually demanded perfection from his helpers. Strength had gone into her, and careful fitting and bolting, as the hull had taken shape; and now the afterhouse was rising upon the largest ship he had built for La Salle. The deck was nearly laid and caulked with pitch, the seams scraped flush, making neat black stripes. She had ports to carry two small brass cannon and three *arquebuses à croc*. The elevated house at the stern was to be tall and highly ornamented; and already the craft had a special rakishness and grace of line that bespoke a French shipyard. There seemed a special sleekness even in the four newly made canoes lying beside her, waiting to serve as ship's boats.
All was well—except for the uneasiness caused by seven Senecas lying on the ground by themselves, watching and being watched by the carpenters. At the sound of footsteps on the portage path, Victor turned quickly and then leaped up, waving his paintbrush. Marc was coming, followed by a line of workmen, all heavily loaded.
"I thought you'd never get here," said Victor.
Marc came up to him, and grinning, swung down his pack. The other men filed on past to the cabins, regarding the wooden figurehead with surprise. "A masterpiece," said Marc, his sincere admiration augmented by contentment that they were together again. "Where did you learn to carve like that?"
"Mostly right here," said Victor. "I learned on this." He lifted the

201

wings carefully and held the figure upright. *"Regard-toi,* it will look something like this on the ship. I think it's pretty good, too."

Marc laughed, but his eyes had gone beyond to the ship. "It's going to be a handsome craft! I expected it to be more crude. Is everything all right? . . ." He stopped to wave a salute to Tonti, who was coming up the slope to join them.

Tonti shook his head. "We're not exactly overloaded with good cheer."

"How can we be cheerful?" Victor pointed to the Senecas, who were eyeing the new arrivals. "The suddenness of their appearance, the way they sit or lie, as if coiled to strike—" He broke off with a gesture of disgust.

"Any real trouble with them?" asked Marc.

"No clashes," said Tonti, "but the larger the ship has become, the more they've pestered us. They show up in numbers at mealtime and of course we have to feed them. It's dangerous to do it when our supplies are so low, but more dangerous not to. They demand other things —blankets, tools, clothes—and when they don't get them, they're sullen. We've given them a lot we couldn't spare."

"Placatingly," added Victor, "as one would worship a serpent, out of fear."

"Meanwhile," said Tonti, "in the guise of friendship they are steadily consuming our provisions. Sometimes they stage fierce debates among themselves, or simply stalk up and down the shore. Their silent movement is threatening in itself—but how is Fort Conti?" The soft Italian voice lingered with pleasure on the name.

"All finished and turned over to Sergeant le Fleur."

"Good." Tonti smiled. "We progress. Two of La Salle's goals achieved: one fort, one ship."

Two steps toward going home, thought Victor. Why doesn't La Salle come so we can get on with the rest of it?

"But La Motte is gone," Marc added. "And he took some of the men with him. I'm sorry about that."

As he listened to the details, Tonti shook his head sadly. "La Motte is no loss, but I hope La Salle hears of this desertion and brings other workmen and sailors when he comes. I'm worried about the discontent among our workmen, too. But I'd better get back to them." He strode away, a slight figure, impressive in his determination and purpose.

"He has worked hard," said Victor. "A lot of the very seams on that deck have been scraped by his one good hand. Night and day he's alert to keep the men in good spirits, but the atmosphere is infested with the poison of desertion. Noel le Blanc—one of those we saw at the Jesuits'," he added significantly, "has actually run away twice, but Messier and Laurent traced him both times and brought him back. Of course, everybody's tired of the food. Our corn is gone and the Senecas refuse to trade us any more. Wild game, meal after meal, makes a monotonous diet."

"They must know there'll be worse discomfort in desertion," said Marc.

"That's what Father Hennepin keeps telling them. The Father has been a pretty good influence, especially with the Bretons. True to pattern, they're more pious than us Normans. But he can't manage to behave decently to Tonti, who is by far the best man of the lot."

Hearing no response, he glanced up. Marc was staring across the clearing. One of the lounging Senecas had got up and was staggering about as if he were drunk; but his apparently aimless circles were bringing him closer and closer to the forge, where the glowing fire lighted the perspiration on the smith's red face and hairy chest, as he laid a red-hot nailrod on the anvil and began to square the end. Occasionally the Seneca knelt and jabbed the earth with a long knife, glaring at the workmen as if wishing his knife were meeting flesh instead. Sometimes with his left hand he gathered his fingers against the thumb and let them spring open as he threw out his arm toward the smith, who was now covertly watching him. And then, as the watchers were beginning to realize that this was no mere gasconade, like the strike of a reptile the savage made for the smith with upraised knife. The boys yelled and ran down the slope as La Forge seized the glowing nailrod in his tongs and held it grimly in front of him, like a fencer on guard. The savage stopped in his tracks, and began to circle, watching the glowing rod. Everyone was converging on the spot at once. Father Hennepin flapped his arms and yelled at the savage, as Tonti ran up behind him and fetched him a clip across the skull. The savage yelled, dropped his knife, and clapped his hands to his head, staring in surprise at Tonti. "Iron-Arm!" he yelped, and turned and ran, completely sober now. The other Senecas, their eyes appraising Tonti with new respect, swiftly followed.

"*Eh bien, l'affaire a été chaude!*" panted Tonti.

The smith put his nailrod back into the fire. "Wish I'd singed him a little."

"They're smart enough to see that without your nails we couldn't

203

finish the ship," said Tonti. "He pretended to be drunk, so if he killed anyone the tribe could say it was the liquor. Brossard says that's a favorite trick of theirs. All right, back to work, everyone." The men, watchful for some moments, drifted back to their jobs.

"Well, Iron-Arm," said Victor gaily, "thanks to you that matter was as soon over as love in Spain."

Tonti laughed. "A good firm hand has its uses."

This incident, the first real show of violence from the Senecas, completed the demoralization of the camp. Discontent, never far submerged, now boiled angrily. Idleness, now that the ship was nearly complete, was an ally of discontent, as was the diet devoid of bread, wine, pepper, or salt. Inadequately fed and poorly housed, the men were restless and moody, afraid of savages and starvation, resentful because no wages had been paid. Tonti was everywhere, heartening and persuading, and Father Hennepin preached to them.

"I'd rather have a bowlful of good pea soup than all his sermons," grumbled Moyse after one of these exhortations. He complained constantly about having no pay, though he was still in La Salle's debt. And since the workmen had respect for him as an able craftsman, they respected his opinions as well. Noel Le Blanc was now so persistent in urging his fellow workers to desert that it became evident he had joined for that purpose, expecting his pay from some other source than La Salle.

Tonti finally threatened the man with severe punishment. That night he deserted again, but Tonti's vigilance made certain he went alone.

Even Father Hennepin took to complaining about La Salle's long absence. "Why doesn't he send me word what he's doing and when to expect him?"

Marc was tired of this oft-repeated litany. "It's his nature to keep his own counsel. And experience with treachery has confirmed him in it."

"Leaving me here with no one to help encourage the men," grumbled the priest. Tonti merely sighed.

Spring came slowly, advancing and retreating, but at last the ice was gone and the forest came back to life. Tonti and Cochois talked of getting the *Cataraqui* ready to sail, but want of an experienced crew made them decide to wait for La Salle. The sound of axes was replaced by that of hoes striking on stones, as Tonti laid out gardens to be planted to corn for next winter's supply. Marc contributed Auguste's seeds. Then he and Victor began exploring the neighborhood for Marc's journal on flora and fauna. It became their Sunday habit to walk down to the cataract, and one Sunday in early May, Marc was sitting near the head of the roaring waterfall, amid its light drifting mist, while Victor wandered back along the rapids, studying birds on the wing to aid him in carving an eagle.

Marc began to feel the peculiar contentment of one who is just where he most wants to be. I'm glad I didn't miss this, he thought. And I would have if the King hadn't sent Victor. Why did he, when so many older, more experienced men would seem a better choice? As he sighed at this enigma his ears caught a slight clicking sound. He glanced idly behind him and jumped, startled, to his feet. An Indian girl was gliding down the trail—the girl from the Seneca village!

She came up smiling, sure of her welcome, as he recovered himself and bowed. "What a surprise! Come and sit down." He indicated the mossy bank, but she made insistent motions that he sit first, and then settled beside him in companionable silence. He saw she was wearing his beads. In her hands were a number of willow twigs. He touched them and asked in Iroquois, "What for?"

"To smoke. *Kinnikinnick*." She explained that a band of Senecas was camped near here now, and she had come to gather these sticks. She showed Marc how the outer bark would be discarded, and the inner stripped off and laid to dry in the sun, before being stored in buckskin bags to use as tobacco. "I make it for you," she said.

"Thank you, but I don't use it," he said.

"No?" Throwing aside the twigs as of no further consequence, she smiled warmly. "I go with you to see queen. You go soon now."

Even in his embarrassment, Marc realized that she was really beautiful. And he saw too that she would fade in Versailles as quickly as one of the new violets on the riverbank.

"You worry about me and your other wife? Don't worry. My father have three."

Baffled by his inadequacy in the Iroquois tongue, he stammered, "I won't go to see the Queen for a long time. First we sail the big ship." He pointed west.

"No. You go home. I think my people will not try again to harm you unless they are very drunk. They think you must be spirits to build such a big canoe so fast. No one has ever seen canoe so big. And you have a medicine man making strong pieces of iron to hold it together. Your chief even has a hand of iron," she added in wonder. "But soon my people will burn your big canoe, before it ever feels water."

"What?"

"Yes," she said with unruffled composure. "It was decided in council. And then you go home and I go with you." Her gaze was as provocative as that of any streetwalker on the Pont Neuf.

Marc rose. He must go back and warn Tonti. But how could he keep this girl from following him? The worst of it was that he was beginning to feel an attraction to her.

"Your La Salle must go back. At once. I have had a dream." She followed him along the path.

He stopped. What was he to do with her? "What kind of dream?" he asked to gain time.

"I saw two trails your leader can take. One leads back to his big fort. If he takes that one he can lead a long and happy life and have many children and grandchildren to tend his grave. If he takes the other"—she gestured to the west—"I do not see him returning. I see no children about his grave."

Marc was impressed in spite of himself. "What about me? Do you see me coming back?"

She made no answer, but stared behind him, her eyes widened in fright. He whirled around. It was only Victor, coming along the path. At sight of the girl he bent himself double in the most gallant of bows.

"*Ai-ee!*" She looked from one to the other, backing away, and then fled through the woods in terror.

Marc mastered his impulse to run after her.

"I thought you had started talking to squirrels," said Victor. "Who is she?"

"The one I got the beaver robes from."

"*Nom du chien!*" exclaimed Victor. "I feel myself surpassed by my infant brother. No dark beauty follows me all over the wilderness."

"Will you shut your mouth? I'm trying to think what scared her off like that."

"Me, of course. Your double. She probably thinks you are a sorcerer and can split yourself in two. Or maybe that your spirit had left your body and was walking by itself."

Marc shrugged. "Well, for once the resemblance was useful. I didn't want her to follow me to the shipyard."

"She ran like one who has no intention of coming back."

Marc nodded, concealing an unreasonable sense of loss. "Well, come on—I have to see Tonti. I'll tell you on the way."

The news of this new threat threw the camp into confusion, out of which Tonti brought order as fast as he could. "We'll set guards, every hour of the day and night." He went to the stocks to confer with Moyse. "How long before she could be launched?"

Moyse looked appraisingly at the hull. "Another day would finish the caulking so she could be put into the water. But you can't sail her until La Salle gets back."

"I don't intend to. But wouldn't the two anchors we have hold her here in the inlet? It would be harder for the savages to get at her."

"Then we'd better put her out there."

Everyone worked at preparing and filling in pitch. By the second day she was ready to be towed out. "We can work on the rigging and sails after she's afloat," Moyse reported to Tonti. "We've got the cables on. But it'll take every man here to pull her out."

"We'll have a launching ceremony first," Tonti decided. "This is an occasion, even if we are in a hurry. Someone call Father Hennepin."

So the stout friar took his place in the midst of the assembled men, with the inevitable half-dozen Senecas watching from the edge of the forest. And while a kingfisher darted across the shade with a flash of blue, Father Hennepin pronounced his blessing on the *Griffin*. The gun crew loaded and fired the cannon, and the Senecas scrambled behind trees or threw themselves flat. As the echoes died away, Victor and Marc led in a Breton sailors' litany.

As the last notes faded, every Frenchman rushed to the cables, and tugged with shouts of excitement. At last they felt her moving down the stocks, and scrambled out of her way. "Thus saith the Lord," shouted Father Hennepin, "who maketh a way in the sea and a path in the mighty waters." They held their breath as the *Griffin* slid down the slope and, with a great splash, settled into the stream. There was pride on every face as they saw their creation actually afloat.

Moyse came up, pride replacing his sullenness. "We've got her anchors set. She'll ride there all right," he said in answer to Tonti's warm congratulations. "And I'm goin' to ride with her. I'll feel a lot safer under her deck." A dozen other voices clamored until, with Tonti's permission, everyone finally spent the night in hammocks slung under the decks.

On Sunday, the 20th of May, Father Hennepin set up his altar on the *Griffin's* deck and conducted Mass, with the men on shore beneath the willows. While they knelt for the benediction, someone was heard coming down the portage path. The congregation sprang to its feet and ran up past the cabins, to break into happy shouts as from the woods emerged two grinning voyageurs in the red caps of Montreal. One of them held a bulky letter. "From Captain la Forest," he said, as he handed it to Tonti.

"Monsieur de la Salle?" demanded Tonti, in a voice choked with anxiety.

"He is well."

"Thank God," said Tonti fervently, "but why hasn't he come back?" Opening the letter, he read the first sheet aloud. La Forest wrote that La Salle had been delayed, but the enclosed sheets were his navigation directions. If the *Griffin* was ready to sail, Tonti was to launch her and, with Luc as pilot, take all the company except a guard for the shipyard and sail through the lakes. At the southern tip of the Lake of the Illinois they were to join the fifteen men sent on the year before.

So La Salle was coming back, and going on with his exploration. That means, thought Victor, that I'm committed by the King's orders to see it through. A wave of desolation went over him. His reunion with Angélique was again pushed far into the future. He felt alone in his depression, for Marc, beside him, was grinning with delight. And when the first wave of disappointment had gone, Victor realized that, in fact, he would not want to miss the sailing of the *Griffin*.

Tonti was plainly aghast at the responsibility that had descended upon him. "Well," said Victor, "we'll soon have a new problem: getting our sea legs."

Moyse turned aside and spat. "What the hell's he thinking about? We need another anchor, and even if we could contrive that, we aint got enough men to sail her."

"We'll have to try," said Tonti with a cheerfulness he was far from feeling. "Did you come alone?" he asked the messengers.

"No. We brought a crew to sail the *Cataraqui* back to Fort Frontenac. You are to send Cochois to pilot her. They've got her launched in the river already."

The longing to be going back leaped into so many faces that Tonti said quickly, "If you have letters or messages, you can send them by Cochois or these men."

"Letters for France, too?" asked Victor. "The ships will soon be coming across."

At Tonti's nod, he turned away with such haste to get paper and quill to assure Angélique of his continued devotion that he charged into the gray bulk of Father Hennepin, surplice and chasuble over his arm. "I'll take charge of your letters, my boy," he said jovially. "I'll be going on the *Cataraqui* myself."

"*Sacré dieu!*" Tonti whirled around in anger. "La Salle's orders are for us all to stay here and get the *Griffin* under way."

"I am under higher orders than his or yours," said Father Hennepin, with a slight imitation of Tonti's accent, glaring as if he hated equally what he said and the Italian intonation in which he said it. "You won't get the *Griffin* out. And I need to go into retreat after my strenuous winter."

"Then you must take full responsibility for deserting your post," said Tonti angrily.

Father Hennepin bristled. "You are not the one to talk about desertion. Any Italian in the French navy has deserted the service of his natural prince. And of course I shall return. I wouldn't abandon my expedition."

"*Your* expedition!" Tonti shook his head in wonder and disgust.

After the departure of the bustling priest, Tonti and Moyse studied the problem of getting the *Griffin* out to sea. It wouldn't be hard to get her out of the channel into the river, they decided, but sails would never move her against the swift Niagara current. She would have to be towed all the way to the open lake, about fifteen miles. With a small crew on board, the rest pulled her out of the inlet; and after days of herculean effort towed her as far as the entrance to Lake Erie. But against the strong wind and current encountered there, they couldn't move her another inch. Tonti had to admit defeat. He hadn't enough men to get her into the lake. With a guard on board, he left her at anchorage in the river under shelter of a nearby island.

24

VICTOR had plenty of time to carve and gild his eagle, while June and July passed with no further word from La Salle, a tiresome and frustrating wait, though the summer was pleasant along the Niagara, and the Senecas gave no more trouble. As soon as the *Cataraqui* began making regular trips with ample supplies of food, the men began almost to enjoy the easy life, with only guard duty at camp and on the *Griffin,* weeding the gardens, and making occasional trips to the storehouse and Fort Conti.

On the 4th of August they were all working on board the *Griffin,* still at anchor near Lake Erie, when they heard a hail and saw a familiar gray bulk in an approaching canoe. "Father Hennepin," said Victor, "and Sergeant le Fleur. The *Cataraqui* must be in again."

"The ship looks fine," panted the stout priest when they hauled him on board. "But I was terribly worried to find no one at the shipyard——"

Tonti interrupted. "But where is La Salle?"

"On the *Cataraqui.* He's having Cochois bring her up to anchor at the storehouse."

"At last! God be praised!" said Tonti. "Did he get everything he needs?"

"I guess so. The ship seems to be full. We brought three more priests."

Tonti turned to Victor. "He'll need us all for portaging. Most of us had better go back to the storehouse."

Victor, Marc, and Dautray exchanged glances. Though Tonti would have died rather than say so, he always suffered immeasurably on that twelve-mile portage, with his slight physique and one hand, since he always allotted to himself the heaviest or most awkward load. "I think La Salle would want you to stay with the *Griffin,*" said Marc. "It's his most valuable possession."

"Very well," said Tonti reluctantly. "Then Moyse and I will get her ready for inspection. La Salle won't lose any time in coming to see her."

Father Hennepin ambled across the deck and stared at the griffin and eagle. "Now you must make me a statue of St. Anthony for my chapel, Victor." There was no need to answer, for he continued to bustle about the deck, giving orders. As they were about to set off in the ship's canoes, he added the last one, "Now, Monsieur Tonti, don't sail the *Griffin* out without further orders."

Tonti answered with a straight face. "I assure you, Moyse and I won't try to get her into the lake by ourselves."

As soon as they had beached their canoes at the shipyard, Victor,

Marc, and Dautray, finding that La Salle had not arrived, set out over the portage path to meet him. About two miles along it, Dautray, in the lead, shouted, "There he is!" and began to run. Coming around a curve that skirted a close-set grove of cedars was indeed the familiar tall figure, followed by Nika, three Recollets, and a line of men all heavily loaded.

"Dautray! Victor! Marc!" La Salle swung down his pack, and returned their salutes. "It's good to see you again."

"And you, sir," said Dautray. "It's been a long time."

"Too long," said La Salle. "But I hope we can go ahead together now. Tonti is well?" Barely waiting for their answer, he congratulated Marc on the building of Fort Conti. "And now to get the *Griffin* out! With all this added help, we'll soon have her in the lake." He turned to the priests behind him. One was Father Ribourde, whom they knew from their stay at Fort Frontenac, and he introduced the others as Father Watteau, who would remain at the shipyard, and Father Membré, who would go with Fathers Ribourde and Hennepin to the West. A pallid youth behind them he presented as the Sieur Boisrondet, so thin he looked as if a breeze would blow him into the river. "Now, let us hurry. I want to see what the *Griffin* looks like."

Since Father Hennepin, waiting at the shipyard, had already seen the ship, he elected to stay and show the new priests his chapel. Meanwhile La Salle hastily embarked in the canoes with Nika, Victor, Marc, and Dautray, taking his turn at the paddles in the hard fifteen-mile pull against the current. After questioning them about their work in the past months, he said, "You'll be glad to hear that the father commissary of the Recollets appointed Father Ribourde to be the superior on the expedition, assisted by Fathers Hennepin and Membré."

Dautray smiled. "Tonti will be glad someone else now has the task of keeping Father Hennepin in his place. Did you get enough supplies to replace what was lost in the shipwreck?"

"Yes, plenty," La Salle called back from his place in the bow, "and my shipload of goods and men should soon arrive from La Rochelle." He fell silent, staring upriver in tense expectancy. They swung around the end of the island that sheltered her, and there she was, full in the sun, gracefully swinging at her anchors, bowsprit steeved upward, her masts raked slightly aft, the griffin's bronze scales and fiery wings springing out from the prow.

"Big canoe," said Nika in a tone of awe.

"She's superb!" La Salle choked with emotion as his eyes searched

out every detail from bow to stern. "Sleek, with fine proportions, tidy.
. . . And that figurehead!" He looked at Victor in surprise. "Did you
really do that?"

"Yes, he did," interposed Dautray. "It took him a long time."

"And it was something you didn't have to do." La Salle's voice
showed how deeply he was touched.

"I'm glad that it suits you," Victor said formally.

Tonti and Moyse, from the deck, saluted, grinning, as they approached. On board, La Salle embraced them both with warm compliments, and hastened eagerly with them from stern to forecastle, touching, inspecting, and praising everything above and below decks, with
a happy enthusiasm in contrast to his usual reserve.

Tonti joined them for the return to the shipyard, and as they were
borne lightly downstream, La Salle's enthusiasm bubbled over. "Imagine how important such a ship will be to the fur trade, now limited
to what can be carried in bark canoes. Who knows what may come
of it in the future? Once the interior is secured for France, perhaps
even the route to China will be found at last."

"I'm glad," said Dautray, "that everything's going well for you at
last."

A slight cloud passed over La Salle's joy. "Not quite everything, I'm
afraid." As the Niagara bore them rapidly downstream, he told them
that at the end of his long journey he had learned that the Jesuit-
merchant factions in Montreal and Quebec, having heard that his
ship was being built in spite of all hardships, had started rumors that
this harebrained adventurer was already penniless and hopelessly in
debt. La Salle's creditors were so aroused that they seized all his property. "Even your bed, Victor," he added with a wry smile. "So you see
how thorough they were. And it was so unnecessary. Fort Frontenac
alone is worth enough to pay all my debts if I don't return."

Tonti murmured his sympathy. "And what will you do now?"

"I had no time to go straighten things out. That was what they were
probably hoping I'd do, because it would be fatal to my expedition. I
had to get these supplies back here. We have a long way to sail before
winter, and a year and two months of my allotted time are gone. I
cannot afford to wait here until spring."

"Your King," said Tonti, "should not make you bear all the cost of
enlarging France's holdings. It is too much for any one man."

Victor listened intently for La Salle's reply.

"Oh, no," said La Salle loyally. "I can do it yet, with just the monopoly on wild oxen hides, now that I have the *Griffin!* Hinaut and his fourteen men should by this time have a lot of furs that I can send back in her to restore my credit." He turned to Marc. "I want to tell you again what a fine job you made of Fort Conti so far. Le Fleur showed me your complete plans and they were excellent in every detail."

"I can't say it's exactly what I'd like to build," said Marc happily, "but we did our best."

"We'll soon have a long string of even larger forts, with the *Griffin* plying back and forth, and then another ship doing the same on the Mississippi."

"There's no hope of getting the *Griffin* out until we have a strong east wind," said Tonti, "and they're not common here. We might be several weeks waiting."

La Salle bit his lip. "Then I believe some time would be saved if we sent a canoe on ahead at once, to join the men on the Illinois River, and bring their furs to the Lake of the Illinois in readiness for the *Griffin's* arrival."

After a pause, Tonti replied, "Very well. And now that you're here to take charge, I'm not needed. I could go on ahead with some canoemen."

Victor and Marc glanced with sympathy toward Tonti. That was a hard offer to make, for it meant that after building the *Griffin* he would not have the pleasure of sailing in her. But it was characteristic for him to choose the harder part.

La Salle nodded. "Good. Take five men with you. The rest of us will fall-to here and get the *Griffin* ready for the first east wind."

Under the stimulus of La Salle's hard-working example, the shipyard took on new life. The portage path was constantly tramped back and forth, Father Ribourde himself making three trips up and down; and Father Membré, for all his slightness and his air of a mystic, proved he had a strong back as well. Young Boisrondet was not so valuable an addition; carrying even a small pack over the portage was too much for him, and he held them all back with too-frequent stops. Inept at everything, he trailed around camp, hindering wherever he tried to help.

"Why do you suppose La Salle brought him?" asked Victor one day, exasperated.

213

Tonti shook his head. "He seems to take everyone who wants to join him. But then," he added cheerfully, "if he selected more carefully, he wouldn't have brought a man with one hand."

By the time Tonti started west by canoe, three days later, the *Griffin* had already taken on new luster with the fittings La Salle had brought: an anchor so large it took four men, well fortified with brandy, to carry it over the portage; cannons of bell metal enough to raise her number to seven; and, as a final touch, three flags—one bearing an eagle for the masthead. The large store of ammunition was divided, part to remain in the Niagara magazine, the rest loaded on shipboard. The ship's bell was attached to the forecastle; and under the poop cabins were completed for La Salle and the pilot. A constant stream of arms, provisions, medicines, extra clothing, and trading goods came over the portage and into the hold. Marc added seeds gathered from the shipyard garden.

Even the weather was helpful, for the fine, cool breezes of the loading days were followed immediately by an east wind suitable for getting her out. La Salle divided the company, thirty men and the three Recollets to accompany him, the rest to stay with Father Watteau. The whole camp accompanied the embarking party to the shore opposite the ship. Here Moyse, looking at the current and feeling the wind, shook his head. "You still can't get her out."

La Salle proceeded as if he hadn't heard. He ordered Luc and the sailors on board; and when all was ready, he seized the two ropes himself. Victor and Marc, the Recollets, and all the rest fell in behind him. The anchors were lifted, the brownish-yellow sails set for every advantage of the wind, and the men heaved, digging their heels into the beach. "She's moving!" shouted Father Hennepin. It was a long pull, but they inched her against the current. And then her canvas moved like the first flutter of wings, the sails caught the wind, and the towrope fell slack. Under her own power the *Griffin* rose upon a wave and slid down it. "By the jewels of Neptune's crown!" yelled Moyse. "She's in the lake!" While the men on shore cheered with what breath they had left, Luc moved her to an anchorage where they could embark. When all thirty-three were on board, the Recollets led the excited company in a rousing *Te Deum;* artillery and firearms were discharged; the anchors were raised, and the vessel turned her prow into waters that had never seen anything larger than a birch canoe.

Victor's vision of home and Angélique was interrupted when Nika crossed in front of him, leaned over the rail and threw something into the water, his lips moving in a brief invocation of his own.

"Now, let's have none of your heathen practices," Father Hennepin protested.

"Leave him alone," said La Salle sternly.

"I would say," said Dautray, "that we can use all the good luck we can get, whatever the source."

"That gesture of Nika's reminded me of something," said Victor. "You know they say in Venice once a year the Signorina, accompanied by Venetian nobility, used to go out to sea to throw a gem-set ring into the water, the wedding of Venice to the Adriatic."

"A good symbol," said La Salle. "The *Griffin* may well be wedded to these lakes."

Nika had not understood all that had been said, but he knew Victor had supported his action. He held out his hand, and Victor, surprised, took it. "You my brother now, too," said Nika.

Victor felt unaccountably as if the King had just bestowed upon him the Order of the Holy Ghost.

In spite of all Luc's grumbling, he managed the ship so well that on August 10 they reached the end of the lake. Everyone on board watched the shores for Tonti, who should have paddled about this far. At the entrance of the channel the *Griffin* turned north into deep, clear water. La Salle ordered Luc to follow the western shore, and strained his eyes into the twilight for signs of Tonti.

"There—a light—beyond that clump of trees!" cried Marc.

"A fire—and there's Tonti in front of it," said Victor. "He sees us now."

Luc brought the ship to anchor, while Tonti and his five men waved and shouted. "So after all," called Tonti, "I'll have a ride on the *Griffin's* maiden voyage." Victor marveled that he showed not the slightest resentment for his long, useless trip.

On the morning of August 27, La Salle summoned the ship's company on deck as he directed the helmsman to put into a sheltered bay. "I want to make a good impression at Michilimackinac. Those who have military uniforms will put them on. The rest, wear the best you have."

On deck again in his scarlet coat and his plumed hat, he inspected ship, crew, and passengers, with a thoroughness that would not have been exceeded by M. Martinet himself, before he gave orders for sails to be set and anchors raised. Out in the channel they passed close to a large island that rose high from the water. Marc pointed out the white cliffs a little back from the beach. "I'd like to explore a bit there. Might be an excellent place for a fort to command this strait."

La Salle laughed. "I hope you'll be as diligent in finding good fort sites when we get into my territory. This would be too close to the Jesuits' stronghold at St. Ignace." He turned to exchange a few words with Luc, who swung the ship to the left to avoid the island and headed it across a channel beyond. La Salle beckoned to the company to gather near the mainmast. "Over in the harbor we are approaching is the mission of St. Ignace. The channel to the left leads to the Lake of the Illinois, where we shall sail in a few days. The channel we are crossing goes north to the settlement of Sault Ste. Marie, at the entrance to the farthest north of these Great Lakes, the *Lac Supérieur*. Your cousin Du Luth would have gone that way, Tonti. St. Ignace, ahead of us, is also a trading center, with an Ottawa and a Huron village, and is in the complete control of the Jesuits. While we are ashore, I shall demand the most circumspect behavior from every man of you. Gun crews, to your places. We'll give them a good show."

Marc and Victor stood at the rail, watching the gulls that now followed their stern. The land ahead was only a dark hazy stretch along the horizon, but as the *Griffin* crossed the channel, low irregular bluffs emerged from the haze, crowned by shaggy pines and firs. Finally a settlement came into sight along a curved harbor, one of the largest villages of New France.

Their arrival was apparently causing as much excitement as La Salle could hope for. Shouting figures came running to the beach in traders' garb, deerskins and feathers, or the uniforms of the garrison.

With billowing sails, the *Griffin* swung into the harbor. At La Salle's signal, his company shouted "Vive le Roi!" The gunners jerked their lanyards and the guns roared. Amid startled cheers from the shore, the hills resounded, the valleys and coves gave echo until it seemed that the very sky rang with the historic news: the first ship had come to this remote northern harbor.

25

BEFORE the ship's canoes could be launched, dozens of their counter-parts had left the beach and were pushing out toward the *Griffin*, their savage occupants jabbering in wonder. The crew was left to guard the ship, with orders to show every courtesy and to let savages come on board in small numbers, while La Salle and his associates went ashore. Through a lane made in the gaping crowd, Victor, Marc, and Tonti formed a small uniformed honor guard behind La Salle in his scarlet suit, followed by Dautray and Jean Michel and the Recollets, as they marched toward the Jesuit establishment.

A priest came slowly out to the gate. Victor thought he seemed a composite of all Jesuits in New France. His black cassock hung on a frame spare from extended fasts and vigils; his somewhat stern face, bronzed and weathered, spoke of good lineage. The Frenchmen re-moved their hats and held them under their arms.

"I am Father Engelran," said the priest stiffly, "and I welcome you to our mission. My associate is busy in the Ottawa village, so I must do the honors alone."

"Thank you, Father." La Salle introduced the others, and added, "We would like to offer prayers in your chapel, in gratitude for our safe journey."

"Of course. And then I shall have the pleasure of entertaining you at dinner."

"Thank you, but we do not wish to impose on your hospitality."

"I insist," said the Jesuit. "We have plenty of whitefish and corn." He turned to lead the way. "Our chapel, you know, was founded by the good Father Marquette, in whose footsteps as discoverer of the Mississippi you are hoping to follow." The priest's tone, though polite, was not without edge.

La Salle's matched it exactly. "Father Marquette was fortunate to be allowed to accompany Monsieur Joliet, chosen by the Governor for that exploration. I am happy that His Majesty has selected me to ex-tend their discoveries and make them useful to France."

Father Engelran walked in silence to the door of the log chapel. "You will find Father Marquette's shrine as simple as the faith of St. Ignatius for whom he named it."

After prayers, they filed out to pause briefly beside the grave of the founder, with its simple record: Died May 18, 1675. Buried in this grave, 1677. The Jesuit explained that the good father had been first buried where he died, on the shore of the Lake of the Illinois, and that his bones had later been moved here.

"Father Marquette was one of your best men," said La Salle softly, as if to atone for his earlier abruptness. "I remember his sensitive face with its dark, earnest eyes—the face of one who had found what he wanted to do and only death would keep him from doing it."

As they left the grave, Marc whispered, "That eulogy was something of a self-portrait, as well." Victor nodded, thoughtfully.

In the Jesuits' house they found none of the elegant furniture of Quebec. At dinner, in a strained atmosphere that silenced even Father Hennepin, they sat on chairs made of a section of log, a thin bark-covered slab left for the back. "This is a very distant post," Father Engelran sighed. "We never have meat or bread, but live on fish and Indian corn. We never have even deer meat—there are no deer within sixty miles and a hunter cannot carry a carcass that far. But it is a healthy place, with good air. And we are fortunate that whitefish is so plentiful. It is our staple all year round—fried, roasted, boiled, or stewed with cornmeal."

An Indian woman brought in a roasted whitefish that filled a whole platter. The snowy meat was flaky but not dry.

"Its flavor is more delicate this way, I think," said Victor, "than when boiled as we had it before. How we would relish such fish at court!"

"I'm afraid it is our only luxury." Father Engelran smiled. "Products of the soil are scarce here, for the season is very short. If you are hoping to replenish your food supplies here, you may have difficulty. I doubt if you will find any corn for sale."

"And not alone because of the scarcity," said La Salle evenly.

Father Engelran shrugged thin shoulders. "The traders here have an association, into which each man puts one or more canoes and shares the profits accordingly. Naturally, they don't care to help you establish posts among tribes that might otherwise trade with them."

"I am by now very familiar with that attitude. How blind, not to see

218

that my plans to make allies and gain territory for France would benefit us all!"

"I agree—if such allies could be gathered into the fold of the Church. And we Jesuits should do it."

Father Ribourde's lips tightened, but he frowned into silence a retort trembling on the lips of Father Hennepin. La Salle ran slender fingers back and forth over a wrinkle in his scarlet coat. "Fortunately we were able to get corn from the Senecas, and we will find more among the Illinois." The startled company tried to hide their knowledge that while he had spoken the truth, there was not a grain of corn on board at the moment. "I am more interested just now," added La Salle, "in finding any possible news of my fifteen men who probably stopped here on their way to the Illinois."

"Indeed they did," said the Jesuit. "In fact, I believe a few of them are still here. And none of them went to the Illinois, I'm quite sure."

La Salle checked a start of surprise. "Do you know where they are?"

The Jesuit's face went blank. "No."

"Perhaps someone in the village can tell me," said La Salle calmly, careful not to reveal what a blow this news had struck. "They had a considerable supply of goods belonging to me, that they were to trade with the Illinois."

"They did their trading here," said Father Engelran. "But I doubt if you find any furs. What trading they did seemed to be for their own purposes. They were much addicted to drinking, gambling, and other . . . excesses. I doubt if they have anything left. Some of them went north, toward the Sault Ste. Marie mission. It is unfortunate, of course, that they did any trading at all for furs here. Your patent expressly forbids it."

"The restrictions on your order, I believe, are even more stringent," said La Salle. "You are forbidden to trade for furs anywhere. Yet there are persistent rumors that you are constantly trading."

"Rumors spread by our enemies. We are not traders."

"It is strange then that so many beaver skins travel in your canoes. Strange, too, while we are talking of it, that I can smell their odor right here."

"The power of your imagination," said the Jesuit. "And perhaps of the smell of our furniture. Red cedar long retains its fragrance. Pleasing, *n'est-ce pas?*"

"Indeed it is. And quite different from the odor of beaver skins."

Victor narrowed his eyes. He had been wondering at this near rudeness to one who was, after all, their host. But he realized now that La Salle was cleverly heading off the priest's reporting him for violation of his patent, for fear of a countercharge.

The priest rose, selected a bottle of red wine from a cupboard, and poured it into glasses. "I have never seen any reason why we shouldn't accept gifts from savages grateful for their conversion. And naturally, those gifts might be beaver. That is the currency of the country and must be accepted in place of ecus and francs. And the hatchets, kettles, and so on, that the Indians expect us to give them can be obtained from the traders only in exchange for beaver skins."

"You feel then that necessity is sometimes greater than the King's laws?"

"Whatever means we use to pay expenses while we win these people for Christ is justified."

"Are you having good results with your mission?" asked Father Hennepin.

"Splendid. It takes much patience, of course. But if we work faithfully, some impression must be made unless the savage mind is harder than stone."

"Sometimes I think," said Father Ribourde, "that we may always have to let them combine the old and the new. As when they feather arrows with the eagle's feathers but use the Frenchman's iron heads."

Father Engelran made an impatient gesture. "Nonsense. In time we will make them as French as ourselves."

"Perhaps," said Father Hennepin eagerly, "we can help while we are here."

The Jesuit looked at him as if he were an insect. "We need no help."

Father Hennepin flushed, and La Salle rose to terminate the uncomfortable visit. Their host accompanied them to the door, and waved aside their thanks. "A rare treat to have you."

Outside the gate, Father Hennepin exploded, "Why, he treated me as if I weren't even a Catholic!"

"Our visit *was* a treat to him," said La Salle grimly, "because he could tell me such bad news. Now to find those fifteen rascals. Tonti, you and I will search the village." He glanced out at the *Griffin,* now surrounded by as many canoes in the water as gulls in the air. "Dautray, go out and get a bale of trading goods and see whether you can get any corn. The rest of you may help him if he needs you."

Victor, Marc, and Jean Michel trailed along for a while, but found that Dautray didn't need them. With his experience at Fort Frontenac, he selected goods and went first to the Huron village, and to the Ottawas'. For a time Marc and Victor stayed to listen to his bargaining, as he moved about among the crowded bark dwellings. Except for the men Dautray spoke to, the whole dark-skinned village ignored them: women pounding corn in wooden mortars, youths gambling with cherry stones on a wooden platter, girls chattering in the shade, naked infants crawling in the dust. Dautray could get all the whitefish he wanted, but no corn. Victor and Marc wandered disconsolately back to the beach.

Victor had brought his journal and inkhorn from the ship, and now sat down, thoughtfully chewing his quill. Marc stretched out beside him. As Victor was entering in his journal an account of their trip and arrival, Tonti came down the beach, frowning. "Bad news," he said soberly. He and La Salle had found four of the missing men, including Duplessis. But they had wasted La Salle's goods in liquor and gambling, and now had nothing but the clothes on their backs. They were horrified to see La Salle here, for they had been convinced by the Jesuits that he was finished when the *Frontenac* was wrecked in Lake Ontario. They said some of the others had gone to Ste. Marie.

"La Salle was so angry he came near to beating those fools," said Tonti. "And when he said they'd have to make up the loss from their shares of profit, Duplessis was in such a rage I thought he might strike La Salle."

"What's La Salle going to do with them?" asked Marc.

"He sent them on board the *Griffin* and will keep them in arms until we sail. I have offered to go and arrest the ones at Ste. Marie."

"No!" cried Victor. "That'll take too long! There's been too much time wasted already."

"They may have some of our goods left. And it's important that La Salle show the whole company that deserters will be pursued and punished. He needs all his men now. We have no way to recruit any more."

Tonti set off the next day with two canoes, six men, and with goods to trade for three more canoes at the Sault. In the days that followed, the boys rather wished they had gone with him. Aside from the scenery there was nothing attractive about this far northern outpost. They knew better than to expect soldiers to be saints, but the Michilimackinac garrison was a little too debauched. The one dirty street of shops and saloons was the scene of constant brawls, drunken orgies, gambling parties and Indian prostitutes plying their trade.

The two Jesuits were polite but distant. They incited the twenty-five or so French traders, *coureurs de bois,* and other renegades into hatred of La Salle by insisting that he would put an end to the flow of furs to this post. La Salle, amazed at their lack of vision, attempted to reason with the traders. "The tribes cannot all come here," the boys heard him say more than once. "Those I shall trade with are too distant. They wouldn't leave their women and children so long without food and exposed to enemies. If I do not trade with them, you won't benefit. The English would, or farther south, the Spanish, who already have trading posts in that country."

But he convinced no one, and the price of corn, already exorbitant, doubled and trebled when he traded for it. Even then he could get only enough to feed his men from day to day. He had to pay more than double for four canoes to be used to go to the Illinois Indians, who were two river trips and a portage farther than the *Griffin* could sail. The rent he paid for a small cabin to be used as a warehouse would have paid for a room in the best Paris inn. What hurt him most was that his achievement in bringing the first ship to the lakes, an enterprise that should have been supported by all Frenchmen, had produced exactly the opposite effect. "What fools they are to oppose the extension of our empire!" he said to Marc and Victor.

"There is a saying," said Victor, "that 'He who sets out to make wise men of fools will be kept very busy.'"

La Salle smiled. "But then they are calling me a fool, too."

"'La monde est plein de fous, et qui n'en veut point voir,'" quoted Victor. *"Doit demeurer tout seul, et casser son miroir.'"*

La Salle laughed, and went on down the street with something close to lightness in his bearing.

"One thing you contribute to this venture," said Marc, "is to make him laugh once in a while. And he needs to laugh," he added lightly. "The old custom of having a court fool had much to recommend it." He moved to dodge a blow that never came. Victor was staring thoughtfully after La Salle.

August passed. September came with winds and rain. The twins

222

watched the southward migration of birds, a constant reminder that they, too, should be on their way. Victor seethed at this delay; and La Salle, fretting at the loss of time and the difficulty of keeping his men in check in this rough frontier settlement, paced the beach for hours daily, watching the channel for Tonti's return. Jean Michel joined the fort surgeon in his daily rounds, but the Recollets were unhappily idle.

Though the traders were reluctant to sell them anything, Marc found a young Indian who could not resist the fine marriage jacket the Seneca girl had given him, and traded him two new red wool shirts. On the same day Victor found La Salle depressed because he could get no more corn.

"I'll get you some." Victor scented a diversion from boredom. "From the very next savage that comes along. Would you bet a new Paris hat?"

"Done!" said La Salle. "I hope you intend to get it honestly."

"More or less." Victor brought some small objects from his pocket. "Know what these are?"

"Cherry stones, marked for gambling."

Victor grinned. "Right. Nika showed me what nice little weapons they are. Let's see, I said the next savage. Well, I guess that's this one." Staggering toward them from the fort was a short Indian with Obijway moccasins and long braids.

"But he's drunk," protested La Salle.

"Try to find one that isn't. They excuse everything by drunkenness, so let's turn the tables. If he has any corn, he's as good as any other. Come, will you interpret for me?"

Victor waited till the befuddled savage stopped in front of him; then brought out the cherry stones and rolled them over in his hand. "You want to play?"

As soon as the savage could focus his eyes, he brightened. "I play."

"I bring beads. Beads and pretty mirrors. You bring corn."

After a little persuasion, the savage wheeled and started unsteadily toward the bark huts. La Salle shook his head, but unlocked the cabin he had rented, and gave Victor an assortment of trading goods. "But I don't think you'll see him again. He'll fall down somewhere and go to sleep."

"If he does, I owe you a hat."

When they emerged, the Indian was nowhere in sight; but as they strolled toward the lodges, he came staggering toward them, two

223

small birch baskets of shelled corn under each arm and in his teeth a wooden bowl. Victor greeted him effusively, and took the bowl. The savage motioned to La Salle and shook his head vigorously, evidently remembering something he had been told. Victor nodded agreement, and maneuvered the savage to a place behind a crude bench near the water. "Tell me first," he said in an aside to La Salle, "what's the word for 'mine' and 'yours'; then sit on the bench and look the other way."

Victor held up a cherry stone, with the marked side up. "Yours." Turning it over to the plain side, "Mine." The two squatted opposite each other; Victor held up a string of blue beads, put the stones in the wooden bowl, and threw them into the air. "Yours!" said Victor.

With a crafty smile, the savage gathered in the beads, tossed the stones, then pointed with an unsteady, dirty finger. "Mine!" he announced, and seized another string of beads.

"Come on, Lady Luck," muttered Victor, and setting out a mirror, tossed the stones in air.

"Mine!" chortled the savage, and seized the mirror.

"I thought you knew how to play that game," commented La Salle from the bench.

"Wait. I haven't got started yet." With a length of red cloth as stakes, he passed his hand over the bowl, as had the savage before he tossed it—and the light dawned. Turn them the way you want them to land; then toss them carefully so they don't change position very much. He failed the first time, but when he was getting near the end of his goods, he got the knack of it, and one after another, three baskets of corn came to repose beside him.

"You aren't cheating that poor savage, are you?" La Salle inquired.

"Of course. But he was cheating like the Devil before I got started. Here comes the last basket! Anything else you want?"

"That's enough," said La Salle emphatically. "As it is, you'll have an irate woman on your trail when he tells his wife."

"*Mon dieu, non!* Anything but that!" Hastily Victor took the other basket, patted the savage on the back, put the bowl into his hands and piled upon it the goods he had won. "Tell your woman—no, I'm not fool enough to tell any man what to tell his woman. You handle it, Chief."

On the evening of the 11th of September the boys took their lutes down to the shore where Laurent joined them with his fiddle. Here an idle crowd gathered to hear the songs of old France—Jesuits and Recollets, voyageurs and artisans, gentlemen and soldiers.

"*Ma chère liberté,*" the boys sang. *Liberté:* the words of the song echoed in Marc's thoughts. How little, until now, had he ever understood its meaning. Great, aged trees made a man stand more erect, until he gradually forgot how once he had bowed before a throne. He felt himself expanding to match the wide horizon. As the color faded from sky and water, they still sat singing until the sky changed yet again, growing light. Broad streamers of radiance spread up from the horizon, shifting and changing, as if giants played with silver ribbons.

"We have brought out the marionettes," said Laurent, laying aside his fiddle.

"You mean *we* did all that?" laughed Victor.

"*Mais oui.* Some think a tune played or sung in calm evening air causes them to dance in the sky. Since we voyageurs know they are followed by storms and gales, I should have kept my fiddle silent."

Nika stirred behind them, and they saw he was making room for La Salle. "Such a night is not often given to mortals to look upon," said La Salle softly.

"I am holding my breath lest it disappear," said Marc.

"You are a fortunate young man," answered La Salle. "One of those rare beings who are happy in the use of their senses and an alert mind."

Marc felt a warm glow at this unaccustomed praise. Before he could answer, Nika said quietly, "Do not sit too long here. My people call it the spirits' dance. Must not watch long, or you will be drawn to join in."

"And if we do?" asked Marc.

"Tomorrow's sun will see you dead upon the beach."

"Indeed?" asked La Salle. "Then we must not. I have other plans for tomorrow."

"My people say dancing spirits are a sign of war."

La Salle lowered his voice. "Then you have heard the rumors, too."

"Yes. Your enemies are sending Iroquois to attack the Illinois."

"If it is not true, it is at least well invented," said La Salle seriously. "Such a war would be ruinous for us. We must have an advanced base among the Illinois. They must not be massacred or driven west."

Marc turned. "Is it so easy to start an Indian war?"

"Sometimes," admitted La Salle. "I don't dare discredit these rumors.

225

They fit the pattern of Iroquois behavior, for they have exterminated or driven out every other tribe near their territory. And they know we'll be interfering with their position as middlemen in the western trade. The Illinois tribe is important and easy to get to. You can be sure the English and Dutch would spur the Iroquois on. And there are French, too, who wouldn't scruple to start an Indian war to destroy me."

"Easy to get Iroquois to fight," said Nika.

"Yes, they don't need much excuse for those murderous raids they call wars." La Salle beckoned the boys closer. "For this and other reasons, I have decided not to wait longer for Tonti. The season is getting late, and the time allotted by His Majesty is being wasted. I want the *Griffin* to make a trip back to the Niagara, and return here before winter freezes the channels. So we will sail tomorrow. I have a task for each of you. Victor, write a letter that I can leave for Tonti. Tell him he is to follow us down the Lake of the Illinois and meet us at the mouth of the Miami. That's on the eastern side, a little above the southern end."

After La Salle and Nika had gone back to the village, Victor commented, "That Nika is quite a fellow. I'd trust my life in his hands, but I don't understand him."

"He's a strange combination of mysticism and practical common sense," said Marc. "It's hard to tell which side of him is speaking."

"What if the Iroquois attack the Illinois while we're there?" asked Victor.

Laurent rose and tucked his fiddle under his arm. "If the Iroquois are about, Monsieur, a great deal of blood will be spilled."

"It was bad enough to watch one of their victory dances," said Marc grimly. "I'd hate to be the center of interest in the next one."

On the morning of the 12th the entire company, including the deserters, embarked on the *Griffin,* sailed out of the harbor and bore to the west through the channel. On the Lake of the Illinois they turned south, the general direction, La Salle told them, of the rest of the exploration. In a bay he called Baie des Puans, La Salle directed Luc to anchor off an island. The wind had risen; no sooner had they dropped anchor than a storm struck, forcing all hands to take shelter below deck.

As soon as the driving rain had slowed to a drizzle, La Salle went up on deck. When Marc and Victor followed him, they found him conversing in a strange Indian dialect with a handsome savage

226

whose dignified bearing even the *grand monarque* could not have improved upon. A birch canoe, tied to the ship, rose and fell with the waves.

La Salle beckoned. "This is Ononghisse, Chief of the Pottawattomies, who used to live near Montreal. He risked his life to come because he fears our ship may be in danger."

The chief pointed to the fleur-de-lis on the masthead. "The sign of Onontio. I, Chief of the Keepers of the Sacred Fires, would always risk my life to save children of Onontio. He my friend."

The boys looked skeptical, but La Salle said, "He is indeed an old and good friend of Count Frontenac. He says there have been some Frenchmen in his village for a long time. Very likely some of my deserters." His lips narrowed as if preparing another tongue-lashing. "There's a Jesuit mission beyond him on the mainland, but only the two priests are there."

When the sea was calm enough to launch the ship's canoes, Marc, Victor, La Salle, Nika, and Dautray paddled behind Chief Ononghisse to the island. Among the crowd at the water's edge were five Frenchmen, hailing their approach with evident joy. "Well," said La Salle in surprise, "they seem to have nothing to hide. There is Chapelle, and Leblanc. Now we'll hear the whole story."

When they reached shore, the five stepped forward to wring La Salle's hand. "Thanks to *le bon dieu,* you are here! You really did build a ship," said Chapelle. "Everyone at Michilimackinac said you had given up and would never come. I said we should go to the Illinois anyway, and if you did not come we would take the furs back to Fort Frontenac. But most of the men were afraid. So we came this far, we five, because we knew Chief Ononghisse. We were so few we didn't want to go as far as the Illinois. But we have some furs for you." He took La Salle into the lodge where he and the four others had been living; and when La Salle emerged, his face was beaming. "You have done exceedingly well! You have at least twelve thousand livres in furs there!"

Victor remembered that La Salle had no right to trade here at all. But my only duty, he thought, is to report to the King.

During the afternoon the chief tried to persuade La Salle to remain, to be satisfied with a trading post here. That night he invited them all to a feast and calumet dance. La Salle sorted out some gifts and gave each of his company a few pieces of tobacco. "They dance and boast of their great deeds, and we have to take part. Use this tobacco to hire one of them to dance for each of you."

A post was set up in the open square, lighted now by a circle of fires. When the drums began to beat, one after another warriors came from the doorways and danced about the post, yelping joyfully. With an occasional grunt the older men moved around with deliberate tread, the younger braves with grotesque postures. Striking the post, they declaimed the warlike deeds and the prowess of their ancestors.

The feasting that followed would have done credit in quantity to the Governor's table at Quebec. Wooden bowls of broth were passed around; drinks of maple syrup beaten up with water; and from huge wooden platters they were served roasted whitefish, deer meat, bear meat, wood hens, and beaver tails.

Afterward, at La Salle's suggestion, Victor and Marc gave an exhibition with their foils, to the great astonishment of the Pottawattomies, who accompanied every thrust with howls of excitement. The boys had never fenced before a stranger audience, or a more appreciative one, and they gave their best, with vigorous *froissements,* delicate *coulés.* When the bout was over, the whole camp roared its approval.

"Merci bien!" said La Salle above the noise. "These Indians will never forget it."

"Nor will we, I think," panted Marc.

Then, with great ceremony the chief presented a calumet to La Salle, to facilitate his reception among the tribes to the south, which, he warned, might have been stirred up against them. La Salle's eyes kept roaming thoughtfully out to the *Griffin,* but when the chief had finished his presentation speech, the explorer took the feather-decked pipe and began to speak in fluent Pottawattomie.

From La Salle's frequent gestures to the south, Victor guessed that he was explaining his plans. Victor's thoughts went back to the day he had listened to those same plans from the antechamber—the day that had so changed his life for the worse. La Salle, he had to admit, was making the same good impression on these savages he had made on the King and Colbert. This chief was honoring La Salle with the same recognition of worth that Louis XIV had seen. Yet there was a difference, in more than costume and setting. Unlike Louis XIV, so distrustful of worth or ability, this chief had so much confidence in himself that he did not fear a lessening of his authority.

On the way back to the *Griffin* that night La Salle was silent while the others chattered about the feast and dancing. Early the next morning he sent for Victor. "I have letters to be written," he said. Victor seated himself at a broad shelf where maps and charts had been pushed aside for ink, paper, and a quill. But instead of beginning, La Salle paced up and down.

"Who will take letters back?" asked Victor.

"The *Griffin*—at once."

"So? I thought we were to sail to the river of the Miamis."

"No need now that there are no furs awaiting us in that region. We can go by canoe." La Salle hesitated, and resumed pacing. "I have been awake all night, making these decisions. I'm going to send our furs back in the *Griffin*. I will write to Count Frontenac, and ask him to use them to make payments on my debts and force my creditors to release my property." He swung around to face Victor. "I am well aware that my patent forbids me to trade on the lakes. But I am forced to it, like a man who steals bread for a starving family. I've been stripped of nearly all my possessions by the same traders the King was protecting when he forbade me to trade in beaver. In order to go on, I must use these furs." He waited a moment, watching Victor, and then added, "I am doing nothing but what I think is in His Majesty's, and France's, true interests."

Victor lifted his quill. "Yes, Monsieur," he said evenly. "Your first letter, then, is to the Governor?"

La Salle sighed, like one who has tried to lift a burden and failed. "Yes. And then one to La Forest, asking him to send the furs directly to Quebec."

Afterward La Salle made his announcement to his company, adding that everyone except the *Griffin's* crew would continue south in canoes.

"Who'll be in charge of the ship?" asked Dautray.

"Luc."

"Luc? You find him trustworthy? After——"

"He's a good pilot. And I can't spare anyone else. I'll need all of you on the Illinois."

La Salle assigned a clerk and enough good sailors to the ship, ordering them to sail back to the shipyard on the Niagara, whence the furs could be portaged to the storehouse and then shipped on the *Cataraqui*. At the storehouse they were to fill the *Griffin* with the supplies and men that must have long since arrived from France. On the way back Luc was to bring the *Griffin* on down to the Miamis' river, to pass the winter.

The *Griffin's* hold was emptied of supplies and shipbuilding tools, and the furs were taken aboard. But when they began loading the canoes, they found they could not take more than half these supplies, so everything that would not be needed before the *Griffin* could complete her round trip—such as rigging and anchors for the new ship, and extra supplies of ammunition—were put back on board. Luc was to take them to La Salle's storehouse at Michilimackinac and pick them up when he came back. During this activity Father Hennepin had been scowling about, wandering from river to huts like one of the tame beavers that came and went like dogs in the village. At first he plied La Salle with questions, only to be brushed off like a persistent gnat. Then he sulked until the loading was finished.

Victor went through a travail of his own. He had to write to the King that La Salle was violating his orders and his patent. In all honesty he shrank from it, because he felt that, in similar circumstances, he would do the same thing. Yet he had been sent to watch for such violations, and it was not his duty to judge them, but to report them. He knew Marc would disapprove violently. Once when they were loading casks of powder, Victor said to him, "La Salle is courting the King's wrath by using that beaver."

Marc settled a cask into place. "Sometimes necessity is above the law! The King could easily make a law that we shouldn't breathe, but we'd find it hard to obey."

And unless La Salle begins to make some money soon, thought Victor, our investment may be lost. Yet, balancing values coolly in his mind, he knew his best profit lay in pleasing the King.

Soon after the *Griffin* was loaded, a morning came that seemed expressly made for her departure. When Victor and Marc went down to the shore to wash, the sun was warm, the sky blue, flecked with white clouds. Shaking the cold water from his face and hands, Marc studied his pensive twin for a moment before speaking: "Victor, I've been wondering. . . . If you want so much to go back, let's return on the *Griffin*. We can hire someone to take our places and send them back to La Salle."

A wave of hope, and astonishment, swept over Victor. "You want to go back to France?"

"No. I don't. I think La Salle needs us, and I'm enjoying this more than anything I've ever done. But you're more important to me than he is. I'll go back if you want to."

Victor was overcome by conflicting emotions. How simple, just to board the *Griffin* and go. And what a joy it would be to see Angélique, and to live the gay life of a guardsman again! But then he couldn't have Angélique, he couldn't remain at court if he disobeyed Louis. He turned and saw how tensely Marc awaited his decision. "Thanks, I appreciate it. There's nothing I'd like better. But I'll stay. You know, D'Artagnan never gave up an enterprise until he had succeeded."

Marc let out a long breath. "I'm glad."

"I just couldn't disappoint the old boy. Now, *revenons à nos moutons,* only our *moutons* aren't sheep but beavers." As they walked back to their cabin, Victor thought with some shame how little his decision had to do with any ideals.

Nika took La Salle out to the ship for final instructions to Luc. When they returned to shore, La Salle stood watching her with pride and affection as the sails were unfurled and the vessel pulled away from her anchorage. With her went the hopes and yearnings of the little band left silent on the shore. To Victor the most significant thing she carried was a sealed letter resting in a chest in the pilot's cabin.

26

AFTER the freedom of the *Griffin's* decks, Victor and Marc found the cramped canoes irksome. By evening they were far out on the open lake, the mainland so far ahead they would have to paddle through the night to reach it. Those not paddling began to doze as well as they could until Victor, wakened by a violent tossing, looked out, half dazed, upon an expanse of heaving black water. "What is it?"

"A storm, m'sieu," shouted Laurent.

"Maybe we'd better stop our carriage and light the lamps."

Laurent chuckled. "All right, m'sieu, you're not busy. Get out and do it."

"Not joke. Go ashore, quick," warned Nika. "When spirits of air and water fight, men better get out of way."

Despite the darkness and the storm, Nika led the way into a cove where they could pull up the canoes. Nibbling a little corn, they waited on wet sand and rocks throughout the day; and then for five more days while wind and rain lashed at them.

"I hope Tonti is safe somewhere," said Marc.

"And what is happening to the *Griffin!*" La Salle's long-pent-up anxiety burst out, as he stared out to sea as if he could conjure up a vision of his ship.

"This Lake of the Illinois has angry autumn moods," said Father Membré. "One of the Pottawattomies called it the 'man-devouring lake!'"

The voyageur Duplessis laughed hysterically. "A good name for this whole expedition—man-devouring."

"Blessed be God," said Father Ribourde, in his slow, pleasant voice. "We must remember that the Devil will offer all possible opposition to our journey."

The others ceased grumbling, perhaps less because of his words than from sight of the elderly man enduring hardship so courageously. "Come on," called out one of the cooks. "Nika got a porcupine this morning. *Mon dieu,* porcupine and rain-water soup!"

"A change from dry corn," said Victor, tasting the soup.

"You'll soon be looking back with longing on that dried corn," said Dautray. "The bag is nearly empty."

Whether the Devil or the man-devouring lake were responsible, sunshine on this journey was as rare as louis d'ors in a poor man's pocket. The explorers spent less time in the canoes than huddled on rocky shores, sheltered only by sodden blankets, while Nika struggled to keep a small driftwood fire burning.

The corn gave out and hunger was added to other miseries. The bald, mustached Duplessis was most vocal in discontent, blaming La Salle for not bringing more food, forgetting that the canoes had had to be filled with such things as the forge, pit saw, kegs of powder and shot, carpenter's tools, and iron, none of which could be obtained along the way. Food became an obsession to everyone but La Salle, who worried alternately about the *Griffin* and the possibility that the Iroquois might be already on the warpath.

On the first of October they were able to start off again. Soon a shout arose from the first canoe. "A village! Just ahead!"

From a cluster of domed huts, savages were running to the water, motioning the Frenchmen to shore. "What are they, Nika?" asked La Salle.

"Pottawattomies."

"How can you be sure?" asked Victor.

232

"I know," said Nika scornfully. "By moccasins, hair, feathers . . ."

"I suppose these moccasins you got me make me a Shawano, then."

"Some day, maybe," said Nika seriously. "When I have time to make you Shawano inside, and find you Shawano woman."

"Thanks," said Victor dryly. "I'll look forward to that."

Meanwhile, the hope of the hungry and discouraged men turned to howls of rage when La Salle ordered them to paddle straight ahead. "They may have been turned against us," he explained briefly. "We won't land in their stronghold, but farther down where our goods will be safer."

The place he chose for landing was a promontory that could be easily defended; but the rocky shore forced them to take to the water and carry the canoes ashore. Father Hennepin had to carry the weakened Father Ribourde on his shoulders. La Salle despatched Dautray and two men with Chief Ononghisse's calumet to the Indian village to trade for food. The rest built a fire on a cliff and sat wearily down.

"We're a long way from reinforcements." Victor shivered.

"Highly improper military procedure," agreed Marc. "Easy to cut us off."

"Keep your guns ready," said La Salle, "and if any savages approach, remember to act at ease."

"I wish I could feel at ease," said Victor.

"In face of an unfriendly savage," said La Salle, "remember two things: to show that you are not afraid of him, and that he has more to gain from you than the fun of killing you."

Only a few minutes were to pass before they had a chance to put his orders into effect. From a grove below them sprang twenty armed warriors. With a quiet command, La Salle led his men down the hill, stopping some distance above the warriors, where, using the same Algonquin dialect as before, he spoke to the warriors until Dautray came back. "When we got to the village, no one was there," said Dautray wearily. "I guess they were afraid of us, too. We took some corn and left goods in its place."

La Salle reported this to the warriors, who, after some consultation, indicated approval and melted away into the woods.

As they moved southward, the weather grew milder. Once they found the carcass of a deer freshly killed by wolves; and from here on game became more plentiful. But at one camping spot La Salle found fresh Indian tracks and forbade the men to discharge firearms. The

233

same day, while La Salle was out scouting, Le Picard and Duplessis fired at a stag. "On such a miserable journey," cried Duplessis angrily at La Salle's later reprimand, "we have at least the right to eat."

"If you expect me to get you back alive," said La Salle, "you'll do as I say. If you disobey once more, I'll have you tied up every time we come ashore."

That night, under cover of yet another storm, Indians sneaked into their camp and stole a quantity of goods. "We'll have to get them back," said La Salle simply.

"Wouldn't it be better to let them go?" suggested Father Membré.

"No. We are so few we can't afford to show weakness. They'd come back tonight and take everything we have." La Salle posted Marc and Victor with three other armed men on the nearby height, and set off into the woods alone, reappearing in an hour with a savage at his pistol's end, saying the Indian had confessed the theft. "He says they can't return everything since they cut one shirt into pieces and divided it."

"It was my shirt!" moaned Victor. "My beautiful, warm red shirt!"

Even in so serious a situation, Marc smiled to see Victor mourning the loss of a garment that a year ago he would not have worn even for a masquerade.

"If he is telling the truth," said La Salle, "they may try to get this fellow back by force." He doubled the guard for the night, and at dawn ranged all his men again on the peninsula, Father Hennepin among them, while the other two Recollets stayed in camp saying *Aves.*

They had not long to wait. Below them, across a sandy plain, appeared a band of about eighty savages, arrows fitted to bows. "That's more than the four-to-one D'Artagnan allowed us," said Victor, his nerves quivering. "I could use a company of musketeers behind me."

"We can echo Henry of Navarre," said Marc, " 'I will be carried out a dead man or march out a conqueror.' *Mais, regardez* those hills along the side of the plain! The nearest one commands all the others."

"Good!" said La Salle. "We'll go and take it. Five of you follow me. Wrap your blanket around your left arm, and let it hang free, so you can raise it as a shield against their arrows."

Marc and Victor were among the five that stepped forward and walked calmly toward the Indians. The savages watched them, retreating slightly; and once atop the hill, the six waited for the next

234

move. Apparently such boldness impressed the savages, for shortly two old men approached with a calumet.

"I'll go meet them," said Father Hennepin. "I have no gun to frighten them." He advanced down the slope with dignity.

"Anyway," muttered Victor, "there's nothing wrong with the fat one's courage."

La Salle nodded, without taking his eyes from the Indians.

"*Tonnerre!*" shouted Victor suddenly. "My shirt!" He pointed toward one of the old men who had a strip of red cloth around his head. In spite of La Salle's warning shout, he dashed down the slope, snatched off the cloth, and shook it in the savage's face. "Where's the rest of my shirt, you cursed heathen?"

Marc held his breath, expecting to see Victor struck down before his eyes. But his very audacity had caught the savages off guard. Hurriedly thrusting the calumet into Father Hennepin's hands, they backed away.

"*Toujours l'audace!*" La Salle let out a breath of relief. "The young fool!" But his lips parted in a half smile.

Advancing down the slope, he began to talk with the savages, and Accau told the rest what was being said. "They say they came to fight because they couldn't return what was stolen. They say they will return the uninjured things and pay for the rest, if we'll accept that." He smiled with a gleam of his crooked teeth. "I think we will."

One savage advanced from the band, unarmed, his arms full of beaver robes, while the old man begged La Salle to accept them in place of the destroyed goods. And the next day they came with the undamaged goods and a feast for the Frenchmen, followed by speeches that caused La Salle some concern. They urged him to remain among them, since the Illinois Indians were determined to kill every Frenchman who appeared at their village. The Illinois had captured an Iroquois, who, they said, had told them that the French had advised his tribe to war against them.

Alarm spread through the camp; but La Salle thanked the savages, saying that he would continue his journey, and was confident he could bring the Illinois to reason.

On the next morning, the first of November, they set off in their canoes again, along the southern shore of the lake. "Tonti should be at the Miami when we get there," said La Salle hopefully. "He had a shorter distance to go, down the east side, and he wasn't so heavily loaded."

But when they pulled up where the Miami falls into the Lake of the Illinois, it was plain that Tonti had not been there. After supper while the men sat about in dejected groups, Father Hennepin began arguing with La Salle.

"See here," he urged, "we can't wait for that Italian. We have no corn, and if we don't get game, we'll starve."

"We shall wait here for Tonti," said La Salle firmly. "When he comes, we'll have a larger force to meet whatever situation we find in the Illinois country. And the rivers here don't freeze so early. We won't be idle. We'll build a fort, where we can store goods from the *Griffin.*"

"A fort!" exploded Victor. "In God's name, why can't we go on about the King's business! The only fort he cares about is the one you promised him at the mouth of the Mississippi. Let's get on to that. We might find a silver mine there that would make us all rich and please the King. Then he'd give you the whole wilderness and a life-time to do what you want with it. I say let's keep moving."

"Remember, Monsieur de Lorennes," La Salle brought him up sharply, "you are not Monsieur le Capitaine here."

27

IN spite of Victor's impatience, Marc enjoyed laying out Fort Miami on a triangular site, enclosed by river, lake, and a deep ravine. In the long wait, through November, they built a palisade-enclosed redoubt, a storehouse strong enough for defense, and near it a chapel, which the Recollets dedicated to St. Anthony of Padua.

La Salle spent most of his time at the river with poles, flags and buoys, marking the channel around a troublesome sandbank, so the *Griffin* could come safely to anchorage. As further insurance of her safe arrival, he drew up a set of instructions for navigating the Lake of the Illinois, and sent Chapelle and Leblanc to Michilimackinac to meet Luc and sail back with him to the Miami. Meanwhile the priests gathered reeds and wove mats to be used over a framework, savage fashion, on the coming winter's journey. While La Salle kept his eyes to the north, hoping for sight of the *Griffin* or Tonti's canoes, his ears were constantly assailed by renewed complaints about food. No game was to be found near the fort except hibernating bears, a tough and unsavory meat for a steady diet.

The weather had turned bitingly cold before Tonti came into sight with only two canoes.

"Sorry to be late," explained the Italian, once the excitement of greetings was over. "We had to pull all the way against a north-flowing current."

"What did you hear of the *Griffin?*" demanded La Salle.

"Nothing."

"Nothing? But you were at Michilimackinac. She must have stopped there to leave the goods I sent back!"

"No, she didn't," said Tonti unhappily. "She hasn't been seen anywhere since you departed in her yourself. I supposed you had brought her down here, until I met Chapelle and Leblanc on the way."

Exclamations burst out on all sides, but La Salle was rendered speechless.

"I told you so. I told you not to trust that Luc——" began Father Hennepin, but Father Ribourde hushed him with a sharp command.

"Maybe he anchored her in a safe place during the storms, and—" Tonti offered, but it was no use. Nothing could have delayed the sailing so long.

"What could have happened to her?" asked Marc.

"Wrecked in the storm, perhaps, and all hands lost," said Victor.

"Struck by lightning, maybe, and her powder exploded," said Dautray.

"She could have been attacked and destroyed by savages, or by someone sent by the Jesuits," said Tonti.

"Luc and the crew may have stolen all the goods and sunk her," said Victor.

"The only hope that she isn't lost," said La Salle bitterly, "is that Luc disobeyed my order to stop at St. Ignace and sailed directly back east."

"If he did, we can still recover the ship," said Tonti.

La Salle quickly seized this thread of hope. "Then for some reason Luc must have decided to carry the goods along to the Niagara."

Moyse's bellows-shaped figure ambled toward them, his broad face grimly set. "You know that if the *Griffin* is lost, there ain't no use goin' on from here. Luc had all the rigging and anchors and half the iron for your new ship, not to speak of all our extra powder and shot."

237

"We're going on," said La Salle. "Luc will bring them down here on his return trip. I'll leave a letter, telling Luc, Chapelle, and Leblanc to make the *Griffin* fast for the winter and bring her cargo and crew on to us in her canoes." He turned back to Tonti. "But the men at the Sault? You didn't find them in all this time?"

"Oh, yes." But Tonti's report only deepened the frown on La Salle's troubled face. The men had taken refuge at the Sault with the Jesuits, together with eight packs of beaver. He had had some difficulty in getting the beaver away from the Jesuits, but it was now reposing in La Salle's little warehouse at St. Ignace. The men were coming, but were about ninety miles behind Tonti, for they had insisted on stopping to hunt.

"What?" snapped La Salle in cold rage. "They'll desert, of course! And take my canoes with them!"

"No, I'm sure they'll come." Tonti was stricken. "Hinaut is in charge, and he's really sorry for his behavior. But I'll go back and get them, to make sure."

"Don't lose any time," said La Salle curtly, and strode off toward the stockade.

Marc hurried to clasp Tonti's hand and console him for La Salle's brusqueness. "We're all glad you got here safely. You just got the brunt of his disappointment over the *Griffin*. Let me go back with you."

But Tonti declined the offer and went alone with two voyageurs, a trip that nearly cost him his life. Another storm drove his canoe against the shore and broke it up, guns and baggage were lost, and the three came back on foot, having lived for days on acorns. A few days later, however, the missing men came paddling into the harbor, lacking only two who had deserted. Hinaut was first to face La Salle's wrath, his long, V-shaped face fearful and ashamed. Surprisingly, La Salle accepted the apology with only a mild reproof.

The sixty-mile trip up the Miami toward the portage was made in a constant snowstorm. La Salle frequently ranged ahead, by land, joining his men again at night. Once, after he failed to return for two days, the men, believing him to be dead, demanded that Tonti dump all the heavy goods and take them back. Nika, hunting in the woods, was missing, too, but on the second day, toward evening, he came into camp telling them he had been waiting at the portage, which they had missed several miles downstream. While they were preparing to go back,

238

La Salle appeared, his eyes hollow above a growth of beard, at his belt two small gray animals. He tossed them down by the fire as he sprawled on the ground, too weary to answer the excited questions from all sides.

Marc ran for a cup of brandy. Victor, watching him and Tonti bend over the stricken man, wished his feelings were as simple; but his yearning to return to France was so strong that he lowered his eyes for fear he showed it. To cover his thoughts, he touched one of the animals lightly with his moccasin. "Is that thing good to eat? Looks like a monkey."

"With paws like hands," added Marc, picking the animals up.

"Very smart, 'possum." Nika's teeth flashed. "When enemy near, he play dead. And look!" He thrust his hand under a fold of fur on the stomach. "Pocket here—carry young ones when danger comes. He can hang by tail from tree branch, too."

"That's why I was able to get them," said La Salle weakly. "With a club."

"Very tasty, 'possum," said Nika.

"There's our Christmas pie, then," said Victor. " 'Possum with imagination for a sauce."

La Salle glanced up with a weak smile. Revived by the brandy, he told them how he had got lost in the storm and kept from freezing the night before by sleeping in a bed of leaves beside a small fire, from which he had apparently frightened an Indian.

"How could you sleep?" demanded Victor. "He might have come back and killed you!"

"I had to take that chance. Without fire or blanket, I'd have frozen anywhere else," said La Salle calmly. Victor shook his head, reluctantly admiring. He knew courage when he saw it; but this was new to him, a kind of scorn for danger, as if the man knew his time had not yet come.

"Tonti, you and the rest pack up at once," ordered La Salle, "and travel back down to the portage. I'll keep one man here with me and join you in the morning when I've rested."

"Good!" said Father Hennepin, and began to bustle about so officiously, that Tonti abruptly detailed him to stay with La Salle. Nika led the way downstream to a great oxbow in the winding river. Even now, no one could see any sign of a portage until they landed beside a giant cedar, and Nika pointed out beyond it a narrow but well-trodden defile leading up to a high prairie.

239

"You did not see these?" Nika pointed to dark round objects like huge flat kettles overturned among the bushes. "Canoes made of wild ox skin. Miamis leave here to use for crossing. Big Miami village other side of prairie."

They encamped again for the night. At dawn Tonti roused them to sort out the canoeloads and make them into packs. Father Ribourde took one of the shipbuilders' wide-bladed axes and blazed rude crosses on the cedars at the water's edge as markers for Luc.

La Salle approved when he and Father Hennepin appeared in the priest's little canoe. Freshly shaven, his hair combed, La Salle looked the aristocrat once again, except for his torn and soiled deerskins.

"We're here only by the mercy of God," exclaimed Father Hennepin. "We had a near-fatal accident in the night. A gust of wind must have blown live embers on our mats, for when we woke they were on fire. We just missed being burned up!"

"But we weren't," said La Salle. "Now let's figure out the portage loads so we can make it all in one trip. We can't divide our party when we're uncertain about the tribes near by. It will take two men for each of the big canoes. . . ."

Victor and Marc, coming to help, passed Duplessis, gloomily pulling at his mustache and staring at the heavy forge and blacksmith tools, the bale after bale of goods. "Hell, I guess he does have a charmed life. Why couldn't he burn up?"

"You don't mean that!" said Marc.

"Better him than all of us," retorted Duplessis. "Look at all the stuff! And he expects us to carry it on our backs for God knows how far, without a decent meal for weeks. But I suppose if he has a cloven hoof one musn't mention it." He subsided into muttering.

One would be forgiven, thought Victor, for thinking that thirty-three men could not possibly transport so much in one trip. Seven canoes required two men each, and one man was needed for Father Hennepin's; somehow the backs of the other eighteen had to be loaded with the clothing, blankets, arms, trading goods, cooking utensils, and all the shipbuilding tools. "We need a train of pack animals," said Victor. "How far is this portage?"

"About five miles," said La Salle. "Not so long as the one at Niagara."

"But we made dozens of trips there," protested Moyse.

"We can do it in one," said La Salle. "It's the only way to keep

240

together and leave none of our goods unguarded. If the Miamis have been aroused against us, they could massacre us with ease if we separate. This is the last portage. One good effort here and we'll have canoe travel all the way."

The goods were finally apportioned with such skill by La Salle that, heavy though the burden was, no one could say it was too much. The Recollets carried their full share, even the aged Father Ribourde insisting on a substantial pack. One after another they hung their guns from a shoulder sling, took up their burdens and fell into line behind La Salle.

Victor and Marc had each a pack on their backs, the D'Artagnan sword on top of Victor's, and they were to carry the pit saw between them. When Marc saw Duplessis swing his bundle of iron on his back and fall into line directly behind La Salle, he was curious at such eagerness and drew Victor into line directly behind him, practically elbowing aside Moyse to do it.

"All right! All right!" said Moyse indignantly. "Go ahead and be the first shot from ambush!"

The trail curved right, then left. At the top of the slope they put down their burdens for the first rest, and blinked in dazzling sunlight on a snow-covered plain. Here and there bones protruded from the snow; and beyond, in the distance, the lodges of the Miami village. La Salle examined it through his spyglass. "No signs of life. Probably they're away hunting."

"Or waiting somewhere for us," growled Moyse.

Dautray called from the rear, "Why so many skeletons here?"

"Wild oxen that starved to death last winter," said La Salle. "The snow must have been so deep they couldn't move around to find food."

"Just like us," said Moyse bitterly. "No food, no way to get any."

Everyone gazed uneasily over the snowy prairie. La Salle took up his pack. "All the more reason to get on to the Illinois. We'll get plenty of corn there." He glanced back toward the Miami. "Now we leave the rivers that flow toward Quebec. When we put our canoes into water again, it will be into a stream that flows into the Mississippi."

As if in happy anticipation, he swung off at an easy gait, Duplessis close behind. The wide trail, in places worn almost knee-deep, offered firm footing; but gradually it left solid ground and entered an area of partially frozen marshes, dotted with little pools. On this spongy and slippery earth they plodded on, hour after hour, silent under their heavy burdens. Ahead of the twins stalked Duplessis, muscular and short like all these canoemen, with chest and arms strongly developed by paddling.

More than one man fell, cursing as he struggled to his feet again covered with mud. Duplessis, too, fell under his pack, the weight of the iron in it bruising his foot. Screaming with pain, he uttered a string of the foulest of oaths. "Hold your tongue!" La Salle called back sharply.

In an instant the unbelievable happened. His face twisted with rage, Duplessis aimed his gun at La Salle's back. Victor and Marc dropped the saw and lunged forward as one, striking the gun aside just as it discharged. La Salle swung around and blanched.

"He almost got you in the back!" panted Marc.

"Thanks," said La Salle. Only a tightening around his mouth showed his emotions. "Glad you were quick."

"Good thing we were," Victor said, and realized instantly that he meant it. The vileness of Duplessis's attack had cleared his own mind; now he knew that he wanted no problems solved by the death of La Salle. "What shall we do with the wretch?"

"Bad dog," said Nika darkly. "Shoot him!"

"Let him resume his burden," said La Salle. "He deserves to be abandoned. But every pound we take off his back will have to go on the back of someone else. We'll send him up front, ahead of Nika, and he'll go unarmed. In camp he'll be tied up."

"I won't carry that damned iron a step farther," mumbled Duplessis.

"Then we'll abandon you," said La Salle.

Marc jerked Duplessis to his feet and lifted the iron to his back. "I watch him," said Nika grimly. "Anyone try to hurt my brother again *I* punish him." He struck his chest, eyes snapping in chagrin that while he was guarding in front, danger to his beloved La Salle had come from behind. "When I punish, it is death—but not a quick one." His rage softened as he turned to Marc and Victor. "You should have the beaver for your totem." His tone gave the words the quality of high praise.

The night camp was actually punishment for innocent and guilty alike. Still in the marshes, they had to sleep on frozen hummocks rising here and there from mud and water. Next day, the burdens were redistributed, and without the pit saw, Marc followed a little way behind Victor, whose tall blond head was as good an oriflamme as a king's plume. Behind them came Jean Michel, whose supplies of salves and physic were long since gone, leaving him to mutter about going back where he could be a surgeon and not a pack animal. It was with almost incredulous relief that they halted at last beside a series of pools where La Salle told them: "This is where the Kankakee rises, and the Kankakee flows into the Illinois."

Once more in canoes, they turned west, through a chain of lakes, into a winding stream. In a few days they emerged from marshes into a prairie, broken by a few leafless groves. "Now we get some hunting!" said one of the cooks. But Nika looked at the patches of bare earth and shook his head.

"Miamis burn it over," he said with a wide sweep of his arm. "Hunt wild ox last fall with fire circle around herd. No game here."

When it seemed they were doomed to starvation, they came upon a great shaggy beast, mired to his belly in a slough. "A wild ox," cried La Salle hoarsely.

The canoes were drawn up and Nika plunged a knife just back of the ribs of the weakened beast. "Bring one of the ship's cables," ordered La Salle.

Laurent, Messier, and Nika, with much thrashing about in the mud, got the cable lashed about the ox, and twelve men heaved it up on solid ground. "A welcome, even if ugly, present from *le bon dieu*," panted Laurent.

"*Le bon dieu* needn't have mired it quite so deep," laughed Messier.

"This was a hunt like none I've ever seen in France," said Marc, watching Nika and the cooks begin to strip the woolly skin from the flesh.

"That day at Versailles," said Victor, "you and Colbert were praising these hides to His Majesty. I had little idea then that such a beast would one day keep me from starving!"

To men prepared to eat anything it came as a pleasant surprise to find the roasted back meat and tongue really tasty, the broth flavorsome. Father Hennepin finally leaned back, hands folded over his paunch. "Umm, I feel as luxurious as a Jesuit!"

The rest of the meat was cut into thin strips and dried on pole frames above a damp-reed fire. Nika stretched and dressed the hide.

As they continued to descend the river, the prairie gave way to hills and forests. Many miles farther, at the base of a high sandstone cliff, La Salle led the way to shore. "I believe this is the great rock Joliet marked above the Illinois village," he said. "We'll camp here tonight."

While camp was being set up, Nika, who had climbed to the top of

243

the cliff, returned with disturbing news. "Illinois village—no smoke rising from lodges. Like village in land of souls."

"That's strange! Father Marquette wrote of meeting just below here five hundred chiefs and old men, and fifteen hundred young men with all their women and children." La Salle was plainly puzzled. "Maybe they're back in the trees."

But when, in the morning, they pulled up their canoes at the village and walked among the arbor-like huts, not even a dog was to be seen.

"And you said we could buy corn here!" Accau voiced the general disappointment.

La Salle shook his head. "This is very strange."

"The corn must be here anyway," said Brossard. "They'd leave it in caches." He and Accau set off toward the nearest hillside. Presently they set up a shout, calling the rest to an opened hole in the slope, filled with corn in rush baskets.

"Cover it again," ordered La Salle. "We can't take their food and seed for next year. Making them angry would ruin my plans. And if they have already been turned against us—no, we'll have to find them and ask for corn."

"*Non! Sacré bleu! Non!*" The men began shouting in defiance. Moyse pointed his pipe accusingly at La Salle. "You promised us corn, and corn we're going to have! If you won't take a little from savages to feed your men, you can build your blasted ship yourself!"

Troubled, La Salle looked from one to the other, all haggard, all weary, all staring hungrily at the corn.

"We're representatives of His Majesty," said Victor. "I think we have the right to live off the land we're taking for him."

La Salle glanced at him sharply. "Very well," he relented. "We'll measure thirty minots, and hope the Illinois will take goods in payment. If they don't we'll die a worse death than starvation."

Provisioned once more with corn, they paddled down the river, now flowing due south.

Every foot of the way they watched for signs of the Illinois. Four more days brought them to New Year's Day of 1680. The priests said Mass, and afterward embraced La Salle, with wishes for his success. Such was the good feeling, the hope brought by a new year, that everyone assured the priests he would be faithful. La Salle nonetheless never relaxed the guard of the night camps.

The fete night of the patron saint of Paris, Ste. Geneviève, found

244

them many leagues to the southwest, and on January 5 the river widened into a long lake, marked on La Salle's copy of Joliet's map as Pimitoui, the place of many wild oxen. Beyond the lake they once more followed the river. That evening they saw the smoke of many campfires on both sides of the river, around a broad curve. "The Illinois!" cried La Salle, and paddling quickly to shore, sent Nika ahead to scout. By the time they had set up their mat lodges, he was back, reporting numerous pirogues and about eighty Illinois huts. He reported that most of the young men must be away hunting, since the camp was filled mainly with older men, women, and children.

"Well, this is the test," said La Salle. "Tomorrow we'll know whether or not we can come to a peaceful agreement."

They stared at the distant smoke, rising in uncertain portent, and many lips moved in silent prayer.

28

"WE won't try to sneak up on them," La Salle announced after breakfast. "Outnumbered as we are, boldness is our only hope. Because of this curve in the river, they won't see us until we are right upon them."

Under his direction the eight canoes were launched and drawn up in line across the river, La Salle's canoe at the far right, Tonti's at the left. Victor caressed the D'Artagnan sword hilt once for luck as, at La Salle's signal, the line set off, letting the swift current carry them without paddles except one for steering. At another signal, all but the steersmen rose and stood with gun in hand as, rounding the bend, they swept dramatically into the very midst of the savage camp. With startled yells the savages leaped away from the shore. Screaming women gathered up their children and fled into the forest. Only a few braves snatched bows and arrows and, from behind trees or lodges, took aim at the intruders. La Salle's party quickly beached their canoes and stepped ashore. Ignoring the archers, La Salle led the way into the heart of the camp, making no signs of peace or of war.

"Stand still," he commanded. "Give them time to recover."

245

"Your calumet?" suggested Tonti in the same low tone.

"Not yet. They'd take it as a sign of weakness. They must show one first."

When the camp was as quiet as a tomb, La Salle shouted a few guttural words, demanding to know whether they wanted peace or war. More than one French shoulder grew tense, expecting the sting of an arrow. At last, a blanket in one lodge door swayed and two old men dressed in skins emerged to walk with dignity toward La Salle, bearing a red stone calumet decked with the white eagle feathers of peace.

"Who are you?" asked the old man with the pipe.

"We are Frenchmen," said La Salle.

"You are men." The old man's tone raised the simple words to the highest of praise. He was Nicanapé, he went on to say, brother of Chief Chassagoac; and in his brother's absence he welcomed them among the Illinois. "My people feared you had brought the Iroquois to attack us. We have heard that they are on the war trail. That is why we left our village."

Smiling, La Salle accepted the calumet and drew his own from beneath his coat, as, with joyful shouts, the Illinois swarmed toward them from all over the grove. Then the travelers were seated about the great central fire, to have their feet massaged with bear's grease. Victor and Marc were special objects of attention because of their blondness and identical appearance. Meat was placed before them, but the tension had quite destroyed their appetites, and the soggy mixture was scarcely an inducement to eat. Still, they had no choice, for one savage attached himself to each Frenchman, putting food in his guest's mouth with his own hand, in no case a very clean one.

The feasting was followed by a dance; and when the last drumbeat had died away, La Salle rose to speak in their own language, Brossard interpreting quietly to the French.

La Salle told them that he and his men had come from the St. Lawrence River to teach the Illinois knowledge of the Great Chief of heaven and earth, the use of firearms, and to give them many useful things. Victor watched the sea of impassive faces waiting to estimate La Salle's quality. The explorer was watchful too, fully aware of the consequences of failure. With ceremonial gravity he presented twists of tobacco and a few axes, his eyes roaming about to read their faces. He assured them he knew how precious was the corn they kept in reserve, but so great had been his need of food when he arrived at their

246

deserted village that he had taken thirty minots, most of which still remained in his canoes. If they were willing for him to have it, he would give them hatchets and other goods in exchange, but if they wanted it returned, he would go on to the Osages with his gifts and his blacksmith who could mend iron tools.

This argument left Victor and Marc with open mouths, but apparently he was playing on a tribal jealousy. He added that he wanted them to keep peace with the Iroquois. "I hold Onontio's voice in my hands, and I am to speak for him, through these presents, to all your nation. The King of France does not wish this river to be stained with blood." He added that if, in spite of their attempts to keep peace, the Iroquois came to attack them, he would defend the Illinois with the few Frenchmen he had; that he could supply them with arms and ammunition for protection; and that he could soon bring up larger forces.

Victor saw that he was impressing the listening Indians. Describing the hazards of the route he had traveled, he said he wanted to build a large ship for going down to the sea and bringing them goods by that shorter and easier way. But as building a ship was very costly, he wished to learn whether their river was navigable all the way to the sea, and whether any other Europeans lived at its mouth.

Nicanapé rose to answer. This was the moment that would decide whether they could build a fort here, the most important in La Salle's plan.

Every movement in the crowd was stilled. "We accept," said Nicanapé, "what you offer in payment for our corn. You may have even more. And we want you to remain with us and not go to the Osages."

Victor felt almost giddy with relief. At least they were safe; and the first part of La Salle's plan could be quickly accomplished. Yet he could not shake off an uneasiness. This Nicanapé was almost too quick to acquiesce. The Recollets, he saw, were exchanging glances as if they already saw a chapel and hundreds of converts under their direction. Nicanapé was still speaking, saying that the river Mississippi was broad and very beautiful, with no obstructions, and that slaves they had taken in war had spoken of great ships which made sounds like thunder, but that people from them had not settled on the coast. If they had, he added, the Illinois would have gone to trade with them, since the sea was only twenty days' journey in their pirogues. Finally, he offered them huts in the village; but La Salle, after making a tour,

247

asked instead for a large empty lodge somewhat apart downriver. While Tonti took charge of moving in their goods, La Salle, with Victor and Marc and the Recollets, stayed in the village, moving about like diplomats at a formal reception. One chief, Omawha, followed La Salle's every step, fondling the knife and hatchet La Salle had given him as if they were kittens.

The air seemed full of good will, but in the morning it became apparent that their troubles had not yet ended. This Omawha came to tell La Salle that a party of Miamis, with a Mascouten named Monso, had come to the village and spent most of the night stirring up the Illinois against him, saying the explorer had already inflamed the Iroquois against them; that he had a fort in their country; that he wanted to go down the Mississippi only to set the southern tribes against the Illinois.

"How did he know," asked Tonti, "that you had a fort among the Iroquois?"

"He was sent here by someone French," declared La Salle, with the calm of white-hot anger. "He has never been within a thousand miles of Fort Frontenac, but he spoke in detail of my affairs there."

"The Mascoutens live near the Pottawattomies," said Father Hennepin, "and their Jesuit missionaries."

La Salle nodded grimly. "They would know these things—and they would also know enough to send a friend of the Illinois—a Mascouten —not a Miami, one of their hereditary enemies." He sat down, his back against an oak.

"Aren't you going to talk to Nicanapé?" demanded Father Hennepin.

"Not until he makes the first move."

In spite of his calm, La Salle was obviously uneasy. As the forenoon wore on, depression and fear spread among the whole party, so that more than one jumped in alarm when a single young savage appeared. Nicanapé had sent him, he told La Salle, to invite them all to a feast.

After they had finished a silent and uncomfortable meal, Nicanapé let them wait in suspense before he rose and began to speak in quite another tone from that of the day before. Accau and Brossard whispered that, scattered among polite phrases, the old man was saying
. . . that he had invited La Salle to heal him of his disease of desiring to go down the great river,
. . . that no one had ever done so without perishing in it,

248

. . . that its banks were peopled by an endless succession of fierce tribes in such numbers that they could easily kill and eat all the French, no matter how well armed or brave,

. . . that the waters were full of huge, man-eating beasts,

. . . and that even if his ship protected him from all these perils, the river was full of rapids and cataracts so dangerous that no vessel could navigate them.

Victor, seeing credulity and fear on many a French face, knew that La Salle did not miss these signs, though he calmly allowed the speech to come to its end.

"Settle yourselves instead here in our country," Nicanapé concluded. "You will possess all our hearts and our trade."

La Salle rose, and thanked Nicanapé for this news, for, he said, the more obstacles there were to surmount, the greater the glory he and his men would earn for their great king Louis. In a more affectionate tone, he added, "But my men and I feel that all you have said was invented by your wish to keep us with you. Or perhaps it was put in your ears by some evil spirit, making you distrust my plans. It is not surprising that your neighbors should become jealous of the advantages of the good trade you will have with us, and that they talk against us to keep you from having these advantages. I am astonished, though, that you are so quick to give your belief to them." Looking Nicanapé in the face he added, "I was not asleep, my brother, when Monso spoke to you last night in secret against the French and pictured us as spies of the Iroquois." With a meaning glance toward the corner of the hut, where the earth was freshly disturbed, he went on, "I know the presents he gave you to make you believe his falsehoods are still hidden in this lodge." A few sidelong glances toward the corner showed he had hit the mark; and he quickly pursued his advantage:

"Why did this Monso run away so fast? Why didn't he speak in the daylight if he had nothing to say that was not true? He told you we were in league with the Iroquois. The Iroquois themselves know how the French can fight, and that if the French wanted to make war on you, they would need no help from the Iroquois! But to make sure in your minds, send someone after Monso and I will wait for him here and uncover his lies to his face. How can he know so much about me as he pretends? I invite you to look at the packs in our hut; they contain only tools and trading goods. You will see that we are not equipped for attack."

After some silence Nicanapé grunted, sent runners to bring Monso

back, and called for more food while they waited. In due time the
runners returned, saying that last night's snow had wiped out Monso's
trail and it was hopeless to look for him.

La Salle withdrew with his men, leaving what he had said to sim-
mer in Nicanapé's mind. "You really impressed him with that 'magic'
knowledge about Monso," Tonti said admiringly.

Nika too was full of admiration. Victor thought how strange it was
that La Salle inspired in the ignorant savage and the cultured Italian
the same affection and loyalty; and he could not help feeling shame,
duty to the King notwithstanding, for the letter he had sent on the
Griffin. If the *Griffin* were lost . . . Angrily he suppressed a hope that
the letter might not reach Versailles. My duty is still to the King, he
told himself, and I am interested in nothing but returning to his personal service.

All through the day workmen and voyageurs, the surgeon Jean
Michel in their midst, kept gathering to talk about the Mississippi,
predicting that all their hardships would lead only to death by a
savage arrow or a sea monster. To counteract them, Tonti led Marc,
Victor, Dautray and the Recollets in ridicule of the nonsense Nicanapé
had uttered, until the men dispersed. But in the morning Jean Michel,
Duplessis, and the four men on the last guard duty were gone with all
the corn they could carry and a pack of trading goods. Fortunately,
they took no canoes.

"The fools!" said La Salle. "Running away in panic, overland! The
chance that they'll die of hunger is a thousand times greater than the
dangers of the Mississippi. To desert when the worst is over and we're
so near our goal! I'm not surprised at Duplessis, but that Jean Michel
should go——"

"That ain't the worst," interrupted Moyse. "The two sawyers are
gone, and there's no use starting any ship without 'em. We've damned
near killed ourselves getting the forge and all this heavy stuff here,
and now—no ship. And if Luc wrecked the one on the lakes . . ."

"We'll manage," said La Salle curtly; but his shoulders drooped.
Victor turned away in despair. Another long delay! He heard La Salle
saying, "I can only appeal to the rest of you to continue in your duty.
This I will promise: if any of you are afraid to venture on the Mississippi, I will give you a full release in the spring to return to Quebec,
and a canoe to make your voyage."

A long silence fell while every man searched his heart. Not mere

250

loyalty to a leader or a contract was in question, but a decision that might mean life or death. Tonti was first to assure him he would stay; then Dautray and Marc, followed by Victor—the only one, he thought wryly, who really had no choice. Moyse declared gruffly, "That's fair enough," and the rest fell into line to shake La Salle's hand; after which they gathered around the fire where the cooks were warming a stew left in the kettle from the night before. As usual, they served the first portion to La Salle. He wandered away, bowl in hand. Suddenly Victor heard a muffled exclamation and turned to see La Salle doubled over, groaning, before he dropped to the earth.

"He's poisoned!" cried Tonti. The rest dropped their bowls as if they were red hot. Tonti and Dautray got La Salle to his feet and helped him, stumbling, into the lodge. The three Recollets came in and knelt in prayer at his feet. Nika ran to the woods and came back with a handful of roots and barks he put to stew over the fire. Victor sniffed at the boiling mixture and drew back, holding his nose.

"Put many kinds in," said Nika. "One may be right to sicken evil spirit so it go away."

Inside the lodge a troubled Tonti was wiping the perspiration from the contorted face of the retching man.

"Here, Victor, rinse this towel in cold water," said Tonti.

On the way back from the river, Victor said to Marc in passing, "Just like Father!"

Marc started. "I'd forgotten. I have that poison antidote from Villette's!" Desperately he sorted his pack for the little vial and, dissolving part of the powder in warm water, helped La Salle sit up to drink it. "Should we bleed him, too?"

Nika shook his head. "No. Blood is the fire of life. Better to put some in than take it out. We make a sweat bath."

Under his direction a small hut was erected, oven-shaped, covered with mats, such as Nika frequently used for himself. La Salle was seated in it and the hut was filled with steam by pouring water over hot stones. At length Victor and Marc carried La Salle back to the lodge and covered him with blankets. Even the praying Recollets were banished so that the leader could rest in peace.

"Will he get well?" asked Marc, when Nika, relieved by Tonti, came out to the fire.

"If the Great Spirit wishes," said Nika.

"He's strong," said Marc. "He ought to pull through."

"A great warrior. But better he were a red man," sighed Nika.

Victor laughed. *"Nom de dieu,* why?"

"White man want to be cured as soon as sick. Afraid to die when he get little fever. Fear make disease worse and it more likely to kill him. Red man patient. He know sickness nothing, death nothing but trail to another life."

"But just not being afraid to die," protested Victor, "won't keep a man from it."

Nika rose to stir the herbs. "Maybe not. But without fear, he live better, die better."

La Salle recovered. And in the week before his full strength returned, the Recollets began their missionary work. Father Membré taught the Illinois children the *Pater, Ave,* and *Credo;* while Fathers Ribourde and Hennepin alternately preached and cared for the sick, dosing fevers and dressing wounds, ever ready with baptismal water to send a dying soul to Paradise. Victor and Marc, with Nika, hunted or gambled with Illinois warriors, but Marc's face really lighted with joy when La Salle announced that he was ready to build his fort.

"Where?" he asked. "I still like that rock above the Illinois village."

"You're a worthy son of Vauban," said La Salle. "We may turn to that spot later. But now we need a site that's also good for shipbuilding. A little way below here, I should think."

Father Hennepin, writing in his journal, pricked up his ears. "I'll look for a site."

"We'll all go," said La Salle shortly.

"Can't we forget the ship and go in canoes?" asked Victor unhappily. "Why not look for some easy wealth along the river? I'd like that better than all this fort building—and so would His Majesty."

"My interests demand," said La Salle coldly, "that we fortify as we go, as centers for future colonies."

"Your interests! But what about His Majesty's?" began Victor, but La Salle cut him short: "As head of this expedition, let me decide what serves His Majesty best." Victor stifled a retort and walked away toward the river.

"I'm sorry——" began Marc.

"Never mind. He just can't stop being Captain of the Guards," said La Salle. "We'll build a ship," he added, raising his voice slightly, "and descend in her to the Gulf, trading as we go. After that we'll sail her, full of wild oxen hides, to France. The cargo will pay for the enterprise. And with a fort well established here, I'll be ready to report to the King and Colbert, bring back a garrison and supplies and make arrangements to start commerce through the Gulf."

Sail to France! Victor turned back, his anger gone, his heart leaping. He could make his own report, and be free of this loathsome assignment! "Then if we build her as fast as we did the *Griffin,* we might go back this fall!"

"Of course," said La Salle calmly. "By the time we get the ship started, Luc will be here with supplies to finish it."

They chose a spot about five miles downstream where a level beach along the water was dominated by a hill suitable for a fort. By the time their camp was transferred, snow had begun to fall. Gradually a palisade twenty-five feet high arose about the hilltop, with lodgings for the men built in two of the corners, the forge and magazine in another, and a cabin for the Recollets in the last. In the center, two lodges were put up, one for La Salle and Nika, one to be shared by Tonti, Marc, Victor and Dautray.

Tonti and Marc, permitted to name the fort, decided upon Fort Crèvecoeur, after the site of Louis's victory in the Low Countries. "Fort Heartbreak," repeated Tonti.

"That's a morbid name," objected Victor.

"Appropriate enough," said Tonti, "considering all our disasters."

"Fort Crèvecoeur it is, then," said La Salle. "Now let's start the ship."

"Without sawyers, rigging, iron, sails, anchors?" asked Moyse sarcastically.

"We'll still get everything we need," said La Salle stubbornly, as if the *Griffin* would stay afloat as long as he had faith that she would. "The lack of sawyers is the great difficulty, as there are none nearer than Montreal. But I'll try sawing planks myself, if someone will help me."

The men exchanged horrified glances. "No, monsieur, not you," said Laurent. *"Moi,* I'll try being top sawyer."

"Moi aussi," said Messier promptly. "I helped a little once. I'll be pitman."

So, with the help of Accau and Brossard, they got the saw set up and started awkwardly on the unfamiliar work. Once more stocks were laid, a keel, ribs, and finally the planking. Although it was cold and they were harassed by an incessant snowfall, Tonti and Marc worked cheerfully, as did Victor, a vision of Angélique before him. But few

253

of the others did. There was none of that pride in workmanship they had experienced at the building of the *Griffin*. Yet gradually a hull arose. "And it'll be seaworthy," promised Moyse. "That is, if you can get her rigged. Luc'd be here by now if he was coming, you know it as well as I do. I bet that Chapelle and Leblanc who went up to meet him have skipped out, too."

"We'll get her rigged," said La Salle quietly; and Moyse looked at him somberly, tapping his pipe against the hull.

The next morning, after the Recollets had departed for the Illinois village, La Salle quietly bade his chief associates meet in his cabin, saying nothing to the workmen. "Until now," began La Salle when the circle was complete, "I had hoped for news that the *Griffin* had completed her voyage and was wintering at Fort Miami, or at worst, at Michilimackinac. I still hope the *Griffin* is safe," he added firmly, "but we can no longer depend on it. Lacking her cargo, there's no iron, rigging, or anchors nearer than Fort Frontenac. And there, too, or at the Niagara storehouse, the twenty thousand livres' worth of goods and the twenty men sent from France last autumn should be waiting. I have decided to go back and get what we need."

One after another they looked up, startled, as if he had just announced a trip to the moon.

"Mais, c'est impossible!" exclaimed Dautray. "Such a great distance, with rivers frozen? You would go on foot?"

"If necessary, yes, I'll go on foot," said La Salle. "Not the long way through the lakes, but overland from Fort Miami to the strait between Huron and Erie. Even so it will be at least one thousand miles. But I must go, or delay the expedition for a whole year; and that would beggar me with expenses."

And he can afford the waste of time even less, thought Victor. Almost two of his five years are already gone, and he's a long way from having flourishing colonies around a chain of forts.

"I shall not go alone, I hope," La Salle resumed. "I'll take Nika, and two or three volunteers. For food, we'll have to depend on hunting."

"But you'll be in constant danger," protested Dautray. "The woods are full of savages. You might meet an Iroquois army coming this way."

"We'll be a larger party coming back," said La Salle. "The twenty men from France—perhaps more if I can hire them."

"If you must go—I'll go with you," offered Tonti.

"Thank you. But I must ask you to do the hardest part of the job—

254

to stay here and keep the men occupied until I get back. If you aren't afraid?"

Tonti smiled faintly. "With only a handful of men, and danger of an Iroquois attack—of course I'll be afraid. But I'll do my best. We must take and hold all this land for France. In Europe they fight over a few square leagues, or a rock in the sea, while here is all this vast space, with fertile valleys, rivers, lakes . . ." He paused, blushing for his enthusiasm.

"Yes," said La Salle softly, and his eyes glowed

Abruptly Dautray said to La Salle, *"Eh bien,* I'll go with you. I'd like to visit my parents."

"I'll go, too," said Marc.

La Salle cast a thoughtful glance over the two of them. "All right, Dautray. But Marc will be more useful here."

His rejection of Marc made the decision Victor had been putting off even harder. The trips to and fro in this country were as arid a business as marching and countermarching, and this one would be worse than most; but once more the King's orders left him no choice. Balancing that ordeal against a year's delay, he felt that he'd rather see it through. He tried to speak lightly when he said: "I'll go with you, if I can be of any use."

"Good," said La Salle promptly. "I'll send off reports to Colbert and Count Frontenac while we're at the fort."

Victor nodded, smiling thinly. Why couldn't he reject me, too? he thought. He glanced miserably at Marc, turning away again in embarrassment before the open pride in his brother's eyes.

"If you want more," said Tonti, "Brossard might be a good choice. And Hinaut. They're both good woodsmen."

"Good suggestions," approved La Salle. "I'll ask them both."

"Of course," said Tonti, "Father Hennepin will want to go. And it would be easier for me if you took him. As soon as you leave, he'll start managing everything. He resents my authority. I don't question his virtue, but I wish he knew when to keep his mouth shut."

"Even when I am present," said La Salle ruefully, "there seems to be some confusion in his mind as to whose expedition this is. No, I don't want him with me. And you shouldn't have to cope with him, either. Fathers Ribourde and Membré will do all the good he could do, without any of the trouble. I think," he added slowly, "I might give him an expedition of his own. I've been wishing I could find out what the Mississippi is like north of the Illinois, without taking the whole party's time. I'll pick a good man to explore the upper Mississippi—and send Father Hennepin with him."

They all burst into laughter. "Perfect!" exclaimed Tonti.

"I'll put Accau in charge," La Salle went on, "because he knows several languages and I can trust his report. While I am gone, Tonti, do as much as you can on the ship, and keep trading for furs with the Illinois. But chiefly try to keep the men contented and busy."

"If only they weren't so desperately afraid of the Mississippi!" said Tonti. "They still believe those wild tales of monsters, cataracts, and fierce tribes that will kill us on sight."

La Salle sighed. "Before I go I must find some way to disprove those tales."

Dinner over, La Salle announced his journey, and asked Brossard and Hinaut to go along. They both accepted promptly.

"I'll go, too," said Father Hennepin decisively. Those who had been in the earlier conference exchanged glances of anticipation.

"No," said La Salle. "There is other important work for you."

"What is it?" asked the friar sulkily. "I don't see any reason to stay here. Three missionaries are more than we need in one place."

"Exactly," said La Salle smoothly.

Father Hennepin raised his eyebrows. "But you said——"

"I said I had other work for you."

La Salle turned to the cluster of voyageurs. "Accau, I'd like to have you select another man, take one canoe, go down to the mouth of the Illinois and turn north, exploring and trading as far as you can up the Mississippi. I'll supply you with goods."

With a look of surprise, Accau nodded cheerfully. "I'd rather have a paddle in my hands than an axe, any time. I'll take Picard Du Gay."

"And Father Hennepin will go with you." La Salle quietly dropped the bombshell.

It was plain that the last seven words spoiled the plan for Accau, but he had no chance to say so. Father Hennepin was on his feet, looking as outraged as if he had been asked to swim all the way stark naked. "You're trying to get me out of the way because you're jealous of me. I won't do it!" he stormed. "You want to send me off where I'll be killed, so you can discover the mouth of the Mississippi and take all the credit. You're sending me right into the country of those dreadful Sioux! No! I won't go!"

Father Ribourde lifted a slender hand. "Gently, my son."

"But I can't make such a ridiculous journey. Send somebody else."
He looked around belligerently. "Anybody else."

"You've said a hundred times," La Salle reminded him, "that you wanted to see unknown regions and convert new tribes. This is your chance."

"But the Illinois say the Sioux are the worst tribe in the world!"

"Remember," interposed Father Ribourde, "that those who die in bed do not always die the best death. The blood of martyrs is the seed of the Church."

Father Hennepin's expression showed that he had no desire to be converted into seed. "But I——"

"I know I am too old and weak for such a journey," said Father Ribourde, "or I would gladly offer myself."

"No, Father, I want you here with our men," said La Salle affectionately. "No need for you to expose yourself when there is a younger priest available. And Father Membré will be occupied with his mission among the Illinois."

"But he hates it!" Father Hennepin protested. "He's always complaining about their filth and stubbornness. He can go on this exploration, and I'll take his place."

Father Membré shook his head. "Thank you for your generous offer. It is true I find the work burdensome and the manners of these savages repulsive, as who would not? The smoke, the fleas, the filth, the dogs—and those boys dressed in women's clothes. . . . " He shuddered. "And when I preach to them, they answer, 'That's wonderful!' but they don't change one of their ways." He sighed. "Nevertheless, I prefer to keep on trying."

Father Hennepin glared around the circle like a trapped animal. "You have no right to order me to certain death."

"Then," said La Salle evenly, "I shall report to your Superior that you refused to carry the cross to the Sioux."

"You can't do that! He'd recall me to France." Father Hennepin's face resembled a round thundercloud. "I know what's behind this. Don't think you are fooling me." He swung on Tonti. "It's all your fault! You're keeping a journal, too. You want to be the only one to write about the discovery of the Mississippi. But it belongs in my book!"

"That's enough," said Father Ribourde. "What has become of your faith, your zeal? You should take this order as a Heaven-sent opportunity to establish our Lord's name among nations that have not heard of him!"

257

"All right, I will go." Father Hennepin thrust out his chin and turned to impress his audience with his fearlessness. "Anybody but me would be frightened. But I believe that God will protect me, even though Monsieur de la Salle exposes my life so rashly. I dread torture only because a maimed priest can no longer say Mass."

The next day a lone Illinois youth in a small pirogue paddled up the river, returning home from a distant war expedition. He had been away since their arrival and was astonished at their presence. La Salle brought him to the kettle bubbling over an outdoor fire, and kept close beside him, offering him food and gifts. "So you have been far to the south?" asked La Salle.

"Yes. Far." The young man's hand flung an arc over the west and south. "Far away on Mississippi."

"In a pirogue?" La Salle added a knife to his pile of gifts. "Then there are no portages?"

"Very broad, smooth river, all the way to sea. No white water."

"Tribes very fierce?"

"No. Fine people along river. Friendly to everyone."

"Friendly to Frenchmen, too?"

"If you go, they all dance the calumet with you. Happy to trade for hatchets and knives. They trade now with white men with long hair who fight on horseback and carry long knives."

"Spaniards with lances." La Salle added a hatchet to the gifts, and asked more details about the river. The youth took a sharp stick, smoothed the bare earth, and drew a map of the river's course, marking distances by the day's journey in a pirogue.

"By gar'," said Messier. "We'll be as safe on the Mississippi as on the St. Lawrence. *Moi*, I'm looking forward to it. We wait here until Monsieur de la Salle comes back. Then we finish the ship and take a nice ride home to France."

The workmen picked up their tools with unaccustomed cheerfulness. La Salle, smiling, turned to the map drawn on the ground. "Marc, copy this on paper as exactly as you can."

258

29

AT dawn on the first of March, two loaded canoes waited to be launched eastward against the swift current. The little band at Fort Crèvecoeur had gathered with serious faces to see them off.

"Think you can make it?" asked Marc.

"Of course," answered Victor jauntily. "Best soldiers on earth, us musketeers. . . ." His attempted banter died upon his lips. The separation would be long; it might be permanent; and only the gods knew whether those departing or those remaining would be in greater danger.

"If you get back to France, and I don't——" he began.

"We'll go back together," said Marc firmly. *"Dieu vous gard."*

After the first few miles of paddling, the trip turned into an ordeal such as Victor would never have faced in a lifetime in France. Across the twenty-one miles of Lake Pimitoui, frozen from shore to shore, they dragged their canoes on sledges. Upriver they alternately broke the ice ahead of the canoes or portaged them through snow and rain. Even La Salle admitted defeat at last. Hiding the canoes on a wooded island, they loaded the goods on their backs and struck out overland.

It was twenty-four days before they saw the palisade of Fort Miami loom through the trees. Chapelle and Leblanc were there, delayed because they had made a circuit of the entire lake looking for the *Griffin*. None of the savages or traders they encountered had even heard of her. It seemed she had vanished into thin air. Furthermore, Chapelle reported that a trader from Montreal had told them the loss of the *Griffin* had been used to ruin La Salle's credit completely. He would get no more supplies at any of the settlements. After La Salle had sent Chapelle and Leblanc on to Fort Crèvecoeur with a letter to Tonti, including orders to fortify the high cliff above the Illinois village, calling this one Fort St. Louis, he led his own party on to the east.

From Fort Miami onward the journey became a nightmare. The

underbrush shredded their clothes. There was almost no game for food. The whole of one day they were trailed by a roving band of Mascouten Indians. And finally two of the party, Hinaut and Brossard, came down with fever. While they lay helpless beside the fire, La Salle went exploring for rivers that might run into the lakes. "If I find one," he promised, "we'll build a canoe and travel by water."

When he returned, he was nearly exhausted, but he had found a river. "I think," he announced cheerfully, "it will lead us all the way to the strait."

Half-carrying the sick men, La Salle, Victor, Dautray and Nika transferred camp to the riverbank. Here, under Nika's direction, they chopped down an elm tree, stripped off its bark with the aid of kettle after kettle of boiling water; and after days of painful labor fashioned a rude canoe, precariously bound and sewed together. "Now there's a craft that will take us all the way to Niagara," proclaimed the indomitable La Salle.

But his optimism was unfounded. After a fine start downstream, they found the river too winding, too full of snags and fallen trees, the makeshift canoe too heavy to portage. In despair they finally abandoned it. But meanwhile, the sick men had recovered sufficiently to continue on foot.

Once, when Victor caught sight of his own reflection in a still pool, he recoiled in horror. His face had become haggard, his eyes sunken and lusterless; his hair hung lank about his temples.

Dautray fell ill next; then Hinaut—and even Nika. When Hinaut dropped to the ground, crying, "We can go no farther! We're more dead than alive," one glance at him showed that he was speaking the truth. "Try to keep on till we reach the strait," said La Salle with unexpected gentleness. "Then you may go up to Michilimackinac and wait till I return. On the way back, of course, I'll be taking the water route."

Somehow, at last, their dogged plodding brought them to the strait. Here, after a rest, Hinaut and Brossard built a canoe and, supplied with provisions, paddled off toward Michilimackinac. The remainder of the party, under La Salle, crossed the strait on a raft; and then set out by foot again on the long trek eastward.

At Lake Erie, Dautray and Nika collapsed. Building still another canoe, Victor and La Salle loaded the sick men into it and paddled laboriously, mile after mile, up the full length of the lake.

It was Easter Monday before they spied the channel to the river Niagara. As they rode its swift current down to the *Griffin's* shipyard, even the sick men clung to the gunwales, watching for the familiar cluster of little bark cabins. When they finally pulled up at the willow-hung beach, Victor leaped out, drew up the canoe, and turned to give Dautray a hand. "We're here!" he exulted. "We've made it!"

La Salle hastened on to greet Father Watteau and a few workmen who came hurrying down the slope with cries of surprise. "Monsieur de la Salle! Can it be?" exclaimed Father Watteau. "Welcome, welcome a thousand times! But you are ill—all of you! Come in quickly. You must have some food. . . ."

The look of shock on the priest's face made Victor realize how ghastly they must appear—ragged, stained, bearded, gaunt.

"We're all here, every man you left," said Father Watteau. "Even the Shawano hunters."

La Salle clasped the little priest's hand. "Good, good. But tell me, have you seen the *Griffin* since we left?"

Victor, helping Dautray toward the cabins, stopped in his tracks and waited for the answer.

"We heard she had disappeared," said Father Watteau sadly. "A mysterious and terrible thing."

La Salle stood dumb with misery, fighting for control. At last he said: "But tell me—by now my ship from France should have unloaded at Montreal. Have her goods been brought here to the storehouse, as I ordered?"

"I'm afraid, my son, I have another blow for you," answered the priest. "That ship was totally wrecked at the mouth of the St. Lawrence and the whole cargo lost."

"No!" At this new misfortune, La Salle stood bewildered, rubbing his forehead with a trembling hand. "The men——?"

"Rescued, but lost to you, I'm afraid. Some were detained by Duchesneau at Quebec. All but four of the rest have gone back home. They were told you were dead."

That night, Victor and Dautray agreed that La Salle must now give up. To their surprise, he began the morning by announcing that he would make every effort to obtain goods at Montreal, despite his ruined credit. Victor could only stare at him in amazement.

He and Dautray were in La Salle's cabin as he stood shaving, Nika holding the bowl of hot water. "I still marvel," Dautray was saying, "at how you came through so much better than any of us."

"You two did nearly as well," said La Salle. "Much better than Brossard and Hinaut. I've always said"—he paused with razor poised over lathered cheek—"that all other things being equal, a man with a trained and developed mind stands hardship better than the uneducated."

He finished shaving and wiped his face.

"You'll all be as good as new with a few days of rest," he continued. "I shall go on east at once, but I'll take three men from here. You take time to get well. Then, Dautray, how would you like to take four men from the camp here with you and start back in two canoes to join Tonti? Father Watteau can give you plenty of food and clothing."

Dautray gave him a startled look, but said after a brief silence, "Yes, I'll go back. I am most uneasy about Tonti and Marc."

"We'll all rejoin them before very long," promised La Salle.

After La Salle and his three men had disappeared down the portage path, Victor, Dautray, and Nika spent nearly a week at the shipyard sleeping, eating, gaining back lost weight and strength. Then Dautray set out for the west, and Victor and Nika, now completely recovered, walked to the storehouse and sailed to Fort Frontenac on the *Cataraqui,* which was still making regular trips on the lake. Here Victor and Jacques had a joyful reunion. Jacques had never been so happy as now, absorbed in his fields and gardens, full of plans for clearing even more land. La Salle, however, had gone on at once to Montreal; so Nika and Victor went on by canoe to join him.

They found La Salle at the little house he owned and used as his Montreal headquarters. Handsome, showing no signs of his strenuous journey, he welcomed them both with quiet pleasure. "You will stay here," he said. "I have plenty of room."

"How are your affairs coming along?" asked Victor. "Are you getting what you need?"

La Salle shook his head. "My arrival caused quite a stir," he said with a wry smile. "Someone had done a good job of spreading the news that I was dead. My credit had been thoroughly killed—and partly by my brother Jean! The Superior sent him back to France last November, and before he went, he seized every pack of furs I had sent down here, sold them for twenty thousand livres, and pocketed the money. And his note was not even due. My other creditors tried to reason with him, but he wasn't interested in their problems or in mine. I could have used those furs to satisfy all my creditors, but now I am completely blocked. Count Frontenac sends word that he is having his own difficulties and can't raise another sou for me."

Victor glanced up quickly, but the explorer's face was impassive. He was looking down at the table before the fireplace, where he had evidently just poured sand over a freshly written page when they knocked. "Oh, that reminds me. That heap of letters on the mantel is for you, Victor. From France. And a note from someone here in Montreal."

Victor seized them and flipped through them eagerly. Several from Versailles, he saw in excitement, but he wanted to be alone to read them. He opened the note first. It was an invitation to a ball at the Château le Moyne for the following evening. "Are you going to this?" He tossed it down before La Salle.

"I'm not invited. Monsieur le Moyne is an associate of Monsieur le Ber's. But one of His Majesty's Guards has the entree, of course."

"Well, then—" Victor crumpled the note and tossed it into the fireplace.

"No, I wish you'd go," said La Salle. "Lucie will be there. You could talk to her and find out if she's well. They've guarded her so closely since I've been here that I haven't had even a glimpse."

"That *is* hard," said Victor. It's as if, he thought, I were back at Versailles now and couldn't see Angélique. "All right, I'll go. I'll wear my uniform and the D'Artagnan sword; and I'll wager my next muskrat that I get permission to bring Mademoiselle Lucie home. If you should be waiting on the route——"

La Salle stared at him as if heaven itself had opened to his view. "You—you will do that?"

"Of course. Nothing to it, for one of His Majesty's musketeers. But if I had a girl of my own, I'd look forward to the occasion a little more. Mademoiselle Lucie's sighs will be all for you. I'd like a pretty girl to flirt with a bit. You must know someone in Montreal."

La Salle wiped his eyes with a fine linen handkerchief. "Yes, I do. My cousin Francois Plet has come from France to manage the business at Fort Frontenac for me, and is at present staying here at Ville Marie. He has a charming daughter."

"Oh—the girl in the carriage!" Victor could remember only a blue bonnet and dress, and peals of laughter at Nika's performance with the hat. "Fine!"

La Salle sat down at the table and took up a quill. "I'll write a note of introduction, so you can call and pay your respects."

Victor tucked the note in his pocket and excused himself, hurrying with the letters in his hand down to a deserted part of the beach, where he sat on an overturned canoe. His fingers trembled at the magic postmark of Paris. There were letters from Auguste, from Madame, and two in a childish hand he didn't recognize. A feeling of disappointment came over him because of the letters that had not come. None from his *bel ange* Angélique; none from His Majesty or even Colbert. Maybe Angélique enclosed one in Madame's, he thought, and ripped open the earliest one with the Orleans crest. Yes, there it was, a note from Angélique, a brief one, written soon after he left; a formal little affair that revealed only that she could put down nothing coherent on paper. He ripped open the other two, encountering there only the strong slanting hand of Madame.

As he read, he learned little of what he wanted to know, though there was news enough. The peace treaty had been signed at Nimwegen the autumn after he left France. Spain had really been the loser, and Louis had retained his place as Europe's greatest sovereign.

Madame's daughter, Mlle. d'Orleans, had been married to the ugly, deformed King of Spain in the Fontainebleau chapel. Montespan had attended in a very daring dress, but was grief-stricken at the triumphant bearing of a certain blond young woman.

Victor let the sheets fall to his knee. Of course Madame had to be discreet and not mention names, for all letters were opened and reported upon to the King; but why hadn't she given him some hint that the young blonde was not the one he feared it was. He ripped open the third letter, and found further scattered references to the new favorite: that she couldn't keep time in dancing; that six beautiful Arab horses had the honor of drawing a new gray coach; that the coach owner had been newly created a duchess. He crushed the letter in his palm. If it was Angélique, she had got her carriage, one even finer than the Comtesse de Soisson's.

Impatiently he hastened through the agriculturally flavored pages from Auguste. ". . . Your little brother is big enough now to enjoy making a good figure at the village dances; otherwise he studies with his tutor, fishes, and takes long walks. I did find your ring and will keep it for you. We are both eager for you to come back. *Adieu,* for I have come to the end of my paper."

The letters in the unknown handwriting, to his surprise and amusement, came from the girl Michelle, still at the convent.

Putting these aside for Marc, he walked slowly back along the shore, depressed by the conviction that he knew all too well who the new favorite was. Full of grief and anger at first, he began gradually making excuses for her. She had been dazzled by the King. How could she remember a distant guardsman? Yet it was not likely to be Angélique, he tried to tell himself, for it was an unwritten law that the favorite must be both married and titled. He took a turn about the narrow stretch of beach. It's all my imagination, he said to himself, something I've been reading into those letters. He pulled the locket from his deerskins, and its diamonds seemed to blink with reassurance. Opening it, he touched the blond curl that brought her presence back, though he could not remember her features. He could only remember that she was beautiful—with a beauty already grown distant, pale, cold, like that of the moon. Everything is going to be all right, he told himself firmly. Angélique is still waiting. All I need to worry about now is how to buy the captaincy.

Not much hope, now, to get it through La Salle. He glanced back at La Salle's little house. That unlucky man was now possessed by his dream in more than one way. I'm sorry for him, thought Victor; sorry for him—and for my own lost investment. Can't he see that the odds are too great against him? Why doesn't he give up?

But the thought failed to carry the conviction it had always borne. Why shouldn't La Salle fulfill his dream if he can? He's so close to it now. Vast profits in furs are waiting there for someone; and as a shareholder in a string of forts and trading posts, I could buy my captaincy in no time. Victor strode up and down the sand, gazing at the broad St. Lawrence. Marc could go to the Sorbonne as long as he liked. And it would mean a lot to Tonti. Someone, sometime, will open up the West. If La Salle fails, it will be a Spaniard or an Englishman who will succeed.

Victor stopped in his tracks to face a revelation that brought order out of chaos. La Salle must triumph. I want him to! I've been wanting it for a long time—and not only for the money in it. He deserves to succeed. Such courage, such perseverance, such vision set him high among Frenchmen. What crowds have joined in celebrations for a Condé, a Turenne, who added only one town to France! La Salle

265

might add a hundred! The King ordered me to watch him, not to help him; but, orders or not, I would help him if I could. I would be proud to have a part in his success. If I only had the Queen's ring, I could sell it. But I have nothing, nothing that anyone here would want to buy. And then a thought struck him, as startling and as painful as a lance thrust in his side: I have D'Artagnan's sword!

No, I can't do it. No one, no one, he argued, would expect me to give it up. But as he stared at the waves breaking at his feet, the thought came to him that D'Artagnan would.

It was a voice he could not deny. With quickening pace, then on the run, he went back to La Salle's house to get the sword.

Instinctively he knew that the one man most certain to be tempted by his treasure was the merchant Le Ber. He had bought a patent of nobility to add a plume to his hat. He had boundless money, ambition, and cupidity. And, Victor admitted wryly, there was a certain pleasure in rescuing La Salle by using one of his worst enemies. But all this, Victor knew, must be kept secret from La Salle. La Salle would never accept the money if he knew.

Without disturbing anyone, Victor quietly stole out of the house with his uniform and sword, took the uniform to a tailor's, had it pressed, and arrayed himself in it before calling upon Le Ber. Victor introduced himself, adding that he was a brother of the Marquis de Lorennes of Rouen, on leave from the King's Guards. M. le Ber listened to his proposition, scarcely able to take his eyes off the emerald in the hilt. "This is startling," he said at last. "And you're with La Salle. Would you give the money to him?"

Victor drew himself up in frigid dignity. Fixing a haughty eye on M. le Ber, he said in his most lofty manner, "Do I hear correctly? Is a tradesman questioning one whose nobility goes back for centuries? What I am using the money for does not concern you. The Marquis de Seignelay has made a standing offer of one hundred thousand livres for this sword. If you pay me sixty thousand, you can make a profit of forty thousand. I can't wait long enough to send it to the Marquis myself. You can. That is all that concerns you. That and the consideration that you will be doing an inestimable favor to the Marquis de Seignelay. I make one condition: secrecy. You must not reveal this transaction to anyone on this side of the ocean. No one is to know I have sold it. I would be displeased, and my displeasure would reach the ears of His Majesty when I return to France."

Le Ber bowed humbly, fluttering his reddened hands. Victor's bearing impressed him as Victor had expected. In the sword he saw only an object of marketable value—something the son of Colbert wanted and would be most grateful to receive. That gratitude he could use. . . . "I assure you, Monsieur de Lorennes, I am very glad to be of service. I have not that much available, but I believe that in a few hours I can raise it from friends."

"Very well. I shall return at four."

Since half the sum would be enough for all La Salle's present needs, Victor kept 30,000 livres. He purchased a cheap sword to wear in place of his lost treasure. With the rest of the coins in a moneybag, he waited near La Salle's house until Nika came out alone. The perfect messenger!

"For La Salle," said Victor, thrusting the bag into the lean brown hands. "It will buy all he wants. But you must not tell him who gave it to you. Just say that someone who does not want to give his name wishes to invest in his enterprise, and will not ask repayment until La Salle is able."

Nika's eyes gleamed. "A man's name is his own, to give or not to give. It will not come to my brother through my mouth."

Victor made a dozen starts on his report to the King. How was he to put into a few words for a busy monarch to read, the meaning of what he had seen and endured in the New World? Finally he reported briefly how far they had penetrated the continent; and listed the forts already established. After much chewing at his quill, he added:

I believe M. de la Salle is the only man in New France capable of carrying out this great enterprise. He is always correct in his behavior and insists on discipline among his men. He speaks and understands many savage languages; he knows native customs so well that he obtains whatever he wishes by skill and eloquence. They seem to esteem him highly. He is energetic, and works harder than any of his men. I believe, Sire, that with Your Majesty's protection, he will found colonies more important than all others previously established by Frenchmen.

Reading the letter again, he wondered whether he had said too much, but reflected that he should trust the good judgment of the

King, who had made use of great talents before. Above all, he rejoiced that his previous, damaging letter had been lost on the *Griffin*.

Nika paddled him across the river to the Le Moyne château, which built of stone and flanked with four towers, was one of the most impressive in New France. Victor was glad that he had worn his uniform, for the ballroom was ablaze with color.

"Come," said Mme. le Moyne, a rather stout, typical French matron. "I'll find you a pretty girl to dance with."

Victor bent upon her his most winning smile. "May I be so bold as to ask your help in finding one pretty girl in particular? Is Mademoiselle Susette Plet here?"

"Oh, yes. Come with me." They made the circuit of the room, around groups conversing between dances. The crowd was much the same as at dinners in Quebec—the nearby seigneurs, rich merchants, military and government officials with their families. From all sides he saw admiring glances directed at his uniform. He smiled and bowed, trying to lift his mood to fit the occasion, but not until he greeted M. Plet and kissed his daughter's hand, did he really think he was going to have a good time.

Susette was dazzling in white satin embroidered with silver. Her eyes reminded him of blue flowers. "You look *ravissante* this evening," he said. "In ancient times you would surely have been goddess of something."

She laughed. "You've been so long in the woods you'd be dazzled by any girl in a ball gown. Father said I was much too dressed up. Do you think so?"

"The occasion honored by such a display is scarcely worthy of it," he said. "But it's a treat to my eyes."

"I'm glad. It's good to see you again."

Such honest directness, without coquetry, took him by surprise. Before he had composed an answer, the fiddlers began a saraband.

By the second dance they were chattering as if they had been childhood friends. "What became of that blue dress?" he asked her finally.

"What blue—oh, that old thing! I'm surprised you remembered it."

"I remember it distinctly. It matched your eyes. You should get another like it."

"But you wouldn't be here to see it if I did. Father says La Salle will be leaving again at once."

268

He swung her through an intricate *pas* in the gavotte. "Something tells me I'll see it—here or in France."

"Then I'll order the silk from Paris at once."

In spite of her being besieged by a dozen youths, and he by as many mothers, they managed to sit out the third dance, talking about France. She knew little news of the court. "You want very much to go back, don't you?" she asked.

"Of course. Don't you?"

She shrugged. "I could be happy there—or here. I like this life, traveling on rivers, going to market. I like the Indian children. They're so quiet, so solemn. When we get to Fort Frontenac I want to help in the mission school."

"I can't understand such taste in one so lovely," he jested, but as he watched the animation of her face, he realized that her beauty was no languorous, coquettish veneer. It sprang from strength, energy and a kind of earthiness. This girl would always be busy at something more than adorning herself.

"Well," she answered, "man needs something he cannot understand —*quelque chose incompréhensible.*"

They laughed together. "Of course," she added, "most of this colony must seem *triste* to one accustomed to the splendors of Versailles."

"Oh, I've had fun here. But usually I suffer like a damned soul."

"What, already, Monsieur?"

He laughed, delighted. The girl had *esprit.*

"But now"—she gestured toward the crowded room—" you must dance with some other girl. Everyone's envying me, you know. I'll have no friends if I monopolize you. You must spread that guardsman's glory around a little."

"If you command it—and if you will help me with a little plot." In a low voice he told her of his wish to get Lucie away early. To his delight she took charge of the whole plan. "First, you must go and pay a great deal of attention to her," she ordered.

Between dances, Victor sought out Lucie, standing with her father. While not so *ravissante* as Susette, she was becomingly dressed in rose velvet with a scarf of silver lace. M. le Ber bowed to Victor and introduced him, stressing all his distinctions of family and his position at court. Lucie greeted him with the gentle, courteous manners that must be part of her appeal to La Salle, Victor thought. He asked for the next dance, and as they moved through the sedate measures of a pavane, the delight of M. le Ber was almost visible, as if he already possessed a son-in-law more to his taste than La Salle.

"It's good that your father can't hear what we are saying," said Victor, for they had at once begun talking of La Salle. She wanted to know everything about him. "I'm so afraid for him," she sighed. "I can't even see him now; and I have a feeling that after he goes back, I'll never see him again."

"No, Mademoiselle, your feelings are quite mistaken. He is as strong as the Pont Neuf. And," he added gaily, "he is my friend, and I do not allow my friends to get themselves killed."

She smiled, her lips trembling a little. "You're very good for him, I know. He is so serious, always so worried. Will you tell him that when he has his colony at the mouth of the Mississippi, I will come to him, no matter what my father says?"

"Good for you!" He bent close to her ear, with an admiring look as if she had just said something extremely clever. "Smile," he added softly, "and show no surprise at what I say."

Obediently, she smiled.

"Would you like to talk to him tonight?"

"But how could I?" She kept sending a vacant smile about the room.

"Wait until Susette joins us, and then do as she says. She has a plan." Susette must soon put her plan into action, thought Victor. It was growing late; the tunes were dragging a little, as were the satin slippers flashing across the floor.

Susette joined them shortly.

"Father is going to take Monsieur le Ber to the library for a game of chess. It's a passion with them, and fortunately it takes a long time." "Now, Lucie, you and I will tell your father you have a headache and I am taking you home. Monsieur de Lorennes and his canoeman will ferry us across the river."

"Father will send my maid with me," said Lucie faintly.

"That's all right," said Susette jauntily. "I'll manage her."

The affair went smoothly. Lucie's flush of excitement fitted the story of a headache, and M. le Ber's scowl smoothed into complaisance when he learned that Victor was to be their escort. As Victor made his farewells to the Le Moynes, both girls appeared, hooded and mantled to cover their finery, carrying their satin slippers now replaced by moccasins. Nika paddled them across the river. But as they started up the beach, Susette said to the maid, "You and I will go on, and leave

Mademoiselle Lucie and Monsieur de Lorennes to sit on this bench for a minute." The maid was about to object, but Susette took her arm and whispered, as to a conspirator, "He's a very good catch."

Obediently Victor sat with Lucie until Susette and the maid were out of sight. Within seconds La Salle appeared from the shadows, all his pride, hauteur, and reserve gone. Now he was only a man in love. "Lucie!" he said, kissing her hand. "Robert!" she answered faintly.

Victor knew all they wanted from him was his absence; and with the quickest *au revoir* on record, he was gone. He and Susette would get rid of the maid, and then walk together until they saw other canoes coming across, when they would warn Lucie.

The date of their departure was set for July 22. In the morning, while they were loading the canoes, Victor was hailed from a craft just beached. In it were Messier and Laurent—here! He rushed toward them but one look at their drawn faces froze him in his tracks.

"What are you doing here?" La Salle demanded.

"Monsieur Tonti sent us with a letter." Laurent tugged at an inside pocket and brought out a paper wrapped in oilskin. Hastily La Salle scanned the lines, his face changing from puzzled concern to pain. "Is Marc all right?" Victor blurted.

La Salle silently handed him the letter, passing his hand over his forehead as if he would wipe away what he had just learned. Victor groaned as he read. Moyse and all the workmen had deserted! They had first destroyed Fort Crèvecoeur, stolen powder, lead, furs, guns, and provisions, and thrown into the river everything they couldn't carry. Tonti, Marc, Boisrondet and the two priests were left in desperate straits, with little ammunition and no food. Tonti was nevertheless sending this warning to La Salle that the deserters were planning to kill him.

"Marc! I've got to go to Marc!" A sick helplessness came over Victor. "What can we do? We've got to——"

"We'll go to them as fast as we can." La Salle's lips were white. "But we'll have to watch for these deserters. They'll be lying in ambush somewhere. So they would kill me, would they? The presumption of *ces-animaux-là!*"

"How did you get here ahead of them?" Victor asked the canoemen.

"They deserted overland," said Laurent, "and we came by canoe. But they may not be far behind us."

Victor grabbed packs from the beach and began loading them in the

canoes as if every second counted. Marc! What has happened to him?
Vaguely he heard La Salle thanking the two voyageurs, telling them to
get food and be ready to start back with him at once. Then he began
rounding up his men and giving orders. But before they could get
their canoes launched, another two-man canoe came rapidly from the
west, and struck the beach with a shudder. Two men in habitant
caps and sashes leaped out.

"*Comment, morbleu!*" said La Salle, "Is something wrong at Fort
Frontenac, too? You both look ready to drop."

"*B'jou, notre seigneur,*" said one of them. "We have traveled night
and day. You tell him, Francois."

"You know, *m'sieu,* we have been trading on the lakes, with your
permission," began Francois, his words tumbling over each other. "We
met some men who have deserted from your Fort Crèvecoeur. On the
way, they destroyed your Fort Miami, too, and they seized the furs
your Monsieur Tonti had stored for you at Michilimackinac. They
met Monsieur Dautray there on his way west, and told him that Tonti
was dead. His four men joined up with them although Monsieur
Dautray himself refused. But the deserters are now nearly twenty men
strong, *m'sieu!* And at Niagara, they plundered the magazine, so they
are very well armed."

"Where are they now?" La Salle rapped out.

The other habitant breathlessly took up the tale. "Eight of them
went along the south side of Lake Ontario to go to Albany, like all
scoundrels. But the other twelve are coming here along the north shore.
They intend to kill you, *m'sieu!*"

"We'll see about that! Victor, pick out seven men. We'll take two
canoes and arrest these devils."

Victor, with a grim face, moved among the men now waiting along
the bank, selecting those he judged best in a fight. La Salle put La
Forest in charge of the rest and told him to follow with the supplies to
Fort Frontenac.

All the way to the fort and then beyond, along the northern shore
of Ontario, La Salle urged the two canoes as if the furies were after
him. Every man kept his firearms close at hand, constantly eyeing
water and shore, for the deserters were desperate men, ready to kill to
keep from being captured. But the great lake was empty except for
themselves. When they came to the mouth of the Bay of Quinté, La
Salle slackened his pace. "I hoped we would get this far! We'll go on

over there." He pointed to a peninsula jutting far into the lake. "They'll have to round that point. We'll camp just this side of it and wait."

In the early morning, Nika, keeping watch on the point, came running back to camp. "Two canoes coming, long way apart."

"Go back to the point and keep well hidden," said La Salle. "Give me a signal when they're almost here."

When the signal came, La Salle's canoe darted out from the shore, two men handling the paddles while he and Victor and the third canoeman held loaded muskets. "I can see Moyse, and La Forge," said La Salle. "We'll take them if we can. But if they fire, shoot the steersman," he added coolly.

"Nom de dieu, I'll be glad to!" Victor's teeth were clenched in rage against these men who had abandoned Marc and Tonti. "I'd like to send them all as a present to the Iroquois."

Confronted so unexpectedly by La Salle and leveled muskets, the first canoe was thrown into confusion. At La Salle's command, they surrendered at once. Submissively they put into shore, where they were disarmed and kept under guard by Nika's men.

The second canoe was as easily captured. Under La Salle's angry interrogation, Moyse admitted that there were more coming in a third canoe, perhaps a day behind. So the entire party returned quickly to Fort Frontenac, placed the prisoners in the guardhouse, and set out again by morning.

At twilight they encountered the last of the deserters on the open lake. These, however, fled to shore; and scattering behind trees and rocks, fired at their pursuers. La Salle signaled Victor to land somewhat farther down the beach. Making a wide flanking movement, Victor and three men descended upon them from the rear and demanded surrender. In the little battle that followed, two of the deserters were killed. The rest gave up, to join their fellows in the guardhouse where, as soon as Count Frontenac should next visit the fort, they would be tried and sentenced.

30

LA FOREST'S party had arrived at Fort Frontenac, and now as fast as paddles could move it, the entire flotilla sped westward over the waters. Worrying about Marc, Victor was in torment at every second of delay; on La Salle's face he read an urgency scarcely less great, for Tonti and Marc were his only hope. "If they have been able to save the ship, the forge and the tools, we still have a foothold on the Illinois," he said repeatedly. "If we can reinforce them in time!"

By recruiting at each settlement, La Salle had assembled twenty-five men in all, as well as adequate supplies.

Taking the shortest route, up the Ottawa they paddled at last along the Manitoulin Islands, and came once more to the curving harbor at Michilimackinac, where Dautray came to meet them with the long-jawed Hinaut and the lanky, amiable Brossard. "We tried to keep those deserters from stealing what you had stored here," said Hinaut, "but they overpowered us. No one here would lift a hand to help us." He jerked a thumb over his shoulder at the mission.

"I know," said La Salle, "but what of Tonti and the rest? Have you heard——?"

"Nothing," said Brossard. "But we know the Iroquois have attacked the Illinois. All the *coureurs de bois* are keeping out of that neighborhood."

Victor groaned. "We've got to get down there! We must go faster!"

"Yes, we must," said La Salle decisively. To free himself from the slow progress of so many men with heavy goods and ship fittings, he divided them, placing half under Captain La Forest, while he, Victor and eleven others sped onward in lightened canoes.

It was early November when they reached the ruined, deserted fort on the Miami. Here La Salle again split his party. Five men, with the heaviest remaining stores, were to wait for La Forest and start rebuilding the fort. With Victor, Dautray, Hinaut, Messier, Laurent, and another expert canoeman, Couture, and Nika, La Salle then pushed along the route followed the year before: up the Miami, over the portage to the Kankakee, and down to the Illinois. They saw no one. The great rock La Salle had written Tonti to fortify was crowned only with its clump of oaks. Grimly La Salle pressed downstream, through the lake to the Illinois village. Here an even greater shock awaited them.

Where the village had once stood there were now only heaps of ashes from which rose half-burned poles and stakes, topped by human skulls. At the approach of the travelers a pack of wolves slunk away. Buzzards circled overhead or settled on branches to await their departure. One emaciated dog sniffed among the ruins. Victor gazed, sickened, on the gruesome sight. Even the graves had been emptied, the bones scattered far and wide. A ghastly warfare against the very dead.

La Salle, white-faced, examined some moccasin prints. "Iroquois!" He gazed off through the forest, where only one crude circular structure still rose above ground. "That's an Iroquois fort." Picking their way among the corpses, they examined the rough palisade of trunks, decorated with skulls to which still clung bits of hair and flesh. Beside it the caches of the Illinois had been opened and their contents burned or scattered.

Laurent, beside Victor, had averted his eyes, kicking idly at one of the piles of rubbish strewn about the enclosure. And then he went down on his knees. "Peste!" he swore. "Regardez-ici, m'sieu!" From the trash he handed La Salle two bits of cloth.

Victor cried out as if shot. The two bits of cloth were remnants of the violet traveling suit, and the red shirt Marc had bought at Michilimackinac. Almost as in a trance he lifted his eyes to the skulls, looking from one to another, dreading to find one on which the shreds of hair were blond. He was only half aware that La Salle was at his side.

"These are all savage skulls," said La Salle. Victor nodded, too numb to speak. "Tonti and the rest have been here, though," La Salle added. "These pieces of cloth inside the fort are all French. Over here is another piece of Marc's shirt that has been used as a bandage. They must have been prisoners here."

"But where are they now?" Victor shouted, and rushed out of the enclosure, through the charred village, pausing at every skull propped on a stake. Wildly he raced from one to another until it became too dark to see. Then Dautray took him by the arm and led him back to the canoes, where Nika had built a fire.

"Is there much use going on?" asked Dautray.

"We must search for them downriver, anyway," said La Salle.

"More likely they've all been—" began Hinaut, and stopped abruptly.

"We won't abandon Tonti and Marc and the others as long as there is the slightest chance of finding them," said La Salle. "We'll go on down the river. Three of you will wait for La Forest here. You'd better hide on the nearest island. Conceal your fire at night, make no smoke by day, fire no guns, and keep a close watch. When La Forest comes, tell him to wait, too, taking the same precautions."

Finding relief in any kind of action, Victor helped convey the goods over to a wooded island, where the baggage was placed in a rocky hollow difficult of access. Here Messier, Laurent, and Couture were left, while La Salle with Victor and the others set off downstream, pausing often to search the shore. Fort Crèvecoeur they found demolished and empty. The ship was whole upon the stocks, but the iron nails and spikes had been drawn out, apparently by the Iroquois, whose tracks were plentiful. Across one of the planks was written in charcoal, *Nous sommes tous sauvages: ce 1 5, 1680.* This was the ship, thought Victor miserably, that was to take us down the Mississippi and then to France. If we could have finished her, Marc and I would now be happily back at Versailles.

Farther down the river they found more signs of savages. One island had some abandoned Illinois huts and other evidence that this had been one of their refuges. Directly opposite was an abandoned Iroquois camp of over one hundred huts. There were marks, too, of Illinois killed or captured, but none to indicate the presence of Frenchmen.

Still farther downstream, they found ten more abandoned Illinois camps, each with an Iroquois camp across the river. Clearly the Illinois had retreated in a body, with the enemy stalking them on the opposite shore.

At last the river broadened, the current lessened, and La Salle said quietly that they must be approaching the junction with the Mississippi. They gazed ahead with anticipation, but Nika, watching the shores unceasingly, grunted and drew their eyes to a meadow on their right. They beached the canoes and raced across ground that bore marks of a fearful struggle. Victor fought back nausea as they approached a row of erect but lifeless bodies—women still bound to stakes on which they had been tortured. Lumps of human flesh still remained in kettles over burned-out fires. Piles of bones and ashes, wooden shields and broken war clubs littered the ground. In growing

276

horror the five men searched for signs of their comrades. On one of the few Iroquois bodies Victor saw a bit of metal hung about the neck. It bore the English King's picture and a few English words. Reminded of Madame's medal collection, on impulse he removed it and slipped it into his pocket.

They continued downstream until before them lay a broad river rolling southward—the Mississippi! La Salle, at this moving sight, stood up in the canoe, murmuring an *Ave*.

"Do you want to go on?" asked Dautray. "We'll go with you to the mouth, if you wish." The others nodded, even Victor; for if he couldn't find Marc, it made little difference now to what point of the compass La Salle led him.

But La Salle shook his head. "No, not now. If we could leave a message here for Tonti, though, in case he came this way . . ."

He chose a conspicuous tree, and, stripping it of bark, hung upon it a slab of wood on which he had drawn the figures of himself and his men, seated in a canoe and bearing a calumet. To it he tied a letter for Tonti, informing him that they had returned up the river to the ruined village of the Illinois.

"Now, quickly—for the love of the Virgin, quickly!" said La Salle; and turning upstream once more, they paddled night and day, covering the 250 miles to the village in four days. From here, after a rest, they paddled upstream again, until, on the 6th of January, La Salle called a halt at the junction of two branches of the Kankakee. "Let's follow the right-hand branch a little way," he suggested. "They may have taken either side of this fork."

Not far above the fork they found their first bit of encouragement. Behind a rude bark cabin lay a scrap of wood that had been cut by a saw!

"They must have come this way!" cried La Salle. "And it couldn't have been the deserters—the fire is too recent. Tonti just missed us, by taking the wrong fork!"

Victor searched the ground with his eyes as if from it he could tell whether Marc, too, had been here. No sign. Yet hope lifted his spirits. "They'd go on from here to Fort Miami! We should find them there!"

"We'll leave the canoes and go overland," La Salle decided. "It'll be faster."

They set out with their packs to plod one hundred and twenty miles in a snowstorm that fell steadily for nineteen days. La Salle admitted he had never known such cold, even in Quebec. Yet when they had conquered the last dreary mile and hastened up the slope to the Miami stockade, they found only Captain La Forest and his men. They had already restored the fort, cleared ground for gardens, even sawed planks for a new ship. But of Tonti, Marc, or the Recollets they had heard no word.

"We must go on! We must find them!" Victor, near collapse, wiped away tears of grief and weakness.

La Forest led him to the fire and knelt to take the ragged moccasins from his swollen feet. "Where would you go? They could be in any direction."

La Salle, too, shook his head reluctantly. "It would be hopeless. We have a better chance for news of them if we stay right here."

As the winter dragged on, La Salle kept busy with plans for recouping his losses, re-establishing a base among the Illinois, and eventually exploring the Mississippi. Victor helped him listlessly. La Salle questioned every Indian who came down lake or river. None had seen or even heard of the missing Frenchmen.

"As long as we don't hear of their deaths, there is hope," said La Salle.

But he did learn that every one of these savages lived in terror that the Iroquois would return. Unless he could dissipate this terror, they would never settle about any fort on the Illinois. Since he could never maintain an army large enough to protect them, La Salle set about traveling from village to village, trying to unite the tribes in a defensive league of their own. On his return, he found Victor impatiently awaiting him.

"A savage who came through here yesterday told us that a few Illinois escaped the massacre and are back in their village. Let me have an interpreter. I'm going back there and find out what happened to Marc."

"We'll both go," said La Salle. "I can get their consent to the league at the same time."

So once more a party set out for the Illinois, this time over glistening snow-covered prairies. About halfway, La Salle and several others developed snowblindness, and they had to encamp in a grove and build crude huts to give the afflicted the relief of darkness. After three days of restless waiting, La Salle sent La Forest and most of the men ahead, keeping with him Victor, Hinaut, and Nika. It was only a few hours later that Hinaut and Nika, out gathering pine needles to brew into a soothing eye remedy, came running back to camp.

"I have news!" gasped Hinaut to Victor. "We found moccasin tracks and followed them to an encampment of Outagamies. Tonti is safe, and so is your brother, *m'sieu!*"

"Safe?" Victor stopped in his tracks, staring. "Are you sure? Where is he?"

"With the Pottawattomies and Chief Ononghisse," said Nika happily.

"On their way to Michilimackinac to find out where *we* are," added Hinaut.

Overcome with joy and relief, Victor stood like a man who had lost the power to move. Then he whirled and ran to La Salle's hut. "Marc and Tonti! They're safe!"

"At last! God be praised for his mercy! And what about Boisrondet and the Recollets?"

"Boisrondet is there, too," said Hinaut. "But only one priest—Father Membré, from their description. They had seen nothing of Father Ribourde. These Outagamies did see Father Hennepin, though, on his way back from among the Sioux. The Sioux had captured him, and were about to kill him, because he had made them angry. But, *voilà,* at the last minute Monsieur Du Luth himself miraculously appeared out of the wilderness and rescued him, Father Hennepin has gone to Quebec, with Accau and Du Gay. But he is through exploring. He's on his way to France!"

As if fate itself had relented, a warm sun came out to melt the snow and clear the river of ice so they could launch their canoe. Downstream they overtook La Forest, told him the good news, and went on with him until they met a band of Illinois. La Salle gave them presents, condoled with them over their losses, and with many oratorical flourishes, offered his plan for safety. "You must make an alliance with the Miamis. Together you can defy the Iroquois, and we French will supply you with all the goods you need."

Respectful, but reserved at first, the Indians were well pleased by the time he finished, gave him corn, and turned back to take his message to their tribe. La Salle was elated. "Now we'll go back and talk with the Miamis."

"What about Marc and Tonti?" asked Victor quickly.

"La Forest will go up to Michilimackinac and tell them to wait there. The rest of us will follow as soon as I can get the Miamis to join the Illinois."

Victor would have preferred to go with La Forest, but he kept silent. The world seemed a brighter place now. Marc was safe, the ship half finished. After that—back to France and Angélique! That is—if she is not the duchess with the new gray coach.

It was May when they set out to paddle to Michilimackinac. La Salle had formed an alliance between those hereditary enemies, the Miamis and the Illinois, which assured the success of his league. As if in sympathy with Victor's joyous anticipation of reunion, the lake offered day after day of smooth passage, and favorable currents all the way up to the northern harbor. Rounding the point when the sun was low in the west, Victor strained forward, his eyes searching among the figures on the pebbled beach. "There! There they are!" He shouted and waved. One tall figure and two slighter ones had caught sight of the canoes and were running toward the shore. Happy shouts went back and forth across the water, until the canoes sped up to the beach. Marc, gaunt and ragged, seized Victor as he leaped out, and they embraced in incoherent joy.

Victor as usual found his tongue first. "I've never been so happy! But *le diable m'importe vivant,* you look terrible!"

Marc burst into shaky laughter. "I know it. But don't say 'Devil take me.' He has a good ear."

"You must have had a terrible time. But at least you can change your clothes now. I brought you some new ones from Montreal."

"My brother is still a Parisian," teased Marc happily. "After about a million miles of wilderness, he thinks first of clothes."

"It's good that someone thinks of them," retorted Victor.

"I'll be all right, now that you can look after me again," said Marc, his eyes twinkling.

"If I didn't, you'd soon be dressed like Adam. But tell me, where have you been? What happened?"

Before Marc could answer, Father Membré and Tonti came to embrace Victor. Even more than Marc they bore the signs of a grueling experience.

"The Lord is good," said Father Membré tearfully, "that he has brought us together again."

"La Forest told us that you hunted for us all the way to the Mississippi," said Tonti.

"Where were you?" demanded Victor.

La Salle came to lay a hand over Marc's shoulder. "We're all glad to see you. We want to hear the whole story. We'll put our baggage in my storehouse, and then go down the beach where we won't be interrupted. By the way, where is La Forest?"

"He isn't here," said Tonti in surprise. "Didn't you know? As soon as he told us to wait here for you, he set off for Fort Frontenac, saying he had some business of his own, and would bring back more supplies. He wants to replace the *Griffin* with a ship he has started at Fort Miami, and build one on the Illinois too."

"He—went back—east?" La Salle looked baffled.

But Marc and Victor were conscious of little outside the joy of being together again. Selecting a relatively smooth stretch of beach, they sat down facing the water. Nika set about building a fire, obviously as curious as the rest.

"Marc, you tell them," suggested Tonti.

Marc hesitated. *"Eh bien,* Tonti and I tried to keep the men busy at Fort Crèvecoeur, but they were depressed by the fear that you wouldn't come back and the danger of an Iroquois attack. And then Chapelle and Le Blanc arrived with your letter." He glanced at La Salle. "They told us the *Griffin* was lost and your credit ruined. The men began raging at Tonti, demanding that he take them back to Montreal. But Tonti assured them La Salle would return because the letter ordered us to build a permanent fort on the cliff above the Illinois village.

"When they quieted down, Tonti and I went upriver to the cliff to make our plans. While we were gone the men threw the forge and tools in the river and ran away with our provisions and furs, saying they were going to ambush and kill La Salle. Tonti sent Messier and Laurent off to warn you, and dragged out of the river all the tools we could find, as well as the forge. But the few of us couldn't hope to fortify the cliff. Then Father Membré learned that the Illinois had grown suspicious, fearing that the deserters had gone to arouse the Iroquois against them. To dispel their suspicion, we moved back to the hut near their gardens. The next few months were mostly waiting. I went back to Fort Crèvecoeur occasionally to tend the garden, while Tonti spent his time learning the Illinois language. The savages seemed friendly, but the priests made no conversions and finally crossed the river to go into retreat in an abandoned hut.

"Later the same day, Tonti, Boisrondet, and I heard shouts from the village, so we took our guns and paddled up there. The riverbank and the square were in a turmoil. Women were loading canoes. A dozen men crowded about us, brandishing tomahawks and knives, shouting that an army of Iroquois was only a day's journey away and that our men had sent it. We expected every instant to be killed, but finally the whole population tumbled into canoes and paddled downstream as if pursued by fiends. They had taken even our canoes, so we walked back to our hut. The Illinois had taken our food and some of our clothes.

"That evening the warriors came back, paddling right past us to the square, and all night we could hear them singing and beating drums. We decided our only hope of surviving was to join them and help them fight the Iroquois. We hoped the priests might be forgotten; we had no canoe to go and warn them, anyway. In the morning we went to the square and offered our services. The chief didn't like it at first, but seeing our pistols and muskets, accepted us as allies.

"Just then a scout arrived, yelling that hundreds of Iroquois were approaching. 'We'll go to meet them,' the chief shouted, and we all rushed for the canoes, crossed the river, and ran up a hill to a dense grove, just as the Iroquois, like a legion of devils, swarmed out of another grove beyond an open plain. The Illinois went crazy, leaping from tree to tree, shooting arrows, while the Iroquois returned a hail of arrows and bullets. I had seen what happened to Iroquois prisoners; so I decided to sell my scalp as dearly as I could. The Iroquois were too many and too well armed. It would be a slaughter, no matter what we did.

"I heard Tonti talking to the Illinois chief, offering to go and try to make peace with the Iroquois, using the names of La Salle and Frontenac. Since half the Illinois were already dead or wounded, the chief agreed and handed Tonti a wampum belt.

"I've seen a lot of bravery," Marc went on, "but never anything like what Tonti did then. Completely unarmed, he walked out into the open, holding up that belt. Boisrondet and I tried to follow, but he ordered us back, saying the Iroquois might not fire on a lone man. The Iroquois did cease firing, but when he was close to their lines, a dozen of them swooped out of the woods and dragged him off. I saw one devil sink a knife in his side. We started to go after him, but the Illinois chief blocked our way, suspicious of treachery. They made it clear that we'd have to stay as a hostage for Tonti. The shooting started again, but we took no part until we saw an Iroquois waving Tonti's hat on the end of his gun! Then we went as crazy as any savage, and shot Iroquois as fast as we could load and fire. I got a flesh wound under my arm, and was behind a tree trying to stop the bleeding when the firing ceased again. Boisrondet pointed across the clearing as if he were seeing a ghost.

"Tonti was coming back, his clothing in tatters, blood running from his mouth and the wound in his side, a necklace of porcelain beads in his hand. Boisrondet and I went out to meet Tonti, laid him under a tree, and dressed his wound with a piece of my shirt. The Illinois chief was exulting over the necklace—which he took for an offer of peace—but Tonti rose up and warned him that it was a trick, that the Iroquois would attack the village later when the Illinois were off guard. Father Membré and Father Ribourde had heard the shooting and were with us by that time. Anyway, the Illinois retired to the village, carrying their dead and wounded. We went along, carrying Tonti.

"That night the Iroquois did come skulking around, so the Illinois set fire to their lodges and retreated in panic down the river. Tonti was too weak from loss of blood to be moved, so we had to take our chances with the Iroquois, who came in, built a fort, and ordered us into it. Then, howling, they started on the graveyard—" Marc stopped, his face twisting in revulsion.

"We know," said La Salle. "We saw the village."

Marc nodded. "We spent two miserable days expecting torture and death. The Iroquois began building elm-bark canoes, so we knew they were going after the Illinois instead of returning home. When the canoes were ready, the Iroquois chief told us to go back to the French settlements, that he didn't want any trouble with Frontenac, but that he was going to exterminate the Illinois.

"We couldn't help the Illinois, so we decided to try to get back to Fort Miami. In the one leaky canoe the Illinois had left behind, we paddled upriver as fast as we could, the two priests baling all the time. After about fifteen miles we had to pull up to repair the canoe, and while we were working, Father Ribourde laid down his cloak and took his breviary to an oak grove to meditate alone.

"He never came back. When we went to look for him, we found only fresh moccasin tracks. Next day we gave up our search for him and went on. When the canoe finally split beyond mending, we set off on foot. It was a rough trip: no food, no game, and the frozen ground kept wearing out our moccasins. Every night we made new ones from Father Ribourde's cloak. We lived on acorns and roots. Twenty-five days later we staggered out on the lake shore—and saw from the sun's position that we were on the west side, not on the east near the fort.

"We decided to go on toward the Pottawattomie village. We know now from La Forest that he and his men were at Fort Miami, waiting while you searched for us. If only we'd known that! The journey north nearly finished us. Tonti's legs swelled so he could hardly walk. My wound opened and wouldn't heal. At last, more dead than alive, we built a fire and lay down expecting never to rise again.

"And then something like a miracle happened. Some Ottawas passing by in canoes saw our smoke. They were as welcome as Elijah's ravens. They fed us and took us into their canoes, saying they were going to visit the Pottawattomies. At the Pottawattomie village Chief Ononghisse remembered us and ordered a big feast. Well, that's about all. We were all right after that. One thing saddened us, though. Father Membré saw a little black book sticking out of an Ottawa's belt pouch. He flew at the savage like a fierce little gray bird and snatched it away. Father Ribourde's breviary! The Ottawa said he had got it in trade from a Kickapoo, who said he was out with a war party hoping to take some Iroquois scalps, when they came on an old man in gray, reading this book. They killed him, hid his body, and took the book and his scalp back to the village, boasting that it was an Iroquois scalp."

Father Membré was quietly weeping.

" 'Except a corn of wheat fall into the ground and perish,' " said La Salle gently, " 'it bringeth forth no fruit.' He used to say so often, 'I am where God would have me, where he sent me, and where he remains with me, and the more I have to suffer, the greater will my consolation be.' "

The little party sat silent in the firelight. Victor was looking at his brother in astonishment. I never before heard him talk so long, he thought. Maybe I never gave him a chance. He felt a new respect and admiration for Marc. "So you've been wounded twice for France," he said softly. "In two different worlds. Once at Ghent and now on the Illinois."

Marc smiled, and between them lay a new closeness.

"Now back to Fort Crèveceour—to restore the fort and finsh the ship," said La Salle.

"And then down the Mississippi and on to France!" exulted Victor.

But La Salle shook his head. "Not to France. First I must explore the Mississippi to its mouth. That will give me the prestige I need in Quebec. With only two years of my five left—and a large part of that to be used for shipbuilding and exploration—I must build Fort St.

Louis before I can go to France." He sighed. "And I must build it right away to support my confederation of tribes against the Iroquois."

Victor's lips tightened, seeing Versailles and Angélique retreat once more beyond his reach. He admitted to himself that now he really wanted the adventure of the Mississippi before he went back, but he had no interest in Fort St. Louis. "I suppose you're right," he said slowly. If La Salle hadn't explored the Mississippi, and hadn't even a foothold beyond the lakes, the King would pay scant heed to him. "But"—a thought struck him—"if we're not going to gather wild-oxen hides to take to France, why delay long enough to build a ship? Why don't we go down right away, in canoes?"

"*Tout à fait,* in canoes!" said Tonti. "An idea! But it may not fit La Salle's plans."

"We know it can be done by canoe," said Marc alertly. "The Illinois do it. And we don't know what difficulties may arise with a ship."

"We could be there and back again before we'd ever get the ship built!" urged Victor.

La Salle strode back and forth on the beach, frowning. "No. I see no reason to change my plans every time Victor feels like Monsieur le Capitaine again."

Stung into fury, Victor leaped up. "That's not fair! I think mine is the best plan. And I think I have the right to say so—even to insist upon putting an end to these delays!"

"Victor!" cried Marc. "What do you mean?"

"Yes," said La Salle, challenging. "Let us hear why you can 'insist.' "

"Very well." Victor looked around at the circle. "But perhaps you'd prefer it for your ears alone. It makes no difference to me."

Tonti leaped up. "I'll take the rest back and arrange for lodgings."

"Marc should stay," said Victor firmly. "And Nika."

La Salle's face was still dark. When the others had withdrawn, he demanded, "Now, explain yourself."

"I want to show you something." Victor drew his pack toward him and unwrapped the long thin package strapped on top. At sight of the cheap sword purchased in Montreal, La Salle looked puzzled, but Marc burst out, "Where did you get that thing? And where is the D'Artagnan sword?"

"Yes, where is it?" asked La Salle. "I haven't seen it since— since——"

"Since Montreal. I sold it there."

"You didn't!" said Marc. "How could you?"

"Because it was the only way to provide a miracle."

"A mir—" La Salle was thunderstruck.

Marc fell silent, intently looking from one to the other.

As comprehension came, La Salle's face turned blank with shock. "That money——"

"It was mine. Nika knew."

The Indian slowly nodded.

"No! You couldn't have. You didn't—" La Salle stammered. "You didn't do that—for me!" He passed his kerchief over his taut features. "Is there any way to get it back? I'm afraid I've spent most of the money."

"Even if you hadn't, it's too late. I sold it to Monsieur le Ber and told him of De Seignelay's offer. By this time the sword must be in his hands. Even double the sum wouldn't buy it back."

"But why didn't you ask me?" stammered La Salle, brokenly. "I wouldn't—I wouldn't have accepted. If it had been anything else!"

"I'm well aware," said Victor coolly, "that it had value beyond its jewels."

"But you should never have parted with it—it should have stayed in your family forever."

"I had no choice," said Victor simply, remembering the compulsion he had felt in that moment. "Monsieur D'Artagnan seemed to want this use made of it. As if he knew that your exploration, your colonies, would do more for France than all his feats of war."

La Salle gazed down into the fire. "I can't—" he began finally, "I can't find words worthy of such a deed. What can I do now?" He lifted his hands hopelessly. "It did mean the difference between failure and success."

"And failure for you meant failure for France," said Marc softly.

Victor clasped his brother's hand. The bond between them had never been so close. Then each reached out a hand to La Salle.

"Such faith in me—" La Salle choked up as he clasped their hands. "Nothing else could prove such faith as that sacrifice did. This is the best moment of my life."

"As the day I sold the sword," said Victor, "was the best one of mine."

"I can never make it up to you," said La Salle, "but I'll do what I can." He glanced down at the cheap sword, "To begin with," he added, "I can give you one a little better than that." He stepped to his

286

pack, unwrapped his own sword, and extended the hilt toward Victor. "Not so fine or full of tradition as the one you gave up, but a fair weapon."

Victor bowed, and took it. "With many thanks, I accept the loan."

"The gift. Keep it. I'll take this plainer one."

"Merci, monsieur." Victor slid it into the scabbard on top of his pack. "For my children, and theirs."

"No, no. It's not distinguished enough for that."

"Let me, and the future, decide that."

Victor encountered La Salle once more that evening, when he was strolling alone in the moonlight along the pebbled beach. The explorer called him to his side.

"There was something more I wanted to say to you," La Salle began, "but I didn't want to say it in front of Marc. No"—he made a protesting gesture—"I'm not going to embarrass you with further thanks. But one reason your sacrifice struck me so hard is that it is not, I think, consistent with your purpose in coming with me."

Victor stared at the handsome face, enigmatic in the shadows. "What," he asked carefully, "do you think that purpose was?"

"You were sent to keep an eye on me."

Victor's nerves tightened. "Then you guessed!"

"I knew of the King's network of spies at court, in Paris, in every city of the kingdom," said La Salle quietly. "If he watches the least actions of a courtier, he would not let a man go out to found an empire without some check on what he was doing."

"I'm sorry." Victor felt the inadequacy of the phrase, and the futility of adding anything to it.

"I'm not." La Salle laid a hand on his shoulder in brief reassurance. "I'm glad His Majesty's choice fell on so good a man. I did ask you to come myself, you remember."

Victor rubbed his forehead, dazed. "I just can't realize that you've known all the time." Yet he recalled, at that interview in the Rue de la Truanderie, La Salle's saying coldly, "You'll do as well as another."

"At times," La Salle said softly, "I have resented it. My feelings were always complicated, because I admire you—and am fond of you, though I do not show affection easily."

"You admire me?" Victor exclaimed. "Why?"

"Your gaiety, partly. I can endure hardships, but I can't make a joke

287

of them, as you do. I'm glad everything is in the open between us now. And—" he added, "even when I did resent being watched, I realized that when Louis XIV has spoken, no one has any choice."

"Actually, I have only once reported anything harmful—and that letter was lost on the *Griffin*."

"So there was good even in so great a loss."

"I haven't been happy about my role," admitted Victor. "Perhaps the sword helped me make the *amende honorable*. I appreciate your not telling Marc. I'll tell him sometime, in my own way."

Back at Fort Miami, day followed day like the drip of soft rain, while the little group planted, tended, and harvested a winter's supply of corn, squashes, and beans. La Salle and La Forest arrived with extra men and what seemed like enough Indians, male and female, to found a new village. La Salle had taken time to put his affairs in order, appeasing his creditors by the sale of furs the *Cataraqui* had gathered around Lake Ontario. He had also drawn up a will in favor of his cousin, M. Plet, who had taken charge of his business at Fort Frontenac. Now he was ready for the great exploration. He had brought these Abenakis and Mohegans to hunt and to carry burdens at the portages.

With further delays for preparation, it was not until the 21st of December that they set out on the shortest route, across the end of the lake to the mouth of the River Chicago. This time the party consisted of twenty-three Frenchmen and forty-odd Indians, including women and children. But despite its cumbersome size, the straggling procession was a cheerful and orderly one. For, unlike La Salle, Captain La Forest had a genius for organization and detail.

They reached the Mississippi on the sixth of February, 1682. Urged by La Salle, Victor now kept the official journal in detail. Gradually, as they swept on down the broad expanse of water, the ice floes vanished. Fish was plentiful. From time to time they passed seemingly endless herds of wild oxen, a wealth in hides beyond anything even La Salle had dreamed of. Sometimes the river was more than two miles wide; sometimes it narrowed to a swift channel. They left the giant forests, the limitless plains behind them and moved into lowlands, where swamps and canebrakes were infested with mosquitoes. Every day the sun grew warmer, the wild flowers along the banks more numerous and brilliant in hue.

On the thirteenth of March, while traveling through a dense fog, they were attacked by Indians. Paddling quickly to the opposite shore amid the whizz of arrows, they felled trees and, in less than an hour, threw up a crude fort. When the fog lifted they could see the Indians across the river, regarding them with open mouths. Beyond lay a savage village.

Advancing to the edge of the water, La Salle made friendly gestures to them. In a little while a dugout canoe came halfway across the stream; an arrow was shot into the air; and when the Frenchmen made no belligerent return, the Indians beached, bearing a calumet. Given a friendly reception, the savages invited the explorers to their village.

An Illinois, a slave, was brought out as interpreter. He explained that these were Arkansas and that they wished to give a feast for the guests. Three days of entertainment followed, and while the Frenchmen sat upon wild-oxen robes they were served fish and meat, preserves of wild plums, and a wine made of dried grapes soaked in water. After the usual dancing, gifts were exchanged, Father Membré led his companions in a hymn, and La Salle planted a cross bearing the arms of France in the center of the square.

From what the Arkansas said, La Salle was now positive the Mississippi emptied into the Gulf as he had thought; but he was surprised to hear that its mouth was still at least ten days' journey away. The Arkansas said that there were Europeans to the east and west of the mouth. They even brought out knives and glass bottles they had obtained in trade with them.

"Spaniards!" exclaimed Victor. "I hope we haven't come all this way to fall into their hands. We could have done that in Europe."

"They say there are none at the mouth of the river," La Salle assured him. "They say also that the Spaniards have no Indian allies, because they enslave them and force them to work in their mines of 'white stone'—silver, of course."

The next day the Arkansas showed them a creature they had just killed, one of the strangest and most repulsive creatures on earth, known to the boys before only in artists' drawings of crocodiles on the Nile. "Then," commented Victor, "at least one story the Illinois tried to frighten us with is true—the one about the man-eating beasts."

On the fourth day, after further exchange of gifts, La Salle's party took to canoes again. On and on they traveled through valleys immense beyond conception, an empire teeming with fertility, awaiting the hand of farmer, trader, trapper, builder.

They passed two other villages that were memorable. The first was the great Indian town of Taensas with its large square dwellings of straw and mud, in one of which they were hospitably received by a chief with three wives and a formal court of sixty old men clothed in white coats made of mulberry bark. The second was Natchez, with its sun temple and sacred fire.

On the sixth day of April, the river split into three channels, running through a network of creeks among cypress groves.

"Gentlemen, I think we have reached our goal!" La Salle sent Tonti down the middle passage and Dautray down the eastern one. He with Victor, Marc and Nika, took the western route. The shore was low and marshy; the water grew brackish; and then the breeze brought to them the first salt breath of the sea. La Salle lifted his head and quaffed as if it were the bouquet of the rarest wine. Their ears caught the unmistakable sound of ocean waves; the shores receded farther and farther; and then they were out of the forest upon the open sea. The gulf lay stretched before them, limitless, devoid of any sign of life. Theirs were the first French eyes to gaze upon it.

"After four long years," said La Salle softly, as if half afraid it was a mirage. "Four long years, but we've done it!"

Jubilantly they coasted along the marshy shore to join with Tonti's party and Dautray's. On a dry spot of ground above the mouth they exulted and embraced one another, chattered, exclaimed and wept. Even the least canoeman could see that their discovery had thrown open to France the richest, most fertile, and most accessible territories of the new world. They fell to the joyous task of cutting a tree into a great column upon which La Salle hung the arms of France. On a plaque Victor carved the words: LOUIS LE GRAND, ROI DE FRANCE ET DE NAVARRE: RÈGNE: LE NEUVIÈME AVRIL: 1682. La Salle put on his scarlet coat, a little too big for him now; Tonti donned his naval uniform; and Victor and Marc brushed out their wrinkled gold and blue.

"I'm glad you two are here," said La Salle, his eyes moist.

"I think that all our lives we will be proud of it," said Marc.

The Indians and their women formed a wondering circle, as the Frenchmen drew up in ranks with loaded muskets. Through the marshy woods the *Te Deum* rang out, after which La Salle proclaimed in a clear, rich voice:

"In the name of the most high, mighty, invincible, and victorious Prince, Louis the Great, by the grace of God King of France and of

Navarre, fourteenth of that name, I this ninth day of April, one thousand six hundred and eighty-two, in virtue of the commission of His Majesty, which I hold in my hand which may be seen by all whom it may concern, have taken, and do now take, in the name of His Majesty and of his successors to the crown, possession of this country of Louisiana, from the mouth of the great river St. Louis, otherwise called the Ohio . . . as also along the river Colbert, or Mississippi, and the rivers which discharge themselves thereinto, from its source beyond the country of the Nadouessioux . . . as far as its mouth at the sea, of the Gulf of Mexico, and also to the mouth of the River of Palms, upon the assurance we have had from the natives of these countries that we are the first Europeans who have descended or ascended the said River Colbert; hereby protesting against all who may thereafter undertake to invade any or all of these aforesaid countries, peoples, or lands, to the prejudice of the rights of His Majesty, acquired by the consent of the nations dwelling therein. Of which, and of all else that is needful, I hereby take to witness those who hear me, and demand an act of the notary here present."

His words fell away into the silence of forest and marsh. Then the muskets roared, followed by shouts of: *"Vive le Roi! Vive La Salle! Vive la Louisiane!* May she become the brightest jewel in the Bourbon crown!"

Yes, thought Victor contentedly, D'Artagnan would be proud of what his sword has done.

3 1

IT is all very well to write one's name in history and add an empire to France, thought Victor, pacing the beach the next morning. His own packs already stowed in the canoe, he wanted for a few minutes to escape the confusion attendant on breaking camp and getting so many people on the move. This moment would be perfect, he thought, if we were going to sail to France. Once back at Versailles I could convince the King that there is no danger to his power from La Salle. At any rate I've been at this task four years—long enough to deserve relief. Instead, there is the long journey north, this time upstream; and only Heaven knows when I'll ever see Versailles and Angélique. Maybe I'll never see France again. Bitterly he turned his back on the river, returning through the cane-brake to the nearly loaded canoes.

La Salle, yesterday's joy undiminished, greeted him happily and held out some sheets of paper. "Will you make a copy of these findings in your journal?"

Victor nodded and took the pages of figures and notes. La Salle had spent the entire day and part of the night after the ceremony taking repeated readings of the sun's altitude with an astrolabe and consulting earlier maps. Feeling that the triumphant La Salle might be disappointed at his lack of interest, he made an effort. "I see you determined the latitude at about thirty degrees."

"I think that is about right. About the longitude I cannot of course be certain, because there are no exact facilities for taking it. But I estimate the difference between here and Quebec to be about twenty-four degrees."

"That's probably close enough." This information will be of interest to mapmakers, thought Victor, but not for me. The only interest this spot will ever have for me again will be if by some improbable chance we sail out this way when I leave for France.

La Salle was now ready to embark. "Next year," he said, "we'll occupy this place with a fort and a colony. But now, we must go back and make the colony among the Illinois as thriving as the one at Fort Frontenac. This time, Marc, we'll fortify your rock at once."

"Good. I have the plans all drawn up." Marc took his paddle, helped Victor push off the canoe, and they settled down for the long pull against the current of this Mississippi—or Colbert, as La Salle insisted on calling it, though Marc remembered that Joliet had called it the Buade and Father Marquette the Conception. All this renaming, he thought, was a laying of French names over the Indian ones like silk over homespun; but sometimes the silk will be too thin and the homespun will wear through. He confessed to an unpatriotic liking for many of the present names. There was a cadence in Mississippi that fitted the roll and surge of the river.

There were days, as they worked their way up against that long, inexorable muddy current, when he wondered if he would live to fortify the rock of St. Louis. Since La Salle had not counted on so long a journey to the mouth and back, they ran out of food and had nothing but crocodile, not a tasty dish. At one Indian village they were surrounded by a huge band of armed warriors, and only fear of the French firearms prevented a massacre. Among the Taensas and the Arkansas La Salle was again well received, but a little farther upriver he fell ill of a malignant fever.

Marc and Victor helped Father Membré nurse him, and Nika stayed as close as his shadow. Week after week the illness hung on, and it was not until the last of April that he could travel.

Leaving Marc in charge of the workmen to build Fort St. Louis, he took Victor along in the party hastening on to Michilimackinac to send word from there to Quebec of his discovery.

They did not reach Michilimackinac till September and there they heard bad news. "Word has come from Quebec that Count Frontenac is to be removed," they were informed. "Most people here think that will be the end of your colonizing in the West. The new governor is Lebvre de la Barre."

"I never heard of him," said La Salle dully, stricken at losing the valuable backing of Frontenac.

"I know who he is," said Tonti grimly. "An old naval officer, inept and corrupt, not the caliber for that job at all."

"La Barre!" said Victor. "I remember him. A black-bearded old nuisance who used to be Governor of Guiana, always hanging around court trying to get another post. Nobody liked him except Madame de Maintenon."

La Salle frowned. "How could His Majesty replace Frontenac with a man like that? I ought to go to Quebec and try to establish good relations with him, but weak as I am now, I'd never get there. And I haven't time. We must get established on the Illinois to keep together the tribes planning to move there."

"What about Fort Frontenac?" asked La Forest. "You remember my lieutenant was to go back to France this fall. What'll happen to the command there?"

"You'd better go back there," La Salle decided. "I'll send a few letters—one to the new Governor, one to my cousin, and a detailed report for His Majesty and Colbert."

But Colbert, he was told, had given up one of his positions, that of Minister of the Colonies and the Marine, to his son, De Seignelay.

So, thought Victor, when Le Ber sold him my sword, he was doing a favor to a very great personage indeed. Aloud he said to La Salle: "You're still all right on that score, then. De Seignelay is one of the best."

When Victor joined Marc in December at the great rock bluff on the Illinois, he was delighted to find the long-planned Fort St. Louis already under construction. Joyfully he plunged into the work. When the buildings were completed and officially christened, Marc stepped back to regard them with satisfaction. "I wouldn't be ashamed to have Vauban himself inspect it," he said.

Through the winter the palisades and cabins were often half-buried in snow, but La Salle worked steadily at establishing a colony. Savages began drifting in by the hundreds to set up their bark lodges below the fort and throughout the Illinois valley. The abandoned Indian village filled again with survivors of the Iroquois massacre. Once more men lay in the shade and gambled, while children played in the square. La Salle went constantly among the tribes, discussing their problems like a conscientious and benevolent seigneur. Tonti took over the trading. Marc and Victor went up and down the river with him, until each had a considerable pile of furs in the storeroom. Almost daily there were additions to the strange colony until it numbered nearly twenty thousand, fused together by La Salle's skill and energy and by a common fear of the Iroquois.

Under terms of his patent as seigneur, La Salle apportioned fine tracts of land to his associates. In spite of Victor's protests, he awarded the twins two adjacent strips of river land a mile and a half long. Included in the grant was a share of the fur trade at the fort.

As they strolled over their new domain, Marc commented: "A beautiful site, and a climate like that of Paris."

Victor shrugged. "It's all right, I suppose."

"One could do worse," argued Marc. "A settler here wouldn't have to spend ten years clearing the forest. He could put in his plow the first day."

Victor frowned. "I can't think what interest that fact would have, even if true. I can't wait to get back to Paris. I adore every narrow street, every crooked dark alley. But I suppose it's all right to take this land, since it's free, and sell it to someone else later on."

"Don't you like anything about this country?" asked Marc.

Victor strode along for a dozen paces. "Yes," he admitted. "I confess I've come to enjoy breathing fresh air, traveling about from one place to another. I've even enjoyed the skirmishes with the savages— since I came safely through. But rather than live here, I'd blow myself up with a barrel of powder. I wonder how long this colony will last.

It sprang up overnight; and if these tribes decide to go somewhere else, it could disappear just as quickly. La Salle is worried about it, too. He knows the unstable character of these savages. To hold them he must keep his promises. They'll depend on him for every blanket and kettle; and for protection against the Iroquois. At present all goods, arms, and ammunition have to come from the St. Lawrence settlements. And the guns and ammunition he has already asked La Barre for haven't been sent, nor have the men he sent returned. And he's had no word from La Forest."

With the coming of the first warm days of spring, Dautray, Boisrondet, Laurent, and Messier were all seized with the urge to build cabins upon their acres. For lack of other occupation, Marc and Victor helped them. Then, when they were well along, Marc decided to build one of his own.

Even Victor had to admit that he could scarcely improve upon the site he had chosen, in a grove of maple and dogwood standing on a little rise that sloped down to the curve of the river. "I can see it with a green lawn and a parterre of choice flowers," he said. "A view that any prince in France would envy."

"Good neighbors, too," said Marc. "Dautray on one side; Boisrondet, Laurent, and Messier on the other."

Victor kept protesting the folly of building. But he carved for Marc's cabin some furniture that would not have looked out of place in a French château; and for one gable end he made the square weathercock, symbol of the feudal banner, its use allowed in France only to those of noble birth. When the dwelling was finished, it was no château, but it was snug and comfortable: a solid, low building, with a steep-pitched roof and fireplaces in each of the three rooms. It had an attic a man could stand up in, reached by a ladder.

"I suppose the children sleep up here," said Victor on a tour of inspection.

"I'll let yours sleep up here when they come to visit," said Marc, in the same bantering tone. "Before I think about the next generation, I'd like some cattle and sheep, horses, chickens, and pigs."

"Scholar, soldier, alchemist, explorer, farmer—is there no limit to the facets of your ability?"

Marc ignored all his teasing. Bit by bit he improved his property, constructing bunks, chairs, tables, ash boxes, racks for muskets, hanging shelves. He cleared away weeds and planted a garden.

295

In spite of the long silence from Quebec, La Salle remained hopeful that he could get along with the new Governor. In April he sent off several canoes with Hinaut in charge, bearing the furs already collected, more than enough to pay for badly needed trading goods and ammunition. "There is no agent so powerful as money," he said to Tonti. "Even my share of these furs, though, is really owed to you and the rest for wages or payments on your investments."

"Let them go," said Tonti, looking around and receiving nods of agreement. "Saving your good foothold here," said Marc, "is more important than anything we'd use the money for."

La Salle also wrote a cordial letter to the Governor. Since they had no more writing paper, Victor found scraps of brown paper from packages of ammunition. La Salle smiled. "Well, the paper will not make an impression on him, but my words must. Let's see what can be done. We must show proper respect to him, but remind him of my authority a little, too."

Slowly he began to dictate.

2nd of April, 1683

SIR,

Although I have not the honor of being known to you, and have reason to fear that those jealous of me have been as ready to represent me to you in an unfavorable aspect as they have been to resort to artifices to prevent until now the success of the enterprises which I have carried out with His Majesty's approval, I hope nevertheless that you will show the same kindness in protecting me as the Comte de Frontenac did during his period of governorship. My devotion to him arose from the same duty which now makes me present to you my most humble services with a zeal and a desire to make them agreeable to you which are as great as was my attachment to him when he filled the position which you now occupy. . . . I was quite aware that that would draw down upon me the hatred of all who were opposed to him, and that I should have their whole power turned against me if he left the country. But I always hoped that I should obtain protection from his successors, when I had had the honor of explaining my action to them, and finding opportunities of proving to them its sincerity."

"I'm afraid," he broke off to comment, "La Barre is doing as he pleases, or as the Jesuits tell him, without keeping contact with the court."

Victor nodded. "Too bad De Seignelay hasn't direct control. He's honest and fair."

"Since he hasn't, I'll have to do what I can with La Barre. Well, let's go on." Continuing with an account of his various successes with Indian tribes, he then added:

The King has granted to me all the forts I build on the route of my exploration by his letters patent, a copy of which I take the liberty of sending you, on the same conditions as Fort Frontenac; and binds me, in his grant of the latter fort, to give a share of the lands which depend upon it to Frenchmen and Indians. I am consequently pledged to do the same at Fort St. Louis, and give settlers permission to occupy them . . . which I have done by making grants to several persons . . . but as some of them must go to Quebec to get what they need, they fear they may be detained there. . . .

This makes it necessary for me to beg you, Sir, to be good enough to permit them to return. Otherwise it will be impossible for me to carry out the wishes of His Majesty or to discharge my debts to my partners, if men are detained when I send them down to bring back here the ammunition necessary for the defense of the fort, which may at any moment be attacked. . . .

I do myself the honor of writing to you to request that, in case you are not willing for them to continue coming down for what they need and cannot find here, you will do me the honor of informing me of your wishes; so that, if I am obliged to give up, for want of men or food, in consequence of obeying your orders, I may know that it is the King's will, and may be able to defend myself against my partners, whose interests will never cause me to fail in the respect with which I shall ever be, Sir, your most humble and obedient servant,

De La Salle

But the men who went down for supplies did not come back. There was no way of knowing whether they had been detained by the Governor, or had encountered the Iroquois, for rumor said those savages were on the march again.

Early in the following June, La Salle wrote another letter, protesting,

The King would not order me to make an exploration and build forts without permitting me to have and to send or bring there, such men and things as are necessary. . . .

We have only twenty Frenchmen left to resist the Iroquois. . . . We have not a hundred livres of powder left, and a proportionate number of bullets. Yet if it comes to a fight, we shall have to share them with the Illinois. If I did not receive any this year, it would be impossible for me to preserve this post . . . which is the key of a country in which a powerful colony can be formed. . . .

La Salle paused. "Maybe it will help if I hint at a bribe."

The colony will be under an obligation to you for having preserved it at its birth and will feel so indebted to you for the favors you have shown to it that it will gladly devote to you, in gratitude for them all, whatever it thinks may be acceptable to you. . . . I have no greater desire than to declare myself with equal sincerity and submission, Sir, your most humble and most obedient servant,

De La Salle

I offer you a thousand apologies, Sir, for the roughness of this paper; but I hope you will be so good as to permit some to be brought to us together with the supplies I am asking of you.

It turned out that La Salle's letters were not worth even their wretched paper. The men he sent back were arrested for breaking the law against trading without a license; their cargoes were seized by La Salle's creditors. La Salle had several letters from his cousin, M. Plet, and from Captain La Forest, carried by *coureurs de bois,* picturing a grave state of affairs in Quebec. The new Governor was completely unscrupulous and greedy. He dealt illicitly in the fur trade, and had joined with the Jesuits and merchants against Count Frontenac's friends, especially La Salle with his favorable monopolies in the West. And worse, while the Governor claimed to be worried about war, he was in fact urging the Iroquois on.

"The fool! The utter, stupid fool!" raged La Salle. "Can't he see that if he encourages Iroquois against *any* Frenchman, he's playing with a two-edged sword?"

Furthermore, a letter from La Forest said that La Barre had not only refused to send soldiers to Fort Frontenac as La Salle requested, but had seized the fort under the pretext that La Salle had not fulfilled the conditions of the grant to maintain a sufficient garrison. Two of his associates, La Chesnaye and Le Ber, had taken possession, lived on La Salle's stores, sold for their own profit provisions sent by the King, and turned cattle to pasture on growing crops. La Forest was heartbroken. He could retain command only if he would join the Jesuits' party, and that he had refused to do. "I will wait for you at Quebec," he concluded, "for you will surely have to come there to straighten matters out."

"I'll have to go farther than that," said La Salle grimly. "With the Governor as our enemy, I must go directly to the King." He turned to Marc and Victor. "Are you boys ready to go to France?"

Victor felt as if all the riches of heaven and earth had been laid at his feet. "*Mordieux!* My foot is in the stirrup! *Haut le pied!* Off to Quebec! Marc, why aren't you more excited? We're going home!"

"I'll stay here," said Tonti before Marc could answer, "and try to keep the fort in operation. *En tout cas,* I'll probably never go back. I can make a living here better than in Italy or France."

"I don't know whether I can stay or not," said Father Membré humbly. "If only I could be back among fellow Recollets for a retreat, I might find strength to come back and try again."

"Then go with us," said La Salle gently. "You can wait in Quebec until I come back from France. And Tonti—thanks. Your staying will greatly relieve my mind. I'll see that supplies are sent out to you, and I'll be back as soon as I can."

Early in autumn, the four, with Messier, Laurent and two other canoemen they hoped to send back with supplies, set their canoes in the water and turned eastward. There, on the upper Illinois, they met a party of canoes as numerous as a flock of geese, bearing uniformed men of the King's dragoons, in command of the Chevalier de Baugis, with a commission from La Barre to take possession of Fort St. Louis. In violation of royal orders, La Barre had also given him a year's trading privilege. De Baugis also carried a letter ordering La Salle to Quebec. "Since I'm on the way now, I can obey that command most promptly," said La Salle dryly, holding back his wrath. He wrote a note to Tonti, asking him to receive De Baugis well, but to stay on as La Salle's personal representative.

After the canoes had gone on, La Salle said, "If I get support at

Versailles, De Baugis won't last long. And if I don't, I'm finished anyway."

If—! thought Marc. If only he were going back with fat dividends for his investors, instead of explanations and excuses.

3 2

WHEN they beached their canoes at Fort Frontenac, only three individuals came down to meet them. M. Plet hastened to embrace La Salle, while Susette offered her hand to be kissed, and Jacques beamed. Victor embraced him, and then devoted himself to Susette.

"How is everything?" Marc clasped Jacques's hand.

"Not good. It was fine until Monsieur le Ber came. I had wheat, maize, barley, and peas, but he let his horses in my fields. Now I have nothing."

"*Fichtre!*" Another demonstration, Marc was thinking, that the feudal system of the weak being protected by the strong was only as good as the lord's character.

"Now, I do not know what to do," mourned Jacques. "I was going to Quebec to get a wife. A ship is due, full of girls to pick from. But now I have no way to support one. Where are you going? Back to France? We heard Monsieur de la Salle had been recalled."

"Yes. Do you want to go along with us?" Marc waited for the inevitable "might as well" shrug. But Jacques soberly gazed back toward his farm. "I'd rather stay, if things could be as before. With a few fields and a gun a man can live very well here."

La Salle had apparently been listening, in spite of his conversation with M. Plet, for now he interposed, "Things *will* be again as they were. I shall have Fort Frontenac back, once I have seen His Majesty."

"Then, *m'sieu,* may I have your permission to marry?" asked Jacques.

"Yes, and my heartiest wishes that you find a good wife." La Salle looked at Marc. "What about your property at Fort St. Louis? Jacques and his new wife could go live under Tonti, and take care of your land."

300

"Merci bien!" exclaimed Jacques. "I would take the best care, M'sieu Marc."

"Good!" said Marc. "We'll send a letter to Tonti, saying you are to be in full charge of our acres. And there's a good house for you."

"You might come back sometime. I'll get everything in fine shape for you."

"Then get your baggage now," said La Salle. "We're going right on to Quebec."

Two more weeks brought them to the capital. The boys stared at the lower town in surprise, for the few scattered buildings were nearly all new, rising among heaps of charred planks and beams, the work of a fire that must have swept the whole settlement. But Jacques had no eyes for anything but the storeship anchored a little way out. "They're here! *Mon dieu!* We may be too late."

"No, the ship's just in," said Marc. "See, nothing's unloaded but the passengers."

"Well, let's hurry."

"Now, Jacques, you've gone unmarried a long time," Victor teased.

"Now that I'm taking the plunge, I want to get there before the best are all gone."

"We'll go to our room first," said Victor firmly. "Give the girls time to catch their breaths from the walk up Mountain Hill."

"The Ursulines will put them up for choice today," grumbled Jacques. "They won't feed them any longer than they have to. So don't take too long."

Ascending the steep pathway to the upper town, they heard the rat-a-plan of regimental drums, and on the cobblestone Place d'Armes a squad was marching in morning drill, in uniforms and jaunty caps of blue and white.

"New ones," said Marc.

"Oui, m'sieu," said Jacques. "They must be the regular troops the new Governor asked for to punish the Iroquois."

The three looked at one another, and then with the pity of veterans at the fresh, spic-and-span youths, deploying so smartly with halberds.

At their former lodgings, Mme. Dumont came nimbly to meet them. She was as fat as ever; her eyes were as greedy; her lips parted in the same toothless smile. *"Bon jour! Bon jour!* A pleasure to see such fine gentlemen again. I have kept your room for you, though the payment you left was used up long ago, and the upper town has been full of people burned out of the lower. Even the new Intendant Monsieur Meules had to take a cabin in the woods, and he's scared to death of being scalped. But your bed! I'm sorry. When the creditors of Monsieur de la Salle came I couldn't do anything. I saved all your boxes in my storeroom. The gleam in her tiny eyes shower she expected to be well paid. "And we will get you another bed, very cheap——"

"I don't care about a bed." Victor cut off her tirade, leaving her open-mouthed. "That 'donkey's breakfast' will be fine. But put some clean straw in it. Is there anything to eat?"

"Oh but yes, wait until you see—a good Norman pot-au-feu, the way they make it at Rouen. I've simmered it all day."

"I can smell it." Marc said, sniffing.

"Your man can take your baggage right up, then," she beamed.

At first it looked as if the girls were overflowing the Ursuline convent, spilling out the doors. Then it became apparent that Mother Mary was herding them to a nearby storehouse where, judging by the crowd of habitants, soldiers, and *coureurs de bois,* the actual marriage arrangements were being made. Victor, who was accompanying Jacques while Marc shopped for supplies for Messier and Laurent to take back to Tonti, looked at the girls who would breed the sons to inhabit Louis XIV's wilderness. Cynically he had expected streetwalkers' faces—and there were a few; but most of the neatly dressed girls had the somber black eyes and stocky build of peasants.

"They look as if they could work like oxen," said Jacques. "That's what one needs here."

"These *coureurs de bois*—will they take the girls along through the woods?"

"No," said Jacques. "They have to become habitants at some seigneury."

Victor raised his eyebrows. So the girls were also bait to lure these men back from the freedom of the woods.

At the door of the storehouse Jacques held back in panic. "I can't go in there," he said breathlessly. "Let's go back and watch the drilling in the square."

"Nonsense." Victor grinned. "Face up to it like a man. You'll need a wife in the Illinois country."

Jacques swallowed several times. "All right. But you keep close behind me!"

Benches were ranged along the walls, filled with girls, some pale and frightened, some rosy with laughter, all of them appraising the gallants that strode about sizing them up. Victor respectfully greeted Mother Mary, who was gliding about from one group to another. "Who are those girls?" He nodded toward a few climbing a twisted stairs at the end of the room.

She gazed at him curiously. "The girls of better class are up there, those who come with good recommendations from their curés, or from convents at home."

"I guess you won't aspire to one of those, Jacques," said Victor. "See anything you like?"

Jacques was hanging back as if he would like to hide under Victor's coattails.

"Don't be bashful," said Mother Mary. "Give me an account of what you have and your prospects, and then you may choose. Here is a nice girl, on this bench."

Jacques gave her one look. "She's nothing but bones. I don't have enough pork to fatten her up."

Victor laughed. "Well, go ahead then and find one that suits you. But remember, a wife is like a horse—it's hard to find a faultless one."

"You be sure to wait for me. You can tell the Reverend Mother about my prospects better than I can."

Victor nodded cheerfully. "I wouldn't think of missing this." As Jacques began to sidle along the wall of the room, looking as if he had come to see if the floor needed repairing, Victor ambled through the center of the room. Apparently the girls were allowed to question a man, and didn't have to take him unless he suited them. The *coureurs de bois* were shrewdly appraising; the habitants plodded about as if dazed; but the soldiers plunged ahead, made up their minds with military directness, and were already lining up before a notary's table. Beyond the table a priest waited in a temporary chapel that had been set up in a large closet.

Victor found himself near the stairs, and out of curiosity he started up to see what the others looked like. The girls upstairs were better-dressed, their broad white collars of finer material. Some looked like demoiselles, quite well brought up. Wives for officers, I suppose, thought Victor.

A nun was posted in the doorway to see that none of the ineligible came up. Wearing a fixed smile with no joy in it, she stared at Victor. "Monsieur wishes to come in?" she asked hesitantly. "Gentlemen don't come here. They usually marry the daughters of seigneurs."

303

"No, *mais non, madame,*" said Victor, startled. "I came with my man —he's down below. I just wandered up to look around."

In a corner of the room two men were wrangling over a girl who protested that she wanted neither. All Victor could see of her between her rival suitors was a pair of pale hands tying knots in a handkerchief. He wondered what that reminded him of. He stepped to one side to get a better look, and was astonished to see the girl jump up from the bench, push the two men aside, and run directly toward him.

"It's you! I so hoped I'd find you, and I did!" The girl threw herself into his arms, nearly knocking him over.

"What is all this?" exclaimed Victor. "You've mistaken me for someone else." He tried in vain to free himself. She's out of her mind, he thought, and was about to turn her over to a nun, when he saw an antique cross hanging about her neck. "Why, you must be—" he stammered, "the girl—with her aunt, in Paris——"

"Yes," she sobbed happily, "I'm Michelle."

Victor drew her to a bench. "Now, let's sit down and talk a bit," he said soothingly. "What are you doing here?"

She wiped her eyes and looked up adoringly at him. "I loved all your letters and presents, and I thought about New France all the time; so when I heard about this shipload of girls, I begged permission to go on it. I knew I could find you."

"You certainly took a chance!" he said in astonishment. "New France is a big place."

"I prayed all the way over. And here you come in on my first day. Oh, *le bon dieu* is good to me!" she said fervently.

Victor was speechless before her joy, but she went rambling on. "I knew you at once. You look different—older, and so brown and strong." She seemed to realize she was embarrassing him with the adoration in her eyes, and let her glance drop to her lap.

"You don't know what you're getting into, marrying one of these fellows. You'll be stuck on some little seigneury farm, or in some tradesman's shop for the rest of your life."

"Even that's better than being stuck in a convent," she said stubbornly. "But I hoped—oh, I shouldn't say this—but I hoped, after all the letters and presents, that you thought tenderly enough of me to— well——"

"Letters and presents?" repeated Victor stupidly. "Oh." Marc must have paid her all this attention. Now look what's happened. I ought to thrash him.

"Well, I don't know what to do," he said aloud. "Your beauty deserves kinder treatment from me, but I confess I don't know which way to turn. If Count Frontenac were here——"

"Couldn't you—couldn't you marry me yourself?"

"What? Oh, see here! I mean—" he floundered. "I'm on my way back to France, probably on the same ship you came on."

"Oh, no!" Tears began to form in her eyes, and he caught hold of her hand.

"Now, don't do that. I can refuse nothing to a lady in tears. We'll think of something."

"I know." She brightened and wiped her tears away. "You can go through the marriage form with me, and then I can stay here until you come back."

I'm not coming back, he was about to tell her, but he hesitated to plunge her into tears again. Then he reached a decision. Marc was the one who had got her into this mess. "Come." He lifted her to her feet. "I must talk to my brother."

"Oh! Yes, you did say you were coming with him."

"Yes, indeed, there are two of us," he answered cryptically.

At the foot of the stair they encountered Mother Mary who peered at him with a hundred questions in her eyes. "I had no idea you wanted one yourself."

"I didn't. This is just an extra present from *le bon dieu.*" He looked around for Jacques and found him, beaming, hand in hand with a pretty plump peasant girl.

"This is Arlette," said Jacques. "She liked the looks of me, and so I said——"

"I know," laughed Victor. "'Might as well.'" He saw that Jacques had really made a good choice, a girl in her late twenties, amiable and pretty in a coarse way, with cheeks like Honfleur apricots. He made a bow that would have done credit to Louis XIV himself. "Arlette! So Jacques was really in time to get the prettiest one. How did you happen to come here?"

"My parents have fifteen children. They were glad to have one less to feed."

Jacques, beaming, noticed Michelle. "You found one, too, *m'sieu?*" His voice rose in astonishment.

"This is someone we—I—knew in Paris. I want to go and see my brother for a minute," he added, turning to Mother Mary. "Could this young lady wait somewhere where she won't be bothered?"

305

"She can go back to the convent. I'll send a note with her. But you didn't tell me about Jacques's prospects."

When he convinced her that Jacques had very good prospects indeed, Mother Mary smiled her blessing on the couple and they joined the line in front of the notary's desk. "I'll be back before you're married," said Victor.

"I hope so," said Jacques heartily. "You can be best man."

Marc, ready to make the rounds of the shops, met La Salle just returned from delivering Victor's journal, as the King's decree required, to the new Intendant.

"Where's Nika?" Marc realized that he had seldom seen La Salle alone.

"Gone to visit his family. He'll be back in time to go to France with us. Come, walk with me. I have an appointment with the Governor, and then I have to go back to the Intendant. I went down to book passage for us, but the captain says he'll have to have the usual statement from the Intendant that the king gives permission for me to leave. I told the Intendant that I have my orders direct from Versailles, and that includes my men. The Intendant knows all that perfectly well but insists I bring my papers to prove it."

"I hope you don't have to bribe him. Remember Victor and I are on leave from the Guards. He can't hold us."

"Good. I'll tell him that."

As they crossed the Place d'Armes, Marc said, "We've covered a lot of territory since the last time we walked here." On every side people were staring at La Salle, pointing him out as the discoverer of the Mississippi's mouth, but he was unaware. "If only Frontenac had won out here, instead of the Bishop, everything would be perfect. But the tables have been turned. There is even a murder charge against me because of the shooting of those two deserters. I don't expect to gain anything from seeing La Barre, but courtesy demands that I pay him a call, and I shall try to get him to let Tonti's men come here and go back with supplies. For anything more, I'll have to have orders direct from His Majesty."

"I hope you can get money from the King this time. Fortification and colonization on such a scale is too much for the purse of any other man."

When La Salle entered the castle, Marc turned to the terrace railing for a look at the river. At his left the St. Charles came down to join the stately progress of the St. Lawrence toward the sea. Below him, among the new buildings of the lower town, sailors were amusing themselves. At least their pastimes are still the same, thought Marc. On the King's ship, repairs were being made in preparation for sailing. The merchant ships would follow and in three days the harbor would be bare. The first snow lay already on the distant Laurentians. Marc thought how much more he knew about that river than when he had stood here before, and wondered how La Salle was faring in the castle.

What would become of La Salle? Brave, adventurous, skillful, he was a dreamer with great capacities for putting those dreams into action. Could he go on overcoming obstacles, or was he doomed to tragedy by the very greatness of his plans? To establish civilization and Christianity throughout the vast valley of the Mississippi was a project too vast and too complex to be more than a goal for the distant future. A mere military occupation would be difficult enough, but to that must be added the civilizing of warring savage tribes, settling them about forts, importing large French colonies when few Frenchmen wanted to leave France. But someone was going to occupy that valley, and if any man could do it for the French, it was La Salle.

Marc realized that the very bigness of the country had fascinated him. Here in the wind of freedom a man could plan his own day. He could *choose*—that was it, that was the essence of freedom. If he followed a leader it was because he chose to, as Nika did with La Salle. The riches of soil and mines and furs were so great that there were enough for everyone in proportion to his willingness to work.

Everyone. What was he saying, where was his vision going? Everyone. But that would do away with the seigneuries as they were. Then let it! The purpose of alchemy was to raise some material to a nobler form than it was. Why transplant an old system to a new world—or any one old religion? There was certainly room here for all, even for those who were not French. Marc remembered that in the Illinois village, when La Salle said, "We are Frenchmen," the chief had answered in higher praise, "You are men." Noble birth was nothing in itself; the dignity of manhood was everything. In this free land no caprice of a monarch should send a man to rot in a dungeon. No individual, not even a Louis XIV, should have so absolute a power.

Now Marc knew he was coming back, and why. Never again could I live in the narrow ritual of the court, he thought. I will come back with La Salle because he has had this vision.

He turned toward the castle, eager for La Salle to come out.

Victor was coming across the terrace. As Marc waited, he realized with a surge of affection that even that domination, that assurance that had made Victor order both their lives, that gaiety so seldom dampened arose from the same source—Victor's boundless confidence that he would be adequate in any situation. He and La Salle were actually kindred spirits.

"Well, did Jacques find a wife?" he asked, as Victor stopped before him, hazel eyes flashing in excitement.

"Yes—but I nearly did, too!" Quickly he related what had happened.

"Michelle—here?" said Marc, dazed, like one coming out of a dream. "How'd she get here?"

"With the girls." Victor pointed down to the ship. "She's very attractive, and I feel sorry for her, but I don't know what to do with her."

"You needn't do anything," said Marc firmly. "I'll do it."

Victor's mouth opened, but he couldn't utter a sound.

"Yes." Marc grinned. "It must have been love at first sight. I saw her only once, and in the dark, at that; but I've thought of her constantly ever since."

"Well, I've always said love was as blind as dice." Victor was shaken by this revelation, but he knew what Marc meant. He'd never forgotten Susette, in spite of his devotion to Angélique. "But you can't be thinking of marrying her!"

"I might. I'll go talk to her anyway."

"She thinks we're both the same man," said Victor thoughtfully. "What's she going to think when she finds there are two of us?"

"She'll find it out sooner or later," said Marc calmly. "I don't think it'll bother her much. Did she seem, well—affectionate?"

"Threw herself into my arms in front of a hundred people, and wept all over my coat front."

"We'd better change coats before I go. It might be better if she didn't know right away that she was weeping on the wrong man."

Victor laughed, a little hollowly. "But you can't be serious about marriage—or do you mean you'll go through a ceremony and later get an annulment? She can't even leave Quebec without the King's permission."

"I don't know that I'll want an annulment."

"But your chances would be ruined in France if you're tied to some girl in the colonies."

Marc drew a long breath. "I might as well tell you. I'm coming back with La Salle."

"Que diable!" Victor stared at him and shook his head as if to clear his ears. "You're coming back here? When did you get that queer notion?"

"I think I've known it for a long time, but I've been seeing it clearly in the past hour. Here I can choose what and how much I want to do. I can be of use to La Salle by building the rest of his forts. Just as Father said, this is the biggest adventure of this century, and I want to be part of it."

Eh bien, thought Victor, I won't argue any more. Let him marry this girl if he wants, and leave her here. Once I get him in France I'll talk him out of coming back. "Well, good luck to you," he said jauntily. "I'm not surprised, really. You've been getting more like an Indian all the time. You even talk like one. But I'll not come back here unless I'm dragged. *Le diable m'en garde!* I freely admit a nostalgia for the frivolities of Versailles, and an abhorrence for swarms of blanketed savages. Go along to your Michelle. I want to go see if we have any mail. I'll come along in time to be best man for both you and Jacques, unless you think I should keep out of the way."

"No, do come. I'll tell her at once that I have a twin."

"I hope she won't run away like that Indian girl."

Marc was already halfway across the terrace. "If she does, I'll run after her."

It was with a stricken face that Victor hastened to join Marc and Michelle in the waiting room of the convent half an hour later. They were clasping hands and upon both faces was a radiance that told all he needed to know. Marc saw Victor enter and stand blinking in the dim light, grasping three opened letters. He left Michelle and crossed to meet him. "Bad news?"

"Angélique's dead," Victor blurted out. "She died giving birth to the King's son. The child died, too."

Marc stood for a moment in appalled silence. "Come, sit down."

Victor dropped on a bench, staring dully into space. "I didn't want to believe it of Angélique."

"I know," said Marc softly.

"She was the duchess with the gray coach the other letters talked about. While I was half expecting it, it's a blow. And now I learn that that was exactly why she had been sent to Versailles. All her relations —father, uncles, cousins—had contributed money to equip her for the court, hoping she would catch the King's eye so they would profit from their investment. And they did, the cursed bourgeois! She was the favorite for two years—" His voice broke.

Marc knew that one of the bitterest pills for Victor was a suspicion that the King had removed competition by sending him, like another Uriah, into danger. "I don't think you would have been happy with her," he said gently. "Especially with her sights leveled on the King all the time. Better that it happened before you married her."

Victor roused himself. "It hurts like the devil. I don't know, though, whether she ever cared about me. Court gossip says Montespan poisoned her. It could be true. The letter says La Voisin has been tried and executed, and there were other poisoning arrests. Montespan was implicated beyond question. Anyway, His Majesty never goes near her now. Because she is the mother of some of his children, he lets her live at court, but he had her removed to the farthest extremity of the palace. There are other changes, too. The queen is dead, and also Colbert and La Rochefoucauld . . . " He passed his hand over his face as if to brush away a cobweb. *"Eh bien,* Angélique got her coach."

Victor sighed. "But I am keeping you from your own plans."

Marc stared in astonishment. Never in the old days would Victor have considered that. He was improving. At the same time Marc wondered how he could ever have felt oppressed by his brother. All his feeling went into an outpouring of love. I hope he comes back with me, he thought. Aloud he said wistfully, "I feel strange getting married without the family's permission. Of course, Father released us, but I would feel better if I could ask brother Auguste."

Victor looked up, startled. "Auguste is dead, too."

"Auguste?" Marc repeated stupidly.

Victor put an arm about his shoulders. "Taken by fever a year ago. Charles writes that he is waiting eagerly for us to come back, to dispose of his future. I also have an imperative letter from His Majesty, ordering me to return without delay. Ironic, isn't it? That's a letter I'd have given half my future prospects to receive any time in the last five years, and I get it only when I'm on my way."

"What does the King want of you?" asked Marc. The truth dawned. "Why, how stupid of me! You're——"

Victor smiled feebly. "Yes, for a year I've been the Marquis de Lorennes without knowing it. Now the King wants me close at hand—with all the others." He rose, wondering why the prospect didn't fill him with more pleasure. Perhaps it was grief at the loss of Angélique:

grief, too, at Auguste's passing, for even though they had little in common, he and Marc had received nothing but good from their older brother's hands. Victor glanced at Michelle who took her adoring eyes off Marc just long enough to give him a shy smile. "I am pleased, my dear brother, to give you the formal approval of your family. But don't crowd in with that press of sheep—" He nodded toward the temporary chapel. "While your bride readies herself, and you make arrangements with Mother Mary, I'll see if I can find Father Membré. You can be married in the Recollet chapel. Let's see. She ought to have a wedding dress. I know—my brocades! I'll get the white one. Not time enough for a regular gown, but maybe the sisters could whip it into a cape or something and find her a veil. I'll be right back. I'll see if I can find some clothes for us." He dashed out of the door.

It was not hard to convince Mother Mary that she was giving one of her lambs into good care, and she agreed, upon hearing Marc's plans, that Michelle should stay with them. She called a cheerful little nun to help get Michelle ready, and said she would turn the problem of the wedding dress over to her sewing class of Indian girls—if Marc could give them a little time.

"I can make it myself," said Michelle firmly. "Just give me some helpers to baste, and I'll be ready in two hours."

"All right," said Marc. "I want to go invite Monsieur de la Salle to the wedding."

He found La Salle in a shabby little boardinghouse, engrossed in a book on navigation, which he put down when Marc appeared. "Victor? Good. I want to write a letter to Tonti."

Marc laughed. "It's Marc. And I'm afraid you'll find the Marquis de Lorennes a little too dazed to be of much use."

La Salle's eyes opened in astonishment. "The Marquis——"

Marc sat in a cane-bottomed chair, and told him all that had happened, including his own plans for marriage, and for returning to New France.

"And what of Victor?"

"I'd be very happy if he would come back, too. But I'll come anyway."

"Then you've found what you wanted here?"

"Not ready-made. But I found what I want to work for. I guess that's a path of my own."

"The best kind, I should think." La Salle was silent for some minutes, rubbing his finger along the edge of the book. "That's quite a bit of news all at once," he said at last. "I'm sorry about your brother Auguste, but Victor should make a good marquis. It's not easy for me—" He clasped and unclasped his brown muscular hands, a sign of unusual agitation "—not easy for me to express affection, but I've come to appreciate him very much, as I have you also. I'll put it like this: By this time I should have sons of my own, and God grant I may before I am many years older. Meanwhile I have much of the same feeling for the two of you. And I might add, Marc, that you're a worthy pupil of D'Artagnan."

"I?" Marc's voice rose in surprise. "But it's Victor who aspires to be that."

"I know. He'll grow up to it, but you are already there." La Salle rose and began to pace the floor, as if driven by the stress of his thoughts. "I wish Victor hadn't given up his sword. It haunts me all the time. It's the kind of gift that obligates the receiver to deserve it."

Marc nodded. "Maybe there's nothing to it, but I can't help a feeling I've had ever since he told me what he had done with it that it has some mysterious power of its own."

"Stranger things have been proven true," La Salle agreed. "But about the question of the moment: your Michelle. You're consulting your heart rather than your escutcheon in marrying her, I take it."

"Yes. A dowry and all that doesn't matter."

"No, I can see that. Nor would it to me if I were getting married today."

"I'm glad that Mademoiselle Lucie is willing to wait. I hope it won't be much longer."

"Only until I establish my colony in the South. But about your problems: you say the law forbids Michelle's going back to France with you?"

"She's willing to wait here until I come back."

"It may be some time before you and I see Quebec again," said La Salle quietly.

"But I thought you were coming right back?"

La Salle crossed to the door and closed it, after looking up and down the hall. "I have never confided my plans to anyone——"

"That's all right—you needn't tell me."

"But it may make a difference to you. With Tonti at Fort St. Louis, I need another lieutenant. I want you to accept the place."

The *cordon bleu* would not have pleased Marc as much. Before he could frame his thanks beyond *"Merci—"* La Salle went on, "If you will swear secrecy—from everyone—I'd like to tell you what I plan to do."

Marc drew his sword, laid it on the table, and placed his hand upon it.

"I plan to take the new colonists directly from France to the mouth of the Mississippi by water, if His Majesty will give me ships, supplies, and soldiers for the garrison. I think I can persuade him, little interested as he is in colonies, of the advantage of a strong military base so close to the holdings of Spain. So we will not be coming back to Quebec at all. Of course, once we have our fort built, you could come and get her—when I come for Lucie. Meanwhile I want nothing of my plans to leak out here in any way. I ask secrecy even from your brother. Not that he couldn't be trusted, but someone might overhear you discussing it—and the fewer the better in any secret."

"I have sworn," said Marc, "I'll keep silent. And now, will you come to my wedding?"

When he left La Salle, his head was swimming with the new plan. With elation, too. La Salle's confidence was something of his own that he had earned.

The ceremony in the modest Recollet chapel was as impressive as Father Membré could make it. After the final blessing, with the Queen's ring on her finger, Michelle's face was radiant.

As they paused in the porch for congratulations, Marc hesitated, as if he had not thought out the next step. As befitting the best man, Victor took charge. "Give me Tonti's list—I'll do the purchasing. You go over to our lodgings and eat some of that good pot-au-feu. You can take our room. I'll find someplace else."

Marc clasped Victor's hand. *"Merci bien,* for everything. I wish you had found someone like Michelle."

"There aren't any more like her," Victor said gallantly. "But don't worry about me. One of these days some girl will have the honor of pleasing me."

"We can find a bed for you here, Victor," offered Father Membré. "If you care to share the humble quarters of Recollets."

Victor raised his arms and let them fall, in imitation of Jacques. "Might as well. Thanks, Father."

As Marc and Michelle went off hand in hand, Father Membré said thoughtfully, "I think he has made a good choice, sudden as it was.

313

She is *douce et bonne,* and has a sensible head on her shoulders. She wasn't right for a convent. She needs a life of action, lots of children, a chance to build something."

"At least," said Victor, "she won't expect too much. All her life she's been practically an orphan, almost a servant, and then a convent inmate."

"Incidentally, I'm going back to France with you," said Father Membré. "Things are very difficult for us Recollets here. The Bishop has always limited our activities. But now, with Governor La Barre also under the Jesuit thumb, we have lost everything. We must take down our bell turret, destroy our monastic apartments, and say no Masses even in private. We are to have as little liberty as if we were heretics. La Barre has declared that before long there will not be one Recollet in the colony. So I must go to France, too, to do what I can."

After her first exclamations of surprise, Mme. Dumont bustled around arranging a wedding supper. Marc was silent, but Michelle chattered about her voyage and the difficulty the nuns had in keeping the two cargoes apart—girls and soldiers. She sighed happily. "I love the clear air and the balsam smell. Is the whole country as fine as this?"

"There are parts I like even better."

"Oh, I want to see it all." She threw her arms wide as if to take it in.

"For a girl like you it can't be very amusing in a convent. I'm sorry I have to thrust you back into one here, for a time."

"I wouldn't mind, with something to look forward to. But I'm not going to wait here."

"What can you do? I can't take you to France."

"You needn't take me anywhere. I'm going with Jacques and Arlette to your property on the Illinois. I've been talking to them, and it's all settled."

Marc gazed at her flushed face in astonishment. As he opened his mouth to protest, the advantages of such a course were so striking that he couldn't speak. She could be useful there, and it was much closer to the Mississippi's mouth than Quebec. He lifted her hand and kissed it. "If you really wish to try it. You can all go with Messier and Laurent—and when you get there, Tonti will help you."

PART III

33

AS the hackney coach made its way through the streets of Paris, bearing the newly arrived Marquis de Lorennes, his twin brother, and his traveling companions, La Salle and Nika, the Marquis leaned out of the coach window, savoring his homecoming. All the familiar sights and noises and smells delighted him. The city seemed possessed of a restlessness and a shrill pitch caused by the crowding together of people and buildings, for Louis XIV more than ten years ago had fixed the boundaries of Paris and its *faubourgs,* decreeing that they could expand no farther.

"Ah, Paris!" sighed Victor. "It's just the same."

"But what did you expect?" scoffed Marc. "Tapestry and banners flung out for us, and a procession of Swiss Guards?"

"No," said Victor, "but many a conqueror has been so welcomed who added far less to France than La Salle has done."

"I am far more comfortable," La Salle assured him, "than I would be in the midst of a celebration."

Victor was watching the passing streets. "Here it is." He leaned out to call to the coachman. "Turn right, and go to the fourth signboard."

Entering M. Tourneau's familiar door, they looked around in surprise. Formerly one stepped from the street into a very rainbow of silks, woolens, laces, and brocades draped for inspection. The bolts of cloth were still there, but the bright colors were gone. Before they could speculate upon the change, the shopkeeper came out of the shadows, peering at them through silver-rimmed glasses. *"Bon jour, messieurs, comment vous portez-vous?"*

The three exchanged glances. He didn't recognize them. Victor took the lead. "I am well, Monsieur Tourneau, as always."

"As always, good," the old man said cautiously. Coming closer, he looked at them over his spectacles. "Why, the Messieurs de Lorennes! Welcome home, messieurs!" He bowed deeply.

"And you remember our friend, Monsieur de la Salle?" asked Marc.

"Ah, oui! Monsieur de la Salle! I made that scarlet coat for you, *n'est-ce pas?* I am most glad to see you. All Paris is excited about your discovery. You have been quite the man of the hour, since Monsieur de Seignelay reported it in the *Mercure.* Ah, Monsieur, my poor shop is honored!"

"I hope," said Victor to La Salle, "that this is the *hors d'oeuvres* to a feast of praise for you at Versailles."

"Oh, but monsieur," said the tailor, "if you go to court, you must have me make another coat for you. It would never do to appear in scarlet!"

"Why not?" asked Victor. "What is all this nonsense, Monsieur Tourneau?" He gestured to both sides of the shop. "Where did you get such a dull collection of materials? Are you tailoring now only for people in trade?"

"Mais non, monsieur, mais non! This is what one wears at court. No bright colors, not for a long time now. *C'est dommage!* You must all have new suits, as soon as I can make them. The King wears only brown and gray, so everyone must do the same. His Majesty has become very devout, and has given up both color and gaiety."

"The deuce you say!" exclaimed Victor.

"You will see." M. Tourneau nodded his head so vigorously his spectacles bounded precariously on his nose. "You think I would display such muddy colors if they were not in demand?"

Victor shrugged. "One must have endless patience with princes and bear with their idiosyncrasies as best one may. Drab it is, then. Do you have anything we can get today? We must go to court at once."

"Mais non, Monsieur Victor, you know it takes many days, even when we rush——"

"Come now! What have you started for someone else that you could fit to us?"

"Pardieu! I never thought I'd see the day, Monsieur le Marquis, when you'd be satisfied with materials picked out by anyone else! Wait, I have two that might fit. But not three."

"Leave me out, then," said Marc. "I have no desire to go to Versailles anyway. I'd rather spend the money on cattle—or other things Michelle and I can use."

"Remember all those portages they'll have to be carried over," said Victor.

Marc, remembering that Victor knew nothing of the plan to sail directly to the Mississippi, said dryly, as he went out the door, "I expect the cattle to walk. And thanks, again, Victor, for giving me half what you had left from selling your sword."

"Just a wedding present," said Victor grandly. "The Marquis de Lorennes is always punctual about family obligations."

M. Tourneau returned from a back room with two partly finished coats, one in slate gray, the other in brown. "If Monsieur will put one on—I think we could finish it in an hour."

Victor reached for the brown one. "If you don't mind, I'd rather not have gray."

"You will need close-fitting breeches and dark stockings," said M. Tourneau, "and hats with very small plumes—all those I have, too. You can have bright waistcoats—they are still in style."

"I have brocades for waistcoats in the carriage," said Victor. "I'll send them in by the driver." He pulled on the coat and made a face at himself in the mirror. "Why in the world does the King like—" he began, but the tinkling bell announced another customer, and the King's valet entered the shop.

"Bontems!" said Victor. "Remember me?"

The severe face relaxed. "Why—it can't be! Monsieur Victor!"

"Yes, I'm back. How are you and how is His Majesty?"

"Both of us are well, but somewhat older," said the valet bleakly. "What are you doing here?"

"Hoping to see His Majesty. Have you an idea when he might receive us?"

"I am sure he will wish to see you at once." Bontems frowned. "Let me see—His Majesty is with the former Madame de Maintenon now—that's why I was free to come for his new waistcoats." He pulled out his watch. "He will be there for another hour, and then will have audiences. But the council meeting has been cancelled because everyone but Monsieur de Seignelay is ill or out of the city. I think he would see one of you gentlemen at eleven. The other tomorrow at the same time."

"You go first, Victor," said La Salle. "I'll be glad to have a day to compose my thoughts and perhaps call first on Monsieur de Seignelay."

"Now, Monsieur Tourneau," said Bontems, "if I may have the waistcoats?"

When he had gone, Victor stared after him. "What did he mean, the former Madame de Maintenon? Has she been advanced again?"

M. Tourneau looked around cautiously, and whispered, "Advanced indeed! They say the King has married her!"

"No!" said Victor.

"Yes, monsieur, in a secret ceremony. The only way he could get her. And Monsieur Victor, if I may be so bold: do not expect the captaincy again. The present captain is a relative of Maintenon. The King does nothing without her advice."

When the coats were finished, Victor took a coach to St. Cloud to wait on Madame before he went on to court. The tailor had told him that neither Monsieur's family nor the Dauphin's now appeared at court except on rare occasions, since both brother and son had bitterly opposed the King's marriage.

Time seemed to have rolled backward when he stepped into the boudoir of Madame, for she was writing letters as before. But Madame showed the passing of five years. She had grown very heavy; her eyes were lusterless in a sagging face the color of brick. But her smile of welcome had its same warmth as she held out a plump hand to be kissed. She wore a man's brown coat and a green and gold waistcoat above the only feminine item of her attire, a long trailing skirt. "Welcome! Welcome back from the wilds of New France. I hear your La Salle was most successful. We are all proud of you, Victor."

"Your praise, as always, is sweet to my ears." He sat down on the stool she waved him to. "I appreciated your letters."

"I could not put into them all I should have," she said.

"I know. I suppose from the hints in your early ones I should have been prepared for the blow when it came, but I hoped I was mistaken."

"I was purposely indefinite. I was afraid if I managed to tell you the whole truth you'd come rushing back, your job undone, and the King would have punished you." Madame picked up a quill and made little circles on the edge of her paper. "The whole thing upset me greatly. I did my best, as I had promised you, but Angélique's own willfulness and the pressure put upon her were too much for me."

"I understand." Victor clasped his hands tightly. "His Majesty has never forced anyone to become his mistress, so that must have been what she wanted. It was a blow—to my affections, my pride, and my esteem for the King. I never knew exactly why I was sent with La Salle, when so many others were more suitable. Why didn't he just have me assassinated?"

She laid down the quill and seized his hand compassionately. "He wanted only to remove the competition of a younger and handsomer man. In such circumstances you know dangers are often thrust on subordinates as honors. But Victor, his affair with Angélique was the most disgusting performance on both sides. I'm glad you weren't here to see it. She wasn't in love with the King, but sentimental as she was, she saw herself as a great romantic heroine. And Louis resumed dancing and dalliance with all the ardor of a young man. He gave her the title of duchess, and a carriage and jewels as good as the Queen's." Madame looked at him pityingly. "Victor, I'm going to tell you some harsh truths. She had never an idea in her head except a new way to adorn the outside of it. She behaved very badly to everyone. Her vanity grew so abominably that when she entered any gathering she passed with her head in air, without curtsying to anyone, even the Queen. She'd never have been the wife for you. And as for her death, what was ahead of her?"

He nodded, unable to trust his voice. Madame reached down to the bottom drawer of her dressing table, and drew out a jeweled casket. "I visited her when the child was born, and she asked me to give you this—her proudest possession. I promised, since she was already in her death agony."

He opened the casket and found a scroll of paper, which he unrolled, seeing first the signature "Louis" and then the lines ". . . we have created our well-beloved Mlle. Marie-Angélique de Scorailles, Demoiselle de Fontanges, a duchess, *pour sa vertu et son mérite*. . . ."

" 'For her virtue and her merit,' " repeated Victor, thrusting the paper back in the casket. "You'd better send it to her father."

"Strange, the things that grew out of that affair. The King seemed to see her sudden death as a warning and became most pious. Of course the revelations that Montespan had been trying to poison him also shocked him into reforming. So Louis sent Maintenon herself to tell Montespan never to enter his presence again. Figure to yourself how Maintenon gloated under that smug face when she went on that errand!"

"At least Montespan's influence is over, then?"

"And about time." Madame was suddenly grim. "She ruined the Duc de Luxembourg completely after you left—did you know? Imagine—one of the heroes of France, and a cousin of the Condés! He was accused of several poisonings and sent to the Bastille. Six months later he came to trial and was found not guilty, but he was nonetheless stripped of his marshalship and banished for a year. When the King let him come back, after Montespan was disgraced, it was only to an inferior position in the Guards."

Victor bit his lip. "There, but for the grace of God, go I! For I could have been ruined with far greater ease. But tell me about the Queen. I heard that she died."

"She had an abscess under the arm, but she died from the ignorance of doctors. And the funeral! From all the carriages you heard only laughter and jokes. The Dauphin went right on to the Palais-Royal for a gay evening, and the King himself went directly to the hunt. He got a swift punishment, though. His horse fell, dislocating Louis's arm. He has been plagued with illness ever since—toothache, insomnia, nightmares. Every day he is becoming more of a devoté, and is at last consenting to grow old."

Madame's devotion to the King had apparently tarnished in five years, thought Victor, but he said only, "So now you are first lady at court."

She squeezed his hand. "Thank you, my boy. I am. But there's an old hag at Versailles who has the idea she is first. He may have married her, or he may not have, but at least he didn't say to France, 'Here is your Queen.' Though it wouldn't be any worse for him to give her the title publicly than to propose as he did that his bastards should inherit the crown!"

"He proposed that?"

"Yes, but it stirred up such indignation that even he realized he had gone too far."

"What is Maintenon's official title, then? In case I happen to see her, which God forbid."

She looked at him fondly. "I'm glad you didn't go there to bend the knee before calling on me, as most people would. Her only title is *dame d'honneur* to the Princess of Bavaria—the Dauphiness, you know, an alarmingly ugly young woman who spends her time in boredom and bearing children. But we are all bored now. The Maintenon has put a nightcap over the crown of France, the pious old hypocrite that she is! God converted her to Catholicism at the precise moment when it was most to her worldly interest; and now she's the greatest bigot the palace ever saw. She has ruined the King. One could forgive his earlier sins easier than his oppressive piety and intolerance. The courtiers all became reformed with the King, so on the surface there are only pious ladies and gentlemen to be seen. All these dull clothes! No entertainments, no plays, no fetes, nothing but eternal going to church! Even Maintenon complains constantly of trying to amuse a man no longer capable of being amused. But go to court and see for yourself."

"As a matter of fact, I'm going this morning."

322

"Then come back one day and tell me of your adventures."

"I will. I'll give you a souvenir of them now." He pulled out the medal and explained where he got it. She turned it over, examining it with great interest. "From around the neck of a dead Iroquois, and with the King of England upon it! Not one of my medals has a history to compare with that. I shall treasure it. And I have one more thing for you." From another drawer she brought out a little box. "I rescued this from Angélique's room after she died—the box you gave her. Since it has your portrait on it, I thought I'd take charge of it."

"Thank you, Madame." He gazed at the portrait, shaking his head. "I was very young then."

"You were indeed." She smiled. "Now run along. I hope the King will be generous."

Outside the St. Cloud gates once more, he ripped the portrait from the box, put it in his pocket, and thrust the box into the hands of the nearest beggar woman. As he was about to step into his hired coach, another pulled up behind it bearing on its panel the white banner with black fleur-de-lis of the Guises. From it stepped the puffy, dissipated Chevalier de Lorraine, arranging his laces as he told his coachman, "I shall be the rest of the day with Monsieur. Come back at midnight." He glanced curiously at Victor, and then as recognition came, exclaimed, "Monsieur de Lorennes! I beg your pardon—Monsieur le Marquis de Lorennes."

"Comment vous portez-vous, monsieur?" said Victor formally.

"I can understand your first step upward," the Chevalier flicked dust from his shoulders as he approached, "but how did you manage Auguste's demise from that distance?"

Enraged, Victor struck the smirking face. The Chevalier staggered, his hand to his cheek. "My seconds will call on you, monsieur!"

"Don't bother me!" said Victor scornfully, feeling that in lashing out at that decadent face he had dealt a blow to the entire dirty world of intrigue. "You wouldn't last ten seconds! And keep a civil tongue in your head when you meet any of my family, if you want to stay alive."

The Chevalier managed a sneer, but his eyes were taking in Victor's bronzed figure. He bowed and sidled through the gate.

The palace seemed to reek with the stench of unwashed humanity, snuff, stale perfumes, and urine. It always smelled like this, he thought, but I had forgotten. He felt like smashing the hilt of his sword through windowpanes to let in air, and for an instant felt nostalgia for balsam-scented forests.

In the magnificent but cold galleries at the head of the stairs, the courtiers were still standing about, waiting. In these drab clothes and with exactly the same wigs, they all looked alike, reminding Victor of herons motionless in a swamp. The scraps of conversation he over-heard as he walked through no longer dealt with scandals and intrigues, but with sermons, processions, and the latest news from Rome. The few maids of honor passing by on errands were dressed in a matronly fashion, their faces rougeless and patchless, their dresses up to their necks, their eyes modestly cast down as if pondering some devout thought.

In the anteroom to the King's cabinet a new Captain of the Guards stared at him briefly from dull eyes sunk in a lozenge-shaped face, nodded carelessly, and resumed staring at his prayer book. Hypocritical tricks, thought Victor in disgust; the antics of a man afraid for his place unless he followed the prevailing pattern. At least this kind of life wouldn't be much wear and tear on the mind. Victor crossed to the window embrasure and tried to calm his uneasiness. What should the rewards be for helping to claim an empire? A lucrative appointment? A sum of money? Costly gold and silver plate? The finest stud in France? The cabinet door opened, a stranger made a quick depar-ture, and the Captain, stepping inside, announced: "Monsieur le Marquis de Lorennes."

Hardly daring to glance fully at the figure in the great armchair, Victor advanced, bowed deeply, and uttered the customary words of inquiry and compliment.

"*Eh bien,* Victor," said the measured voice he had not heard for so long. "It is good to have you back. You look remarkably fit. Come closer."

Victor bowed again and advanced. The royal smile increased in a mixture of approval and envy of such perfect physical condition. Victor, *au contraire,* could scarcely hide his dismay at the dimmed glory of this sun around whom so many planets revolved. In a ponder-ous black wig, a plain coat and breeches of drab brown, the Sun King, though still of noble presence, was only a relic of his former splendor. Time had indeed laid a heavy hand upon him. His face was fleshy and as flushed as a Norman peasant's.

A hitherto unnoticed figure in black now rose from a desk in the corner of the room, and Père la Chaise came forward. "May I join His Majesty in welcoming you home?"

"Thank you, Father," was all the startled Victor could manage. Smiling, the priest resumed his place, apparently intending to stay through the audience.

"Well, Victor, your report? Have you changed your mind since you praised Monsieur de la Salle in your letters? Tell me everything that happened."

Victor launched into his account, uncomfortable because of the antagonistic presence so prominent in the room and the difficulty of making the wonders of the New World known to one who had never left the soil of France. But he told of them as well as he could, hoping to see a smile of satisfaction dawn on the King's face. The King did not interrupt, but he did glance frequently toward the corner. With relief Victor came to the end. "I do not believe any other man than La Salle has the combination of qualities that are needed to colonize and hold the West for France. Furthermore, he firmly believes he can do it."

"And," said the King slowly, "you are convinced that he has no plans dangerous to the crown." In his eyes was the still unfulfilled need to have complete confidence in someone.

"No, sire, I am sure he has none. You have been ill-served and worse-informed by those who made you suspicious of him." Victor tried to pick his words with care, knowing that advice to be useful must be adapted to the character of the person to whom it is offered. "You said once, Your Majesty, that if you were well informed, you could always rule wisely. Then I tell you on the honor of my family, that Monsieur La Salle seeks nothing for himself but a reasonable livelihood so he can marry. He wants only to serve France and you. Sire, it is my humble entreaty that you listen sympathetically to his reports and his requests."

The King nodded. "Tell me again about the location of the Spaniards nearest to your discovery." And when Victor had complied as best he could, the King said, "A naval and military establishment on the Gulf could secure to us, then, free navigation of those seas, as well as form a base for attack upon Spanish treasure ships in case of war. You have done very well, Victor, and now I shall know what to say when La Salle appears before me. One of the merits of his discovery is that my purse contributed nothing to it, which makes it a unique colonial project, when every Quebec fisherman who wants a new net writes to ask me for it. But now perhaps I shall help La Salle a little. Tell me, what do you think of La Barre as Governor?"

"What can one think? Incompetent, greedy, weak, no imagination, too old for the job—!" There goes my head, thought Victor ruefully.

"Yes, I am afraid he is." The King sighed. "He kept pestering me and the Jesuits wanted him."

Victor thought with foreboding, the Jesuits want other things, too. "Le Comte de Frontenac, sire, is the ideal man for the job, if he were left alone. You'll have a hard time finding a better man."

"Well, I couldn't know," said the King almost petulantly. "He and the Intendant kept flooding me with paper every time a ship came back—requests, grievances—and most of them sounded like petty squabbling. I couldn't see anything to do but to relieve them both. *Eh bien,*" he flexed his fingers restlessly, "maybe I'd better send the Count back by and by."

"The Comte is the most capable man—if he has your support."

"I am glad to have your opinion," said the King graciously. "Now, as to your plans. We must find something for you." He glanced again at Père la Chaise. "For the moment, positions at court are all filled. But as a beginning I shall give you a captaincy in the Gray Musketeers."

That's not so bad, thought Victor, though it's below what I had before. Still, if it is only a beginning. . . . "Thank you, sire," he said. "May I ask where the Musketeers are? I saw no drilling in the Place d'Armes."

"They're on the road between Chartres and Maintenon. Their present Captain will explain what they're doing. I want to replace him with someone who will maintain discipline and make the men do what they're supposed to."

Mystified though he was, Victor understood that he was to have no more information.

"You might return here at the same time tomorrow, to get your commission. In the meantime, Bontems will find you a room in the palace."

"Thank you for the honor, sire."

"Not your former room, of course, but something on the floor above it."

Victor's heart sank. The next floor was a collection of filthy cubbyholes. He should be flattered at being installed in the palace, but how could he stand the confinement and stench? For the first time he felt how ridiculous it was that a noble who has a palace of his own should lodge in a wretched hole under the stairs just to be under the same roof with majesty. "Please do not concern yourself with it just now. I hope to have Your Majesty's permission to go first to Rouen to settle Charles's affairs, and take care of any necessary business for the estate, and then for a time I would be camping out with the Musketeers."

"Let Marc go to Rouen, and you go to the Musketeers tomorrow," interrupted the King fretfully. "Now does that take care of all I promised you? No, there is the matter of your pay for five years. Bring me paper from that desk." When Victor complied, the King scrawled a few lines, signed them, folded the paper and handed it to Victor. "Although finances are now in the hands of Louvois, the Minister of War, I have written an order on certain funds Monsieur de Seignelay holds as Minister of Colonies and the Marine. You will present it to him for payment. And here"—he wrote a line on another sheet—"is an order to the stables for a suitable mount. Now, is there anything else?"

The King's cool disregard of his request to go to Rouen made Victor reckless in his bitterness, and he reminded the King deliberately, "You also promised that I could have the hand of any lady whose permission I could obtain." Immediately he wished he could recall the words. Why did I forget that no matter how familiarly he may chat with me, I am in the presence of my master, and he can send me to rot in the Bastille? Tensely he awaited the King's displeasure, but when he dared raise his eyes, His Majesty was composed, a thoughtful look on his fleshy face. Victor could hardly control his tongue as the truth struck him: the King had put the whole Fontanges affair out his mind, as he always banished from his thoughts everyone who died. Victor's father, La Rochefoucauld, Colbert, the Queen, Angélique—no memory of them would be allowed to remind the fourteenth Louis of that vacant niche awaiting him in the tomb of the Kings of France.

At last the King spoke: "When you have recovered the youthful good looks that your years of hard living have somewhat marred, you can find plenty of women."

Victor clenched his hands, fighting back in panic a rising hatred of this callous man.

"But I have a suggestion about your marriage," the even voice went on. "Do you remember the daughter of the Duchess of Gèvres?"

Victor wrinkled his brow. "I'm not sure. The one who's tall and lean and walks like an ostrich?"

Louis smiled. "But with a very fine estate."

"She stank like a skunk, even from a distance."

"Her money smells all right." The King was frowning slightly.

Victor said quickly, "I appreciate Your Majesty's giving thought to my problems. I will take another look at the lady. Perhaps she has aged like good wine."

The royal brow cleared. "Then we have everything settled. Now will you bring me the little velvet-covered box in the top of that cabinet?"

When Victor, wondering, had found it and placed it in the royal hands, the King rose, snapped the spring to open it, and said, "Kneel before me."

In amazement, Victor knelt, and in growing wonder saw a light blue ribbon placed about his neck, from which hung a dove with outstretched wings, set with diamonds. The Order of the Holy Ghost! The King drew his sword, laid it on Victor's right shoulder, and began to speak, "In recognition of your services to the crown of France . . ."

Victor was trembling now, unable to contain himself. As the King went on through the presentation, a surge of joy at this highest of of honors was mingled with disquieting thoughts. One was a bitter realization: My father should have had this, not I. Or if anyone deserves it now, La Salle should have it, but he will never get it because of his low rank. And then other thoughts crowded in: Is this an honor, or is it a bribe to stay here at court? Praises and honors are the least costly of rewards.

Silence fell as the King finished and replaced his sword. Victor rose. "I am overcome, Your Majesty. I cannot express my appreciation in fitting words, this has so taken me by surprise."

"I usually confer honors in private now. I am tired of public ceremonies."

He's tired of everything, thought Victor, as he said truthfully, "If I am to receive it at all, I greatly prefer it in private."

"Then tomorrow you will call for your commission." Louis's tone dismissed him.

From one of the peddlers outside the gate he bought a pair of gloves *à la mousquetaire,* befringed, embroidered, betasseled, and entered his hired coach. "Drive to the Grand Ecurie." Even though I haven't yet got my commission, he thought, I'm going to get my horse now and ride out and see what kind of maneuvers the Musketeers are performing between Chartres and Maintenon.

When he reached Pont Gouin on the Eure he saw what looked like a construction camp. Masons were chipping huge blocks of stone, workmen were carrying buckets of water for mortar, laborers were digging the frozen ground near a stone building. No, not a building, he saw as he rode closer, for there was only a series of high arches stretching up from the river. Shabby, emaciated workmen were trying to raise another ponderous stone to the crown of a great stone arch. When the men dropped to the ground in exhaustion, others were herded forward to replace them. Victor watched aghast at the grueling nature of the work. He noticed, too, that most of the men were in rags, but some of the rags had once been familiar blue tunics.

"Well, let the damned stone down," bawled the voice beyond the arch. "Take a rest, and we'll try again. We've got to get it up there, and another one, too, before night." The unhappy wretches let the great arched rock to the ground, and threw themselves down, some lying as if dead, some nursing rope burns on their hands.

Dismounting, Victor approached an officer.

"I'm Victor, Marquis de Lorennes, formerly of the Guards and the Musketeers."

The officer saluted. "Welcome to our camp, Monsieur le Marquis. But if you've come like all the rest to tell us that the King is displeased with our slowness, I can only tell you that we can't go any faster, especially with the slim food rations we have been sent. You can see for yourself it's no joke to raise from four to eight hundred weight of stone to the top of an arch seventy-four feet high."

"No, the King sent no message. I am to be your captain, but I don't have my commission yet. I just rode out to see what you were doing. I've been away for some time. I supposed you were on maneuvers."

The officer laughed bitterly. "Maneuvers, indeed. I'd rather serve in the galleys than drive men all day to work beyond their strength and then spend my evenings burying good French soldiers. We take dead men out by carloads, every night, and bury them secretly, over there." He pointed to a field beyond the encampment. "The King doesn't want any news to get out that so many are being killed on his favorite project. No workman is allowed to leave, and let me warn you, no officer is either. I don't know what will happen if war comes, we're losing so many musketeers. I've buried nearly eight thousand of the best soldiers of France, and for what?"

"Yes, for what?" asked Victor. "It looks like supports for a vast bridge, or an aqueduct."

"It is an aqueduct, monsieur. It is designed to bring the water of the river Eure to Versailles. In the summer months there isn't enough water for the fountains. So Louvois hatched this scheme of diverting the Eure to the palace grounds and using soldiers to build the aqueduct. Forty-five regiments were detached from various fortresses—twenty-two thousand men—to work as excavators, laborers, and wheelbarrow men. It'll take forty-seven arches and we've put up only ten so far. You can imagine the casualties before the thing is done!"

"But they aren't used to this kind of work, and they're not even dressed for this weather!" said Victor angrily.

"That's one reason they're dying. During the summer we had a lot of malaria, too."

"But doesn't the King know what's happening?" demanded Victor.

"Of course he knows. And so does Maintenon, but they don't care. 'What does it matter?' says Maintenon, 'whether soldiers die on enemy soil or that of France?' "

Victor shook his head. "Just to satisfy a whim," he said under his breath.

"When will you be taking charge?" asked the lieutenant.

"I don't know. I must—" He broke off, watching an exhausted little workman pushing a wheelbarrow full of heavy rock, inching it over the ground until he came to a slight upgrade that stopped him completely. Victor stepped to his side and shoved it up the slope.

"Merci, monsieur," said the workman wearily. He stood there, barely alive, reminding Victor of the way a wild ox, fatally wounded, props himself up and dies on his feet. "Mordieux! It's Victor!"

Startled, Victor looked closely at the thin wrinkled face, covered with scratches and dirt. "Dreux! In the name of God! What are you doing here?"

"The same as all the rest." The thin chest was rising and falling from the exertion, tears streaking the dirt on his cheeks. "It's good to see you."

"Come over here and sit down." Victor led Dreux to a huge rock awaiting the masons' chisels. *"Par le sang dieu! Tu es maigre à faire peur."*

"No, not thin enough to scare you." Dreux tried to rise to their old bantering. "You look strong enough to face a dozen ghosts like me." In his emaciated face, his eyes were feverishly bright. "But how did you find me?"

"The King has suggested that I take command here."

Dreux groaned. "How can you?"

Yes. How can I? Victor thought. It's against my self-respect as a Norman, as a De Lorennes, as a man, to drive these soldiers to death so that the King's fountains may have more water. A vision rose before him of La Salle, carrying as heavy a burden over a portage as any of his men, never asking a man to do what he would not do himself. And then the realization came, sharp and clear: Between the King and La Salle, La Salle is the better man. How could I stay here, even with some other assignment, knowing what the King has done to his proud musketeers? No Indian chief would so neglect his warriors.

Dreux was wavering as if about to faint. Victor moved over to the end of the rock. "Lie down. I want to think for a minute."

Gratefully Dreux stretched out across the stone, murmuring, "I'm too dirty to touch your fine clothes."

Victor pulled his head down, and stroking back the matted hair that was once so carefully dressed, said, "Just rest!"

"I wish I could die right now," Dreux sighed. "I'm so happy to be with you again."

"Nonsense. You're not going to die. I'm going to get us both out of here."

Dreux moved his head slightly. "There's no hope for either of us. Madame de Maintenon makes all the appointments now—she and that Jesuit."

In the old days, Victor recalled, the King's mistresses had had no voice in the affairs of France beyond suggesting decorations for the palace or statuary for the gardens. But this Maintenon was a new kind of mistress who was ruling France behind the name of Louis.

"Well," said Victor at last, "I can't pull a long face all day to please Maintenon. I have to be where I can laugh when I want to."

"But if you refuse this commission she'll probably have you sent out with the soldiers quartered on Protestants."

"They're not doing that again!"

"As bad as ever, and getting worse. The Jesuits and Maintenon are constantly trying to persuade the King to revoke the Edict of Nantes that gave us protection against persecution. They tell him that to placate Heaven he must destroy all the 'heretics' in France."

Victor's revulsion was so strong he was almost dizzy. He knew what had happened before the Edict. Quartered with Protestant families, the worst type of soldier was encouraged to make their lives miserable until they abandoned their religion. Protestants were driven naked

331

into the streets, sent to loathsome prisons, and their women raped. Victor had looked on these things as belonging to the past century.

He remembered long ago hearing the slow pronouncement of the King: "The Jesuits shall not dictate to the crown of France. The temporal and spiritual run in parallel lines, but they must not be tangled. I will not have France run like a religious order. Heaven should not weigh so heavily upon earth. . . ." How could Louis have so passed from one extreme to the other, with the caprice of an eastern despot?

Slowly, surely, Victor made a decision. "I'm going back with La Salle," he said, "and you're going with me!"

Dreux sat up, hope springing to his features, despite his trying to deny it. "How can I go with you? Huguenots are not allowed to emigrate. And what could I do over there?"

Victor gave him a brief summary of La Salle's explorations and, as he described the property along the Illinois and Marc's plans to develop it, Dreux's face lit up as before a vision of the Promised Land. "Oh, it would be wonderful! But you're too late. I'm so weak I couldn't last that long, anyway."

"Nonsense! One can never count on a Gascon dying that easily. He's more likely to live to be ninety-eight."

"You'll have a hard time getting permission to go yourself. You musn't make it harder by trying to get an impossible permission for me."

"I don't know," said Victor. "I have a feeling that anyone who speaks as favorably as I have of La Salle will not be welcomed by Maintenon and her Jesuits. His Majesty may let me go. And we won't ask permission for you. Could you escape from here, do you think?"

"The punishment is being branded and sentenced to the galleys for life, but I'll take that chance. I might get away tonight while they're burying the dead. If I'm missed tomorrow, they'll think I was one of the bodies. They don't keep any records. But where shall I go?"

"Toward Paris. If anyone asks, you're carrying a message to the new Captain. La Salle can get you a room where we are, and when you're stronger, we'll help you get to La Rochelle. You can find some work there until we come. It's a good Protestant town."

"When will you come?"

"I won't know until after La Salle's interview with the King tomorrow. His Majesty will help him, but I don't know the details yet. And

332

we have to go to Rouen, Marc and I, to see what needs to be done there. I'm head of the family now, you see."

"Oh, I forgot." Dreux rubbed his forehead. "I have a note from your brother Charles for you, but it's back at the barracks. He wrote it when he made a visit to court six months ago."

"Do you know what's in it?"

"Yes, he talked it over with me. He didn't like the court, and wants your permission to marry a nice Rouen girl. They want to live on the estate and manage it in case you and Marc prefer to stay at court. But didn't you get any of my letters?"

"No. They must have been intercepted. Don't worry about anything now. We'll soon be in New France, with all this behind us. But I must go. What time will you try to get away? I'll ride out and meet you."

"No." Dreux was firm. "I'm not going to get you in trouble. I won't try it unless you promise to let me get to Paris as best I can."

"Then I'll tell the officer to let you lie in your tent the rest of the day. He'll do it. He thinks I'm going to be his superior tomorrow."

On the way back to Paris Victor's thoughts were occupied with this seemingly abrupt change in his plans. Yet he wondered if his decision had not been forming all the time even if he had not found the court ruled by a petticoat and a cassock. What was the use of an extra ribbon, the right to enter a certain door, the favor of holding the candle as Louis XIV gets into bed? Only to people cut off from real living, who have nothing useful to do, could these trifles hold value. Father was right. He knew that if one cannot take these follies seriously, one should stay away. The poison that killed him was not the only kind at Versailles; I was imbibing a slow poison myself. If I had stayed it would kill me as surely as it did Father, even if I lived to be a hundred. The wilderness has discipline, and etiquette, but they are real, based on the stark necessity of doing one's share, of not being a burden on others.

I'm going back, he told himself; that's the important thought for now. Even if I leave my heirs not a cent in my coffers, I'm going. I want to see Nika again inspecting every detail of a new camping place, like a cat in a strange house. Whether or not I have the King's favor, I'll have the companionship of brave men. And not only men. For now memories came flooding back of an evening in Montreal and the peculiarly satisfying companionship of a girl with a gaiety to match his own, the honest directness and charm of a girl who loved river travel, housekeeping, and Indian children. She belonged in that country, he saw in his new awareness. Her beauty needed no patches or masks, no foot-high coiffures; it was like the new country itself. She was a part of it; and he knew now she was a part of his own feeling for it, too. He decided to write to her at once and tell her so.

Back in Versailles, Victor presented himself at the palace of Sceaux, home of De Seignelay, and was admitted to a long gallery full of paintings and statues. A footman led him to a library at the far end of the gallery.

From behind a large, cluttered desk, backed by a huge fireplace, De Seignelay rose to meet him, his long pale face filled with pleasure. "This is a rare treat, Victor. Most of my days are spent in receiving people I don't want to see at all."

Victor shook his hand and murmured a polite response, but he could not take his eyes off the wall above the mantel, for there was the D'Artagnan sword, its emerald winking in the candlelight as if in greeting. De Seignelay followed his stare.

"You see that it arrived safely." He scrutinized Victor closely. "I never thought it would be my good fortune to see it where it is."

"Nor did I think to see it there," said Victor, as calmly as he could. "But circumstances were in your favor." Forcibly he wrenched his eyes away from the sword, and remembered his manners. "May I offer my condolences upon the death of your father? And congratulations on your new position."

De Seignelay waved Victor to an armchair beside the fire, and took an identical one opposite. "I miss my father greatly, and so does France. But tell me about yourself. I don't mean your adventures in New France. Monsieur de La Salle was here today and gave me a full report, to supplement his letters. But about your plans now—did you have good luck at court?"

"I found many changes."

"Ah, yes." De Seignelay leaned back, his long thin hands resting on the arm of the chair. "Where everything was roses before, you perhaps see a few thorns now?" Victor nodded.

"You may speak freely here," said De Seignelay. "These walls have no ears, and if they had, they would already have heard much worse than anything you are likely to say. Perhaps we can sum it up: Louis XIV grows old and decrees that all the world be old, too. He grows devout and decrees that everyone fast, pray, confess, and hear eternal sermons as he does. The glamour has departed, leaving a tyrant, selfish, exacting, and intolerant. They say in Paris that the King is ruled by 'the old woman, the Jesuit, and the bastard.' "

"Which bastard?"

"The Duc du Maine. He has grown into a complete villain, with a soul as misshapen as his back. And the King adores him—I speak with special bitterness because His Majesty is constantly pressing me to sell this palace to the brat. And under Maintenon the priests have become more important than ducs. Père la Chaise overtops all of us ministers and makes more decisions than Louis himself."

"Everyone says the King has married Maintenon."

"Probably. Those things have a way of getting out. Secretly. He's not going to face Europe's ridicule by putting Scarron's widow on the throne of Charlemagne. Madame de Maintenon's apartments are now those at the top of the Marble Staircase, opposite the King's. She seldom leaves them except to go to Mass every morning. She always wears the same smug pious face, as if she took it out of a box in the morning and put it back at night. Being in a peculiar position halfway between queen and commoner, it's difficult for her to live amid court etiquette, so she never appears at public functions. She and the Jesuits have pushed the King—who used to be merely rigidly Catholic—into bigotry, and have convinced him he can obtain pardon for his sins by extinguishing heresy."

"One would think," said Victor, "he'd attain that goal more surely through acts of mercy and kindness."

"No bigot ever entertains that thought."

"A sad blow to France then." Victor mused a moment and then asked bluntly: "Do you think the King will really help La Salle?"

"Maybe—but for the wrong reasons."

"I know," said Victor. "I could see his mouth turn down and fire leap into his eyes when the Spanish possessions in the new world were mentioned. Any plan to hurt Spain is attractive to him. But it will be a long time before any colony will be strong enough to make any aggressive move against the Spaniards."

"Don't let La Salle tell him that. Let's get our colony at the Mississippi's mouth, and hope the King will sometime tire of war and turn to developing the empire. But enough of these problems that keep me awake nights. I didn't give you a chance to answer when I asked about your plans."

"I have decided to go back with La Salle."

De Seignelay sat up, his eyes gleaming. *"A la bonne heure!* I'm glad to hear it! But tell me why."

"I think I would have gone back sooner or later, but today's events hastened my decision. I may be foolish to leave the service of a Louis XIV to attach myself to someone who may fail, but it will be a better use of my life."

"Good," murmured De Seignelay.

Victor tried to lighten the moment. "Of course I would be glad to know what is ahead for La Salle, and for Marc and me. Last time, I at least had La Voisin's assurance of travel and violence, and I had plenty of both."

De Seignelay took out a jeweled snuffbox, but laid it on the edge of the desk without opening it. "It's queer that you should say that. I had intended to invite you to stay for a little gathering this evening. The center of attraction will be La Voisin's daughter, who has made some remarkable prophecies for us before."

"Her daughter?"

"Yes. That trade is passed on like every other. Even if a sorcerer knows she may die on the rack, she will bring up her beloved daughter in the same profession. I hope you can stay."

"It's tempting," said Victor, "but I think I'd better go on to Paris. I want to talk with La Salle about his audience with the King." And, he thought, I want to be there when Dreux comes.

"You are quite right. But wait—perhaps we can persuade her to give you a private reading." Before Victor could protest, De Seignelay had leaned back and touched an embroidered bell pull.

At a soft tapping at the door, De Seignelay went to open it. Certainly the creature who glided in had nothing of the witch about her. She seemed very young and was dressed like a schoolgirl.

"You wished to see me, messieurs?"

"Yes, mademoiselle," said De Seignelay. "This gentleman cannot stay for this evening, so I wonder if you would tell him now what you can see of his future."

Her dark eyes flew in alarm to Victor. "I don't know. Sometimes, as you have seen yourself, I can tell nothing at all."

"That's all right, mademoiselle," Victor assured her. "It doesn't matter."

"Oh, of course, I'll be glad to try." She sat down in an armchair that almost swallowed her up, and arranged her skirts.

336

"Don't you need appliances of some sort?" asked Victor.

"I know what you mean." She smiled warmly. "My mother's rooms were full of them—all kinds of queer instruments hanging on the walls, dried plants and seaweeds, lion and panther skins, stuffed animals and birds, especially owls and vampire bats."

"And on the table," said Victor, "parchments filled with lines and curves, horoscopes, magic wands, waxed figures stuck with pins, all the tools of the astrologer."

"I have all those things still," she said, "but if I can tell you anything I can do it without them. If we might have the candles out and just firelight? And if you will sit quietly and not speak until after I do."

De Seignelay extinguished the candles. For a long time there was no sound but the soft snapping of wood, while the fire made strange patterns on walls and ceiling. Victor began to think the girl was asleep, but at last a voice came from the depths of the great chair.

"You are going on a long journey." She sighed and fell silent again. Victor was disappointed. The usual cant of a fortuneteller. But when she began again, a tremor ran along his spine. "Your journey will be like the one you have returned from, with the same dangers, the same troubles, and because you go with the same leader, the same enemies and the same faults. He will make the same mistakes as before. It is not clearly set forth, but I see hunger, cold, a long search for a river's mouth. I see your leader continually dividing his men, sending them here and there, often to no purpose. I see a priest who causes trouble. I see shipwrecks, quarrels, desertions, and deaths. But not your death, or your brother's. You will come back to visit your family, but you will never stay long in France again. And after long lives you will die in bed, uniforms packed away in a chest, swords on the wall. But your leader will not come back."

"You mean he'll never visit France again?" asked Victor softly.

"Never any place on earth again. I see one with murder in his heart going with you."

In spite of his skepticism Victor felt himself shiver, remembering the Indian girl who told Marc, *I do not see your leader returning.*

"Tell me more," he asked.

"Many will die when disaster comes, and the one who could help them will not. A colony will be founded sometime, but not by him." With a start, she sat upright, like a little girl startled out of her sleep. "I'm sorry. I fear I was no help."

"You told us many things," said De Seignelay, and Victor added, "Thank you, mademoiselle."

De Seignelay lighted the candles, escorted her to the door, and came back to his chair. "Well?"

"I don't know . . . I'm confused. I feel as if I had lived through a long journey while she spoke, but how much was in the past and how much in the future, I have no idea."

De Seignelay stirred the fire, sending up a shower of sparks. "Even though she looks like a child, many people have great faith in her powers. Some things she may know. The servants may have told her who was here. She may have heard other things she has put together. But there's always something one can't account for."

"Maybe she heard of the attacks on La Salle's life, and is guessing it might happen again. But even if every word she says is true, I'm still going with him. If it's going to be so difficult, he'll need me even more."

"I must not keep you longer," said De Seignelay, rising. "You and La Salle both have need of time to plan what you will say at Versailles tomorrow. You have the order for your wages?"

Victor produced it. De Seignelay crossed to a wall safe and brought a gratifyingly heavy sack. "I think you will find it correct."

"Indeed, I feel as if a golden shower had descended upon me." Victor rose to take the bag and go, but the minister set it instead on the desk.

"One moment longer. I have a contribution to make." He crossed to the mantel, took down the sword, and held it out hilt first.

"Monsieur!" exclaimed Victor. "What do you mean?"

"It is yours."

"But you can't do this! You've always wanted it!"

De Seignelay stood with his back to the fire, hands behind him, a smile on his face. "Having it has taught me I have no right to it. All it does is reproach me every time I look at it. I am not proud of the life I lead, bowing before a sovereign for whom I have no respect." He glanced oddly at the sword. "Do you know I have never worn it? I couldn't. Several times I put it on to wear to the palace, but I couldn't go outside this room with it on. It was as if someone prevented me."

"But," protested Victor, "I can't pay you what you spent for it."

"I don't want pay. Why, I spent one hundred thousand francs for fireworks at a fete I gave last summer. I just wanted to own the sword, and now I have done so. Maybe I wanted it because it is a symbol of a kind of greatness that I know isn't in me. I think there may be more than a little of it in you and Marc. D'Artagnan's sword, for whatever reason, would never really belong to me. D'Artagnan would understand why you sold it, but he would think better of me for giving it back."

Victor ran up the stairs two at a time and knocked on La Salle's door. Inside he found Marc and La Salle in earnest conversation. Both of them caught sight of the D'Artagnan sword at the same time and leaped to their feet together. "You got it back!" exclaimed Marc.

"Yes, but that's not what I'm excited about. I'm going with you!" With a cry of joy Marc ran to embrace him. "Yes, I'm going, if I can get permission, and I'm trusting to luck for that. I have something to tell you, Marc, about how I happened to go the first time, but that doesn't matter now. This time I am going of my own free will. And the D'Artagnan sword goes with me." He patted the hilt, puzzled as Marc and La Salle exchanged a glance that was not only joyous but significant, their eyes regarding the sword as if it were a thing of magic.

"I can't tell you how glad I am, on both counts," said La Salle. "And I am sure D'Artagnan would have no doubt that the sword is where it belongs."

There were mysterious overtones to that speech, but Victor was too full of news to search for them now. "I've a thousand things to tell you." He drew a third chair up and sat down with them. "All this about me can wait. I want to talk about someone else. This afternoon I saw Dreux. . . ."

When it was nearly dawn, Dreux came up the stairs and knocked feebly at La Salle's door. He was so ill and tired that Victor and Marc undressed him and put him to bed, wondering if he would ever rise again. In the early morning, while he slept, Marc went out to get food, and some clothing for him to travel in. Later La Salle left for the court, and Victor followed an hour later. The three were to meet at noon at the gates of Versailles, to dine together and report to Marc on the interviews with the King.

Victor arrived early, and to avoid the indoor stenches, walked through the garden. Even in winter it had formerly seemed to him imposing, but now the park with its marble statues, its bronzes, the

339

bizarre complications of its waters, was boring, and the Grand Canal was a dull little pond. He laid his hand on the emerald of his sword, and then clasped the hilt firmly. "Come, Monsieur D'Artagnan; help me once more! I've got to get free to do what I must."

Then, his heart strangely at rest, he walked quickly to the anteroom where he found La Salle, his audience already over, in serious conversation with De Seignelay. They beckoned for him to join them, and after ascertaining from the Captain of the Guards that other audiences were scheduled ahead of his own, Victor crossed to them. "It must be that you weren't successful, or you'd be surrounded by courtiers. I'm sorry."

"Not at all," said La Salle softly. "I got far more than I asked for."

De Seignelay added, "I hinted to someone as we came out that the King had not listened with any interest. You see, the plans must be kept secret for a while."

"Victor is one of the few I must tell, though," said La Salle. "He won't give it away."

So Victor learned the really astonishing news. La Salle had asked permission to voyage to the mouth of the Mississippi by water with a colony of settlers and enough soldiers for a garrison, thus avoiding the Quebec route. "And His Majesty was most generous," said La Salle quietly. "I asked for two ships, and he is giving me four. I have permission to recruit a hundred soldiers, all the mechanics and laborers I need, families to found a colony, and several priests—none of them Jesuits. And His Majesty is paying the entire cost! Furthermore, I am to be governor of all the territory from the Illinois to the border of Mexico."

"Wonderful!" said Victor.

"You have been with me in the depths," said La Salle. "I'm glad you are here when I am at last on the heights. Incidentally, Victor, I got permission to take Dreux as a lieutenant. So he can go openly to La Rochelle with you."

"Again, wonderful! He can go with us to Rouen first and get his health back. But what about Tonti and the forts?"

"The best of news. La Forest is in Paris now, and the King will send him back to Quebec on the first ship. All my property, including Fort Frontenac and Fort St. Louis, is to be restored to me under La Forest's command and Tonti's. Also damages are to be paid me for all losses suffered because of La Barre's acts. One other detail will

340

surprise you: La Forest is ordered to march four thousand warriors at Fort St. Louis to the mouth of the Mississippi, to aid us in an invasion of Mexico!"

It taxed all Victor's control not to burst into laughter. "Doesn't he have any idea how far that is? You can't march four thousand Indian warriors of a dozen different tribes two thousand miles from their families and hunting grounds. And you can't invade a country they know nothing about, with bows and arrows."

"The King," said De Seignelay, "knows nothing except what he wishes and orders. *Je veux, j'ordonne.* But all that matters is to get the colony established and control the Mississippi."

"Impractical details can then be forgotten," said La Salle. "Everything is most satisfactory—unless, Victor, the King refuses to let you go."

Victor laid his hand confidently on his sword hilt. "It is time for me to find that out. And I'll meet you and Marc at the stroke of noon."

In spite of his confidence, Victor was quaking inwardly as he presented himself once more before his sovereign. While making his bows, he looked at the King, sitting with his back to a window, shadowing a face which was dissipated and prematurely aged. And as Victor stood rigidly waiting for the King's sign of recognition, he dreaded the despotic *je le veux.* If this was not the sun, it was a gilded torch at which one good man after another had scorched his wings.

The royal hand beckoned him closer, the royal smile was bent upon him. *"Eh bien,* Victor, you have come for your commission."

"I have been to the aqueduct," said Victor. "And I desire to trust to the judgment of my sovereign whether I could not best serve him elsewhere."

The King sat as cold and mute as any of the marble gods presiding over his fountains.

"I neither can nor wish to do anything without your consent," Victor went on. "But I feel that any of your officers could do as well as I at the aqueduct, while perhaps my experience could be best used in the new colony. I should like a chance for active service so I may earn my laurels before I come here to rest on them. It is not enough for me to plume myself on my birth and the services of my father to Your Majesty; I ask permission to add services of my own. I believe the needs of France just now are in the colonies, to establish our strength against the Spaniards." He smiled, with an attempt at the old jauntiness, and added, "And I am ill-supplied with pistoles, livres, and louis d'ors. I humbly ask for a chance to replenish that lack."

Louis's mouth, surrounded by deep wrinkles, began working with a nervous spasm, as had his father's in old age. "I would not like to lose you again so soon."

"That is most gracious of Your Majesty. But I feel that my work in New France is not finished. And if I do not go back, my five years' experience there will be wasted, when it could so well be devoted to Your Majesty's service."

The King lifted his hand in a gesture that was half annoyance, half frustration. Victor, watching closely, guessed what was passing in his mind, for the King regarded him with a mixture of affection, regret, and exasperation. But he obviously had no answer for Victor's arguments, and something in Victor's mien seemed to be restraining him from petulantly ordering him to stay. The royal gaze roamed about the cabinet, changing almost imperceptibly when it came to the little desk where the Jesuit, fortunately not there today in person, could still be felt as a guiding spirit.

"I need you here." Louis paused, and Victor, tense within, met the royal look. Strangely it was the King's eyes that looked away. "Very well. If you prefer, we can alter the commission to make you captain of the hundred soldiers La Salle is to take with him."

Victor bowed deeply. When he had control of himself, he saw that the King was holding out his hand. He advanced, dropped to one knee, kissed the ring that had wedded Louis to France, rose, bowed, and backed to the door. He had got just what he wanted, he thought in elation, from the most powerful king in the world; not by meaningless flattery but by the same appeal to reason that La Salle used in dealing with the savages. And he realized, too, that this time he stood before the King with the same kind of independence and self-respect La Salle had shown when he first came to lay his plans before his monarch—the self-reliance a man must have to keep alive in the New world.

The King lifted his hand in farewell, as to his own lost youth. Then he sat staring before him, his heavy features settling into great weariness.

In the royal court the sky was overcast. In this dull light the great white palace rose ghostlike above the dead foliage of the garden, with the coldness of a prison, its symmetry signifying only weariness and monotony. But as Victor emerged, the sun found an opening in the

342

clouds, and he glanced up at it. Close to high noon, he thought, and smiled as he recognized this use of a skill he had learned in the wilderness. It was time to meet La Salle and Marc.

On the Place d'Armes, the two brothers smiled at each other, and fell in one on each side of La Salle, to stride down the long avenue and out upon the highway, never once looking back. The wrought-iron gates had no magnetic power for such as they.